Third-class Ticket

In 1969 a group of forty elderly Bengali villagers undertook a remarkable journey. Their adventure was made possible by a benevolent landowner, Srimati Uma Sen, who left her wealth in a trust fund to enable groups from the village to travel around India in a third-class railway carriage. Her desire was that the villagers should see all of India: 'My village is a small, poor one in Bengal. The people there know nothing except that they are very poor. They listen to the old stories, but they do not know that there are places of temples and ruins and palaces which they could visit and touch. They do not know that India is very big and very beautiful as well as very poor. I want them to learn that, and to find out how other villagers survive and teach their children. I want my villagers to see India, then the village will no longer be small.' For a distance of 15,000 kilometres and over a period of seven months Heather Wood travelled with the villagers and *Third-class Ticket* is the absorbing story of that journey.

Heather Wood was raised in Red Deer, Alberta, the daughter of the Canadian author Kerry Wood. She studied history, religion and anthropology in Montreal, California and Oxford. It was her researches for a B. Litt. on Bengal anthropology which first took her to India. She is married and has twin sons.

HEATHER WOOD

THIRD-CLASS TICKET

with illustrations by Beryl Saunders

———

PENGUIN BOOKS

PENGUIN BOOKS

Published by the Penguin Group
27 Wrights Lane, London w8 5TZ, England
Viking Penguin Inc., 40 West 23rd Street, New York, New York 10010, USA
Penguin Books Australia Ltd, Ringwood, Victoria, Australia
Penguin Books Canada Ltd, 2801 John Street, Markham, Ontario, Canada L3R 1B4
Penguin Books (NZ) Ltd, 182–190 Wairau Road, Auckland 10, New Zealand

Penguin Books Ltd, Registered Offices: Harmondsworth, Middlesex, England

First published by Routledge & Kegan Paul Ltd 1980
Published in Penguin Books 1984
Reprinted 1985, 1986, 1987, 1988

Printed and bound in Great Britain by
Cox & Wyman Ltd, Reading
Set in Janson

To Patrick,
who worried and waited

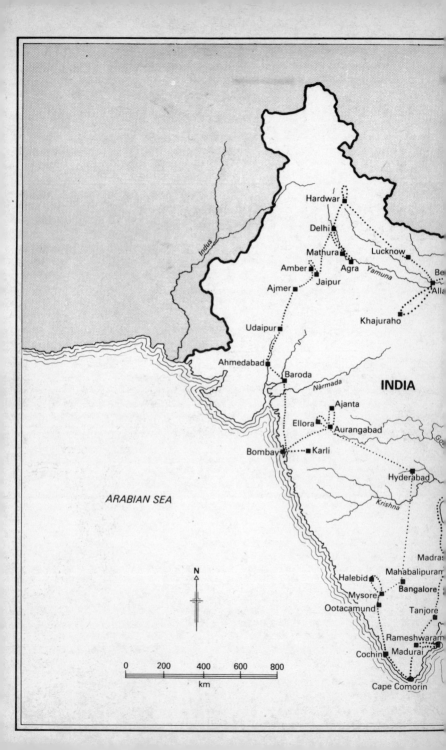

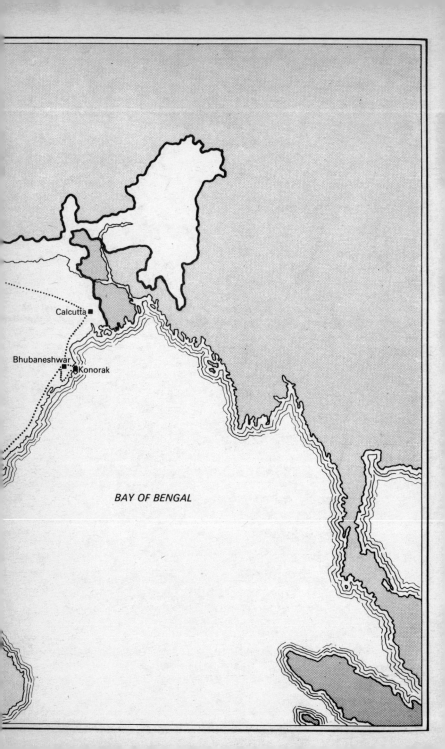

Contents

Author's note

This tale is the story of a real journey made in 1969 by a group of Indian villagers. For a short time I was able to travel with them. I travelled 15,000 kilometres in the third-class carriages of Indian Railways, over a period of seven months. For me, this was a confirmation and culmination of studies in Indian history made possible by the generosity of the Woodrow Wilson Foundation, the Danforth Foundation and the Canada Council. At various times all of these supported my studies. To the villagers the journey was an adventure thrust upon them by unexpected fate when their kindly landowner died leaving her wealth in a trust fund for her villagers. Many of them found the confrontation with the world beyond their village alarming and unsettling. After their travels they returned to the years of crisis and war which resulted in the formation of Bangladesh and the tidal wave, famines and struggle which followed closely upon that war. I returned to Europe to continue my studies, marry, and wander the world.

Always the tale of these villagers has haunted me. It has now been written because of the help of many friends. In particular I wish to thank the scattered family of L.C. Jain, who adopted me as a daughter in Calcutta and gave me friendship wherever or whenever we met. Mr P.K. Jain, not of the same family, saved my life by pulling me out from under a train during an ugly moment. Miss Helen C. Reynolds, Alan Held and Alice and George Park have been patient and helpful in their criticism of the manuscript. Adam Kuper gave unexpected assistance and generously of his time. The understanding of Fräulein Hannelore Bock and Schwester Elizabet Reinhard, kindergarten teachers of my sons, has allowed me the time to write. Most of all I wish to thank the villagers who shared so much and who asked that one day their story be told. They would forgive the liberties I have taken to protect their identities, and the alteration of their beautiful language. To those who still live and remember—a fond salute.

Prologue

The small figure hesitated before the iron gates. Beyond was the palace where she wished to go. Now that she stood alone before it this goal of her journey looked terrifying. Delhi was so much less friendly than her own village in the delta of the Ganges. Even Calcutta felt less alarming than these gates, despite the crowds and the beggars who always made her feel angry at her own wealth. Srimati Uma Sen gathered her white widow's sari more securely about her and stepped up to the guard of Baroda House, the headquarters of Indian Railways.

'Please, Sir, where do I find a tourist director?'

'Tourist Information Officer, Room 111, second floor,' he snapped and swung wide the gates.

She crossed the courtyard, went through the big doors expecting great grandeur, and rather braced herself for it. Instead the dingy hall contained nothing but rows of grey filing cabinets, and a staircase led away from the betel-splashed marble floor. Slowly she began to climb, and at once began to pant and strain.

'Oh Ma, this illness,' she thought. 'Always it is the same: when I wish to do something important it tries to stop me. There is always more pain. I must get this done before it is too late. Will this officer understand, or will he be just another impatient clerk?'

She paused on the landing to catch her breath and clutched the rail as her dizziness began again. A crowd of clerks rushing off to their coffee pushed past her and she struggled against the wall. After another effort she stood in an upper hall lined with filing cabinets. Many men squatted patiently, all holding wads of fluttering paper with which they occasionally fanned themselves. It was not hot, being November, but fanning was a reflex to pass the time. Srimati Sen smiled when she saw it.

Smudges on one wall indicated that Room 111 was to the left so she began to move slowly down the crowded dark corridor, trying to see which was the door she sought. There was a line of people outside one door and loud voices came from within. This was the place, no doubt, for there were tattered posters of some famous ruins on the walls around the door. She took her place at the end of the line and sank squatting to the floor. She tried to calm her panting. The journey from Calcutta seemed long ago. She had gone there hoping to arrange this business, but they had told her, with a scorn she still found irritating, that she must come to Delhi and Baroda House. No one believed that the little widow could mean what she said about her plans and her money. At last she was here, a week later, banker's notes and proofs of her wealth tied in the cloth by her side. If anything she was even more frail after the trying journey.

It was pleasant in the village, she reflected. Especially just now in the evenings when the grey wispy figures gathered in the mists around the fires, and someone told stories or they just chatted and sang. She liked to walk about then, much more than in the day when it all looked so poor, and the faces were so much more lonely and withdrawn than night. In the day one could not forget that the people would never know anything better, as she had done, but at night the mists and the old tales drove away the limits. We all dream together, she smiled. She was the rich woman of the village. She had been the only child of a rich landowner. When he had died he had left all the wealth to her, recognizing that she had greater ability and sympathy for the running of his lands than any of his nephews. There had been a long court battle after that, but she had won. Soon she had married the richest young landlord in the district, a marriage arranged by her uncle, he thought for his own benefit. But the couple had found that together their love for the crops and the river which ran past the villages was very great. From that love they came to be friends, able to work together and eventually able to think of each other with that warmth of respect and trust which not often happened in childless marriages. For years they had hoped for a child but when none came they did not withdraw from each other, but became more considerate and even gentler in their regard for the village. Last year only, her husband had died suddenly. Soon after, Srimati Sen found that with every effort she panted, became dizzy, could not go on. Over the months of struggling to get the estate entirely in order she had neglected her own worries until, towards the end of the summer, she had realized that she could do so no longer. What was it the specialist in Calcutta had said? 'Next, please, hurry along now,' a brisk voice broke in, and she realized it was speaking to her. Srimati Sen looked up. The man was frowning down at her in disdain:

'This is not a village tree. Want to go see your married daughter, eh? Desk 2. Hurry. It is our tea time.'

She stumbled across the doorway into the bright light of the office and for a moment could not see past the dizziness in her eyes.

'Another last-minute pilgrimage,' muttered a voice.

Srimati Sen grew angry and drew herself up. She glared at the speaker, at Desk 1 she saw, and then turned, hoping not to be sent away by the man at the second shabby table. The name card said H.R. De.

'Ah, Bengali, too,' she smiled.

The man was busy writing, looking down. He had a smooth, young face, and smelled of soap. When he suddenly looked up and met her eyes, she realized that here was the attentive officer she had feared she would never find.

'Sit down please, may I help you?'

'Yes. Can you arrange trips around all India?'

'Of course. What kind of trip? To the pilgrimage places? What class? For yourself? Ladies Reserved?'

His questions came too fast, she was still dizzy. She soothed herself again by slowly taking out the papers and smoothing them on her lap:

'You see, I want my villagers to see all of India. I want them to go to the great ruins, and the temples, and the places of the great gods. I want them to come here and see Delhi. To visit the government houses. I want them to go on the boats out to Elephanta in Bombay, and then up to the dairy farms of the north. I want them to go from Himalaya to Cape Comorin and back again. They must see it all.'

Suddenly she could not breathe and broke off gasping. The little man rose, fetched a cup of tea and sat down again. The tea was for her, not him, and she looked at him in surprise. She could not tell what he was thinking. She began again:

'You see, my village is a small, poor one in Bengal. The people there know nothing except that they are very poor. Sometimes, if they are very lucky maybe their children can go to school, and maybe the children will not be so poor. But they do not send the children much to school. They do not know that India needs them to do so. They listen to the old stories, but they do not know that there are places of temples and ruins and palaces which they could visit and touch. They do not know that India is very big and very beautiful as well as very poor. I want them to learn that, and to find out how other villagers survive and teach their children. I have been to America and to England and seen many fine things, but I want my villagers to see India. Then the village will no longer be small. Can you do it, can you make a tour of all India?'

He looked at her in genuine confusion and waited while she stopped panting:

'I hope I can help you. I do not know what you want me to do. Shall I write out tickets for all the people of your village? I think they will find such a journey impossible, much too confusing.'

'No, no forgive me. I go too fast, there is so little time. You must arrange a special railway car. A place where they can sleep and where a cook can make their Bengali food for them. The car could take only some of the villagers first. After the first journey, there will come others, until all my villagers have seen India. But they must go all around. The journey will be long, about two months, and they must do it in winter before planting time. They should see Calcutta first, then Benares and

Sarnath, then Lucknow and Hardwar and Kashmir, down to Chandigar and down here to Delhi.'

Mr De was writing very quickly, though she spoke slowly, savouring the memories associated with each name:

'From here to Agra, Jhansi and Khajuraho, then to Sanchi and Mandu, and across to Gujerat and up to see the Rajput ruins, Ajmer, Amber, Jaipur then Bombay. No that is wrong, you will have to make a better route. But Bombay and Elephanta and Karli. Across to Ajanta and Ellora and Aurangabad. Down to Hyderabad and Mysore, Halebid and Belur. Then up the hills to Ooty and down to Coimbatore and Cochin. To Cape Comorin and Madurai, Trichy, Madras, Mahaballipuram and Rameshwaram. Then north to Puri and Bubaneshwar, Konarak, up to Darjeeling and Gangtok. Home again to Calcutta.'

She stopped. Mr De continued writing. Then he stopped, looked over the long list, looked at the frail figure in front of him and looked down again in confusion:

'I do not understand. A railway car to make such a journey would cost very much money.'

'Yes, yes, of course. But I have it. You see . . .' she handed him the banker's letter and the laywer's statements of her holdings. His eyes widened as he read the documents and he gazed at the lady in dismay:

'But is this your will? You want all this money to be spent on giving your villagers this journey? Is there no son or nephew? This is your will. It is all your money, all your own money,' he repeated in amazement.

'Yes,' she said with amusement, 'my father and my husband were very generous to me. All is to be made into a fund to pay for these journeys. They must go on for years so that the children may go too.'

'A railway carriage and the stops and the tickets I can arrange,' Mr De reflected in astonishment. 'But who will go with them? Who will explain what they see? Will you? But this is your will?'

Again she smiled at his confusion and then, quietly, she said:

'Mr De, I am dying. I will die within maybe two months or less. I cannot make such a journey. The will is good and will be read in time to pay for the first tour this winter, I tell you. There is a schoolmaster in Calcutta who comes from our village. He knows my dream and he will go with each of the tours. As soon as you have arranged the carriage and planned the route he will come to you to learn what he must do in each place. He is a good man, he will learn what you can teach him. But can you do it? Can you make it possible for my villagers to see India?'

'Yes,' he almost murmured, 'yes, I can arrange it. But it is you who make it possible.' Then he looked up to her and she saw that he was weeping.

The week in early January was clear and cold on the banks of the Ganges.

Prologue

There was a ring around the moon. One evening as the villagers huddled around a fire, not speaking much but comforted together, one of the old farmers looked up, saw the ring and said:

'There is going to be a big change, a miracle is going to happen.'

The others laughed and mocked him:

'Ours is no village for miracles!

'Don't be silly, Surendra, Krishna will never sing in our groves.'

'Ah, he must have found something to drink. Where is it, friend?'

'Hush, fools, a ring around the moon always means a miracle, or a death.'

'Or both maybe?' They laughed. The night grew colder, the teasing stopped. They again sat silent. Suddenly from behind the high walls of the Sen compound, there came a wail. A servant came running out:

'Srimati Uma is dead, Mataji is dead.'

There was a low sigh from the group.

'At last then she suffers no more.'

'You see, it was a death, Surendra, and not a special one. We knew it was coming.'

'What will become of the money?'

A week later the will was read in the village compound and the widows, the older men and women, and the elders of the village found that in the second week of February they were to begin a journey in a special carriage around India.

'We are going to see where Siva lives,' one woman whispered to another as she came away from the reading of the will.

'Why spend all that money sending us on a journey that will only be trouble and pain?' grumbled another.

'Ah, she must have gone mad in the end. Going to Delhi to give good money from Bengal to Indian Railways. What good can come of that?'

The old man remembered the ring around the moon and thought to himself, 'Maybe I shall even see the great Himalaya.'

1

A walk across Calcutta

The ferryman had sent word up and down the banks to all the boatmen to come to the village pier before dawn that morning. Now the men were running back and forth among the mists and the tiny boats, greeting friends, competing in the excitement. The boats looked even more flimsy than they were with the canvas not pulled over the mid-ship hoops as protection against the sun. Only the skeletal hoops themselves and the grace of the crafts conveyed a feeling of structure. Fires were lit and the boatmen stood chatting and warming themselves, concerned that there was as yet no sign from the village asleep at the edge of the trees. The mists began to lift a little, then dip again, then teasingly rise to show more of the great wide water before descending upon it once more. Here the river was wide and slow and it took a man forty minutes to pole across the current. Most of that time was spent coming back up to the pier, carefully, cowardly even, for all who lived upon it trusted this most holy stream not at all. It was grey-brown here and low at winter's ebb. There was a smell of dank, stale decay in the black mud where first the boatmen stepped, but then there was clay and grass and the smell was lost, slowly, in the cover of the village smells.

Suddenly around the corner of the compound they came, walking with all the grace of generations trained to bear great burdens, but this morning with great embarrassment. Usually the village was a noisy place and departure a time of much shouting and argument. In this dawn there seemed no place for protest at the adventure ahead. The women were wearing their special saris with deep red borders. Each had a shawl for warmth. Each was heavily laden with assorted bundles of clothes and bedding and extra food which must be necessary for the journey. The men wore dhotis and shawls and carried big bundles and around them crowded children and grandchildren, families and friends, silent too in the strange moment, but each laden with something more to be crammed into the waiting boats. There were brass pots for cooking and clay water pots filled from the village wells, bundles of pan leaves, little packets of sweets, a bottle of the best local toddy, firewood, garlands, and a child's wooden horse, tucked into grandma's parcel in the excitement and then forgotten.

Loading the boats brought out all the passions and frustrations of the village and it took the ferrymen much patience and some brutality to load everything but only those villagers who were supposed to be going. By the time they were seated and the boats sunk low in the water, the mists had lifted and the broad river reflected and distorted a meagre, clouded dawn. It was cold. The boatmen picked up their poles and called to the villagers to help push them off.

'Buy a Benarsi sari for Jhunu's wedding.'

'Toss me your pot of gold first.'

'Don't forget to see Cousin's mother-in-law and ask for more medicine for the baby.'

'Feed it properly for a change.'

'Remember to make an offering for more sons in Benares.'

'Who can pay the priests there?'

'Don't take any drink in Delhi, Grandpa, those Jats poison everything.'

'Don't go barefoot in the south. They have diseases there.'

'Bring back a husband for old Rhupa.'

'I don't want a husband.'

'Of course you do, silly girl.'

'If it comes warm before we return, be sure to plant the small field to pulses.'

'Try to get the back kitchen thatched before the rains.'

'We'll manage, we'll manage.'

'Ashin-dada will meet you at Howrah station, remember, not Sealdah.'

The calling and waving continued until the little fleet was well downstream from the crowd on the bank and beginning to make its wide arc to come back up to the far pier. The crowd began to disperse to the waiting tasks of the day. A few children who stood and strained to see the far bank wondered what might be the thing called a train which all the old people were going to ride. But the river began to shine and the smells of morning began to reach them so they, too, drifted off. On the boats the groups compared stories of the incompetence of those left behind to keep the village in order during their absence. By the time they reached the far bank, the elders were thoroughly convinced that they had no business going away, but were doing so just to spite their ungrateful families. They were a happy band of cynics, colluding in their betrayal of family duty, each knowing too well the fear of what they must now do which prevented them from saying more.

Once they met Ashin-dada there would be forty-five of them, enough to fill a third-class carriage, but not to crowd it. As they loaded themselves with bundles from the boat, they began to look at one another as fellow travellers for the first time. These ones would know them day and night without the protection of house walls or village work. They joked a little with the boatmen about the riches and wonders they would bestow when they returned, and began to mount the bank, not at all convinced by themselves. The women grouped together a little behind the men, wives not walking with husbands, brothers avoiding brothers. Surendra set the pace, delighted that he still recalled the way through the two villages and across the fields to the town and train station. It was only about eight miles, but it took them most of the morning, walking single file, steadily, like a patient but determined snake. Sometimes they stopped at a well to shift their bundles and drink, but usually they only drank the village water from the clay pots, three of which were already broken. One or two of the older women were beginning to limp. Most of the men had taken off their shoes and were walking barefoot, silently, enjoying the feel of the earth and dust which they had worked since they were toddlers.

The provincial town was decrepit in the noon light. Cream and beige paint peeled off the houses. The dust was thick. Many scrawny dogs licked ugly sores. From every shop there blared a piece of film music, loud, shrill, too fast, each in competition with at least four others, so that eventually the din became an accepted and tolerable background to all thought. The villagers moved more slowly, and kept closer together. They knew this town from market days when they had once come to buy for a wedding. Some of the men had come here every year during the war years to work on the roads and the railway. Two of the women had been in the convent school for a year and giggled together as they passed it. They had fled when there were riots and the Muslim girls had suddenly disappeared from the classes. The villagers knew the little hospital, and they looked shyly at Amiya whose smallest grandson was the latest to have died there. The tall figure did not falter, though she was crying. They were glad to reach the bare station.

Surendra asked a guard when the next train went to Sealdah and was told to ask the information officer. The information office was closed, so he asked another guard, who said he must ask the station master. The station master was having lunch and not to be disturbed. Surendra went to the ticket master who looked up and said, 'Third-class ticket, one way, Sealdah'. Surendra was confused. The master repeated his statement and slapped down the ticket in front of the old man. Surendra fumbled and thought, 'Do I have to pay after all?'

The ticket master waited a moment enjoying his omniscience and then said:

'Old man, you come from the village of Srimati Uma Sen, don't you?'

'Yes, sir.'

'And all those ones, forty-four it should be, have come too?'

'Yes, sir.'

'All your tickets are here. You do not pay. Just have each come up to

9

me here so that I can count out and be sure none of those damn beggars gets one.'

Surendra stepped back: 'We do not pay?'

'No, Srimati Uma Sen paid. I have it here, with big directions to be good to some group of stupid villagers from the Sen lands. Baroda House sent us a letter. Seems a terrible waste of money to me.'

He looked scornfully at Surendra's muddy, dusty feet, at his crumpled dhoti, and the worn shawl pulled around the knotted shoulders, and at the old man's grizzled head and puzzled eyes.

'I must ask Elder De,' murmured Surendra and shuffled away from that scorn.

'Oh no you don't, old one. You get your ticket now, or you don't go. I want my lunch.'

Surendra took the small green piece of cardboard gingerly.

'Hang on to it, and it will get you to Sealdah. Now go send those others to me, and quickly.'

Away went Surendra to show his ticket to the group. He found it soiled and crumpled when they returned it to him. He had rather liked the crisp freshness of it. He slid down to his habitual crouch and held the ticket between his knees while he tried to see the blurred name: Sealdah.

Each of the villagers went to the ticket master and said, 'Srimati Uma Sen's village, Sealdah, please.' They had agreed this was the safest approach. Each time the ticket master slapped down the green card from his pile, checked off something on a list marked in bold letters ATTENTION FROM BARODA HOUSE, and said: 'Third-class ticket, one way.' By the time they had all received them he was shouting with impatience at their slowness. To get a ticket and not to pay was strange enough in itself, but to get a ticket and not pay and then be slow about it was just intolerable. He shouted, 'A damn waste of good money,' slammed down the grating and went off to his lunch.

The villagers sat down on the cement platform and began to look around them.

Behind was the vaulted station, dilapidated now, but once an imitation of something grand. The tall, arched windows were opaque from the dust and soot, so that inside the building one had to grope carefully, half-blind, across the piles of post, luggage and sugar-cane which littered the floor. There were few lanterns and they would be lit only at night, not now in the noon brightness. In front of each of the wickets and offices was a heavy iron grating, gleaming and slippery from the oil of the hands which had clutched the bars while making a simple request. The gate to the platforms hung off at one side and people wandered through it without hindrance. On the wide first platform where the villagers now sat and ate leisurely from their bundles there were rows of crates and battered steel trunks and patched canvas bags, labelled ostentatiously, but forlorn and forgotten. In front of them some porters—gaunt men with great red turbans—were sleeping against one another. Across the first pair of tracks under some stairs a group of beggars was boiling something over a small fire; occasionally one of the ragged children who wandered up and down the tracks would dart back and drop something into the pot. Amiya was watching them while she ate. Finally her curiosity overcame her hunger and she stood up, moved a little away from the group, adjusted the folds of her sari, and tried to see what the children were putting in the pot. Simple Deepaka who often trailed Amiya in the village quickly licked her fingers, rose and followed. They stood together. Deepaka was puzzled as to what she should look at, sleepy after the long walk. Elder De finished his lunch and drew near, smiling at the women and wondering what he should say.

'The train will not come for some time yet, you ought to rest yourselves,' he managed.

The women ignored him as two more children darted past them on the tracks and put something into the pot. Amiya clutched Deepaka's arm:

'It is rubbish. That was a lump of dirty rice and an orange partly eaten. They picked it out of the dirt there. Those people are eating rubbish,' she was almost screaming in her shock. She shouted at the beggars to go away. Others of the villagers began shouting that the beggars must move out of sight. Amiya picked up a lump of coal and threw it, as she would have done at a village dog. She managed to hit the cooking pot and overturn it. The beggars scrambled for the bits of food. Some of the children burned their hands on the coals now spluttering. They whimpered and were briefly comforted by the older beggars while they fetched the pot and their rags and moved off down the dim platform. For a moment they stood dazed in a patch of sunlight before they found refuge in the shadows of another set of stairs. Amiya and Deepaka turned back to their places. Sometimes as they finished their meal from the village they muttered in astonishment to each other:

'It was rubbish thrown on the tracks.'

Then, like the others, they slept against their bundles, for a moment at peace between the village and the journey ahead.

At last there was a clamour of porters, of chattering women buying tickets, of children trying to see everything at once, and of the villagers preparing to board the train.

'Have you your tickets? Have you your tickets?' shrilled Elder De as he paced back and forth among them, getting in the way, falling over bundles, and trying very hard to appear composed. The forty-four huddled together in a sudden convulsion of surprise as the shrill whistle of the train blasted and echoed under the vaults of the old station. There it was, steaming down in noisy mechanical efficiency. It slowed, and the sigh of steam scattered a group of chickens that had been loosely tied together by a farmer not going far. Passengers rushed for their baggage, chickens rushed for one another, and Surendra murmured over and over:

'Oh Ma, look at the train.'

The panicked villagers pushed and fought and scratched, thinking that it might go off without them. Always suddenly when needed there would be Surendra grinning wildly, his dhoti tucked up as though he were out in the paddy, throwing up the bundles, pushing stout Deepaka up the stairs, and settling them all into the third-class carriage.

'Where is Reena?'

'Where is Jaydev?'

'Where is Babla?'

'All are here, or there.' Surendra scrambled back and forth counting heads. He checked the platform and saw that nothing had been left behind. His glance took in the rush of porters, the waving groups of family and friends, the red splashes of betel juice on the cement, and one lone chicken abandoned by the farmer, happily pecking at some spilled grain. He looked over the villagers crowded on the benches, spreading out their bedding on the upper bunks, trying to stow away all the bundles and parcels. Then he took his own bedding roll from near Elder De, moved it to the space near the door which smelled of the latrine, but was big enough, and settled down to light his biri and enjoy every moment ahead. A guard came and slammed down the heavy grating in front of him:

'Going far, old one?'

'Yes, to see all India.'

'And the moon too?'

'No, that I have already seen,' shot back the farmer. The guard went away grinning and Surendra rocked back and forth on his heels in secret pleasure at the humour of the truth. There was a last ripple of porters to one end of the train, a blast of the shrill whistle, a sudden jerk, another, and another. They were rolling slowly out under the roof of the platform, past the banished beggars, into the open evening sunlight and the edge of the town.

'I've lost my ticket, my third-class ticket.' A wail.

'No, there it is, Deepaka, tucked in your waist string.'

'Ah. That is where I keep paper notes when we have them.'

'Silly one. You are too fat. It is not a safe place.'

'Don't you tease me. I've had twelve children and that makes any woman soft in the waist.'

'And in the head too, Deepaka?'

'Only when they are all young,' she smiled back, and then thought 'or when they die'. Six of her twelve still lived, four daughters and two sons, they ran the little land well. She rolled back and forth with the train, not yet interested in anything out of the windows, and thought of the grandchildren at home and the married daughters scattered far. Soon she was crying silently. Feeling foolish she looked around and saw that the other women were also crying into their sari ends. Silly women, silly Uma-didi to include women on this journey. Strange that we all called her Uma-didi, though she was not elder. I had five children when she was not yet a bride. Poor Uma-didi, such a lonely life without children. Maybe that is why she gave the money to the trains instead of to some temple. Well, it is done for good now and we are going to Sealdah. I wonder if Ashin will remember Deepaka? Too fat, too ugly, too old now to sing with him.

Surendra glanced behind him at the full carriage. Some of the women were drying their tears and beginning to look out of the window. The men had already brought out the cards. Elder De was trying to read a map. Forward in the other car some villagers were talking with the farmer, who still held his chickens.

'Same as at the well in the village,' grinned Surendra and lit another biri. He liked the rocking of the train as he squatted on his heels and leaned against the metal wall. He could see out of both doors this way. The land was very dry. The rains would have to be heavy. He gauged the soil well from the flickering glimpses and wiggled his toes as if he were walking in his own plot. He caught a glimpse of a village ahead to the right and realized they were turning back again towards the river.

'Same as our own river, always the same.'

The telegraph lines flickered orange and silver in the afternoon sun, each pole beckoning to the next as the train sped south. The low trees thickened as they drew nearer the villages and sometimes Surendra caught sight of a cooking fire, or the curve of the thatch of the squat houses. There was a goat tethered. There some buffalo were being herded home by boys playing tag with the tails of the beasts. Sometimes through the green screen he could see a woman walking slowly with the big brass water pot newly filled balanced on her head and cautioned lightly by one upraised hand. The train began to speed up a little now and Surendra watched the river glittering through the trees along the banks. Gradually it grew dark. In the long haze of twilight the ticket collector came roughly through the train.

In the back of the third-class carriage the collector punched the tickets of the family going only to the next station. Then he came to the men of the village still playing cards with studied attention. They spilled the cards as they fumbled for the demanded tickets and cursed the collector loudly for destroying the game. He cursed them at length and individually for slowing his duty and told them how undesirable they were as passengers. Thus was a friendship established and the collector dallied long, hearing the news, learning of Uma-didi's will and of the journey ahead. He chided the women for not having brought enough village sweets to last the trip and was at once given the best they had tucked away in their bundles. He teased Amiya that she would find the village in chaos because of her absence, and flirted with Deepaka over the wondrous length of the grey hair which she was letting down to comb. Surendra complained when the official punched his first ticket, so the happy man felt in his pockets until he found another, unpunched, but cancelled, which he had confiscated two carriages back. He gave it to Surendra as a souvenir and the old man waited until he was out of sight before flicking it disdainfully out the window. Then he tucked the crumpled punched ticket which bore the name Sealdah away in his bundle next to his supply of pan.

The train began to slow and rumbled into the glare of the lanterns of a town station. Tea wagons jangled their bells. Great trays of fried savouries brought spicy, oily smells to the window. Beggars whined at the windows and doors, and above all, new passengers pushed and screamed while a few of the old ones got down slowly to the platform. The villagers leaned from the windows and bought tea, and looked at this station. They were disappointed that it seemed so like the first. The shrill whistle blasted again and they were off, this time into the night. A happy sing-song of talk made the food last longer, and the small brown clay cups were cradled in their hands affectionately long after the tea had been finished. The latrine was beginning to smell intolerably so Surendra picked up his bundle and pushed into the crowded carriage. It was hard to find a place with all these newcomers sitting along the corridor and filling all the luggage racks. Between a group of card players and the open ladies' compartment he found a space for his bedding and curled down upon it for the night. He turned to the villagers, lit a biri, and asked Mitu how long it would be before they reached Sealdah:

'Long, we do not get there before midnight is passed.'

'Where will we sleep?'

'In the station I suppose.' Mitu reflected for a moment on the prospect and then added, 'There will be many people, Sealdah is a big place. My father and I used to come down here once each year with dolls and pots to sell. We used to sleep with a cousin in Ballygunge, but that is too far to go tonight, and he must be dead by now.'

Mitu was of the family of potters in the village. He was thin and wrinkled to the tautness of a threshing flail and bronzed deep red-brown from his hours sitting—legs extended—around a mound of clay while he pummelled and then caressed it into shape. He was a good potter and loved to mould the fragile shapes around the village temple each year after the rains. But now stainless steel was cheap, even in the village, so his sons were making less and less, and bringing more playthings of plastic into the shop. The coloured stuff sold well, but it offended old Mitu's eye and was ugly against his searching fingers. His grey hair and sad eyes matched Surendra's precisely. They had been boys together, but

14

were strangers now, since Surendra was a cultivator and the potter caste was not much respected. Now that was behind them in the shadows of the night and they talked long about the village as they had known it as boys, the changes that had come, the dwindling of the crops as more and more of the young men went off to search for work in the jute mills or the streets of Calcutta. They spoke of their wives, long dead, and of the failures and hopes of their sons and sons-in-law. They talked of the foolishness of grandchildren who would not now learn the old ways. Long after the noise around them had lulled into snoring the two men murmured. At last they saluted each other solemnly, turned away into themselves and slept.

In the darkness Amiya stumbled down the corridor of the swaying car, found the latrine awash with the contents of the blocked pipe, and was sick out of the window. Again and again she retched, unable to will herself to move away from the smell around her. Finally, she pulled the soaked edges of her sari up to her calves and moved back into the corridor. There she leaned against the cool metal, looked out into the darkness and let herself be soothed by the rhythm of the train. She thought back to the early events of the day, and enjoyed the memory of the long walk over the fields to the station. When she recalled the beggars and how she had overturned their pot, she was sick again. She turned back to the ladies' compartment where she had settled herself, rummaged in her bundle for one of her dull, working saris, and changed from the wet one she had worn in salute to the beginning of the journey. Once she was clean again she poured some water from her last jug and washed her face. Then she cried a little, washed her face again, and sat down to compose herself for sleep. She noticed a glow of dim light in the darkness ahead, and that the train was slightly slowing. For almost an hour she watched alone while the train wound its way through the northern slums of Calcutta. She covered her head with her sari and trembled occasionally. When she saw lanterns swaying ahead, she moved forward and shook her sleeping friend:

'Deepaka-didi, waken, we are here. It must be Sealdah.'

Deepaka wakened in shock and looked out in surprise. It took a long time for her to realize that Amiya had just used the respectful term of address for the first time.

The villagers were too tired and dulled to take in the size and crush of the northern city station. They tumbled from the carriages, laden with hastily assembled bundles. They followed docile and uninterested, while Mitu led them to a huge waiting hall. There they fell again amongst their belongings, against strangers, and were asleep. It was a restless night with much whistling of trains and a constant rumble of people coming and going, but still they slept. Dawn brought a horde of sweepers, and with them the villagers moved to waken, wash and prepare for the walk across the city to where Ashin-dada was to be waiting in Howrah. As they bathed hurriedly before the water taps and changed into their village clothes they looked about them and noticed the huge cavern which was the station. It was dark, endless, filled with running porters, pushing crowds and beggars. Sometimes a man with a blue jacket over his grubby shirt and dhoti could be seen arguing with groups of worried travellers. He must be an official, certainly. The villagers gathered together and ate the remains of their food. The man with the blue jacket suddenly stood above them:

'You come from Srimati Uma Sen's village?'

'Yes,' they replied in chorus.

'How many of you are there?'

'Forty-four,' replied Elder De.

'No one lost, no belongings missing since you left the village?' the man smiled slightly.

'No, no, only the water pots.' They looked about them, patted the bundles and were reassured.

'You know you must go to Howrah to meet Ashin Mukherjee and board your own carriage by ten this evening?'

'Yes, yes, Ashin will be waiting.'

'Here is a map and how you must go,' he spread a torn and yellow map before them, traced a simple route naming the districts and the streets which he wrote on a paper and gave to Elder De:

'If you are not able to walk, then take a bus to here, and a tram from here, but it is best to walk across Howrah bridge. It is too crowded for wheeled traffic. Is anyone sick, are you able to walk?'

'No, no, we will walk. It is not far. We have not seen the city.'

'Yes, it is very far, and the city is tiring. What of him? And her?' The man pointed to Surendra and bent, wiry Reena.

'He sets the pace for our marches, and she herds in the stragglers,' laughed Jaydev. Reena grinned, for she knew it was true that she could stick longer to the walk than many of those years younger.

'If you want anything before you go, come to the station master's office. We have instructions from Baroda House to take good care of you.' The man went off in a rush and was immediately beleaguered by another group with a petition.

'Are we ready?' murmured Elder De. Then, Mitu and Elder De leading, the villagers stepped out, one by one, into the fresh dawn before Sealdah station.

The vast square before the old station was a jungle of bicycles and rickshas, the operators squatting beside them, some eating, a few still asleep, most smoking and watching for possible fares among the groups leaving the station. The sun glinted across the wheels and came to rest against the side of a high stagecoach, pulled by two horses, with the turbaned driver sitting on top giving orders to a large family loading trunks and baskets and cloth bundles into the space behind him. Everywhere there was colour and movement, but for this instant it seemed united to a purpose and the noise was still even, almost rhythmic. The ripples of activity moved forward, greeted the amazed villagers and rested, for more and more of the pedi-cab and ricksha drivers were coming up to them, bowing and speaking of the rates of travel. Elder De was stunned by the size of the square and looked this way and that as he polished his glasses, trying to determine what the centre of this metal jungle might be. It was Mitu who scolded the ricksha men and told them to be off and Mitu who gathered the villagers to follow as he led the way across the square. Surendra and Reena this time together herded the stragglers, chivvying along someone who stopped to gaze at the confusion, helping another to readjust bundles. As they moved through the carts and the flock of black, flapping carriages, the villagers perceived that the square was hemmed by shops and buildings, joined one to another, by balconies, washing, colour, and the overlapping morning shadows. Directly before them was a pump on the top of a small platform, and there people were washing brass pots or taking their morning baths. In the opening beside the well Mitu came to a halt and the villagers gathered around him, stunned by the size of the space they had just crossed. Elder De found the slip of paper from the station master and started to read the names of the streets and route they must take. Immediately the villagers started murmuring about the difficulty and how they could not manage. How could they find the names of the streets? Finally Mitu rose and in his deferential way suggested to Elder De that it would be best if they walked in small groups, not such a large one, and if each smaller group carried a copy of the directions. Arguments ensued, but subsided when the shock of what they were about to do again overcame the group. Babla said he would like to see the shops of Chowringhee, and Mitu said he would like to visit the potters of Kalighat. At the mention of Kalighat all the villagers shouted at once. So it was decided that they should proceed to go and worship at Kali's temple, and after being blessed find a way to Howrah.

By now the villagers were surrounded by a crowd of beggars. Women, ragged and ill, carrying grey and tattered children, perhaps led a blind toddler. Men with crutches, bandages, and missing limbs or eyes. Children alone and bellowing in their scrawny desperation. They cried, they chastised the villagers, they pulled at the women's saris, they touched the bundles, they locked their eyes to the villagers' and would not quiet their pleas even for a moment. Gradually the villagers' bewilderment turned to frustration with this new distraction, and thence to anger. Insults were shouted and returned, commands given and ignored. Mitu moved off down a small lane, still dark and smelling of the incense used in morning worship in the homes above each of the crowded shops. The villagers followed him in a straggling confusion trying both to see and to follow.

Behind came some of the beggars, close enough to wheedle, far enough not to threaten. It was a thoroughly frightened procession.

At the end of the street was a small shrine. It was whitewashed, and on one side was a garish but entrancing portrait of the goddess respected within, done in the sensuous black lines which only the Calcutta artists have mastered. The villagers paused to look and recalled their own little shrine, concealed by the banyan tree, brown and crumbling, but with a little frieze of figures around its shoulder which marked it as the home of the guardians of all living things. Mitu sat beside the picture and traced the lines, black to green to red and back to black, with his fingers. With the pause the women decided they too must perform their morning worship here at the beginning of the day. The men sat down with their bundles to smoke. The women went up the three steps into the dark shrine, one by one, waiting in a contented group as the familiar activity conveyed a calm. Mitu pulled out from the folds of his shawl a new pad of paper and a stub of a pencil. Carefully he drew a miniature of the portrait on the wall, taking special care to match the slant of the staring eyes and the flowing rotundity of all the lines. Surendra watched him with interest, as did Harischandra, the village scribe.

'Why do you make a picture?' asked Surendra.

'As a reminder. Maybe I can use it someday on a sara for a wedding, or on a pot.'

'I did not know you could draw,' commented Harischandra.

'Draw, model a toy, make a pot, it all comes from the same hands,' Mitu muttered as he finished, licking the pencil now and again to keep it strong.

'It is very different from the shapes on the temple, not so much like what we see,' offered Surendra.

'Yes, this is Kalighat painting. Not very old I think,' returned Mitu.

'Come, come ladies, let us get on with the journey,' Elder De fussed as he noticed the women beginning to settle down contentedly as they finished within the shrine.

Again they moved off slowly, without fear now. The familiarity of the shrine and the disappearance of the beggars had restored their native cheer.

'Maybe we should have brought a goat from the village since we go to Kalighat.'

'He would not have liked the train ride.'

'It did not bother the chickens.'

'Chickens are without thought, anyway.'

'Were you sick, O wisest one?'

'Look over there. What is the garland before the gate?'

'Must be a wedding.'

'No, no. See they prepare for Saraswati-puja.'

'Yes, this afternoon and tonight they do it at home, too.'

'How beautiful she is.'

'See there is gold in that sari, I am sure.'

'No, it cannot be. But see how well they have made the eyes.'

'The crown is not tasteful. It looks like a foreigner's hat.'

'Isn't it grand with all the coloured electricity?'

They stood, peering into the little compound at the image being dressed and decorated by several young men. This time it was Surendra who warned that the sun was beginning to be warm. The winter morning was late and they must move on with determination. They teased him for his anxiety, but followed Mitu once again. Occasionally a yellow taxi rumbled by, bellowing like a water buffalo and always driven by a large Sikh. The villagers shied from these more than from the gaily painted lorries loaded with men going off to work.

As they walked from street to street, through bazaar after bazaar, the size of the city began to oppress the villagers. The houses here were all together, there was no shelter of trees between, and everything seemed to be done in the streets in view of everyone, family and strangers alike. Old Reena cursed the disgrace of it and asked Harischandra why the people had no shame.

'Some of them have no homes, but live here on the street. You see over there is a pile of rags in a doorway. One of those washing must have slept there last night. Most of these houses are for many families together. There is no other place to wash but here at the tap.' He paused and looked around, remembering his one year as a college student when he had learned to do the accounts and write the letters by which he earned his living in the village. It had been a lonely time. He remembered how the village had haunted him as he walked these streets. It was a relief when the famine had ruined his family and forced him to return.

'It is very dirty. I wish I had my broom,' grumbled Reena as she hurried on.

Now they were moving with many people, and often were separated as they tried to keep Mitu or Surendra or Elder De in sight. No one could lag, for this was the morning rush and the traffic moved more slowly than the crowds on either side of it. The villagers crossed a small bridge high above the almost dry bed of an old river. At once the smell of a cremation ground surrounded them. As they descended steeply from the bridge into the pushing crowd they knew they had arrived in Kalighat. Harischandra waited at the entrance to a small lane and counted heads. Soon they were together. Some sat down to rest but were at once told to move on by the burly forerunner of a cluster of fancily dressed ladies who could not push through the crowd. The villagers shifted, the ladies passed, and Elder De commented that Mitu was missing. Babla laughed that he would find difficulty even finding forty-three in these crowds.

Harischandra urged them forward to the square before the temple: Mitu
would know they would be long at the temple. Again they counted
bundles and began to move away from the roar of the taxis and traffic on
the big street into the lane of temple shops.

First they passed a dark shop without a display, but down the alley which
ran beside it they could see piles of clay and wood, shards of broken pots,
and trays of small images of Kali, set out to dry. This would be a pottery
and indeed they could hear Mitu shouting in excitement beyond the
shutters.

Elder De stepped up and banged on the shutters:

'We go to the temple to worship, Mitu, do you come?'

'Oh Ma, I will come later, later. I must see all,' Mitu replied, his voice
shrill and trembling in the din.

They moved on past rival shops selling puja items, flower stalls dripping
garlands of jasmine, marigolds and roses, the basket maker's shop where
plain winnowing fans leaned like rows of horseshoes against the walls.
The maker was busy painting the sara with brilliant pink designs of
flowers around Kali herself. Reena bent further to watch.

'No, no, you do not put Kali on a fan for grain and rice,' she scolded.
'You must put Lakshmi-ma, who guards our wealth.'

'Do you want to buy this sara?' the shopkeeper asked.

'No. It is bad luck not to have Lakshmi-ma there.'

'Then if you do not wish to buy do not bother me,' he spat.

'Your mother was a sweeper's laundress to teach you such manners.
Why do you make such a bad picture?'

The shopkeeper smiled at the overture and responded:

'Here we are at Kali's temple.' He pointed to the egg-coloured domes
soaring above them at the end of the lane. 'Many tourists come here to
see our temple and they want a souvenir which shows Kali-ma, so that
they can show their friends that they were here. They do not know that
this is a sara for grain, and if they know they do not use it anyway since
it is painted. They probably live in some city house with all stainless
steel in the kitchen.'

Reena squatted beside him listening and watching the villagers mingling
with the crowd in the lane before the toy shops and the flower stall:

'Who are tourists?'

'Tourists are people who go travelling just to see new things, not to
visit relatives or attend a wedding. Mostly they are foreigners who have
much money to come here to India, and they do not know anything.
Kali, Lakshmi, even blue Krishna, all the same to them.'

Reena looked at him keenly. 'If they spend much money to come and
see, you should tell them what is right so they can learn.'

'They do not want to learn, only to photograph. Kali's tongue is easier to sell than Lakshmi-ma's smile.'

'But it is wrong.'

'Yes, it is wrong. I must feed my family, too. There are many others willing to paint everything, even verses in English on the saras.'

'These tourists have all much money?'

'Yes, of course. Who can leave his work and family and wander like a cow if he is not a paisa-wallah?'

'Pilgrims also just go to see and make puja. They do not have much money.'

'No, they must have more money than you or I, Mother, or they could not leave their work to go to a strange temple.'

'But you are wrong,' grinned Reena. 'I am also a tourist.' She enjoyed the new word.

'Where is your home place, Mother, and whither do you go? Where do you hide the great pot of gold?' The shopkeeper raised his voice towards the mixed crowd of villagers and strangers who had gathered to listen to the repartee and watch his deft strokes on sara after sara.

'We come from Srimati Uma Sen's village up in Burdwan district. We go now to see all India. We pay no money, there is no pot of gold. It all comes from Baroda House.'

Reena watched the confusion and attention grow around her and settled herself comfortably. She was the village storyteller and alert to every nuance in the crowd. Someone offered her supari and said:

'Tell us old woman, how can one be a tourist without money?'

'It happened thus, from the beginning,' began Reena. She told of Uma-didi, who had inherited her father's wealth, married a rich man, but remained childless. The crowd encouraged her with common proverbs about the ill fates which must accompany greed, but she countered them with a great paean concerning the character of Uma-didi, and told of how the village had come to replace the children she had wanted but not had. Sceptics in the crowd shouted:

'But she still collected your taxes, eh?'

'She gave us our seed grain with no interest,' shouted Surendra.

Reena quieted them all with a practised look and began the second part of the tale, of the death of Uma Sen's husband, of the beginning of the long, wearing illness, of her sudden mysterious visits to Calcutta and Delhi, always refusing to take servants, just one man as guard. She told of the nights just a month ago when they had all waited for her to die. Surendra interrupted:

'There was a ring around the moon.'

A great, knowing sigh went up from the crowd—it was always so with mysteries.

Reena elaborated on the death and sorrow and then built up the tension of excitement over the reading of the will before the village temple, a strange place for the reading of any rich person's will. She told of the carriage that awaited them at Howrah, of how all the villagers were to go around India. They, the oldest and wisest, were being sent now first to prepare the way for the others. She told of the money being given to Baroda House in Delhi to pay for the journey, the food, and for the tickets each of them had already carried.

The crowd sat stunned and then fired questions and comments:

'Has all the money gone?'

'Who is to go with you to show you India?'

'How long can you leave the village?'

'What are you going to see?'

Each question was answered at least by ten and sometimes by twenty villagers all talking excitedly and eager to share the stage.

Finally the shopkeeper turned to Reena and said: 'O wisest tourist of all, you should go and give a goat to Mother Kali that she has let you live to see this great journey. And take my wrong sara to remember this beginning,' he smiled.

Reena chuckled in delight, took the sara of mistaken praise, and led the villagers away to the temple. The lagging crowd talked over the tale and bought sara after sara from the host. It was a good bit of business to listen to a mystery, he grinned, especially a mystery about money.

In the compound before the temple they found the small gate which would lead them to the real place of worship, and quietly formed a line to go in. Harischandra decided to sit beneath a tree with the luggage. He never had been one to visit temples, and he alone among them had seen Kalighat before. He was joined by other men, who decided the line was too long. They squatted smoking, or sat against the bundles watching the crowds and the business in the stalls which lined the square. As the others went through the little door they found themselves in an enclosed court, the high towers of the temple looming above them. Immediately to the right were galleries where they were to wash, and a locker room with guards where they must leave anything of leather, and all their shoes. Among the worshippers washing there was subdued excitement and little talk, for down the alley directly ahead of them they could see the small groups and the blood running on the stones, and sometimes they could hear the bleating of the kids which were sacrificed there. Deepaka and Amiya washed together, glad that they had bathed at Sealdah. When finally they were ready, they joined the line before the steps up into the temple. Through the tiny door they could glimpse only darkness. All around them was the constant pounding of the ceremonial drum.

It was Deepaka's turn to bend and enter the cavernous inner sanctum. She looked at her feet for she was unsteady on the narrow stone steps and found she must quickly descend into a throbbing, swaying crowd. As she adjusted to the light she realized that the roof of the cavern was high above her in the domes, and that the sound was coming down to her, echoing and re-echoing for emphasis. She turned to her left where there was the greatest activity and realized with a start that this great red and black stone was the goddess herself. Deepaka bent low in salutation and stumbled as she was pushed from behind by the others tumbling in after her.

'Oh Ma, not too close,' she murmured and moved a little back into the darkness.

But she was swept on and around until she could see the priest receiving the devotion of each worshipper, placing garlands before the stone, sometimes bending to give a worshipper something before each stepped out into the sunlight. People shouted their salutations, the great drum did not stop, and from outside came the frantic, high drumming which preceded the fall of the sacrificial knife. Deepaka waited and let the other villagers go ahead of her. She was frightened to be so close to the goddess. The great crude eyes were too familiar from the picture she had on the wall at home to be disregarded. She watched as Reena went forward, curtly saluted the goddess and the priest, and was gone. Then Babla, then Amiya, then Rhunu and Arundati, and the others one by one. Deepaka watched the priest, who seemed so rushed and yet interested in what he did, unlike the priest in the temple she had visited with her mother to ask for a son. That one had seemed stupid, this one was alert and keen and looked at each who stepped before the stone with a querying gaze. Deepaka wondered what he was asking, aside from the name and Gotra of each of them. She watched for a while and gradually moved forward until she was swept into the moving assembly and found herself before the stone. She looked at the red daubs of paint (or was it blood?), at the solidity behind the eyes, and she could not turn to look at the young priest for a long time. Then, shyly, she bent, hands together, before the stone. When she looked up she found the priest's keen eyes almost smiling at her. She thought, 'He looks like my boy who died of the smallpox when he was not yet three.' She smiled at the priest. He bent, touched her feet and handed her a white lotus. She stared at it in confusion, but was pushed out into the sun before she could ask what it meant. The high drum-beats from behind the temple were rapid again, so Deepaka turned away, stepped down across the bloody gutter and into the open court. She still gazed at the lotus.

Amiya came up, saw the flower and started in surprise.

'The lotus,' she whispered, 'Deepaka, he gave you the lotus.' She was in awe of the most holy of flowers, simple and waxen on Deepaka's old hand.

'Yes, and he smiled and touched my feet,' replied Deepaka, also whispering despite the din.

'I never took you for a saint,' said Amiya, and the moment was gone.

They found their sandals and stepped again out of the little gate into the square where the men were eating. Most of the villagers were waiting, too, including Mitu, who was showing Harischandra the sketches he had made in the potters' shop. Deepaka sat down and began to cry silently while smiling at her lotus. Amiya and the others bought a large bunch of green bananas and began to eat. Deepaka tucked the lotus into her bosom beneath the sari and joined the silent group.

Elder De and Mitu were consulting a map with the papers given by the man at Sealdah:

'We are not yet half-way, Mitu. We cannot go to the National Museum. We must eat and then walk all this way to Howrah so that we are there before it is dark. Otherwise we will not find Ashin.'

'But the student said there were many wonderful figures in the museum, and things from the times of the emperors.'

'But we shall not meet Ashin if we come in the dark, and few here wish to look at stone figures.'

'No, that is true,' Mitu agreed sadly. He put away his notebook, shook himself and suggested they find somewhere to eat. The men who had waited long began to assemble the loads, but the women lingered in the shadows of the temple they had just left and took a long time to pass the wares spread out around the square. There were necklaces and cloth pieces, puja ornaments and clay images of the goddess, toy shops and tool shops, and finally, just out of the square, sari shop following sari shop with their wares hung out like banners above the heads of the passing crowd.

'Surendra, you'd better stay behind and be sure we don't lose any of the women here.' Elder De tried to smile.

'And that they don't lose all our money on foolishness,' grumbled Babla, with a short look at his wife Arundati, who had already stopped to finger a shawl. Slowly they moved down the lanes, broken now into small groups by the press of other crowds, but all somehow knowing that they must reach the busy avenue ahead and then turn along it. Surendra moved as he would behind his buffalo, patiently, with a determination which dissuaded all from stopping long under his gaze. His patience was more compelling than his speed, for they knew that Surendra had never shirked his labours.

'I have nothing else to do,' he always grinned as he went first to the fields and came last home from them.

Arundati darted into a shop to ask the price of a sari, but was shooed as a leper would have been from the village.

'Get out, get out,' shouted the owner, sparkling slightly in his white shirt and trousers. 'This is no place for street people,' he grumbled. A group of ladies dressed in silk were drinking Coca-Cola and laughed at the man and at Arundati.

She turned to Surendra in dismay: 'Does he think I have no money?' She and Babla were the misers of the village, and no one really knew if they were richer than the others.

'Of course not, village crow, look at you. You are a tourist from the train, not a lady buying wedding saris,' scolded Reena.

Arundati hung back, looking at the cloths waving above her head.

'Come along little one, there is a fine Saraswati ahead.' The group assembled before the gate of a small compound. This time a blast of music was playing from an old gramophone set up near the image. Finding they could not hear one another's comments on the goddess of learning they moved on, but not before the beggars from the celebration had come forward to the lure of the laden strangers.

Villagers and beggars walked on together, the first trying to hurry, the second trying to hinder and gain attention. A young mother covered with open sores moved close to Arundati and held out her blind baby to the plump woman.

'No, no, go away,' shuddered Arundati. The mother was persistent, the baby squirmed and whimpered. Arundati gave it the banana she had tucked in her bundle. Immediately several other beggars who had been petitioning others dropped back to Arundati and surrounded her, each whimpering or crying. The little woman was frightened and turned this way and that, holding her bundle of bedding and clothes tightly and trying to cover her face with the end of her sari. Surendra moved up with sure mien, pushed two of the beggars out of the way and led Arundati on quickly until she was beside Amiya.

'Let us stop, I must rest,' she panted. But Amiya glanced at her once, shifted her bundle to her head, straightened her back and moved on with the long swinging stride of one who is in the habit of crossing fields. Arundati struggled and shuffled and complained constantly of how hard it was, but she kept pace. Surendra smiled to himself:

'Same as the buffalo, always the same.'

All through the afternoon they walked, along great wide avenues, down dingy lanes, past rows and rows of dark little shops and offices. Always they paused briefly when they came to a pump. At one of these water stops Elder De counted heads and found that Reena was missing. Harischandra turned back to trace their route and found her only a few hundred yards away, squatting on a street corner, her bundles beside her. She was watching a strange procession on the other side of the street.

'Look, Harischandra, what kind of saints be those?' She gestured at a group of young people dressed in orange homespun robes, dancing and singing at the door of a fancy eating place. Harischandra squatted beside her to watch.

They were young, their heads were freshly shaven and gleaming white. They danced in a circle, slowly, singing a chant in which Reena and Harischandra could only recognize the names of Krishna and Ram; it was not like other chants they knew. Suddenly they stopped, turned toward the doorway and held out begging bowls.

'Harischandra, those are foreigners, begging?' Reena almost whispered, she was so shocked.

'Why do they sing of Sri Krishna and Sri Ram? Why do they try to look like sannyasis?'

'But begging, Harischandra. Foreigners have money. Otherwise they cannot come across the seas. Why do they beg?'

'They are very dirty.'

'Look, the cook knows them, he is giving food.'

They watched while the bowls were filled and then stared in astonishment as the group sat down where they were, without washing, and began to eat in sight of all. The last to sit stood before the cook, lifted his hand as if to bless and muttered something Harischandra could not hear but which caused the cook to grin. Then the boy turned away and, facing the others, began to eat.

'Ai, Ai, Harischandra this is bad. Who is that child to bless the cook? Ai, let us go away. I do not like this sight.'

When he caught up with the old woman he was laughing:

'Is it not always so with those who would be saints without work, Mother? The pan seller says they come here to gain enlightenment, but not by study, by the way of the dreaming drugs. When they become sick from too little food and too few baths, they send word back to their parents who send money, and then they go home on the big metal aeroplanes.'

The two had joined the waiting villagers, most of whom were half asleep in the sun. Elder De was pacing up and down polishing his glasses and looking down the big avenue before them. Arundati was massaging her legs, groaning slightly. Amiya and Rhunu were arguing over something they had seen. Reena told the story of the foreign saints, much embellished, until all who listened were weeping with laughter. Surendra stood and stretched:

'Come, it is but two hours to twilight, and we must cross the great bridge before dark so that we may find Ashin-dada.' Hoisting his bundle, he led off down the street without hesitation.

Elder De came running after, waving the map: 'But Surendra, which is the way? How do you know where to go?'

Surendra paused briefly and waved to the green space opening before them. 'That must be the maidan, the lungs of Calcutta. There we can walk on good dirt to rest our legs after this hard road. To the right beyond, past the tall buildings, must be the bridge, for on the other side of the maidan is the fort and then the river. So we just follow this way to the bridge.' He waved simply as though in the village, and moved off again. He was eager to remove his shoes.

The others had gathered themselves close to hear Surendra. Many followed him. Babla, Mitu and Elder De walked more slowly, Harischandra waiting now and then for them to catch up.

'How does Surendra know, he has never been to the city before?' grumbled Babla. 'Now we will all go wrong because of the silly old man.'

'Well you know Surendra is not silly, Babla,' cautioned Elder De. 'It is the right way for us, and much simpler than the hard streets marked by the station master.'

'But how does he know? Does a ring around the moon bring dreams with maps in to our farmers?'

'I think I remember that Surendra went to the mission school for a time. Of course he had to stop and work in the fields as soon as his elder brother died, and he did not go to the pukka school. There were many tales told then of Calcutta and the palaces of the English. He would remember anything to do with the river. I recall the tales of the fort and the maidan, too.'

'Yes, it is true. He went to school for a season. My brothers and I could not go because of the pottery.' Mitu spoke wistfully. In the Kalighat potters' shop he had met a student of art who had shown him many beautiful books with pictures of statues and paintings and strange mysterious carvings on coloured stones. It was the student who had told him of the marvels in the National Museum. He flexed his hands; it was odd not to have had them in clay for two days together.

'What good does it do to read?' muttered Babla. 'Amiya could read once too, and Rhunu was sent to the school, but what are they as scholars when they cook and pat the dung? You, Elder De. Over and over again you read the account figures and write them for the money-lender. You do not read anything else, nor could you, look how you fear the map. And here is Harischandra supposed to keep his family by his letters, but he plants his pulses and works in the paddy, and his family wears rags like the rest of us.'

Elder De wrinkled into a smile: 'Maybe if you learned to read, Babla, you would not have to pay me to do your accounts.' The shot reached its mark and Babla puffed in anger:

'There is no point to the schooling. We give money for our children to learn to write, but who can pay for books? What use is letter learning in the village? We need the work of the children in the fields. Each who goes to school is lost to the crops.'

'And they must come back in order to live, anyway,' Harischandra said quietly, remembering his own sorrows. Once he had owned some books, but his wife had left them on the floor and white ants had eaten them. Sometimes in the first years after his return, he had bought a little magazine or a paper, and read it over and over aloud. But the ease of it had vanished. Like Elder De he now read only when it was required, and that was seldom.

'But perhaps if our young did learn at school we would not have disasters like the mechanical well,' the younger voice of Jaydev broke in.

'That was not my fault, Jaydev. If the technical man had left spare parts you could have fixed the pump. It was not the reading of the book of advice that was wrong, but that there were no parts.' Elder De bridled whenever this last failure in village improvements was brought to mind. He thought it great foolishness to install a complicated metal pump and then leave without showing them how to run it without breaking it, or how to find replacements for the pieces that were faulty. But whenever the officers were there in the village, with polished vans, and wearing boots in the fields, he could not say anything but yes, yes, yes. Later he would shout at his grandchildren about the stupidity of the man with the machine. It did no good.

They were walking on the maidan, strung out in small clusters like beads on a child's necklace. Most of the men had followed Surendra's example and had taken off their heavy shoes, put them over one shoulder, and were walking like dancers, gripping the soil with their toes for the sheer relief of it. It was late afternoon. The traffic whirled around the maidan. The taxis still bellowed like buffalo, each driver competing with the others for inches of space. Safely in the middle of the open park, where goats were grazing and beggar families were settling to their meal, the villagers stopped to watch the confusion. The buildings of Chowringhee, higher than any they had seen before, were partly concealed in the dust and haze of the traffic. There was a glow of pink from the Raj Bhavan, then a scar of black of the huge Writers' Building, then the big hotels, the carpet and jewel shops, the alley down to a market, and more shops, all joined by an arcade under which flowed a shimmering river of people. Behind them were the tall trees and roads to Alipore. Before the Victoria Memorial the ice-cream sellers and stalls were waiting for the rush of the evening promenade.

A goatherd asked them where they came from and whither they went. They told him the little story of their wanderings and he saluted them as they moved off. First he had milked two of his goats and those who had wished had refreshed themselves with the warm milk. The boy had refused payment, flung wide his arms to embrace the maidan and said: 'No, here you are my guests. This is my village.'

It was the first time, but would not be the last, that they heard themselves addressed as that most privileged of orientals—the honoured guest. They thought about it and wondered what would become of the boy as they walked on to the end of the maidan and entered the busy streets of the business district. Office workers crowded past them in their rush to leave their work, and often the villagers lost a bundle, or had to pause to find one of their members who had become confused and lost in the rush. They were not much separated, and frequently called back and forth about where they should turn. Once they stopped at a fruit seller and bought more bananas to refresh themselves, chittering like bats over the price.

Twilight began to creep about them on dusty paws, and the business region was emptied of crowds long before they had wandered their way through it. Now there came the smell of the river, the tantalizing smoke of evening cooking fires, the pall of exhaust and oil and dung which hung suspended between the hedges of buildings. The groups moved closer together as they emerged from the quiet of the alley and saw before them the converging confusion at the entrance to Howrah bridge. The bridge loomed sternly black into the mauve of evening, and there was no end to it. Far below was the river, leisurely now at its appointed meeting with the sea, but still a battleground for ships and skiffs and little fishing boats.

'This is our river?'

'Yes, with others like it all together.'

'Oh Ma, look at the ships.'

'We shall be lost in that.' Arundati gestured to the crowds flowing up on to the bridge and to the traffic slowly moving behind an ox cart.

'We know we must descend on the other side to the station, so if there is space let us gather again at the end of the bridge.'

'What if it falls under the weight of so much?' Arundati whined.

'Then we shall all be washed of sin in that holy water, and Calcutta corporation will have another big worry,' grinned Reena.

'Has it ever fallen before?'

'Does it look so, blind one?'

'Can we not go down and cross by boat?'

'Look at the bank, Arundati? Would you rather slide down the stone wall than walk?'

'Well, at least we only have to do this once.'

'And what about the return journey, wife?'

'That is far away yet.'

'Look out, the traffic goes both ways.'

Babla pulled Arundati roughly out of the way of a bus as it rattled down towards them from the bridge. The couple moved forward together in their accustomed silent antipathy, each trying not to watch the other, but doing so out of habit and a consideration they did not admit. Reena followed a few paces behind, amused by them at first, but alert to the new world moving around her. Soon she was silent, and her eyes wide without fear as she moved up under the iron girders and stood, high above the water on Howrah bridge.

The greater wheeled traffic stood in two lines in the middle of the bridge. Around it and sometimes between it whirled the walking crowds: back and forth, up and down, round and round, dipping and swaying, nodding and bowing one to another in a strange ballet suspended between all other realities. Beyond the moving groups, at the walls of the bridge, were the beggars, the incoming hopeful poor and the departing vanquished. They had collapsed here on the bridge, unable to move further, unable to find any shore. They were the dirtiest, the most helpless of the people Reena had seen this long day. For the first time she saw people who had lost their hope and abandoned all dignity, who sat huddled against the cement, not daring to plead any more for the benefits fate had given others.

'Ai, oh Ma, what is this, what is this?' Reena repeated often as here she saw a boy withered with starvation, draped in a few grey rags, his eyes staring with the listlessness of those soon to die, there a group of lepers, a bundle by their side, collapsed and immobile beside the girders. A little farther on three children and a girl in the late stages of pregnancy were trying to light a fire. They had little clothing and their brown-gold skin was rippling grey with shivers as they bent to their work. Reena, stopped, watched, bent to help and they scattered, running from her in terror into the concealing folds of the crowd. An old man, bent and knotted, slowly pulled a cart along with the traffic. About him arose a cloud of abuse though it was no more his fault that the traffic was slow than it was the fault of the oxen ahead. A man leaned helplessly against a long crutch. He was numb with illness and age. Reena looked at his hands, misshapen with the knots of pain, at the chest shuddering with the effort of breathing, and at the foot wrapped in straw against some further injury. She paused beside him, quickly removed her own slightly tattered shawl, and wrapped him in it. Then she moved on. For a moment the old man seemed to turn and flicker in awareness. One hand moved up and clutched at the shawl. He hopped on again. Reena was cursing as only a practised storyteller can. Harischandra moved up from behind her:

'Mother, mother, shall I go back and get your shawl? It is a long cold journey that lies ahead of us.'

'Ai, in a big carriage, like rich tourists, with food paid for and all.'

'Have you another shawl?'

'Yes, child, one just like the old man's—to be carried to the river when my time comes.'

'No one will carry him to the river.'

'No, but at least if he lives through tonight he will be warm.'

'Wait until your daughter hears of this, mother, you will never know peace again.'

'Maybe that is the purpose of the journey, Harischandra.'

The man fell back, thinking of the crone's remark. She was sometimes thought to be a witch, this Reena. Her simple words seemed to have no meaning or too much. Harischandra remembered nights when they had sat listening to her, enthralled by a tale. He would have sworn with the rest that the figures she talked of walked and talked there in the space before her. She was often a lone figure in the village, frequently at war with all her family, rarely placid and content as became one of her age. Harischandra wondered why she had given her shawl to the old man. He moved up again:

'Why did you give it, mother?'

'It was mine to give.'

'True, but I have not seen you give to many beggars.'

'He did not beg!'

'Then why give?'

'Maybe he was my husband.'

'But your husband died three years before my wife died, and that is the whole lifetime of my grandson away.'

'You are still a simpleton, Harischandra.'

'Perhaps I want to learn again.'

'Remember the tale of how the Lord Siva cut up his beloved Sati in grief?'

'Of course, it is well known. We go to see the places where she fell.'

'Ai, and who can tell what form is Sati now, eh?'

Reena squatted, found a last slightly browning pan, and waved him away. Here she would watch for a time before going on. She wanted, as often, to be alone with the world about her.

Surendra matched strides with Harischandra:

'What is Reena plotting now?'

'I do not know,' and Harischandra told the tale of the shawl. When he had finished, Surendra stopped. He motioned Harischandra to go on:

'I will wait for her here.'

He smoked through his cupped hand and crouched, peering back into the dust and twilight. Harischandra moved forward and sensed that most of the bridge had been crossed. There was a wall of noise ahead of him. When he came to the end of the flickering of the girders above him he looked down to the left and saw the reason for the wall of noise. Ahead of him slightly the villagers were gathering around Elder De as they withdrew from the strangers who pressed on around them and beyond. They were looking down to the left, and all looked stunned, silent, fearful. Soon there were twenty or so together. Then perhaps thirty, and then a long wait as the dark of night came closer.

'That is the Howrah station,' murmured Elder De.

'There Ashin is waiting.'

'We will never, never find him.'

'Yes, he will watch. He knows how we will come.'

'How many people are there there?'

'I do not know, I do not know.' Amiya was shocked. She looked around at the faces of the villagers. They were on the edge of panic, a panic she had often seen on the faces of girls about to give birth for the first time. She reacted quickly:

'Here now, come, we must go down two by two and follow this path.' She gestured. 'You, Narend, lead with Rhunu; Babla, find your wife and go after Mitu. Come along, come along.' She sent them forth one after another to support old friends in the long descent into the whirling confusion below. At the sound of her voice ordering them calmly, the villagers did as bid. Soon all but Amiya herself, Elder De, Surendra and Reena were moving slowly down towards the square. Surendra and Reena came down from the bridge and with that Amiya and Elder De began their descent. The two oldest ones followed quietly and did not comment on the sight. It was nearly dark. They were very tired. Calcutta was behind them already, nearly asleep in the early dreams of the winter night before Saraswati's image.

Below them row upon row of hooded rickshas rested, their drivers crouched between the poles. The red turbans of the porters marked them as buoys in the deep sea, all running to or from the enormous façade of Howrah station. From the height of the bridge one could see the trains stretching and stretching against the faint glimmer of the rails. As they descended, the villagers lost sight of the trains and became part of the battle of trying to find a place: to run, or walk or park, or lay one's luggage or turn about in search of someone lost. They moved reluctantly at the quickening pace of the crowd around them, so that by the time they were in the square they, too, were nearly running with the crowd. They did not pause to look back at the bridge, nor for their friends and fellow travellers. They rushed ahead, dodging cars and the abuse of porters until they were within the doors and stood huddled beneath the soaring vault of the station hall. After a few moments Elder De arrived, caught his breath and counted heads. They were still forty-four. The frightened elder sighed, polished his glasses, and peered before him at the station. It was bigger, better lit, and even more crowded than Sealdah. He was very frightened.

Suddenly he was embraced by Ashin, freshly bathed, smelling of coconut oil and sandalwood, gleaming in a white dhoti and shirt.

'Welcome, welcome, uncle. Blessings, aunt, was it a hard journey? So you have come?' Over and over again the words of welcome brought smiles and relief to the villagers. Ashin had found them, soon they would sleep. It had been a long day.

Two officials in blue jackets waited until Ashin introduced them to the villagers and then made long, formal speeches of welcome and of how great a trust Uma Sen had placed upon them all, but especially on Indian Railways. Little of what was said was heard. They only smiled at Ashin, noted how well, though older, he seemed, and vaguely nodded at the rush about them. Finally Ashin and the two men led them along a confused path to a side track up in the back of the station. There was a blue carriage with lights within. They boarded, found it all newly painted and filled with the smells of cooking food. At the back they found a young cook busy. He welcomed them, asked them to take their places, and began to heap rice and pulses and curds on tali after tali. They sat to eat, but Deepaka looked up to the end of the carriage and saw a magnificent photograph of Uma-didi smiling down on them. Jasmine and marigolds hung about the picture in the traditional garland of honour. Ashin shook hands with the two officials, stepped up the three high steps into the carriage, looked at the peaceful scene and closed the door. At the sound the villagers looked up and greeted him again in chorus.

'We will leave in the night,' he said. 'Now you must rest.'

2

Holy Benares

Deepaka woke with a start. At first she stared at the confusion of sleeping bodies and bundles around her, not remembering quite where she was. Then she saw the flicker of light on the garlands swinging from Uma-didi's picture. She smiled at her own dreaming.

'We must be moving now. The train rocks like a cradle.' She lifted the curtains and looked out, starting back for a moment in surprise. She settled again by the window and watched the shanties of corrugated iron, thatch and old matting flicker past. They were on the outskirts of Howrah, moving slowly north-westerly. Sometimes Deepaka would see a fire and a group of figures huddled in the warm light. Once she saw the high spires of a lone temple in an open compound and she folded her hands and bowed to it.

'Perhaps it is the temple of Sri Ramakrishna.' The gentle voice of Ashin startled Deepaka. She smiled to him in welcome as he lifted down one bundle and settled himself across from her.

'You are not asleep after all your troubles over us?'

'No, I have waited to see the train move on. It seemed important.'

'Yes, yes, it does. But you look worn, Ashin. Has all this preparation been too much for you, or have the children been naughty this term?'

'Perhaps both, sister, but are we all here not more grey than when last we met?'

'Ai, yes, and some more bent, and many more frightened.'

'Did Calcutta and the long walk frighten you?'

'No, no,' Deepaka paused in thought, 'but the first wait for the train did frighten me. There is so much ahead that I wonder if we are ready for it, Ashin?'

'I suppose just as ready as a girl for her first babe, or a man for the death of his father.'

Deepaka strained to see in the darkness if Ashin was teasing her, but his face was shadowed and still as he gazed out at the fields sheltered by the winter night. The lines of his face were softened by a serenity deeper than any Deepaka had known, but none the less they had been etched

35

more clearly by time. 'There is even grey in his hair,' Deepaka noted with surprise.

'If you are right, we should be frightened. But I cannot think of Uma-didi wishing us to be . . .' she too looked out of the window.

'Did you notice—' they both began at once and then smiled, remembering all the times over the years they had been teased for saying the same thing at the same moment.

'What, sister?' Ashin asked quickly to break the memories before the tears came.

'Did you notice, Ashin, how we all just ate and curled to sleep like children, without even questioning our places or what will happen in the morning? And we are the old, used to going to bed last of all after the breakfast has been made ready!' There was shy wonder in Deepaka's voice which gave it youth again and reminded Ashin of the days when he was a student, she a young mother, and they had sung together.

'Yes I saw, but not all slept at once. Surendra and Mitu talked long. Elder De tried to stay awake while I read the paper. And Amiya saw to the cook's cleaning.' He smiled as he thought of the tall form quietly padding the length of the carriage almost as though she needed to tuck each sleeper in safely before she too could rest.

'Yes, Amiya-didi is restless still,' Deepaka looked to where her friend was tossing and murmuring.

'Do you think, sister . . .' Ashin paused and looked away from the attending eyes.

'What is it, dada?'

'Do you think Amiya will bend to the breezes upon us in these weeks? Much will depend upon her.'

'Why, Ashin? What worries you?'

'She is the strongest in the village. She is not used to being alone and away from all that is known as shelter. She has lost now the little grandson. Perhaps she needs to weep more than she has done.' Ashin did not go on, but he thought of the story of the beggars' cooking pot told to him by Harischandra while Amiya had been scolding the cook at the other end of the carriage.

'You mean, dada, will she be as frightened of the beggars, and so ashamed that she is sick in the night for the rest of the journey?' Deepaka smiled kindly at the teacher's embarrassment.

'Yes, that is what I mean.'

'Perhaps. Who can tell? We all have much to find in ourselves before we open Uma-didi's gift.'

'Open the gift?'

'Yes. Now it is a mystery, like the ring around the moon before she died. But in some days we will each know what we have been given, and each will have a different gift.'

'It is you who should be the schoolteacher, not I.'

'Hear the boy! Remember, I am the simple Deepaka, not one of the wise ones.' She laughed and turned away from him to the window and the darkness. She found it comforting, like the darkness by the little oil lamp whenever she had watched by a sick-bed. She did not understand why her daughters found that darkness frightening. She had always liked the night.

Ashin looked away to the figure huddled on the other end of the bench. That was Rhunu, of the sharp tongue and clever hands. Now she slept covered by her shawl. Across from her, Narend, her husband, sighed and pulled the blanket close. Ashin wondered about each one and at what Mr De had said in Delhi when he had gone to learn of all the arrangements:

'It will not be an easy journey. You will all bring much to it, just as you will have to learn from much. I hope you will have strong hands and hearts to help you.' Ashin frowned as he recalled the bitter quarrels among the women in the village and the slow hatreds of the men, festering over years and inherited unwillingly by cousins and sons. He looked searchingly at Deepaka, but her head was back against the window, her mouth open as she slept.

'A tiger on the shore and a crocodile in the river, eh little brother?' Reena startled Ashin. She was above him, having been the first to climb to the space of the top bunk. Her eyes twinkled in the night light from the corridor, and he could not tell if she was laughing at him. He was still slightly afraid of her, as he had been when a boy, but like all the rest he was fascinated by her strange, magic way with words.

'Have you been listening, mother?'

'To the train, to the words of the sleepers, to my own thoughts, O curious peacock.'

'Then perhaps I must take my thoughts away and let you sleep.' Ashin rose to go.

'Do not brood, boy, settle yourself in your music. We will find strengths as well as weaknesses. It is out of your hands to guide us. This is Saraswati's day, she who gives wisdom.'

'Truly, and she who gives music. I must withdraw before I sleep, thank you for reminding me.' He stepped out into the corridor, paused, closed the door behind him and walked to the end where his own suitcase and bedding had been stowed. Surendra roused when he entered, but seeing the thoughts on Ashin's face did not speak to the younger man. He watched while Ashin spread his bedding on the bunk above Jaydev, clambered up, sat crosslegged and pulled out a string of beads from his waist band. Peace caressed Ashin's face as Surendra watched him pray, and there was silence in the train.

Surendra looked away from the meditating figure across from him. He stretched and wriggled his toes wishing they were pressed against the warm mud of his house instead of this cold metal. How long had it been since he had prayed like that? He could not remember, but what did it matter anyway? Prayers were for women and schoolteachers, not for the likes of him. Ashin had been like that since he was the odd, quiet boy who haunted the schoolrooms like a lonely ghost. Surendra watched the sleeping Elder De in the flicker of the match. Silly old man, he wants too much and is always sad because he finds too little. Surendra reflected on the headman. But he was a good elder, fairer with the taxes and seed grain. He tried hard to make things better even though he did not know how.

Surendra smoked and, as he watched the shadows changing on the ceiling of the carriage close above him, he remembered the last time he had prayed. It was soon after his wife had died, when his daughter lay in childbed. She was weak from the grief just past but the boy had been born strong; the fourth she had had, making seven with the girls. She was still lithe and often led the village girls in their walk home from the well swinging gracefully below the heavy water pot. Amiya was there to help as always after a birth, and there was the foolish old mother-in-law who kept getting in the way of Amiya and the midwife. Something had gone wrong. Amiya said they must get the doctor from the town. The mother-in-law said that would only bring death, she would have no doctors. Amiya had sent the son-in-law off to fetch the doctor anyway. Surendra remembered how he had walked the banks of the river waiting for the boy to return. He returned to sit by the wall of the compound, for the women would not allow him within.

Amiya had come out in anger and told him that the cord was stuck and the afterbirth would not come. She had said the mother-in-law wished to pull it out and would not listen to the words of danger.

'No, Amiya, you do as I do with my buffalo, massage her belly with warm oil. It will come.'

'I know, Surendra, but she will not let me. She says I am not of the house.'

'Then tell her I come myself to do it, or she pays me back the dowry.'

He had waited long. Then there were screams and he had started to go in to his daughter when the shrill wailing which greets every death told him all was over. The mother-in-law had pulled. His daughter had bled to death. Then Surendra prayed for his daughter, his head bent against the mud wall. Now as he wept and smoked he recalled the prayer:

'Take her to a better father and a better husband. Take her to green lands and a clean river. Take her to mother healthy children. Take her gently and with a smile, for she has taken that smile from me.'

Strange that the words should come to him again, of a sudden, as they had in that moment. He never thought of his wife or his daughter at the village, not even when walking with the little terror of a grandson who liked to twist the tails of the buffalo. He spat, turned his face to the wall and resolved to sleep.

Arundati was being sick again, Babla realized as he wakened. She was not sleeping below him as she should be and he was annoyed. He shifted his blankets trying to find a more comfortable position. There was none. The train seemed not to move quickly and he wondered if they would soon stop. He would get out and breathe a little when it did. He thought of the fields at home in the village and fretted at what would be squandered by carelessness. He had not wanted to come on this foolish journey, but there had been no choice. The will had said all the elders. He would not stay back if the others were to have a free journey. But he grumbled to himself that there was no point and he would soon be ruined because of it. Arundati swayed in the doorway and groped forward into the compartment. He looked at her with scorn:

'Foolish woman, wasting good food.'

'You are awake?'

Babla made a face at her. She shivered slightly and looked at him.

'This is a time for prayers, not insults.'

'And what do they get us? Wealth? Sons? Healthy grandchildren?' Babla enjoyed the pain of his own regrets and did not notice that Arundati was crying. Their wealth, Babla knew, was much less than the villagers thought but best to keep them thinking it was great. The only child, a daughter, had died when her own children were small. Her husband had deserted the village years ago. The two grandchildren were an ugly girl and an idiot boy who had fits and whom old Reena protected from Babla's hatred. The girl was always crying and Babla thought now that that was one good thing about this journey, he was away from that horrid wailing which punctuated every day. He looked at Arundati clinging to the bunk and saw her tears.

'Go to sleep and stop that snivelling. We have to get this journey over with and you might as well resign yourself to it.'

'Maybe the train will crash and we will all die.'

'There is no creature on this earth more foolish and more timid than you. Go to sleep and do not waste any more food.'

Arundati crept to her own bunk and pulled the shawl around her. She tried to recall the sights of Calcutta but she could only remember the billowing saris. If only she had bought just one: they would certainly never see anything as fine again. She would put it away in the metal box for her granddaughter's wedding. Ai, where would they find a husband for that girl? If only she would smile at the families when they came to view her. But no, the girl always whined and pushed her fumbling brother in front of her so that the candidates rushed away in horror. Arundati cried on and on, regretting the saris more and more. She fell asleep thinking of the beautiful blue one with the gold border which she had touched for a moment before being pulled forward. A light flickered across her face and she seemed, in sleep, to be smiling.

The train slowed and the whistle whined at the far-off dawn. Mitu rose and watched as they pulled into the small station. Babla pushed past him so Mitu waited a moment before swinging down to the platform. Some porters were drinking tea in a corner and Babla realized how thirsty he was as he watched them. Other travellers were getting down from the other carriages of the train, but few were getting on board. Mitu went over to the porters and squatted with them. Soon he was fondling a clay cup of tea. Babla stalked over to him and asked:

'How much did you pay for that?!

'Why nothing, Babla. They share it for friendship.'

'Friendship? With porters of a station? Ask them how much for a cup.' Babla looked away. To his embarrassment he heard Mitu quietly telling the porters that he, Babla, was feeling unwell from the train and could he too share in the comfort of the tea, please? One of the porters rose and thrust a little hot cup into Babla's hands saying, 'Drink and recover, Brother, the train is a noisy thing.' Babla turned away, gulped down the tea, smashed the cup, and climbed on the train. He was not ill. How dare the potter make fun of one who worked his own land! He pulled his blankets to order and let the warmth of the tea lead him to sleep. He did not hear the chuckles of the porters as Mitu bade them farewell and apologized for the ill manners of the village grouch.

The train began to move, hissing with the effort of leaving the station. Out of the window Mitu could see a line of palms against the purple night. He got out his pad of paper and with sure strokes sketched the repetitive grace of the trees. Then, without pause, he turned a page and turned to look at the sleeping friends about him, his hands putting down what his eyes saw: a confusion of cloth, here a thin leg and arm dangling down from a bunk, there a flickering movement of a woman's hair blowing away from her sari. He watched the bitter face of the sleeping Rhunu and sketched into the portrait a rare beauty which perhaps he alone saw.

'Wake up, wake up, my beauties. Do you not know you are leaving Bengal? Come, come friends. Greet the sun and show me your tickets.' The conductor stood happily surveying the confusion. He watched and laughed and harried the villagers awake, and asked again for the tickets.

'But we have no tickets.' Arundati spoke in horror.

'What, no tickets? And asleep here like kings?'

'No, we have no tickets. We come because Uma-didi gave the money to Baroda House.' The confusion echoed from one to another and then the cry went up for Ashin, who was washing himself at the other end of the carriage.

'Here are the tickets,' said Ashin, producing a briefcase full of blotched sheets of paper. 'Forty-five third-class tickets for a circular tour in this carriage. We go around India.' With great pride Ashin handed over the tickets and the letter explaining things from Mr De.

'Yes, we have been told to expect you,' said the conductor. 'Is everything in order for you, is the food good? Do you want anything?' The conductor turned to the worried faces and tried to reassure them with his friendliness.

'No, no, it is as you said, for kings.'

'The food is good, we have a Bengali cook.'

'Will you punch the tickets?'

'Yes, if you wish. Let me see, where does it say we are in Bihar?' The conductor looked over the smudged typing until he found what he wanted. Then with a flourish he pulled out his clumsy punch and made an impressive hole on one of the place names. He handed the ticket to Surendra.

'Is this mine?' Surendra asked Ashin.

'Yes, if you like. Do you want to hold your own tickets? You must not lose them.'

'Yes, please let us hold them.'

'Don't give them to the women, it is not safe.'

'Yes, we shall hold them.'

'Uma-didi wished it so.'

The conductor punched the forty-five tickets slowly, counting them out of Ashin's case. When he had finished the smells of the tea and the warmed rice were strong and he wrinkled his nose in pleasure. At once Ashin bade him sit and eat. While the others washed and dressed, the two talked of the arrangements in the train and for the first stop in Benares. There was quiet as the cook served each with his small breakfast.

'Someone is not an idle guest, look at Uma-didi's picture.'

'Oh Ma, is that not beautiful?'

'Ai, who could have done this while we slept?'

'Uma-didi, I salute you under a strange sun,' and with that little Uma bowed and was imitated by the rest. Around the portrait hung a fresh garland of roses and jasmine and before it, tied to the frame burned a stick of incense. The conductor rose to go, shook hands with Ashin and Elder De and bowed to the others.

'You will be more comfortable, my friends, if you store your boxes and bundles here, underneath the bunks, and put the bedding up in these hammocks.' He showed them by lifting Babla's suitcase down from the end of the bunk and pushing it out of sight underneath Arundati's bunk. Then he unhooked a mess of string and tied it across the little compartment so that there was a wide, soft storage place swinging above their heads.

'Is that rope good, my son?' asked Reena with obvious agitation.

'Yes, mother, it would even hold you without falling.'

'Then I shall sleep as a babe for the rest of this journey,' and so saying Reena scrambled back to her compartment, unwound a similar mess of rope, tied it across in perfect imitation of the conductor and, crouched like a monkey on the edge of the upper bunk, began to arrange her few possessions on the bedding she spread on the hammock.

'Reena, you cannot sleep there. It is for the cases.' Amiya was stern and scandalized by this new impropriety.

'Nonsense, you guardian of my reputation. I shall travel better than all of you. I suggest you do the same in the next compartment, Amiya, maybe you will waken in good humour.'

'But, Reena, perhaps it is not good for your body to swing like that with the train.' Deepaka's concern was obvious. Reena was now stretched in the hammock grinning like a boy at a successful prank:

'Do we say that to our children when we tie them to the trees? No,' Deepaka, you are a better mother than to question how to care for this old baby,' Reena laughed, enjoying the scandal she had created.

The morning passed quickly as the villagers sorted themselves into the compartments, set up their little treasures: here a picture of a saint, there a string of beads, across the way a tiny brass image of a goddess. Each one made at least one remark about Reena as they came to look at her sitting on the hammock. Harischandra found that he could make a bookshelf in the corner of his bunk and soon his ticket was displayed with pride and he sat wondering if he would ever own another book. Mitu made a pillow of his bedding and sat with a good view of both the window and the carriage, his sketch book on his knee. Babla and Arundati argued over where each bundle and small comb should be placed and harried those who shared the compartment, until Amiya stormed down upon them and told them to settle themselves or separate in disgrace for the rest of the journey. Babla did not reply to this powerful cousin, but he continued to mutter as he sat on Arundati's bunk. Amiya herself took great care in arranging her own place and then helped anyone who would let her. She was restless and could not sit. Soon she was by the cook, watching and scolding and giving unnecessary directions. Elder De questioned Ashin without pause about what was to come, how they were to arrange things in Benares, where they would sleep and when they would depart again. Surendra listened and then interrupted with a question of his own:

'Ashin, this boat on the river or the great museum you speak of will cost money. How do we pay?'

'I have the money for all those things with me.'

'That is not good, for it could be stolen and then where would we be?'

'Surendra is right, nephew, you should not carry so much money.'

'What shall we do? We must have money for the fees. I cannot leave it in a bank.'

'Divide it now amongst a few who can conceal it and then we will always be sure to have enough.'

'Who shall carry it, uncle?'

'When we carry the tax money after harvest Harischandra carries some with the accounts, I carry some, Babla and Surendra the rest. Babla is very careful, and no one would ever think that Surendra guarded something of worth,' Elder De smiled at the scruffy cultivator, content and grizzled, swaying with the train.

'Then we shall do the same now. I shall carry what we need for each day, and you four must guard the remainder. We collect more in Bombay and Madras where there is a safety deposit from Baroda House.'

'I shall get Babla,' and Harischandra moved down the carriage to fetch the miser. When he had explained his news and the task to be given to Babla, the older man's humour changed and he strutted back to Elder De and Ashin.

'You want my help with the money?' he said to Ashin.

Ashin explained. Babla gave good advice about the keeping of records of how much each man carried and how much Ashin spent each day. The little council enjoyed the new business. Soon they were smoking and as at ease as the gamblers playing cards along the corridor. At the end of the carriage some women crouched around Amiya, each with a cooking task, each happy with the familiar work. The cook smiled sleepily at the women. Somehow they had all forgotten that in the village they would never prepare food together. They had confidence despite the strange freedom. Rhunu sat alone, still holding the little horse, sometimes tracing the painted lines with a careful finger.

'Did you make the horse, Rhunu?' Mitu dared to break her silence.

'Perhaps.' Rhunu snapped and hid the horse in the fold of her sari.

'It is a fine one, may I draw it?'

'Draw it?'

'Yes, here, in my book.' Mitu took his pad and showed her the sketch of the temple painting, the boy with his goats on the maidan, Howrah bridge in shadows looming high above them all, and the views in the train he had made in the night.

'Why do you do that?'

'It passes the time, and keeps my fingers loose. Maybe it will be helpful with the pots when we are back again in the village.'

'It is just what we see here,' Rhunu looked around her and then again at the sketches.

'Like your horse, each has a beauty or something I want to remember.' Mitu carefully concealed the page where he had sketched Rhunu herself, but his concern was unnecessary, for she was carefully removing the horse from the hiding place and looking at it.

'Then draw it,' she said abruptly and thrust the horse at Mitu.

Arundati had moved to the group of men. She waited until they could ignore her no longer and then asked Ashin when the train would come to Benares.

'This afternoon, before we eat.'

'Will we go to see the sari shops?'

'Ah, mother, I could not keep you from them any more than Lord Siva himself.'

'But will we have time to see and to buy?'

'Yes, tomorrow or the day following. We stay four days in Benares, there will be time.'

'Benarsi saris are expensive,' growled Babla.

'But cheaper there than in Calcutta.'

'Do you buy a wedding sari for the little one?' asked Uma.

'Yes, if I can find one.' Arundati sat, eager to chat.

'Is a wedding agreed?'

'No, but I must be prepared.'

'It is always difficult to find the right husband for these silly girls,' Uma responded. She and Jaydev remained poor, for both their sons were students who did not, they said, wish to marry. Uma recalled to Arundati their difficult attempts to find wives for the boys. Gradually the two women became friends. The one was frail, thin and quick in all her movements, her eyes hidden behind thick glasses. The other was plump and stolid, inclined to whine and complain. Uma, like Jaydev, wanted to reform the village and she was ambitious for her student sons. Arundati yearned for the happy days in her father's house when all was easy and she had had many saris, or had at least in memory. She had refused to send her granddaughter to the village school because she dreaded being alone with Babla. Sometimes when she was busy cooking a special meal, she thought it might be possible that Babla was disappointed with himself, but most of the time she just thought he was disappointed with her. The two women had shared nothing in the village, occasionally meeting at the well, often hearing complaints about the other's husband from their own. Along the carriage many who had remained strangers though living within sight of one another now were talking together and planning to share the adventures ahead.

The meal was served. The groups ate in silence, turned away one from another, wife waiting for husband to finish before beginning her own meal. The food was not rich, but there was more of it than in the village. Reena thought it like festival food, Babla complained that it lacked the pickles and sweetmeats which he enjoyed. The land they passed was dry, rolling hill country. Sometimes the scar of a coal mine could be glimpsed, sometimes the station at which they stopped seemed crowded with strangely garbed tribal workers, eager to find a place on the train. The heat increased, the fans failed, there was much dust this winter. Reena slept in her hammock. Surendra smoked and patted the bag of money at his waist. Ashin tried to read a newspaper but soon he also slept. Amiya was sick and tried to find comfort on her bunk. Failing, she looked to Deepaka, who went back to the cooking stove and made tea, carefully including some of the herbs she had brought in her bundles. Amiya was not the only one skilled in curing. Amiya drank the tea and lay down again. Deepaka fanned her friend and hummed one of the songs of Tagore. Amiya grew quiet at last. The fan grew still, Deepaka's head sank low and she slept. Rhunu watched the passing scenery and every now and then her eyes stole to Mitu.

They were wakened by the conductor banging on the door:

'Come, get ready. We come to the holy city in less than half an hour.'

Little needed to be packed, but for the next minutes the group was a confusion of preparation. Suddenly Rhunu called out:

'We come to a bridge, there is Ganga.'

At the windows they called back and forth in excitement as they saw first the bridge, then the great river low on its banks but embroidered with a complex pattern of boats. On the farther side they saw the steps, dotted now in the late afternoon with many white-clad figures. The skyline was a confusion of temple towers, modern blocks, minarets, and derelict palaces. When they had crossed the bridge they could see only alleyways and dense traffic. They were in a field of rails and a station loomed ahead. The train stopped and from the carriages on either side rumpled travellers and sick pilgrims struggled forth. When some of the rush had subsided the villagers climbed down and clustered together. Ashin went ahead to find the station master and ask what they must do and where the carriage would be put for their stay. He returned with a bustling man who carried a great sheaf of papers and seemed eager to be free of this new responsibility. He gave the villagers a nod and told them they must sleep in the carriage and not on the platform. He gestured to the back of the yards near a water tower and said that the carriage would be placed over there and would they please come and go through the gate to the yards not through the station. Clearly the villagers offended his tastes. Ashin asked him about the arrangements made to take the group to Sarnath and south to Khajuraho. The man waved his papers at some offices up above the station hall:

'Not my job. Ask the tourist officer.' He hurried away. Ashin advised the group to move out of the station and wait for him in the great courtyard before it. He went to find the tourist officer. Elder De watched him go, removed his glasses, and rubbed them again and again. He turned to Rhunu's husband, the tall and quiet Narend:

'We must stay together. I do not think he will find the officer.'

'No, it is late.'

'What shall we do without more help?'

'Plow the field as usual.' Narend beckoned to the villages to follow and led off, Jaydev beside him waving his umbrella as a banner. They walked two by two. Before they had gone far Deepaka began to sing a song of fishermen well known to them all. It made the walking easier, and they smiled with delight as other travellers stopped to look at the strange procession. Ashin looked down from the balcony above and smiled, too.

'They will manage it, they truly will,' he thought as he banged more firmly on the office door. Eventually a scrubbing woman came past and told him that all the officers had gone home. Ashin sat down in the corridor and spread out his map. After some time he folded it, rose and found his way to the courtyard. The villagers were sitting eating something hot and fried, he could smell the tang of it long before he saw what it was.

'Where now, little brother? May we walk to the great ghats to bathe, or is it forbidden for farmers?'

'We will do that at dawn. There are to be boats to take us along the river. Now we will walk to Viswanath. How we will stay together I do not know.'

'Just as now. Narend led us, for he is the tallest, and we sang to keep pace. We can do so again.'

'Which way, Ashin?'

'Let us be off, which way?'

Without hesitation they set off, singing, the rhythms of village work refreshing their legs wearied with sitting. They wound through the streets, pausing now and then while Ashin consulted the map. Sometimes the singing faded off into chatter when they saw some new strange temple, or a crowd of foreigners being addressed by a guide with a megaphone.

When they were ready to return, Narend strode before them and tried to lead them home. But eyes were greedy for the colour of the city, and hands would touch the saris, the dolls, and the beautiful carvings. It was fully dark when they emerged from the alleys of the inner city and the longest part of the walk was still before them. It was impossible to stay together, impossible to see Narend. Cries of 'Wait, Wait' brought the movement to a halt.

'I am frightened,' Arundati moved close to Uma.

'I, too, a little. But we will reach the station soon. Narend remembers everything and is never lost.'

'It was he who brought the doctor in the night of the flood when their son had the cholera, was it not?'

'Yes, on a little raft across the angry river with the doctor praying aloud the whole time,' Uma laughed. Several others joined her in the memory.

'He must have been a fine doctor all the same, for he won over the cholera.'

'No, it was not he who won, it was Rhunu herself. She it was who made the boy drink salt water. He was better by the time the doctor came.' Amiya had never forgotten the strange determination Rhunu had shown.

'Come, mothers, we must move on. See, Surendra and Narend have bought torches from the ricksha men, now we will go easily.'

It took another hour to find the station and then a long period of confusion in which many were lost before they found the side gate and the carriage by the water tower. At first the station guards did not want to let them in, but Reena gave them vivid descriptions of their ancestry, and with laughter and admiration the guards bowed before the storyteller and her followers. The cook was angry when they appeared so late and told them all the food was ruined, but good smells belied him.

'Here Deepaka, your tali is laden, come in and eat,' Amiya called.

'No, it is after sundown, Amiya, I may not eat now.' Deepaka smiled as she climbed the steps, 'besides I have had the best food of all, the sight of Ganga at Kasi, and the blessings of the temple.' Amiya was startled, for she had never known a time before when Deepaka had insisted on following the rules for widows.

'But you must eat, it has been a long day. My head aches from hunger.'

'Then eat quickly, before the food is cold, and here, eat my portion too. I will sing the evening prayers for you all.' Deepaka settled serenely before the portrait of Uma-didi and from the folds of her sari brought out a fresh garland of marigolds. After placing them around the portrait, she bowed and then began to sing. The others had paused in their eating to watch her and some of the widows had withdrawn to eat in the shadows. Then the familiar song and the soft voice removed the strain from the moment; the villagers smiled secretly and bent to eat. When the prayers were finished and Deepaka turned slightly from the portrait, a deep voice singing from the other end of the carriage made her start. She turned further and recognized Ashin's turn of phrase in the evening song of Tagore they had sung together as children. On her cue she joined him and from this melody they went on to others, sometimes joined by other voices, most times just the two harmonizing and vanishing into the night beyond the light of the carriage. A group of beggars crouched listening to the music though the villagers did not know it. Finally Ashin began his favourite of Tagore songs, in which the traveller knocks on every door of the outer worlds before he finds his own. The lilting Bengali words were heard afresh and brought deep stillness to the listeners. At the end Deepaka rose and tried to move to her bunk but the clamour of praise was loud. Before she was half-way Ashin had met her and was wringing her hands:

'That was beautiful, didi, you see we are not old. We can still make music for the village.'

Deepaka blushed and suddenly was young and glowing with beauty.

Then she pulled her sari over her head and moved into the darkest corner of the sleeping compartment. Rhunu watched as Mitu concealed the sketchbook where she had seen him drawing the scene. Narend watched his wife as he stretched his long frame on to the bunk beside her. Above them Deepaka combed her hair and Reena was silent in the hammock. Deepaka was Narend's cousin. Though they shared a similar temperament, he had paid her little heed over the years. She was called Simple Deepaka by some because she asked the questions and said the things that no one else would dare to for fear of being called stupid. Her husband had laughed much and had died too early to see the success of the sons Deepaka raised, or the hard-working mothers her daughters had become. Narend's stomach growled and he thought to himself that Deepaka must be hungry though she did not complain. Even when he had pulled her hair and frightened her when they played as children she had never complained.

'Keep that stomach of yours quiet,' Rhunu murmured. Her voice was muted but still sharp and he thought there was a quaver in it. He reached out until he found her head against the pillow, and then with a gentle finger found the tears on her cheek.

'What is it, wife?' he whispered, his hand still resting on her face. There was silence and Narend could only hear the heavy breathing of their sleeping companions. Then Rhunu's calloused strong fingers grasped his and he knew that though she could not say what was troubling her, now she would sleep. Their hands parted. She turned under her blanket. Narend stretched again, still wakeful. As often over the years, he wondered what his wife was thinking. She was so often sharp, so often scolding, yet she took more gentle care of him and of their sons than any woman in the village. They were both silent people, perhaps that is why their parents had matched them. Now it pained him that she had been weeping. He swung off the bunk and again found her face in the darkness. She was sleeping. He took great care not to waken her as he carefully wiped the tears from her face and neck and then pulled the blanket higher around her. She stirred slightly. He stopped. When she was still again he rose and walked slowly down the corridor to the door of the compartment. They were all sleeping. It was cold as his bare feet sought the metal floor at the end of the carriage. Like a village dog he sniffed a little before slipping through the door and stepping down the steps on to the cinders. A few more strides and he was against the wall of the railway yards. There he stopped, squatted and bent to light a biri. Reena found him by the light of the match.

'Mother, you come to me like a ghost, be careful that I do not die of fright and haunt you,' teased Narend. They were old friends, often sleepless, often meeting by chance in the darkness. Reena was the youngest sister of Rhunu's mother and she liked her difficult niece and was liked in return. It was with the silent Narend that she could talk.

'Rhunu is restless.' Reena was squatting beside Narend.

'Yes.'

'You must ask Mitu to help her.'

'Mitu? Does she need his help?' Narend knew he would be given a sensible answer. He had no fear of Reena's words as the others had.

'She wants to draw, in the book, as he does.'

'You mean making alpana?'

'Yes, only not the same thing over and over.'

'No, she is never pleased by that.'

'She studied drawing for a time when my sister still lived, when there was the teacher at the Trader's House.'

'But she said they only did alpana and embroidery and women's work. Does Mitu now do that?'

'No, he makes pictures.'

'Ai, I understand. She said he had made a picture of the little horse of my grandson. The boy will be sad to have forgotten it, Rhunu made it for him last harvest.' He smoked in silence and said nothing more. Reena knew he would find the right way and moment to help Rhunu. She looked around the yards, noticed the beggars sleeping nearby, and then spoke again.

'Strange to be in Kasi and to think only of the foreigners.'

'The ones we saw on the walk this evening?'

'Yes, and at the temple.'

'You saw others in Calcutta.'

'They were different, they were fools of the dreaming drugs. Today these people were not the same.'

'But we saw some very dirty ones wearing clothes from the bazaar.'

'Still, they did not look the same.'

'Teach me.'

'No, not yet. I do not understand. Perhaps I am too old.'

'That is the first time I hear you say it.'

'Foreigners are stranger sights for old eyes than even these holy stars above Ganga.'

'Come, it grows colder.' Narend led the way back to the carriage and the two returned to bed silently. The tall man noticed that Reena's old shawl was thin. It was her only covering in the hammock and he remembered the story Harischandra had told of the old man on the bridge. He fell into a sleep plagued with dreams. Several times the sleepers were disturbed by shunting trains and whistles. Just before dawn when the dogs began foraging and barking, Surendra rose and began to move down the carriage. When he reached Ashin he bent to waken the younger man but drew back seeing the tired face.

'We have waited a lifetime to wash our sins away in Ganga. Another day will make no difference, nor add much to the sins,' Surendra laughed to himself. Now would be the time to rouse his buffalo and go out to the fields. He watched the sky and wondered if this year there would be good rains. He went back to his bunk, pulled some cloth from his bundles and went out into the dim morning. The cook found him there washing out his clothes.

'What old man, do you now do the washerwoman's work?'

'Quiet, fool, they are still sleeping,' Surendra jerked his head towards the carriage.

'You do not sleep.'

'No, I would be out to my fields by now. One cannot break old bones to new habits.'

'Have you always washed your clothes, then?'

'Sometimes my daughter-in-law does, but it is no trouble to me, and they dry in the sun with the smell of dew and earth still in them.'

'Ai, he is farmer, washerwoman, and now poet. Next I will find he is a demon.' The cook reached out and filled the tea pots with water.

'You should have found that out first, lad. Tell me, is this water good for drinking?' Surendra had an instinctive distrust of all town water.

'The station guards said so, but I will boil it long to make sure.'

'Trust no one about food and water. Remember we are far from Bengal now and you must be your own guardian.' Surendra moved to a space of weeds and grass and spread his clothes out with practised hands. Then in the mist he washed himself. There was movement inside the carriage. Some of the women noticed Surendra's clothes drying and quickly fetched their own garments. Soon there was a long rainbow of wet garments spread along the edge of the station yard. Ashin came out before the sun was up and hurried into the station itself. Uma scuttled away from the train and came back with a group of sweepers who cleaned the two lavatories quickly and to the relief of all the travellers.

'Where did you find them, Uma?' Jaydev was surprised that she had gone off alone.

'By the station toilets, where else?'

'Will they come again?'

'Yes, I have told them to come morning and evening every day as long as we are here.'

'Why twice, and not once as in the village?'

'We are forty-six who use only two latrines. We must be clean or we shall be sick.'

'And if we fall sick will you make us line up for a needle from a strange doctor?'

'Of course,' Uma was serious and Jaydev teasing, but he saw that she was right.

'Come, come quickly. Are you ready? We go to the river to the dawn.' Ashin returned excited with a man in a blue uniform. No explanations were needed, at once the carriage emptied and the villagers hurried to keep up with Ashin and the official. Narend walked with Surendra and

Mitu at the back and it took the three of them to keep Babla and Arundati at pace with the group. The two were still arguing over the price of the sari Arundati was sure she had to buy. They had gone to sleep the night before amidst the same argument, not even the thought of the washing away of their sins by Ganga could distract them. When they at last tried Surendra's patience, he gestured to Narend and Mitu to circle in front of the arguing pair.

'Now we go forward, you two, we do not want to miss the dawn's blessing. You are so cantankerous that not even Ganga can save you.' With that the three men strode away forward to the rest of the group. At once Babla ran on, past the angry figures, until he was in the midst of the villagers. Panting, Arundati at last caught up with Surendra while they waited for a bus to cross a square.

'Do not leave me, do not leave me,' she pleaded. Once again Amiya came back and set a pace which Arundati was forced to keep. Within a remarkably short time Ashin and the official led the way into a small gulley and then the group emerged on to a long terrace. Below them were the steps. Before them was the river. Across it came the yellow dawn, the first dapples of sunlight now at the middle of the river. As one they raised their hands on high and recited the salute to the sun. Then slowly, just as hundreds of others along the bank were doing, they walked down the steps and into the river. With cupped hands they bent and brought the water above their heads, pouring down over their faces. Then each in his own way performed the ritual of washing, watching the priest ahead in the water. When the gestures were finished they stood and watched in awe as the dawn sunshine splashed over them, blessing and warming and greeting them as it had never, quite, done before. Some went out of the water and sat on the steps watching strangers. Others repeated the ritual in the name of someone at home. Reena chanted to herself the line from the story she had told the night before and when she was as drenched as a Bengali fish, she splashed out of the river and up to a platform to dry. After a time two long boats, each with a canvas canopy, appeared and pulled in to the shore where they stood. Ashin explained that these boats would take them the length of the city. They boarded them dripping and watched critically as the boatmen poled out into the current. They turned to look back; for the next hour they were mesmerized by the strange, moving frieze before them.

Up and down and across the ghats moved the crowds, now vivid in the dawn. At first it took a moment to realize that the ghat which the villagers had just left was now full of strangers. As the boats swung from the bank and pulled further away the villagers strained to see a group of priests descending a flight of steps in procession. Each carried a furled umbrella, each held his skirts above the damp of the steps, and each walked solemnly directly into the water, the pile of umbrellas mimicking the firewood on the next ghat. This was the central burning ghat where those who died in the city were burned, and their ashes given to the holy river. Already three small family groups were waiting beside their draped corpses. A priest sat near each. Someone was struggling to light the first fire, a body was moved forward. The flames caught and jumped. The villagers sighed. For an hour they moved slowly past the bathers and they did not tire. Surendra joked with Reena about the women washing their saris as they stood in the places of prayer. Elder De was teased by them all when he admired the peace of a group of priests sitting asleep on the sunny steps. Finally the boatmen began to turn toward a bank where a boy was washing his buffalo. The great black beasts were restless, and when the two laden boats appeared behind them, the herd split and one branch began to swim downstream, bellowing and snorting the while. The herd boy jumped up and down in the water and screamed at the villagers, whereupon Surendra and Narend and six of the others sprung from the boats into the water. With practised slaps and much joking they expertly herded the animals together and up on to the bank. They enjoyed their lark thoroughly and when they climbed out spent much time scolding the boy for his neglect of the beasts, pointing to an animal with a sore foot and to one with an infected eye. The boy went off, shouting, behind the herd.

Beggars had a fire going, they urged the farmers to dry themselves beside it. This they did, laughing with their hosts. It was colder here than in Bengal on this February day, and though the sun and wind dried the bathers, they shivered as they climbed up the path the buffalo had taken to find again Ashin and their guide.

3

Of fear and foreigners

When the villagers finally reached the square where the buses waited they were hungry, and frightened by the secular rushing of the city. Ashin suggested they all go and eat in a restaurant before going out to Sarnath. Amiya was not alone in her horror at this idea. Ashin found himself facing an angry crowd. Many of the villagers who had stayed silent and slept much of the way from the village now shouted and denounced the pacific teacher for this new blasphemy against their customs. Ashin explained that it would be a long ride and that he could not promise food when they arrived.

'We do not eat the food of strangers in the village, we will not do here.'

'We will wait until the cook of the train gives us food.'

'He is not of the village.'

'He is known to us.'

'Hush the talk of filth. We will not eat. We will ride the bus.'

'When will the bus go, Ashin?' little Uma asked as the others climbed aboard the vehicle.

'Not for an hour.' Ashin was shaken by the stubborn resolution of the villagers and all that it implied for the future.

'Come,' Uma led Jaydev, Rhunu and Narend into the crowd. They went back along the route they had come. Ashin persuaded the others to stay on the bus and himself paced outside. When he saw them returning he and the bus driver laughed together. Each of the four carried a huge basket. Each basket was piled with fruit. Narend held an enormous battered teapot from which the steam was curling. Rhunu balanced another basket on her head and when they reached the bus the villagers could see that it was filled with little clay cups, fresh and still grainy from the potter. A lumpy parcel was tied with Uma's shawl and she was often nearly knocked down when she swung it too far.

'Where did you get the food?'

'Is it cooked or can we eat it?'

'How have you paid for so much?'

'Are we to smash these cups as on the train?'

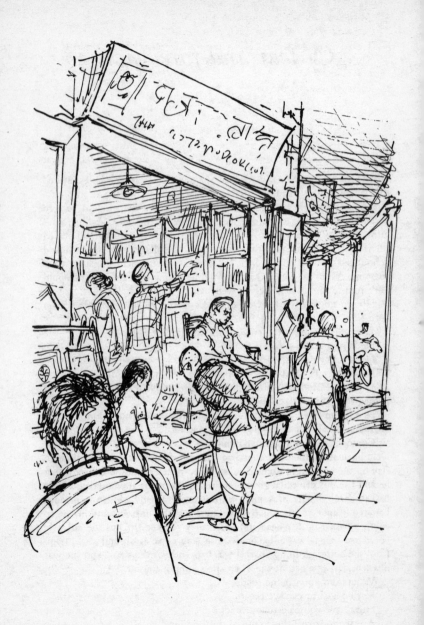

'Must we wait while you return the pot?'

'Show us, show us, what have you found?'

'I have bought the pot. Now we can make tea wherever we are.'

'Do not smash these cups. Tie them safely in the end of a shawl or sari.'

'Here, pass down the fruit.'

'What is in Uma's bundle?'

'Look, the bread of the Muslims we sometimes eat at festivals. See, it is warm. The cook spoke Bengali, he came from Murshidabad.'

The villagers ate well, but their providers had been wise and kept much in the baskets so that there would be no repetition of the protests later in the day. The bus driver started off as Uma told Ashin that they had returned to one of the markets they had passed in coming from the river. She laughed as she related how Narend had bought the teapot from an office boy who had been sent to fetch it by some sleepy clerks. The boy had been unwilling to sell the pot but Narend had explained that by selling it to pilgrims he would acquire virtue and by not taking tea to his clerks he would help them to work harder. With gusts of laughter the boy had given the pot to Narend. Rhunu had seen a potter's stand in the market and had quickly purchased enough from the startled owner. Ashin asked where the money had come from and Uma looked shocked.

'Why, from Jaydev! He said he carries some of Uma-didi's money for the journey and that we should pay for the food from that. Is it not so?'

Ashin blinked. 'Yes, of course, that is right. Jaydev, I must keep accounts. What did you spend?' Jaydev told him and the guide in the blue uniform whistled.

'You must bargain well in your village, friend. That is half the price we would pay for that fruit here in Benares.'

'Then you are daily cheated, for it is not worth more than we gave. Rhunu just refused to understand the prices said by the man until she felt it was right. Then she understood.'

The bus took them across the city, though very slowly, for the morning traffic was thick and bicycles would not give way to the bus no matter how plaintively it might bleat. Eventually they were travelling past larger compounds, and it all looked more like a village. Late in the morning they still did not feel warm and they asked the guide and Ashin to tell them of Sarnath to distract them from the discomfort.

Briefly Ashin reminded them of the story of the Buddha and that it was here that he had preached his first sermon. They looked doubtful until Reena chirrupped that they all knew the tales of the elephant who adopted the orphaned calf, and of the lion and the mouse.

'Those are tales of the Buddha, and it is the same Buddha here. We go to see where he taught of the wheel and the right way as he saw it.' Reena stepped forward to leave the bus.

'But I do not know of the wheel and of what he taught,' came the complaint from several.

Under the noon sun a splash of orange shimmered. It took the villagers a few moments to realize that this was some sort of holy man. He was unlike any they knew from the village. His head had recently been shaved, he was small and trim from much walking and little food. The robes he wore were richly bright against the deep brown of his one bared shoulder. Throughout the long explanation of the history of the stupa given by a guide, the villagers kept looking toward the stranger. When the lecture finished they asked first about the strange priest:

'Why would a priest come to the stupa of the Buddha?'

'He has walked the length of India to sit before the place where Buddha preached,' replied the guide.

'May we address him?'

'Yes, he likes to meet those who come.'

Deepaka led the way across the terraces. She was always eager to meet new priests. Many of the others laughed at her, and a few settled themselves to sleep against the warm stone rather than listen to more talk. Shyly Deepaka bowed to him. The priest smiled in return. The villagers behind her pressed a little closer and Deepaka backed into their midst. Ashin asked the man if they might speak with him. The stranger replied in English that he would be happy to speak with such a large group of pilgrims.

'We are not pilgrims of the Buddha-puja,' Nirmal declared sternly.

'They say you come from Sri Lanka, the land of Ravana,' Harischandra tried the English hesitantly.

'No, my home is in Thailand to the east. I came over the sea to Sri Lanka to speak with the monks there.'

'Are you a family priest of puja in your land?'

'No, no,' the monk smiled. 'I am a monk serving in a temple in the city of Bangkok. There we meditate upon the teachings of the Lord Buddha. I write prayers for those who come to worship.'

'But you have a begging bowl.'

'Yes, here I am a pilgrim, and even in my country we monks must beg for our food.'

'And the belly of a priest is always empty.'

Ashin translated this for the monk and he guffawed with pleasure to the delight of the villagers, who had only laughed nervously. Adjusting his seat he began slowly to tell them of the Buddha. The courtyard was warm in midday. Most of the audience soon slept. Deepaka and a few others attended and they were sorry when the young man's voice began to tire. He rose and collected his staff.

'Do you go now?' Deepaka spoke in English and Ashin started with surprise.

'You, with your friends must rest. It is tiring to listen to sermons.'

'Will you bless us first?' Nirmal and Amiya exclaimed in shock at Deepaka, but the old woman was serene in her request.

'What blessings are mine to give I give you gladly,' said the monk and bowing he stepped gracefully across the stones and was gone, only the soft swish, swish of his robe echoing gently from the rocks.

'Why do you tempt the gods, Deepaka? You must not ask priests of other lands for a blessing.'

'He seemed a simple man and as I am simple, too, perhaps his blessing is good for me.'

'I had forgotten Deepaka that you learned English.'

'She is not alone,' grinned Reena, also speaking the foreign tongue. 'Amiya and Surendra should also remember it for we were taught by the tutor at the great house on the river.'

'Do you remember?' Ashin turned to Surendra.

'A little, a little,' replied the old farmer enjoying the confusion of the schooled men around him.

'Let us wake the sleepers and see more of the place. We have had our sermon, now let us find enlightenment,' Surendra joked as he looked about him. 'What is that place?'

'That is the museum,' remarked the guide.

'A museum? Like the one in Calcutta, with statues and pictures?' Mitu was awake and on his feet in one quick spasm of excitement.

'Yes, yes. This is about Sarnath and those things found here about the times of the Buddha.' The guide started off to lead the villagers away towards the building. It took a long time for them all to waken, struggle up stiffly and then cross over to where the guide waited. Mitu was already inside the hall, impatient but not quite confident that he should go on alone. At last Ashin and the guide arrived and the villagers slowly wandered from case to case and statue to statue. Mitu sketched the smiling head of a young man so vividly moulded in stone that the smile seemed to flicker. The potter led the guide from case to case until each new wonder had been admired. They assembled again outside.

'Did you see the jewels the women wore?' Arundati was astonished.

'Did you see they had money pieces with writing on?'

'How could their potters make such figures, Mitu, when now our temples are so plain ?'

'I do not know. The figures must have been carved by the gods of those days, not by potters.'

'The Buddha was a prince, too, did you see the finery he wore as a boy? Aye, and then to become a monk! What a pain for his mother,' Uma sighed.

'But to have such a saint for a son would be a great honour, Uma!'

'Not at first, only after his fame was great, I think.'

'Do not speak so on the holy ground.'

'It is not holy ground, it is only a place where a sermon was given.'

'To others it is holy.'

'Not to us.'

'Tell us, Ashin, tell us of the times when men could make the stone come alive,' Mitu pleaded.

'No, no more sermons. I am tired of so much talk. Let us go to the bus. The sun is already sinking. All of me aches from hearing of all these holy men.' Babla gestured to the long shadows and the villagers realized how quickly the day had gone. Slowly they moved across the square and through the gardens. They turned often to look at something new, and Deepaka always searched for the monk. Then, suddenly, they were on the bus, counted, and moving away from the town.

Benares was bustling in the last shadows of twilight when they returned. The crowds were out for the evening promenade, traffic swirled to take the workers home. Lights came on around the tiny shops which crowded the streets with vendors, noise and a brilliance of colour which the villagers found oppressing after the stillness of the afternoon. They were glad to reach the station after their long walk from the terminal and found the carriage quickly. The cook was waiting on the steps. It was cold and they were grateful for the steaming rice he served them. Deepaka looked to the dusk and wondered if she must not eat. Amiya stepped forward and pointed:

'See, the sun has not yet set, it still hits the tops of the spires. Come and eat.' Deepaka led the evening prayers, but then she ate. After the meal there was a little quiet talk, but before Ashin had had time to get out his paper the villagers were preparing for bed. Ashin joined Surendra.

'What do we do in the new dawn?'

'More temples and then the university, I think,' said the tired teacher.

'Why the university? We are just farmers, not learned folk?'

'Yes, but it is a place of books. Many people come to learn Sanskrit and the old tales.'

'Then it should please Reena.' Surendra saluted Ashin and retired.

Ashin sat on, making notes by the light of the watchman's lantern. This business of food would be a problem. They could not spend the journey eating fruit and tea. Some already, after only two days, were looking ill and older. What was to be done? Ashin picked up his beads and thought of the moments of song with Deepaka. Strange that she did not meditate upon the music as he did. Did she find peace in her prayers and blessings? Ashin thought of her eagerness to find new words of worship and of his own solitude. Perhaps there was truth in each of the prayers she gave. Perhaps that way was a solace to her. But in following the raga with his mind did not he too find the same truth? The same knowledge of all that was hallowed moving in harmony within him? Ashin drew in his muscles, exhaled, and from somewhere deep within hummed the first syllable of his raga. He closed his eyes and his being vibrated imperceptibly as he once again drew strength and peace from the music. Within the carriage, Harischandra strained to hear the tone and, failing, slept again in envy and loneliness. Across the city the guide who had spent the day with them was telling his wife about the strange group of poor villagers who had today herded buffalo in the holy Ganges, gone and bought fruit in the market for little money, and then asked a monk from across the sea for a blessing.

'They must have played with you, husband,' she scolded. 'Only rich men go around India and behave so foolishly. Tomorrow you must ask them for money.'

Surendra wakened before dawn and found that Deepaka and Reena were already washing at the tap. Amiya followed him down into the dew and the darkness.

'Surendra, do you remember the way we walked to the river?'

'Yes, it is not far.'

'Could you take us now?'

'Truly, but why? You bathed in Ganga yesterday.'

'We would do so each dawn while we are here.'

'I will take you. Do others wish to come?'

Amiya went back into the carriage and after a few moments she returned, followed by a sleepy procession. She had wakened all the widows from the village and the two old teachers, Nirmal and Bankim, who spent their days chanting to the temple. So far, they had spent this trip praying and trying not to participate in the changes around them. Amiya viewed them as exasperating and irresponsible. She never could forgive them their idleness. The newcomers washed at the tap in the cold and were surprised when Reena stepped across from the station carrying the steaming teapot.

'Where did you find tea, Reena?'

'In the station supervisor's office. The fee was the story of the snake prince. It took as long as the pot took to boil.'

'The sky pales. Come, we must hurry.'

Surendra led them down beside the dark wall until they came to the station square, eerie with its rickshaws stooped like scavenging birds keeping vigil over their prey. The band was draped in grey. They drew close together as they walked, the shawls which had warmed so many children and grandchildren at last too thin to warm old bodies. Each carried a little water pot. They did not talk in the chill, but walked quickly behind Surendra, intent on the task ahead. When they reached the alley at the top of the ghat they paused and took off the light sandals or slippers they wore. Then, once again, they stepped forward on to the high terrace and looked down to the water. This morning a mist lay along the river like a feather coverlet. Reluctantly, as the sky turned from purple to green to pink, the river gave up the mist. The villagers watched, fascinated, as the white clouds swirled upon the water. When the first orange hint of the rim of the sun was visible they moved down and stood in a solemn line in the water. Then the sun rose suddenly, demanding his homage. Before they had finished the first prayer the villagers were bathed in the light. The last of the mist rose, bowed, and retreated. Ganga mocked the solemnity of the praying figures along her banks. Suddenly, it was morning. From behind and above them the villagers heard the waking sounds of the city, growing from a growl to a barking, belligerent roar. Surendra, who had been watching the villagers in the water, stepped down to them, said a hasty prayer to the sun, drenched his head, and asked Nirmal:

'Shall we depart now? We do not wish to alarm those in the carriage, and we must not be left behind.'

'No, no. Oh Ma, I must finish another prayer.'

Slowly the old ones ascended the steps, turned for a farewell look at the river and then disappeared among the other pilgrims. Not long thereafter they reached the station and the carriage to find Ashin worrying, breakfast ready, and the clothes washed and dripping. They explained the nature of their absence and Ashin shyly smiled his respect for the worshippers. Soon they were off, weaving here and there through the crowd, noticing a more colourful shop, a funeral procession, a garland maker, as they walked. Through the labyrinth of alleys they found a way to the Durga temple and were shocked when a family of monkeys appeared on the wall to greet them. This was an old temple, rather dingy to the villagers' eyes. Amiya, who had stopped to watch a mother monkey feeding her baby, suddenly looked up and realized that once again a crowd of foreigners was watching the worship from a neighbouring house. She fumed, she shouted, she raged at Ashin, and all that happened was that one of the foreigners raised a camera and appeared to take a picture of Amiya pointing at him. The shock of this effrontery made her recoil, she ran away from the sight of the window. Deepaka came and tried to distract her by pointing out a seller of coloured powders who had made his wares into a line of beautiful little mountains, gracing the edge of the temple wall. Amiya would not respond, nor would she talk. Ashin led the rest of his charges from the temple. Over and again Amiya asked Ashin:

'But do they pay to watch worship in their own countries?'

Over and again she received the same reply:

'I do not know, Amiya. They come to learn and do not know what they do is an insult.'

Amiya's distress was contagious and it was a confused and somewhat sullen group which made its way down a wide avenue to a wooded park. They left the main road and followed Ashin up a flight of steps. Everywhere there were priests and holy men. And everywhere there were groups of foreigners taking pictures of the priests.

'This is the Hannumanji temple,' announced Ashin.

The villagers started forward eagerly along the cobbled walk. They loved the monkey helper of Rama, and to pay him homage in his own temple caused them great excitement and delight. Amiya walked a little more slowly than the others, Deepaka beside her trying to remind her of the wonderful nonsense of Hannuman. A cluster of women who always tried to imitate Amiya stayed close to the friends. They were walking behind a pair of foreigners, a boy and a girl. Amiya was stiffening with anger, and Deepaka was trying to hurry her past them when a voice addressed the foreigners:

'Good day to you. Do you like our temple?'

Amiya watched the couple pause and then saw their confusion as they looked at the wizened little holy man smiling to them from under his umbrella. The two bowed and waited. Amiya and the others paused to watch.

'You spoke to us in English,' the girl said hesitantly.

'Yes, once very long ago I was a student in England. Where do you come from?'

The boy replied, 'I am from the States and my friend is from London.'

'Why have you come to India?' asked the little man.

'We want to reach . . .' but Amiya and the others did not know what he said. Harischandra could not translate. The little man bent forward to the boy.

'I beg your pardon. I did not understand. Please say it again.

The boy blushed and said 'You know, enlightenment, release,' and then again the strange word.

'Ah, you mean you wish a revelation of God, or as we say, to be absorbed in unity.' The old seer sat back, pleased to have understood, but the boy and girl were distressed.

'No, no, enlightenment, nirvana, release into nothing, like in the old books, you know.'

'But enlightenment is recognition of unity, or in your tradition, knowledge of God.' The old man stated this flatly.

'No, we learned all about it, the big self and and the little self, and finding nothingness.'

'But my young friend, the great self is the Universe, or God, and absorption into that unity is what we are all seeking.'

'We spent time in Rishikesh with a guru,' the girl tried to explain. 'He said we had to meditate to make ourselves empty.'

'Yes, as vessels for the god, or unity, within and without.'

'No, to be not attached to life, so we can be released. You know, initiated.'

'But you are young, you have not yet begun to live, this is not the time to be released. You must wait until you are old like me, and all your duties done, then you can go out to seek release.' The old man changed his attack. His audience was growing and they murmured approval at this remark.

'We have no duties, we just want to get released.'

'Of course you have duties: to learn, to work, to marry and have children, to raise them as best you can. Then when they have children you can choose to take this path.'

'But we don't want all that. We don't have to do it. We want to get released now.'

'My friend, I do not understand this phrase 'get released'. Here we view enlightenment as an achievement of study, discipline and devotion. One earns release, or revelation, one cannot be made aware by any other agent than one's mind, or the tools of one's spirit. First you must master the languages of revelation, either in our tradition or in your own, and then you must practise hard until you are able to reach that one moment of joy. Nothing can obtain it for you except work and constant awareness.' The small man was revelling in the phrases of the foreign language. Harischandra struggled to translate.

'But does not a guru do that? He releases you and you get enlightened. It is not hard, they said so in Rishikesh. We have been looking for a guru who will take us together.' The boy put his arm around the girl. Amiya looked away. The old teacher smiled and then his face grew sad. Slowly he withdrew into himself and the Indians knew that the interview was over. The couple looked confused as people started to walk on and as the old man began to murmur, oblivious of them all.

'Why did he stop talking like that? Why did he look so sad?'
The couple turned to the remaining watchers. A studious-looking man looked at the holy man and at the boy's honest bewilderment. Finally he spoke:

'I think he fears that you have only disappointments ahead, and he does not wish you to go from our country with this disappointment. There is no easy way to truth.'

'But we won't go until we've got enlightenment. You Indians know about spiritual things and the easy ways to get release. That is why we came here.'

'Then I must wish you a happy time. But please, remember that the holy man here in Benares had studied too, and that he recommended work. Perhaps he was once an engineer.' The clerk moved away and Amiya and Deepaka with the other villagers followed him up the path.

'They were not like the watchers at the temple,' said Deepaka.

'No, they were dirty.' Amiya did not like to be puzzled as she now was.

'They said they had come to learn from Indians.'

'And they said they had no duties.' Amiya spat. Someone else muttered. 'Where are their families and how do they feel about these children wandering about in dirty clothes, to get released?'

Deepaka paused and looked back. The couple was walking hand in hand along the path. They looked like small children returning home from a party; sad, tired, depleted.

'No wonder the old man wished to weep,' sighed Deepaka. She caught Amiya and the others as they were about to enter the temple and for the next hour she forgot about the couple. When she came out of the enclosure a monkey plucked at her sari and she squealed in fright, to be teased at once by the others. The villagers were gathered under a tree eating some fruit. Amiya related the tale of the couple with bitterness and scorn, and was shocked when Harischandra, Ashin, Reena and Deepaka expressed pity for the young couple:

'They come to learn, Amiya, they do not come to offend.'

'They were dirty. The girl was wearing blue trousers like the man. Why do not they learn from books in their own lands?'

'Perhaps they tried.'

'No, they come to be lazy and not wash. There is much work to do here and in their own countries.' Amiya grew more stern as she saw her supporters nodding.

'They must be rich, or they could not come here and not work. How much does it cost to come across the seas?'

'Thousands of rupees.'

'You see, they are just mocking us like the people at the temple who took pictures of our prayers. They are rich but they pretend to be poor. They say they have no duties and come to find an easy way to be released into nothingness. Foolishness. Would they not offend fewer if they just cast themselves into a river in their own lands? That is the easy way to nothingness!' There was uncomfortable laughter for a moment and the villagers were relieved when Ashin urged them to move on to the bus.

There was little traffic in the early afternoon. Despite the winter chill there were people sleeping in doorways. The villagers commented whenever they saw such a figure and were astonished when the guide told them that most of these people were pilgrims. He explained in detail that the costs of lodgings in the city were very much higher than elsewhere because there were always too many visitors. Several times they passed groups of foreigners and the guide explained that the foreigners came on tours or to study, and that very rarely did they come alone. Ashin asked about the large buildings ahead of them.

'This is the university. Now we shall get down and one of the professors will show you about.'

The villagers spoke to one another scathingly of the guide's foolishness in bringing farmers to a university. Some of them drew Amiya's attention to a crowd of students:

'There are foreigners here, too. Look they walk there. They must be part of the class.'

'They all carry books. All of them. Ai, they must be rich,' Harischandra sighed.

A gentleman came forward with their guide. He addressed them at length in Hindi, bowing and smiling. Suddenly he stopped, looked at them carefully and then said, in English:

'You do not understand. What language do you speak?'

'Bengali.'

'Ah, Bengali.' The man rolled around his mouth a few lines of Tagore. The villagers were delighted. The professor gave again his speech of welcome to the university. He told them that education was the hope of India and that they, by coming to see the oldest and best place of learning, were setting an example to all the villagers of India. The villagers were cynical but they listened as they were told of the antiquity of the place. At the end of the speech one of the villagers asked the professor why there were foreigners in the university.

'They come from many lands to study our ancient Sanskrit. They are very interested, too, in our philosophy. Usually they stay but one year so must return to their own places just as beginners. Many of them come after they have studied years, they are earnest students.'

'Who pays the money for their studies?'

'They must pay, either with family money or with scholarships.'

'What is a scholarship, please?'

The professor talked as he walked and told them of scholarships, examinations, courses and classes. He led them into a building which smelled of dust and age.

'It is a house of books.' Mitu stared in disbelief. Their host explained that this was the library and that here the students studied or borrowed the books. He showed them how it was ordered.

'But who takes the money for the book?'

'No, no one pays. They take the book when they need it and then bring it back for another student to use. The library owns the books, and they are not for sale.'

'Do you have pictures, too?' Rhunu spoke almost in a whisper.

'Yes.' In a moment the gentleman showed them scrolls and manuscripts. In one he found some of the Jataka tales of the Buddha.

'See, here is the young elephant standing under the legs of the bull. The words tell,' said the professor, beginning to read the words.

'But that is my tale of the elephant who adopted the orphan who was the Lord Buddha,' interrupted Reena. 'Oh Ma, it is written. The picture shows it all.' Reena pointed along the scroll and the villagers crowded forward against the table to share her excitement. Reena bombarded the professor: did he have this tale, did he have that, were there books of the snake tales? When the professor was unable to answer he turned to the librarian and together they tried to please the old storyteller. They went off to another section, Reena's voice shrill in the still hall. The librarian was subdued from habit and with amazement at her knowledge. Mitu was once again sketching. This time his fingers moved hesitantly as he tried to copy the miniatures illustrating the story of the elephant.

'That is good,' said the professor to Mitu,' have you studied drawing, then?'

'No, I am the potter of the village.'

'My wife studied drawing once. She makes the best alpana in the village.' Narend's voice startled the villagers and they turned to stare at the couple.

'Come, then, and see the books of design,' said the professor led them to another room. Here there was better light and as the volumes opened Rhunu and the other women lost their embarrassment and moved to examine the books.

'May I touch it?' Rhunu asked the professor.

'Of course, turn the pages and see it all.'

Rhunu and Mitu stood at the table for a long time, astonished at the variety suddenly before them. After looking in silence, they began to show each other special things, a cloth piece, a mandala, a familiar toy horse such as Rhunu had made, a clay pot decorated with a line of parrots just as Mitu might make. The other villagers moved away with the professor to one of the windows and were listening as he told them which building was which and where the students went to eat and how difficult it was to run the university with too little money. Harischandra walked carefully from one set of volumes to another, his hands sometimes reaching up tentatively to touch the bindings. His eyes were wide with shock at the revelation that there existed so many books yet to be read. When the professor wished to lead them away from the library Ashin had difficulty persuading Harischandra and Mitu and Rhunu that they must leave. Harischandra turned to the professor and asked:

'Must one be a student to read the books?'

'No, we have many scholars who come to spend their last years in the city and they stay in a hostel while they come to read our books.'

'There are few scholars,' Harischandra spoke wistfully.

'Any man is a scholar if he truly wishes to learn the truth and gives himself to that search,' replied the professor.

'But not in one lifetime can one man find the truth from so many books.'

'Perhaps he could, if he started with a little truth,' the professor was amused. Reena was waiting for them at the bottom of the steps:

'Come, the man says there is a book store where we can buy books of tales for only a few paisa. He says there are books of stories from foreign lands too.'

'We will go to the book store after we have seen the rest of the university.'

The villagers moved away from the library only after Reena and

Harischandra had touched the feet of the librarian. The professor was embarrassed and bustled them officiously into a larger hall.

'These are the classrooms,' the professor explained as they walked through a long corridor and looked into the dark rooms at the rows of chairs and mess of paper. Then they entered a long, low hut lined with many tables. The professor said this was the eating hall.

'You mean the students from different families, even foreigners, eat here in sight of one another and of the same food?'

'Yes. There are cooks who prepare the meal. They all eat together. There are also meals served for those who stay in the hostels.'

'Students live also under one roof with strangers?'

'I will show you.'

They left the cafeteria and walked until they came to a building where laundry was hanging out and a great blare of noise and voices dominated everything. The professor led them into a hallway where they had to step carefully around all manner of possessions. He knocked at one door and was answered by a young man. The boy saluted the professor and stood looking at the crowd of strangers.

'Lakshman. These are villagers from Bengal who go around India to learn about education. May they see your room?' The professor turned to the crowd: 'This is Lakshman, he comes from Bhopal. He studies grammar and is a good student.' The villagers bowed, which confused the boy. He stood back from the doorway and gestured that they should come in. The room was already crowded with a bed, a desk and a chair. Everywhere there were books. A metal trunk was just visible under the bed. Above the desk was a large map with many stars made upon it in ink. Each group of villagers carefully removed shoes before entering, and bowed before leaving. When Harischandra entered, he gazed in astonishment at the books. Shyly he spoke to the boy:

'Do you own all these books?'

'Most of them. Some are from the library.'

'Do you read them all?'

'Oh yes, some more than once.'

'What do they tell you?'

The boy was confused, but the eye of the professor was upon him.

'They tell me about the beautiful Sanskrit language and about our great poets who wrote in India before the rest of the world had any alphabet.'

'Soooo,' came the appreciative response.

'But you have newspapers, too.'

'Yes, I want to know all about politics. And democracy. India is the biggest democracy in the world.'

'What is democracy?'

The boy looked blank, appealed to the professor in vain, and then replied:

'It is what we have since independence. India is the biggest independent democracy in the world. And the oldest.'

'Why do you study grammar? Do you wish to be a priest?'

'No, I wish to be a professor. My family has enough priests.'

'Lakshman wants to teach Sanskrit in the University of Bhopal.'

'What does that boy study?'

'He studies philosophy. And that one studies modern literature. He wants to go to America.'

The villagers thanked the boy and moved away from the residence. Deepaka asked Ashin:

'What was the strange picture above the table? I have never seen a god like that.'

'That was the map of the world, Deepaka. The blue was the sea and the coloured bits the many lands.'

'Which was India?'

'The red triangle sticking out into the sea on the right.'

'But that was just a small red piece.'

'The world is very big, the lands seem small to get them all on one piece of paper.'

'The boy said India was the biggest.'

'No, he said the biggest democracy.'

'Are other countries bigger than India?'

'Yes, many are bigger.'

'What were the stars?'

'I do not know. The boy must have made them.'

'Yes, they are the places he reads about. When he reads of a new place he finds it on the map and makes a star,' the professor explained.

'Are there maps which show only India?' asked Surendra.

'Yes, and of each part of India, too.'

'He should have had a picture of the gods, especially Saraswati, if he is to learn.'

It was not until they had seen several more buildings and Jaydev had exploded with excitement when shown a laboratory with instruments and tools, that they finally did come to the book store. Twice Ashin had to go back to fetch Jaydev.

'Look, Ashin, they can weigh just one grain of rice. See, here, when the light goes in this glass, a rainbow comes out. Look, look!'

Many of the villagers remained outside the book store. The men smoked, the women gossiped. Inside Mitu and Rhunu looked at books full of pictures. Reena hopped from one counter to another examining books of tales. Surendra was bent over a stack of paper, Narend beside him. Deepaka and Amiya laughed and urged the others to hurry. Harischandra opened one text and appalled, muttered, 'It is too small, too small.'

The professor found another and said:

'This is easier, try this one.'

Hesitantly Harischandra took up the bigger book and found that indeed the print was larger and he could read it. Ashin sent Surendra back to fetch the readers when the bus arrived. It took much arguing to pull them away. They departed and the professor stood alone.

'They are very simple. It is a pity to waste such a journey on them. I would rather my students could do it.' And he walked away.

This time the bus took them to a large factory and having deposited them, rumbled back to the city.

'What strange wonder do we see now?'

'This is a weaving factory. Here they make Benarsi saris.'

For the next hours the women exclaimed over the silks while the men climbed about the machines and were shown the mysteries of the mechanical looms. Mitu sketched as fast as he could. Arundati was in a trance. In the corner of one room there was a pile of brightly coloured wool cloths like the shawl the student had worn.

'What are these?'

'They are shawls made from the waste ends of wool. We dye them with chemicals from America. They sell in the market for about ten rupees and the students wear them.'

Surendra draped a red one around himself and pranced. 'I am a prince in my finery.'

'Just be careful you do not turn back into a snake,' laughed Reena.

'Is it warm, Surendra?'

'Yes, I shall show you,' and the cultivator curled up on the pile of shawls and slept while the rest wandered around the looms and shops.

'Do we buy your saris here?' Arundati asked eagerly.

'Here, or in the markets of the city.'

'Come, Uma, let us go and buy.'

'Do we come back to this place?'

'No, tomorrow we shall see more temples and go to a printing house.'

Narend stepped away and Ashin realized that it would soon be dark and they must find their way across the city alone. He began to try to assemble the villagers but the task was impossible. As dusk descended the workers stopped, locked the machines for the night, and a guard came around asking them all to leave. Ashin found the weavers' foreman and asked him directions for the long walk. The foreman was appalled that the villagers should walk to the station. He told Ashin to wait and rushed to the office. Ashin found the shop and the villagers plucking at the silks, the embroidered slippers and the soft shawls. He urged them again to come out into the darkness. Narend and Rhunu came each carrying a neat bundle. Uma came with a small packet clutched tightly. Babla tried with all his roughness to get Arundati to leave the piles of saris. At last he pulled her away, still empty-handed and still comparing one piece with another. When they were all outside and Ashin had counted them

to be forty-five the foreman appeared and declared that the company
lorry would take them to the station. A painted van rattled forward and
there was much laughter as the villagers climbed up into the open back.
Ashin thanked the foreman profusely and was dismissed with the
comment:

'You are our honoured guests.'

The dust and noise of the lorry prevented conversation. Through the
city they journeyed until at last they reached the station and their angry
cook. When the meal was finished again the questions were asked:

'What have you in your bundles? What did you buy?'

Little Uma was the first to speak:

'We bought a sari for the girl who becomes the wife of the elder son.'
She unwrapped the silk and it rippled as it fell from her lap. It was
brilliant pink with a deep yellow border. Uma had never seen anything
quite so magnificent and she fondled it while the others praised it.
Arundati returned to her bunk and sulked:

'I have come away with nothing. I wanted to buy the one with the
gold in the border. No one in the village except Uma-didi has ever worn
a sari with gold in it. Now I have nothing.' She turned on Babla and
poured forth her anger until he too flared and shouted at her. They
quieted only when they realized that the others were listening to the
fight. Then Surendra said:

'I too have bought something, but not from the weavers.' He took
from his shirt a small packet of paper and the others pressed around to
see what treat was in store.

'Look. It is a map. Like the boy Lakshman's.'

'No, it is different. It has just a little blue around the edge.'

'It is my map of India,' Surendra's pride was obvious. 'Ashin-dada, let
us mark with your pen where we have travelled so far. Then each night
I can mark it and when we return we will all be able to see where we
have been. I shall put it on the wall of my daughter-in-law's house.'
Slowly and carefully Ashin followed the road from the village to the big
town, then the railway to Calcutta, and then again the railway to Benares.
He paused and at once the audience ordered him to go on and mark the
journey to Sarnath. Harischandra bent forward and read off the names of
all the places they had passed.

'Hai, what a fine souvenir.' Mitu was delighted. He withdrew to his
bunk, brought out his sketchbook and tried to draw the villagers looking
at the map.

'What have you, Narend?' Jaydev slapped the bulky bundles.

'Those bright shawls for the ones at home. They gave us their shawls
for the journey. Is it possible for me to send them by the post?'

'Not tomorrow, but the following day is our last here and I had
thought to leave it free for those who wish to shop. We could go together
and send letters or your parcels.'

'Oh Ma. Letters!'

'Harischandra, have you a pad?'

'Write one for me to my son.'

'I promised you would write from the holy city.'

Harischandra was kept busy late under the lamplight. Gradually the villagers settled to sleep. Arundati resolved to make a list of all the things she would buy. Deepaka wondered if it was a blessing to have held a book of the *Gita* in the library. Reena watched Narend as only one of the parcels was wrapped for the post. Eventually when there was quiet Narend removed from the package two small items and handed them to Rhunu.

'What is this, husband?'

'You draw a book record of the journey, like Mitu. I bought the coloured sticks because they are chalk and you are used to colour not ink pens.' Rhunu scowled in concentration at the book. It contained sheets of blank but very soft paper. Then she opened the other box and found that there were little coloured sticks in neat rows. She looked at Narend. Then she picked up one stick and carefully in one corner made a mark on the paper. After a moment of surprise, Rhunu quickly sketched an alpana there on the first page of the book. She drew easily and the familiar form glowed under her hand. When it was finished she looked at Narend with fear.

'Yes, like that. Now you make pictures. It is late. Let us sleep.'

Rhunu closed the wonderful box and the book and placed them carefully beside her. She turned from Narend and began to pull the blanket over her hoping he would not notice that she was weeping. Then she heard Reena sigh and knew her old aunt had watched. There was no use in keeping secrets from Reena. Turning, Rhunu saw that Narend was not on his bunk, but knelt and was removing something from the parcel. She watched as he rose and unfolded what looked like a blanket and spread it over Reena in the hammock.

'What is this, Narend?' Reena was at once awake.

'Only a shawl, Aunt, you will need it since you gave the other away.' Narend stretched out to sleep.

'But, Narend, it is bright purple. What is an old widow to do with a shawl of purple? Why did you not buy a white one or a grey one?'

'They do not make them.'

'Aunt, the storyteller in the drawings of the books at the library wore a purple shawl.' Rhunu spoke softly but she could see Narend tense and grunt as she gave him away.

'Oh Ma, so she did. Then I shall wear it too,' and Reena settled to sleep laughing to herself.

Rhunu reached over and touched Narend's shoulder.

'Bless you, my lord husband,' and then she too turned away.

The night passed slowly, for both Arundati and Amiya kept rising to

be sick and others were restless. In the early morning the same procession
made their way to the river, but this dawn was grey and no sun came to
the river. Clouds hung low over the city as the wet worshippers hurried
back to the carriage. When they reached it there were few others about.
They made a late start to trek again behind the tourist guide. The morning
was quickly gone. At midday they were standing beneath trees looking
up at the Tibetan temple, a modern place where there were many strange
pictures and demons glared from every gable. A group of tourists came
with a man carrying a megaphone and stood beside the villagers. Some
of the foreigners began pointing at some of the pictures. Amiya moved
away and waited for the others out of sight of the foreigners, followed
as usual by her obedient admirers. Deepaka followed the gestures of the
tourists and found they were looking at pictures depicting the acts of
love. Deepaka gasped with shock. She was horrified. She came upon
Amiya suddenly.

'They are dirty people,' said Amiya, 'they do not smell of sandalwood
or coconut oil.'

'Yes, they must be very dirty people to make such pictures,' Deepaka
replied thinking of the tiny statues and the mysterious people of the
mountains who worshipped at such a temple.

'Yes, and they show these pictures in foreign countries and people will
think we are beggars and that we act as they do.'

'Why do they make such pictures?' Deepaka was still preoccupied.

'Why, to show to those who do not travel these ways.'

'You think those are the ways of real people?' Deepaka looked astonished, but not directly at Amiya.

'Well, I do not think those foreigners are the same as we are in the
way they feel, but I think that is how they all behave. Yes, I am sure.'

'But Amiya, they had helpers!' Deepaka stared at her friend.

'Yes, but rich people here have helpers as well.'

'Rich people?'

'Yes, they behave like that in Calcutta I think, going about with helpers
to carry their parcels and speak with megaphones and help with everything, I suppose.'

'Everything?'

'Yes, they do not do their duties themselves, as you and I do.'

'Oh Ma, those are duties?' Deepaka sucked in her cheeks in shock and
confusion. Amiya's smug tone was echoed back and forth among the
villagers. No one spoke to Deepaka of what she had seen. Ashin led the
way with the guide and Babla had a hard time keeping Arundati from
going into the sari shops. Deepaka lagged behind, sometimes turning to
look back. Reena fell back and walked with her. Reena had draped the
bright shawl proudly around her bent shoulders.

'What bothers you, Deepaka?' Reena asked suddenly.

'Did you see what the foreigners were pointing at on the temple?'

'You mean the statues of the dancing girls with their men?'

'Were they dancing girls?'

'Who else could be so acrobatic or smile while doing it?'

'Why are such pictures on a temple?'

'To keep the evil things out, like the demons, say the wise ones.'

'But if that is so they would be on more temples. This is the first we have seen.'

'There will be more. Perhaps in the times when men built the temples there was another belief.'

'The foreigners took pictures of them.'

'What?'

'With the cameras. They pointed them up and made pictures. I am sure.'

'Ai, it must be a terrible thing to be a mother of a foreigner.'

'I am frightened by these things. Let us join the others. It is not good to recall the night of the flower bed when we must follow the rules for widows.' Deepaka hurried to catch up, and Reena followed her with a keen look.

At the end of an avenue, where they had to dodge many bicycles, the villagers turned into a large building and crowded the reception room. A tall man was waiting. He addressed them in Bengali and gestured to show that they should follow him. This they did with care for he led them along a narrow balcony over a huge room in which there was much machinery, clattering and pounding so that the whole balcony shook. After some time the machine stopped and then the man led them down to it. First they saw the desks where men worked over sheets of paper, making red marks here and there. The paper was passed to another man who had a machine with many small levers which he pushed. There was much noise from this thing until at last a small piece of grey metal fell down from a slot into a basket. A boy came to fetch the basket when it was full and another man carefully put all the bits of metal into some order in a tray. Then the heavy tray was put into the machine in the centre of the room. It was very strange. The tall man explained that this was how books were made. He showed them the ink which was poured into a hole in the machine and picked up some paper at the end of it and showed them that the words which were on the first paper were now there, printed and lined just as in a book.

The villagers stood silent in confusion. Mitu saw that one of the plates was a map made in metal. He showed the others and they were intrigued to see the map shown on the paper at the end of the machine. After a time the foreman directed them all to step back and he started the press. Everything shook. The villagers laughed in fear as they watched the paper rolled out of one end, hidden somewhere in the centre, and come out with the words and drawings showing clearly. The foreman stopped the machine, went over and tore a piece of paper out of the printed sheet.

He handed it to Ashin and said, 'There is your letter and keep it as a souvenir.'

Ashin stared in astonishment, for it was a printed copy of a letter he had written long ago from Calcutta. It told the story of Uma-didi's will, of the journey around India, and even gave the names of the travellers. He showed and explained it to the villagers but they could not believe that there was not some magic here. The tall man brought a basket and from it began to pull the little plates of metal. Each time he pulled one up he read a name and after a moment the villagers realized they were their own names. At last each went forward to take the little metal from the man. When each had his own, they thanked the men of the press and emerged into the evening rush.

'Why are they all so kind, Ashin?'

'They say we are their guests.'

'And it makes a good story to tell the other workers.'

They were again on the way back to the station. Without difficulty they found the way. The cook harangued them on their irregularity. Last night they were late, now they were early. What was he to do?

'Just continue feeding me this well,' said Elder De. After the meal Uma urged Ashin to read from the history book. Elder De interrupted:

'It would be better to leave the history book until we are moving on the train. Tell us what we will see tomorrow so that we understand a little better when we see it.'

'That is sense, uncle, but tomorrow is a free day for prayers at the river, or shopping, or more temple-visiting.'

'Do we not stay as one group?'

'No. Enough now know the way here so that we can go out without the guide to lead us.'

'I wish to go back to the university book store, who goes with me?' asked Reena.

'Please, I will go with you,' Harischandra was eager.

'And I,' said Deepaka.

'I go to the museum. Do I go alone?' Mitu looked around.

'I will come,' said Rhunu quickly.

'I wish to buy saris,' said Arundati.

'Many will go shopping. You had better stay with me, cousin,' said Amiya firmly.

The travellers sorted themselves according to their interests and Ashin was able to be sure that with each group went one who knew the route home. Suddenly Bankim asked Deepaka to sing the evening prayers. Once more Ashin joined her. They sang the fishing songs and the tunes of the village festivals. When they finished the carriage was deep in darkness. Each found his bunk, reflected but briefly on the day, and slept.

In the morning after the little widows' procession returned, Ashin reminded them that they must be back at the train by sundown, for in the evening the train would depart.

'We go to central India to see the temples of Khajuraho. It must be done quickly for the following night the train will go north to Allahabad, Lucknow and the Himalaya.'

By mid-morning the carriage was empty and Ashin walked alone down the tracks to the station master's office. For many hours the two of them talked and sent telegrams to stations up the line telling them of the coming visitors. There were many interruptions, but Ashin was able to leave in the afternoon and go out into the city. He sought a book store first, sat alone in a café listening to the chatter of the students around him, and thought of his wife. Gradually he realized that the midday rest was over and the streets were filling. He found some of the craft shops and bought toys for his children. He had written Sundara-devi a long letter telling her everything of the journey so far and wishing he could talk of his worries with her each evening. She had told him not to buy a sari in Benares but to bring one from the south. Still, he bought a fine piece of red silk and had the man wrap it for the post. How had Narend managed with all the letters? Ashin began to hurry but he saw a crowd going down to watch sunset over Ganga, and he knew that he must stay and say his own farewell to the river. He descended and found a ghat. Shadows were long and there was a plume of smoke blowing ashes to him from the burning ghat. When he had finished his salutation Ashin sat in the sun and sang to himself. It was very good to be alone.

'Hail, dada, it is good that I have found you so. I am in disgrace.'
Ashin was shocked to find Babla so earnest and subdued beside him.

'What is it, Babla? Are you ill?'

'No, that would not bear telling. Last night you heard Arundati wailing about not buying a sari? She was louder than a triumphant mongoose.'

'Yes, I heard.'

'Well, I fear I do not trust my silly wife. You have a good calm wife in Sundara, you may not understand.'

'Yes, I miss Sundara-devi, but I think I do understand.'

'Last night I hid my money, Ashin, for fear that she would take it and spend it all on some silly sari for the girlchild who does not wish to marry. We have all the journey to make yet.'

'That seems sensible.'

'Yes, but I did not know my wife's evil. Now I have been with Jaydev and Narend watching at a mechanical place—'

'A mechanical place?'

'Yes, one of those shops where men get under automobiles and where there are many tools. It was Jaydev's idea. He thought we might learn how to fix our pump at the new well, and how to make one of those motor ploughs. He was right and I think we have learned.'

'A fine thing, uncle. I praise you for that.'

'But then I wanted to buy one of the tools, one of the wrenches with adjustments so that you can fix all machines, not just one kind. I went behind the shop to get my money, so these Benares men would not see it, and I found that the Uma-didi money, which you gave me to keep safely, was open.'

'That is all right uncle, you have not lost it.'

'Ashin-dada, it pains me. Arundati has taken a 100-rupee note from it.' Babla clucked with the shame of it.

'She has taken 100 rupees?'

'Yes, I knew exactly how much was in the Uma-didi money, and how much was mine. She has taken a 100-rupee note.'

'Did she have any other money?'

'Yes, that is why it is so terrible. I gave her 100 rupees this morning because she said she must buy a wedding sari. It is much, but maybe with a fancy show we can catch a husband for the silly girlchild. Now there will be nothing.'

'Perhaps she has not spent it. It would be a very expensive sari for 200 rupees. Let us walk past the shops on our way to the carriage. Perhaps you will find her still shopping.'

'We must go. But first, Ashin, while we are alone, take back the Uma-didi money. It is a disgrace that I cannot keep it safe. I am ashamed.'

Ashin was astonished at Babla, but he took the money from the hands of the farmer and together they went up and into the shadows of the city. They walked quickly along several busy streets where there were many shops, but turned and made their way to the carriage. When almost there they met Elder De with Nirmal and Bankim and some of the others returning. The old men were exultant and poured forth a tale of a miracle on the river, of music in a temple, and of being given five rupees each by a group of foreigners who passed them.

'Imagine, Ashin. They thought we were begging when we raised our hands in salute!'

'See, here is the five rupees.'

'Don't tell Amiya or there will be no sleep for any of us.'

'Bankim, you are a scoundrel.'

'No more than you. What is that parcel you carry, Babla?'

'A wrench for fixing the pump at the well.'

'You have wasted your money, Babla, for the first time. When I see that pump working it will be another miracle.'

'No, I do not think so. Jaydev and some others worked long with the men at the mechanical place and he said he was sure we could mend it. Jaydev has some drawings which he will get Mitu to make better tonight.'

'Look, Reena and Deepaka are back.'

The women were folding the washing beside the carriage. Inside many of the villagers were impatient with the cook, who had counted on their being late. Reena captured Ashin and took him to see the books she had bought:

'See, here is the story of Rama, and this little one gives translations of tales from across the sea, by a man named Grimm. They were a few paisa, and now when I die there will still be stories in the village. Listen to this one from over the sea.' Reena wanted to tell the tale then and Ashin had difficulty in persuading her that she must wait until she had a better audience.

'Ashin, what is wrong with Babla? He sits outside and I think he may weep.' Deepaka had never seen the miser moved, and was alarmed.

'Babla weep? Never. You must be silly tonight, Deepaka.'

Ashin rose and went out. He met Amiya and a large group of the villagers returning. Each told him tales of terrible prices. Amiya was startled when Ashin asked her where was Arundati.

'Is she not back? She left us and went with Uma when little Uma said she was tired. I thought they would return. Arundati just kept seeing saris. She had not bought anything, not even fresh supari, when they left.'

Mitu and Rhunu and Surendra arrived happy. They were followed closely by Narend, Jaydev and the remaining others. The cook handed out the meals just at sunset. Uma and Arundati were still not back. Babla could not eat and Jaydev asked Amiya constantly where she had left the pair. He dared not set out in search. Suddenly Uma-didi came up the steps, grey with fatigue, carrying two parcels.

'Wife, wife, you are late! Are you ill? What has happened?'

'Where is Arundati?'

'Has there been an accident?'

'Away man. Uma, drink this and rest. Then tell us.' Amiya commanded and held out a cup. Gradually Uma revived.

'We walked and walked. Arundati wanted to go into every sari shop. She would not stop for tea or to rest. At every sari place we sat long for the sellers thought we were beggars and would not show us saris until Arundati showed them her money.'

'She showed a seller her money?'

'Not just one, many, many. And she had much money.'

'Babla, what have you lost?' The remark was intended as a joke, but Babla turned away and slumped against the window.

'Then I was bitten by a dog. I think the beast was hungry.'

'Let us see, Uma, is it a bad bite? Was the dog ill?'

'No, no. But it makes the walking hard.' Uma showed Amiya and Rhunu the nasty sore at her ankle and immediately hot water was summoned from the cook. Amiya and Deepaka delved into bundles until they had assembled an impressive array of medicines. While Uma talked, Amiya bathed the wound and bandaged it. She was skilled and wasted no gesture.

'So I found Amiya and said I would return here. I had bought some Hannumanji toys for the children and fresh pan for the journey. I wanted nothing more. Arundati said she would come with me. The moment we were out of sight of the others she said now I could help her find the wedding sari for the girl. She was so urgent I felt sorry, so as long as I could I stayed with her. But the foot started to bleed and I could not and went to say good-bye to the river. I thought she would also make a last puja, but she vanished. She must have gone off as I went down the ghat. I could not find her. Now I have walked back along all the ways I recall, but the shops are closed and there are few to ask if they had seen her return. Those who were still open remember her when we were together but none has seen her again. I am sorry. I was too tired to do more.' Uma bent against Amiya's big frame and wept.

'Babla, I think we must search. Now it is late and dark. Arundati will not find the way alone.' Narend beckoned Surendra and the two went out and began to prepare torches. Ashin gave directions to Elder De as to when the train was due to depart and what to tell the station master if they were not back. Jaydev remained with Uma. Babla reluctantly joined the three men outside. As he left Reena gave a sharp farewell:

'Thrash her when you find her, Babla. Then keep the money. We must get through the journey without hindrance from the wailer.'

The villagers waiting in the carriage did not try to sleep. The cards and souvenirs were left aside. They gossiped about the village and lapsed often into bitterness about the miserly couple and their unhappy fortune.

Babla, Ashin, Mitu, Surendra and Narend made quick time. There was still much activity in the centre of the city. Along the small streets pan sellers were still open.

'A little Bengali lady, you say? Slightly fat? Wearing a white sari with a red border? There are many people in Benares, and they all come to my shop for good pan. How should I know this lady from the others?'

'She wanted to buy a sari.'

'So do all the women who come to Benares.'

'She has a high voice and weeps much,' Babla tried to describe his wife more closely.

'I cannot help you. Have you asked the police?'

From street to street and square to square they walked. Sometimes they wakened a beggar to ask if any had seen the woman alone. The police offered no help. After more than an hour the men stopped. Surendra lit a biri and crouched to think.

'It is unlikely that she has spent the money, Babla. The sellers would remark someone with a parcel.' Ashin tried to be of comfort.

'The money does not matter, I will pay it back if it is lost. What of the safety of Arundati? She is alone. Someone might hurt her or try to steal from her.'

'No, no she does not look rich. No one would try to steal.'

'But she showed money in the city. Many will have seen. She is not a good wife, but I would have her back,' Babla muttered the last and did not realize the others had heard.

'Come, let us make a plan,' said Surendra. 'She wished to buy a sari and when most shops closed she still had not bought one. Where would she try to go?'

'Why, to the factory where she saw the saris being made!' Mitu exclaimed.

'We came away by that great lorry. What of the route would she recall?'

'Nothing. She does not notice what we pass, like most of the others.'

'No, Babla, you are wrong. She saw the big pink building and thought it was the house of the richest man in Benares but the guide said it was a school.'

'Then we must go to that building and see if she has tried to find the factory. Do you know the way?'

'No.'

'I do. We visited that school today. It is a place run by foreign ladies for girls without families. Rhunu wished to see it.'

'I remember the way. It should not be far.' Narend led them off, pausing at the doorways and alleys to light the figures and see if any held a familiar face.

Another hour passed as they walked. They found the pink school and walked on towards the factory. Ashin kept looking at his watch and wondered if they would journey with the train. Finally they stopped. No one had responded to their queries. It seemed impossible that Arundati could have come so far. They walked slowly back. At the school Narend stopped.

'Let us ask here. She might have got this far and they might have seen her alone.'

'But they are foreigners. They would not notice an old woman,' Babla was sullen. 'Perhaps the police have found her now.'

'There are still lights, I will ask.' Narend mounted the steps with Mitu close behind. The others stayed on the street. After a little time a nun answered the door.

'Yes?'

'I am sorry, I do not speak Hindi. Do you know English or Bengali?'

'English, yes, I know.' The nun spoke with a heavy accent.

'Please, madam, have you seen a little Indian lady? This high, fat, very frightened. She went to buy saris and is lost.'

'One moment. I have just come on the watch. I must ask the others.' The door closed.

'Will she come back?' Mitu asked.

'Yes, she has gone to ask others.'

'When did you learn English?'

'In the war when we worked on the railway for the soldiers.'

The door opened and a more authoritative nun stepped out:

'You lost a woman?'

'Yes, a little Bengali lady. This high, a little fat. I think, also very frightened.'

'You speak the truth. She is here. We found her on the steps in the dark. She had cried herself to sleep. Shall I waken her and bring her to you?'

'Yes, yes, please.' Narend turned back to the darkness. 'Babla, Ashin, she is here.'

'In the house of the foreigners?'

'They found her on the steps. She is asleep. The lady in the hat has gone to fetch her.'

In a moment Arundati was on the floor patting their feet and weeping. Babla raised her and she stood forlorn but safe. She had no parcels. The nun listened to the story told by Ashin and again asked them to wait. When she returned she carried a packet and some keys.

'It is too late, and she has had much shock, for you to walk back with her to the station. I will take you in our bus.' She hurried them through the darkness to a sturdy new bus and then expertly drove them through the streets. Arundati told Babla she had spent none of the money and handed him the little purse of notes. He put it away. She was surprised he had not scolded. At the station they again thanked the nun, who shared their relief and pleasure. She gave the packet to Arundati and said:

'Good-bye, child. This is to remember the house of the foreigners where once you slept.' She was gone and the little party moved to their boisterous welcome at the carriage. When Arundati opened the parcel she gasped. Folded within the paper was a magnificent cotton sari embroidered with peacocks in the border.

'Look, it is what the orphan girls learn to do there. They showed us in the classroom this afternoon.' Rhunu traced the beautiful work.

'What is the cloth? It looks like silk and feels like cotton.'

'It is a mixture, like the wedding saris of the Santali women the peddlars sometimes show us.'

'Why did the foreign lady give it to me?'

'She said you must remember them.'

'It is very beautiful, Arundati. You must fold it away and keep it. No girl of our village has worn such a sari. It will be fine for the wedding.' Uma tried to settle the weeping lady. Babla sought Ashin. The train was about to leave Benares.

'Ashin, here is the 100 rupees. She is a foolish woman. We must write a letter in English to thank the foreign ladies.'

'I can write English, but now it is time for sleep. Let us do it when there is light.'

'Peace be with you, Ashin-dada. It has been a strange day.' The miser rocked back to the compartment along the moving train. Arundati was asleep. He bent and covered her with his blanket. For most of the night he lay on the upper bank watching the shadows on the ceiling. Towards dawn he fell asleep and anyone passing would have seen tears on the old man's pillow. But no one passed and the train moved south.

4

North to Himalaya,
home of the gods

Ashin sought the station master of the town where they stopped at dawn. He awakened that gentleman and at once the official was eager to please this strange visitor whose coming had been announced by Baroda House itself. Ashin found himself eating sweets with tea at this early hour. The bus was parked in the courtyard. The driver was a good man, now asleep. There was a government guide who had been engaged for the day, he would wait for them at the Tourist Rest House. The carriage would be cleaned while they were away, and yes, all the connections with the northbound train had been arranged for the night. Ashin was surprised and began to relax a little as the gentility of the station master flowed over him. The two walked towards the carriage as the villagers were assembling on the track. After a gracious speech of welcome they were off in a cloud of dust. The driver gestured at the passing scenery, telling them of the battles and gods who lived on these plains, and too pleased to have an audience to notice that they did not speak his language. By mid-morning they were in Khajuraho and met the uniformed boy who sat waiting on the steps.

'There are twenty-two temples to see, we must hurry,' and he led them off at a trot. The guide directed them to the side of the first temple, and began explaining the history of the temples and of how they came to be rediscovered. He spoke quickly and nervously and often lost the thread of his memorized lesson. It mattered little, for the villagers did not understand him. They stood looking up at the temple which was covered in small, but very detailed, figures. Gradually the vacant expectancy on their faces turned to recognition, then to shock, then to withdrawal, and suddenly they were divided into a group of men and a group of women, carefully apart, carefully not looking at the temple. The guide, oblivious, droned on.

'What is it, what does it mean?'

'The figures of dancing girls on a temple!'

'It must be of gods, not of men.'

'They are not decorated as for gods, only for princes.'

'But it is on a temple!'

'It is to frighten demons away with the disgrace.'

'No, it cannot be. This is a place of worship.'

'What is it like inside?'

'Just an ordinary temple inside. There is a small lingam.'

'Let us do our puja.'

'No, no, not here.'

'Not with those things outside.'

'The others might think we were worshipping those things.'

'Ai, cannot we go from here?'

The morning turned to midday and then to afternoon, each temple becoming more puzzling to the villagers. When they could bring themselves to ask one another, they knew no answers. None of the women dared to ask Ashin what was meant. They kept to themselves and looked away when they found that a new temple also had some of the sculptures. The men shyly joked with one another that the student could not be married so could not know of what he was speaking. Occasionally one or another admired jewels on a figure, but usually they sat with their backs to the temples, pretending to enjoy the sun. A priest came to them and asked if they would like him to recite prayers on their behalf. He assured them it was a good place to pray for sons for their daughters, that the worship given here was especially pleasing to the gods. Their embarrassment was oppressive and the priest went away. Before them on the path a cart was moving slowly. The farmer made no effort to pull aside and let the villagers pass. The villagers recovered some of their spirit as they thought of their own carts and teased the farmer. At the next temple they saw that the cones represented Mount Meru, the abode of the gods, and they laughed to see all the hundreds of figures of demons and servants of the gods. Reena told a story of the arguments on Meru and the temple seemed to move as she spoke. Mitu moved forward and carefully copied one of the lines of flowers decorating the lowest level of the temple. Deepaka watched as local women entered the inner temple and performed their worship. Then she followed. It was only a temple. The god was within, not among the strange figures. The guide became aware that he was being ignored. He fumed to Ashin about the stupidity of these people and the antiquity of the art before them. He led them down the dusty track through the village and back to the bus. As the travellers boarded the bus Ashin thanked the boy, and he was startled by the venom the lad expressed.

The bus rolled north. Tiffin carriers were opened and the travellers ate a little cold rice. There was not enough to feed them all. There was silence as the bus journeyed slowly towards the train. A few men commented on the tools of the village. A few women spoke of the prices in the souvenir stalls. They were relieved to see the station. Each sought the privacy of bed and blankets. Before the train moved out in the night the villagers slept. Again Amiya and Arundati and little Uma and others

were sick. Again Surendra and Mitu lay awake watching, listening, wondering. The train was shunted and transferred to another track at a large station. At dawn a cold mist concealed the landscape. The cook tried to light the stove, but as the train rocked it first sputtered and then went out. On the second try it toppled and quickly the flames caught the rags near by and the cook's own clothing. Elder De was closest, and without a pause he grabbed the cloths and threw them out of the window. He doused the cook with the water bucket from the lavatory, and all was over. There was a clamour as the villagers gathered to see the damage. The cook's wailing prevented most from hearing what was said.

'It was well done, uncle.'

'It is foolishness to light the fire while the train moves.'

'Then there must be no meals while we travel.'

'We can buy food in the stations as we pass.'

'It is the food of strangers.'

'We must learn to eat it.'

'That we dare not.'

'Does no one help me?' The cook cried until Amiya was sent forward. She saw that he had burns along his leg and ordered the others to clear a space and a bunk for the man. When she had cleaned the burn and bathed it, Rhunu applied a dressing. The cook limped back to his corner.

'Your hands are skilled in healing, Amiya-didi.' Ashin was impressed.

'Come Uma, while my medicines are out. Let us see the bite.' Amiya had noticed that the injury was not healing and had become discoloured.

'Where do we next stop, Ashin?' she asked.

'In Allahabad where the rivers meet.'

'Then there Uma must go to a doctor. This bite is fouled.'

'There will be a university hospital, I am sure. But you are as good as any doctor I have seen, can you not heal the wound?'

'There is medicine to do it quickly. I can only keep it clean. That is not enough.'

'You speak as one who knows the healing secrets. I have always thought you were but a helper of the healers,' Jaydev tried to joke.

'As a girl, I wished to study to be a doctor. I begged my father to let me go to Calcutta. My mother laughed and found me my husband. We walked to the town to buy the saris and a special sara. I bought some books from a student who had failed the medical course. My father whipped me very hard and my mother sold two that I could not hide. The rest lie in my trunk. Do not withdraw the foot, Uma. It must hurt before it will be better.'

The villagers listened to this secret of Amiya's past and realized the meaning of her stern direction whenever there was illness or accident in the village. They knew Amiya had been suddenly, and most unhappily, married and that her husband had mocked her learning from his deathbed. Harischandra thought to himself that she at least had known she could have done it well, but life had given her only disappointments. He had had the year in college before the disappointments came, but he had never known if he could have done it.

He was about to speak when Arundati came before the group:

'Didi, is there anything in your bundle to settle my stomach?'

'Ai, my stomach rages too.'

'Chew this while I look.'

Amiya was kept busy by the travellers until the train slowed and stopped in a station. Several of the men collared the tea seller and filled Narend's huge pot. The cook fetched fruit and limped the length of the carriage passing it out. Later he was able to buy chapattis, but most of the villagers refused to touch the cooked food. Ashin was worried. When they pulled into Allahabad his fears were not allayed, for the station master had gone home without leaving directions. The villagers walked on the siding before sleep. Hunger did not bother them. They were used to going with less food in the village. Ashin's worry was contagious. It was hard to settle to sleep seeing the teacher poring over his notes. Elder De called out:

'Reena, we are wakeful children. Tell us a tale before we find some mischief.'

'Ai, Reena tell us a tale.'

'A good one, Reena, to fill us with dreams of princesses.'

'Do not be a fool, she will tell us one of princes.'

Reena laughed and arranged herself beside a fire. No one ever missed one of Reena's tales, unless they were dying. Tonight she told them not a village story, but the classic description of the wedding of Uma, daughter of Himalaya, with Lord Siva. She made it bawdy and hilarious, she made it uplifting and sternly moral, but best of all she made it alive before the villagers there in the flames and shadows of the fire. Reena sang of Uma's tears as Parvati waited for Purush, as the young bride longed for her husband to remember her.

'By the door of the hut I pounded grain until the dust was so fine that the wind blew all away from me. Still you did not come.' The villagers did not know if Reena had made the song or learned it, but they wept together. No one dared to move as Reena reminded them of Siva's dance. Even the earth shook as she spoke, the incoming train beyond was not noted. At last the tale quieted as Siva remembered and came home to his Uma and the two found joy and slept. The villagers shook themselves like waking puppies and then found their ways to deep sleep. No one was ill that night, and only Reena herself was restless.

Before dawn Deepaka rose and went out to bathe. She wished she knew where the river was. She was joined by Nirmal and Bankim and some of the other widows. Together, yet separately, the little assembly prayed beneath the lightening sky. The cook began to make breakfast. Surendra's clothes were again the first laid out to dry.

Ashin found the station master, a nervous but well-meaning man who was anxious to help, but unsure how to do so. He arranged for a boat to take the villagers to the sangam, the junction of the two holy streams. Ashin asked for directions to the hospital. The station master was alarmed and backed away as he asked them if they carried disease from Bengal.

'No, no. One of the women was bitten by a dog in Benares and the wound does not heal. She needs medicine.'

'I will send my servant to show the way.'

Soon Amiya and little Uma were gone. A guide came to Ashin and then the boatmen arrived. Eventually the villagers set off for the river. During the walk they purchased little garlands of marigolds and jasmine. They looked like one of the Khajuraho friezes as they swung along. Mitu was struck by the grace and colour of the little procession. He sketched a little but it would not come right. When they paused he spoke to Rhunu:

'Didi, have you your coloured sticks with you?'

'Why?'

'When we move again, see the way the garlands swing. I have tried, but see, the black is not good.'

Rhunu looked at the rough picture and said nothing. The group moved on again and she hung back until she saw what Mitu had seen. She squatted, took out her book and box, and with quick strokes caught the line and movement of the women and the garlands. Mitu was astonished at the sureness of her hand, and said so. At once Rhunu closed the book and ran on until she was in the midst of the group and her garland was also swinging.

They reached the bank of the river and settled themselves in the boats. From this point it looked like any river, perhaps a little bigger and without exceptional beauty or strength. The boatmen kept to the bank and only gradually began to cross the current. As he did so the villagers realized that the far bank had ended and another river was flowing into Ganga. They arrived at the sangam. The guide showed them where to throw their garlands so that they would be caught by the joined waters. Suddenly the water became a tapestry as the garlands landed and were moved in patterns down into the wider stream below. The guide recited some prayers and reminded the villagers that here Gandhiji's ashes had been given to the waters. Then the outing became a party as the boats moved easily. They were sorry when it was time to return to the shore. A student welcomed them. Jaydev asked if they would return to the station and see if Uma had found a doctor. The guides told him that a strange village woman would be lucky to see a doctor before sundown, if at all:

'It takes many hours. But do not worry, the servant will be sure they return safely.' Reluctantly Jaydev boarded the bus and went with the others to see the Congress headquarters. Ashin tried to warn the student:

'We had a discussion on the train some nights ago. The villagers want to know what is democracy. And they want to know what is independence and why we now celebrate independence from the British. They ask also why India is one when we do not share a language, nor gods, nor even food with all those who live in this land.'

'But India is the biggest democracy in the world. Do they not know that?'

'They have been told. No one has yet said what is democracy and why ordinary villagers are part of it.' The student reflected and began to look curiously at the people behind him pointing at the sights of the city they were passing. He turned again to Ashin:

'Maybe there will be a politician who can explain these things.'

'I hope so, I find it difficult. I no longer know myself, for the things I teach in school are rejected by these people, and rightly.'

At the hospital Uma sat on a bench, the servant was asleep, and Amiya watched the crowds. They had been given a number when they entered and were told to wait until it was called. There were few people then, but now it was crowded and it seemed to Amiya that no numbers had been called. Certainly no one had departed. The servant had suggested that Amiya go forward and pay the nurse some money, but Amiya was horrified and scolded him for suggesting that doctors were the same as clerks and government officials. Hour after hour had gone by. The room smelled of soap and wood smoke, of oil, pan and disinfectant. Amiya sometimes drifted into memories of the hospital in the big town where she had so often waited for a child or a grandchild to die. The last grandson had died there. Amiya had had six children. Four had died before reaching the time of marriage.

She thought of each one. Two had lived only a few days and were not named. A little girl had been a joy to them all with her bright eyes and quick laughter, but one winter she had caught a fever. She had had stiffness and had cried in the pain. Amiya had searched the books to learn what to do, for her husband said it was not worth going for a doctor just for a girl. When the girl's screams increased, Amiya had smuggled her down to the boat and had carried her across the fields to the town and the doctor. The doctor had been gentle, but he showed Amiya how her daughter struggled for breath. It took two long days for her to die. Amiya still remembered the walk back to the river, her arms empty, her husband scolding on the far shore. Then there were the two, the boy and the girl, who lived still and had children of their own.

Last came the son who was her hope, the best in the school, the leader of the village children in mischief. When he was twelve and spoke often with his mother of the day he would take her books and go to study medicine, she noticed that he seemed to darken in colour, and he no longer played so well. One night she stirred in her sleep and wakened alert with worry. The boy was unconscious. Without pause Amiya had called the boatman and she and her protesting husband had carried the boy through the night to the hospital. The doctors listened to all she could tell them. They questioned her over and again about when he had first weakened. The second night he died. The doctor told Amiya it was kidney failure from a disease long growing but unnoticed. He showed her pictures in the books and her husband screamed at her for looking at the texts. There had been no line on his palm to forecast the death. Amiya had sent two other children to the doctor and they had been cured of the disease, but that dawn after death the couple had returned to the village slowly. Within a year, Amiya was a widow. She looked at Uma and around the waiting hall again.

At the nurse's desk a group spoke loudly and drew Amiya's attention. There was one man, about her age, who looked familiar. Amiya watched, looked again, and then remembered. He was the doctor who had been the student when her last son had died. It was he who had showed her the pictures in the book and explained why the boy had died. Amiya rose and moved stealthily across the hall. When she reached the doctor she bowed to him. He turned towards her ready to dismiss her interruption. She spoke in Bengali and the sound of his mother-tongue made him pause:

'You were a doctor student many years ago on the river. I brought to you my twelve-year-old son. He died of kidney failure and you showed me the pictures in the book.' The doctor put on his spectacles. He was puzzled. The others watched the scene with amusement. Suddenly the old doctor smiled.

'You were the mother who did not believe in the palm lines and who asked me why. And you sent me two other children who were sick and they lived. What brings you here from the village when our hair has greyed?' Amiya told him of the will and at the name of Uma Sen he nodded recognition. She told of the journey and led him to Uma. The foot was indicated and he bent to examine it:

'Ai, we must treat it, an infection has started. What have you used so far?' Amiya told him. He was surprised.

'But that is very good, you have not made the wound worse with foolish salves. Come, help your friend to my examining room.'

When the treatment was finished the doctor turned to Amiya.

'Mother, you must take medicine for this foot. The wound should heal in a week. If it does not, you must find another doctor and show him this medicine.'

'We travel now to the north, and then to Delhi, and from there south. Here I have found you who speak Bengali, but soon there will be no one, and I cannot speak of wounds and medicine in English. You must tell me what to do for I must do it myself.'

'How many are you together?'

'Forty-five, and the cook has a bad burn on his leg.'

'What medicines do you carry?'

Amiya listed the things in her bundle. The doctor listened and wrote them down. When she finished he was quiet. Then he sat down:

'Look, mother, you must learn quickly. You go to places where there are other waters than you are used to. Soon the villagers will be tired and then they will fall ill easily. Some things you must watch for.' It took the doctor over an hour to explain what sicknesses might plague them and to tell Amiya how to treat them. At the end of that time there was a large collection of pills and tubes and bottles in front of Amiya.

'Tell me what each is for and I will feel it is safe to give them to you.'

Uma listened in awe as Amiya picked up one preparation after another and recited the conditions requiring its use and the dosages needed. She did not falter once. The doctor bowed when she finished:

'I wish my students would be as attentive as you, mother. Come and have tea and tell me of the big town. Is it much changed since we were young?' The three chatted happily to the consternation of the attendants. The doctor bade them a safe journey as they approached the nurse's desk.

'We must pay now, for the foot and the medicines.'

'No, only for the foot. The medicines I give you in respect for the wishes of Uma Sen. She was very beautiful, I remember her well.' He was gone. Amiya and Uma turned to the nurse. She charged them fifteen rupees, which made Uma gasp.

'What do you think this is? An ayurvedic dispensary? This is a teaching hospital. It is costly to be treated by a professor.'

'Can you tell me the name of the doctor?'

'That was Professor Raichaudhuri. You should not have wasted his time.'

'Let us go back, Uma.' They emerged from the waiting room into the rush hour. The servant found them a tonga and they rode to the station, giggling at the excitement of the vehicle. No one was in the carriage when they arrived, so the two women devoted themselves to ordering their belongings. Uma rested while Amiya helped the cook. The station master came to check on them:

'Did you find the hospital and see a doctor?'

'Yes, they were helpful.'

'A Bengali. Dr Raichaudhuri.'

'He is the professor. He has been to America. Did he speak?'

'He treated Uma's foot, and gave us some directions for the care of our health on the journey. How do you know him?'

'My son studies to be a doctor. My eldest daughter is already a doctor. She works in the children's clinic.'

'Two doctors in one family? You must be a rich man.'

'No. My children have worked very hard. They have both had scholarships. If a student is good and works hard, the university gives

89

money to pay the expenses of the student if the parents cannot. It is very common here, for the foreigners give money to our colleges.'

'Foreigners give money for our people to study?'

'Yes, much money for books and buildings, too. There are some rich people across the seas, but even the students who come here come with scholarships.'

'And your daughter had a scholarship? They give them to girls?'

'If the girl is good in her studies.'

'Maybe we do not have them in Bengal.'

'My sons have never spoken of scholarships.'

'I do not know how it is in Bengal. Here the student must compete for the scholarships.'

'Then you must be very proud of your children.'

'We are blessed, they work hard. The little one is a problem, she wants to be married before she finishes college. Who can find a husband these days for a girl without a degree?'

'Ai, do all the girls go to schools?'

'Of course, there are many ladies' colleges and the girls are well looked after by the teachers.'

Uma and Amiya were embarrassed by the contrast between what they knew and what the man felt was normal. He bowed to them, about to leave, and then remembered:

'I must tell you. The others are to return early for the meal, then you will go to a dance drama at the university. It has been arranged.'

'What kind of drama?'

'I do not know, it is by the students of classical dance.'

While the cook and Uma finished the preparations for the meal, Amiya retired to her bunk, where she sat lost in thought. When the villagers returned from the political discussion at the Nehru house, they were disgruntled and eager for the food. Jaydev pressed his questions upon Uma and Amiya, and then told them of the excursion:

'First we were on the river and said our prayers. Then we were taken to Pandit Nehru's house. There was a student who tried to explain about independence, but some local political-wallah kept interrupting and arguing, so we came away early.'

'We are to go to a dance drama at the university. The station master came to tell us.'

'I must wash.'

They ate in silence, one turned from another. Before they had had time to relax the student came running:

'The bus is waiting. Come, we can have a tour of the college before the performance.'

Quickly they followed him, their clean clothes shadowed in pink and gold from the deepening sun. The bus took them to the college while the student shouted of the antiquity of the place of learning. He recited the names of lawyers and famous men who had graduated from the college.

'Does no one ever learn how to drill wells or make better ploughs?' muttered Elder De.

'This is not a technical school.'

'What is a technical school?'

'A place where boys study about wells and industrial things.'

'Do we not visit such a place?'

'No.'

They had reached the auditorium.

'Is it a wedding? Look at the saris.'

'Come, we must find our places.'

'In that hall?'

'Ai, see the rich ones.'

'Look, the woman carries a purse of gold.'

'Oh, Ma, they must be wearing all the jewels of the dowry.'

Carefully the villagers followed the boy. The crowd grew silent and stared at the villagers. They were scrubbed clean, their worn clothes still smelt of the morning sun, but there was not a jewel nor a piece of silk amongst them. There were titters as Reena walked in with her bright purple shawl. Elder De walked stiffly in his distress. Surendra was amused by the discomfiture of the rich ones at being so disgracefully invaded. Inside the auditorium they looked at the painted ceiling, the brocade curtains, and at the dress of the people coming in to take their seats. The villagers did not dare even to whisper. Ashin hoped they would not become frightened. The lights dimmed. As the stage setting of a palace came into view they gasped in delight. The music started and for the next hours the villagers sat enthralled as dancers created princes and demons, gods and heavenly messengers. They did not understand the sermons, but they recognized at once that a saint was being rewarded for his trials. Often they called out, sometimes they beat the rhythms of the drums, at the end they shouted just as they would have done for a jatra troup of entertainers in the village. The audience laughed. The performers turned and bowed to the villagers. A gentleman came out on stage. He spoke of the traditions of music which had lasted through the generations, ascribing again unwarranted antiquity to the drama they had just seen. He praised the teachers and dancers and then turned to the villagers. He described the visit of the Bengalis as a blessing to the university and said that because they had maintained the village traditions they had made such a performance possible in modern India. The audience clapped and the lights went up.

'What did he mean, we made it possible?'

'Those were just polite words.'

'He meant the storytellers kept alive the tales before there was writing.' Reena took the compliment to herself.

'Our tales are not like this. Our dances are not for a palace.'

'The great ones learned from our ways.'

'The night air is too much for you. It is time you found your bed.'

'What have you planned for tomorrow, Ashin?'

'The train goes to Lucknow. In the morning we shall hear of the great mela.'

'Hush, do you not see it is time for sleep.'

In the morning at the river it was Rhunu who first drew aside to make a picture of the water. Some priests were gathered waiting for them. The villagers were summoned near and listened to the tales of Prayag, of gods and emperors, of pilgrims and battles and terrible punishments. The chanted tales chased morning away and only the cold wind from the river drove them back to the station at a run. Ashin had forgotten his appointments, Jaydev had not organized the food. The station master pushed them aboard the steaming train and the conductor came to see why they had been late. Elder De panted:

'Priests,' and with laughter they left Allahabad.

By evening they had watched the rich farms for many hours, and the men argued much over the mechanical aids to irrigation. They entered Lucknow and came down towards a bridge. By the time they stopped at the station it was night. An aloof official welcomed them and suggested they take the evening walk according to local custom and led them towards the Imambara.

Two men, bearded, weathered brown, sat waiting beside the carriage for dawn to break. Deepaka, stepping down to wash and make her morning puja, jumped in fear. She paused, came forward and peered at them in the darkness.

'Are you bhuts?' she asked.

'We are your guides. The elder is a teacher here in the city. We want to take you to morning prayers. Would you tell your people to hurry, we must be in the mosque at dawn.'

Before the two men expected it, the forty-five stood ready. Again an exchange of salutations, again a quick walk through a city not yet awake. They stood before the doors of the mosque. The older man turned to the villagers and explained that the men must go forward and the women must remain behind on one of the mats. Hesitantly they followed and obeyed, aware that many of the glances turned their way were hostile as well as questioning.

For a moment they could see nothing in the mosque. Then the size of it made them bow. From one side to another was as broad as the whole village at home, from the floor up, up, up to the vaults of the dome was higher than even Kalighat itself. Suddenly from high above them came a wail, held, lowered, then high and held again. Over much of the world a muezzin called the faithful to prayer. The teacher spoke softly in Bengali and translated the words. The men only understood 'God is one'. The villagers sat alert, watching and listening as the figures before them bowed and recited in unison, always led by the strong, strange voice. Suddenly sunlight shot in the high windows. The praying figures raised their faces in salute. Then again the soaring, mournful prayer. It was over. The teacher and the guide stood, the villagers followed. They stumbled into the light. Outside the mosque no one spoke. Deepaka moved to the teacher, bent and touched his feet. Nirmal and Bankim shuddered in shock. Now Deepaka had broken the spell of the mosque.

'No, no, Deepaka. It is wicked. They would kill us if they could.'

'Silly woman do not tempt them.'

'Hush, they worshipped as you do in your own place.'

Hour after hour, step after step the teacher led them from bridge to palace, from mosque to residency, from tomb to garden. Rarely did they pause except to listen more attentively. Evening drew in and they found themselves again before the mosque of Aurangzeb. This time sunset prayers ascended to the great vault and the glow departed from the tiles and left them in darkness. Exhausted, drained of their tension, they emerged to say farewell to the teacher. He wished to go home. But there were questions:

'Where did you learn Bengali?'

'Why have you shown us your prayers?'

'How is it allowed that we, the infidel, can enter your temples?'

'Why did the Persians and English come to our land?'

'Why are there no dancing girls, no princes, in the tiles of your temples?'

'Why was this city a place of battle?'

'What does it mean, that there are Muslims and servants of Lord Siva, and Christians who keep their ladies dressed as widows to teach our children, all together in India?'

'Why do women sit behind in your temples? In our puja we lead, and we pay the priests!'

'Where is the picture of your god? Why does the singer sound so sad?'

'I remember when Bengal was divided and blood ran between brothers and cousins. You are a peaceful man. What makes the blood flow?'

'My niece married a Muslim man and we vowed never to speak of her again. Yet your daughter could marry a worshipper of Siva and still be a good woman. Why do we hang our heads and speak of disgrace?'

The next day they retraced their steps and visited the museum. In the afternoon they were taken to a literary gathering where poets recited and the villagers could follow only the sounds, not the meaning. Surendra complained that misery was more exalted than delight, and went alone to buy more biri. Babla turned to Ashin as the two sat outside the carriage in the evening:

'Ashin, my eyes are heavy from all that we have seen, and my head too full. What must we do tomorrow? Can we not rest? Is there no time for us to talk with each other of what we have done?'

'Tomorrow before daylight the train will move north. We go to see the birthplace of Ganga. The journey is long, you can rest as we travel. There will be many stops.'

'We have seen too much these days. I feel I would know India better if I had my hands upon a plough.'

When the train began to move, few of the villagers stirred. None but Ashin stood and watched as they moved towards the mountains. In the morning the villagers watched the richness of the country with envy. It was fine land, the houses were bigger, bullocks glistened with health, the crops were heavy. Toward noon Ashin fetched a newspaper and tried to read, but he was interrupted:

'What does it say, dada?'

'There is fighting near the border of Kashmir again.'

'What does it mean?'

'Perhaps someone has had a blood feud.'

'No, the paper gives word only of armies and men of power.'

'Is there an army?'

'I do not know.'

'Why do they fight?'

'They want the land, each for themselves.'

'Is it good farmland?'

'Those who live there do not wish to be ruled in one way and others do not want to be ruled by them.'

'Will they always fight?'

'If it is over land, yes. Look at the Ghose case. That has been fought since the time of my grandfather, and it is only a little piece of land.'

'Little? Who says little? It is as far as a man can walk in a day in all directions. None of us ploughs such a piece.'

Surendra got out his map and found Kashmir. Then he found Bengal:

'Look how far we have come. There is still much more before we have even crossed India from side to side.'

'Where is Persia where the armies came from?'

'Where is England?'

'They are not on the map. This is just India. England is across the sea. Here is Bombay, the boats sail from Bombay.'

'The teacher said the Persians came by foot with horses. Which way did they come?'

'Here over the mountains.' Ashin tried to show them, and Harischandra tried to read, but everything had to be questioned and explained, and made real by comparison with the village. Many of the villagers would listen to nothing about the reform movements of the Sikhs and shouted down Harischandra's attempts at explanation. Others wanted to know more of the rulers, so Ashin told them of Akbar, of his tolerance, his building, and his introduction of new ways and new ideas.

'Was this king not Indian?'

'Of course he was Indian, he was born here and raised here. He must have loved his lands.'

'But he was a northerner.'

'And we are little Bengalis whom no one trusts and whom all call cowards. Who is Indian?'

'There, you see. We are Bengalis, and all think of us as Bengalis. It is only those who go to other places who are called Indians. We do not call ourselves Indians.'

'That is true, and around us are the Jats and the Sindhi peoples.'

'Why do we need the name India?'

'We do not need it. We have our own place. Who would wish to be a Madrasi?'

'Only a Madrasi.'

'It is a sad joke. We are on a train, half-way across India. Bengali is our language, but Bengal alone is not our country. We have been treated as guests and brothers and sisters by all we have met. We are still afraid of the foreigners, but not of the people who work these fields. Now, why are we without fear for these people?' Elder De spoke earnestly.

'I was afraid in the mosque.'

'I, too, they were angry to see us there.'

'But you were not afraid of the teacher and he was of their faith.'

'There was no need for fear, and that we learned.'

'We were right to expect trouble. There have always been wars between us. We are shamed by having been in their temples.' Bankim spoke with a hiss and at once began to mutter a prayer.

'That is not right, uncle. You found the teacher a wise man. He was as faithful to his worship as we wish to be to ours. I do not believe wars have been between faithful men. They have been over land and money and power, but not over obedience to prayers.'

'There is truth in that. In the early times the Muslims were strangers and did not hold the lands. Why was there so much blood when the British left?'

'It was madness. It was wished by the madman. If he could not have India, he would destroy her, so they gave him Pakistan and he died.'

'What you say, Amiya, is a riddle to me.'

'She speaks of Jinnah.'

'Do you not remember how all the Muslim children disappeared and then the huts were left empty? Ai, it was terrible.'

'Does government make orders which can cause one man to kill another? That is blasphemy—it is the destruction of all his future lives.' Nirmal was truly horrified.

Ashin struggled with definitions. His audience was restless. Elder De spoke softly:

'But are we ourselves not the government of our village? We settle matters which involve us all and which no man can settle alone. We keep the rules for order, is it not so?'

'Truly, and the money-lender and the landlords tell us just how to do it.'

'Is not the government of the district or of Bengal or of India like our council?'

'No, for the people who sit on the councils do not farm, so they must be rich men.'

'How can a rich man know what concerns a poor one?'

'Gandhiji was not rich.'

'Oh Ma, he was. He was a lawyer with much money and he was always cared for by rich men. Besides, a saint is a saint whether rich or poor.'

'But Gandhiji was not of the government. The British were the government. He wanted them to go away.'

'How could the British be the government when there were so few of them?'

'There was only one family at the trading house but they kept the seed grain, solved the quarrels, and brought gifts at festival times. Now you must start a year before to ask a question about tax, there are so many clerks. How did the British govern without papers?'

'Are there more Indians than British?'

'Yes, many more, and there were always few of the British sent to India.'

'If the government is now of Indians there must be more of them for each man must employ his family. It is so.'

'Did not the British have families?'

'Their families stayed in their own place. Only the young came here.'

'Must younger brothers wander there, too?'

'If there is land to be worked, surely.'

'It always comes back to land. And still I do not know what is Indian.' Babla walked away. The group dispersed. After a little while when the card games were noisy and the women were fighting over their bargains, Amiya moved close to Ashin:

'Dada, may I question you?'

'What is it? Does Uma's foot not mend?'

'It mends well.' The stately grandmother twisted the end of her sari.

At last she asked: 'Ashin, are there scholarships for village girls to go to college in Bengal?'

'Yes, at some colleges in Calcutta there are scholarships.'

'How does a girl get one?'

'First, because her teacher recommends her as a good student. They do not give scholarships to girls whose families will make them stop to be married.'

'So the family must promise?'

'No, but the teacher must know and trust the family. The girl must be very good, for the examinations are for many.'

'Are the examinations given in Calcutta?'

'I believe they are also given at your old school now. Some girls from the big town now come to college in Calcutta.'

'Truly?'

'There are two who lived with my wife's sister last year. They came to study at Loreto College.'

'How much does it cost, to send a girl to school?'

'I do not know. Perhaps 100 rupees per month. It is not so expensive for a girl, for the girls do not go out and they live with families and help in the house.'

'Are teachers very rich?'

'No, they are badly paid. Government servants get much more.'

'It seems much.'

'You are used to the village where you do not pay for your house and where you do not need to buy food in the market. In the city there are too many people, it is very costly.'

Amiya moved back to her bunk. Ashin watched her and would have spoken again but Arundati and Babla sat down before him. They looked hesitant and Ashin realized he had not heard them speak loudly to each other since Benares:

'Ashin-dada, we have not yet written to the foreign ladies.'

'Yes, you wanted me to write in English.' Ashin found his writing case and asked: 'What do you wish me to say?'

'First, tell them that I am an old man, now with grown grandchildren.' Babla waited while Ashin wrote.

'Say that I had never been to Calcutta when we began this trip and now we are tourists going to see all India. Say that I am often frightened by strange sights and strange people. I want to be home with my feet in my ploughing.'

'No, Babla do not say that, foreign ladies do not understand about ploughs and being tourists. They teach sewing to girls.' Arundati interrupted.

'Write as I said. They will understand when I finish. Say that my wife is very foolish.' Arundati covered her head. She was swaying with the movement of the train and Babla watched her before going on. 'She has always wanted beautiful things and little work to do, but she has never had them. Thus did her eyes grow wide and greedy when she saw the saris in Calcutta.'

'Do not say that to the foreign ladies.'

'Say that I have always been a fearful man. I fear not to have seed grain, and not to have a new bullock or a new cow when my old ones die. I have always hoarded our money and never let Arundati buy the little dolls at festivals, or the coloured cloth from the pedlars. Sometimes she does behind my back and then I beat her.' Babla hung his head. Ashin kept still. Babla continued:

'When we came to Benares, Arundati was devoured by greed. She could not even pray calmly to the river without thinking of the saris. I was devoured by fear. I felt she might spend all my money foolishly and then we would have nothing in the weeks ahead or to take home if the crop fails. She hated me for my fear and I hated her for her greed, and we both became blind. Then, she went out in search of the best sari of all, though it is only for an ugly girl who will not like anything anyway. And she became lost. When we went out to search I did not know which fear was greater in my heart. The fear that she would spend my money, or the fear that my silly wife would die alone and frightened somewhere in the holy city. There would be no one to scold her, no one to ask her to cook, no one to find her and carry her to the river. I did not know until I walked those streets in darkness that this foolish wife is part of me, and if she died alone then all I would have left would be my fears. There would be no one to fight with, no one to speak with about the children, no one to comfort me by teasing.' Arundati was looking at Babla with wide eyes.

'Then we came to your great palace. The others said it was a school run by foreigners and I knew that there was no use looking there. No foreigner would care about a greedy and frightened wife out in the night. They might even think she was a thief or a beggar. When you came out with her I was disgraced. You, a stranger in my country, had given her comfort, and I had not believed it possible. Now, I have a further disgrace, for you have given her this most beautiful sari of all, made by your own hands. It is a gift for an honoured guest, not a gift for a thief or a beggar or a silly village wife. I cannot pay you for this sari, for I know there is no price on the work of your students. Also I think you would be angry to get money, just as I would be angry if a guest tried to pay me for the food we give. Thus I say to you, thank you for giving an old man peace with his fears, and thank you for giving my wife the only truly beautiful thing she will ever own. I am the cultivator Babla, of the village of Uma Sen. Written this day on the train from Lucknow going north.' Ashin finished writing carefully. Babla held out his hand for the papers and clumsily wrote his name. He handed the pencil to Arundati and she made her mark. Then they rose:

'Will you mail it from the next station?'

'Is it right to say such things to foreign ladies?'

'It is right. I will mail it for you,' Ashin turned away suddenly and Babla and Arundati walked together down the carriage.

Deepaka was mending the hem of a sari. She watched the country passing, turned to her stitches and worked again. Rhunu was sitting opposite her and very carefully was drawing the old woman. The lines caught the curves of her plump body with her knees tucked up beside her on the bunk. There, too, were the folds of the sari being mended. On one wrist was the widow's bangle. She leaned slightly against the window and Rhunu had caught the glow of sunlight on her face and the shadows behind the grey head. It was a portrait of great peace. Rhunu's hand grew still as she realized it was complete and true.

'May I see, Rhunu?' asked Deepaka.

'I did not know you watched,' Rhunu replied sharply and tried to close the book. In her haste she spilled the chalk sticks and Deepaka bent to retrieve them. It took a time to collect them all but when the box was full Rhunu was calm. The book lay closed upon the bunk. Deepaka returned to her sewing and did not ask again. After a few moments Rhunu opened the book and solemnly passed it over. Her hand now shook. Deepaka looked at the picture, then at Rhunu, then again at the picture.'

'But Rhunu, you have made me look like a saint!'

'I only drew what I saw.'

'It is very beautiful. You do me much honour.'

'My hand is very slow.'

'Child, child do not always mock your gifts. They are from the goddess. By giving your best, you do her honour.' Deepaka closed the book and handed it back. Rhunu looked up at her:

'You truly think it is good?'

'Of course. You make me live and look out from the paper. That comes from the goddess.'

'I always fear to offend. When the alpana are done the others say too quickly that they are good, before I can judge myself.'

'Then you must make peace with the gift of the goddess within you. You alone can know when you have used the gift well. The offence of others' remarks must be as nothing. So is it too with puja. What is done from a true heart is pleasing to the gods. You must not doubt your gift just as you must not doubt your goddess. To do so is a mistrust of all.'

'It is not easy to trust one's hands to portray what the eyes or the heart sees.'

'Then you must learn. Do I not trust my old fingers to sew even though I talk to you and watch the country we pass?'

Jaydev and Narend had been talking. They passed Deepaka and Rhunu

now sitting at ease, and sought Mitu from his bunk. Then they went
back to Babla:

'Waken brother, and help us direct Mitu to draw the ways to fix the
pump.' Jaydev shook Babla and the four, surrounded by many other
curious men, sat in the corridor and tried carefully to create a faithful
picture of their pump, and of the repairs the mechanic had forecast might
be necessary. It took them a long time. They argued over each of the
little pictures. Many comments were made by the observers and Mitu
had to start again to correct the drawing. At last they were content and
began to smoke. Elder De had been watching with interest:

'Mitu, can you make a map of the fields of the village with the water
channels?'

'Yes, if you all guide me.'

'But why, Elder De, do you wish a map? We all know where the
water goes for each of our fields.'

'Look out of the window. See the sprayer which pushes water all over
the land?'

'Yes, all the field is watered evenly.'

'It must be costly. See the metal pipes.'

'Our fields are watered unevenly. The parts near the channels get too
much, the edges get too little. Is it not so?'

'Truly.'

'Could we not make these sprayers?'

'There must be a pump to force the water.'

'But we have a pump. You have had Mitu make pictures of it. Can we
not fix pipes to the pump so that it could spray out water?'

'It could be done.'

'There are the old pipes the foreign technicians brought which did not
fit the pump.'

'Yes, they might be used.'

'Let us try to visit one of these farms.'

Midway along the carriage a group of women had been gossiping over
what might be happening in the village, but the gossip had turned to
biting accusation and now they were fighting in full voice. In the corridor
some men had been playing cards, but they were shouting, each accusing
another of cheating. The din grew. At first the noise amused the other
travellers. Quickly it became a threat. Amiya rose and walked calmly
down to the men. She pushed passed them and stood silently over the
screaming women. They did not notice her. She shouted:

'Hush you. The train is not the river bank. Shall the northerners know
of your foolishness?'

'Always interfering, Amiya. Haven't you enough family of your own
then?' The jibe was cruel and meant as such. Before Amiya could recover
and join the fray, old Nirmal who had been sitting near by, spoke to
them all and to no one:

'How can a man enter heaven when he is surrounded by demons?'

The old man did not know why the whole carriage suddenly echoed with laughter. The card players laughed until the tears came. The women hung to one another in their mirth. Amiya went back to her own place. It grew peaceful again, there were no disputes for the moment. Deepaka leaned over to Amiya:

'It will not be well if they fight like that often.'

'No, but the hours are long. They have little interest in these miles of country. There will be other journeys even longer.'

'Let us urge them all to walk at the next stop.'

'Reena, can you not tell a story to pass the hours?'

'Ai, ai, I have been reading one of the foreign ones from this book. Come, come, my children, and hear the story of the Snow Queen.'

Reena's summons had never failed to bring the villagers hurrying to her. Now they came especially eager, for this was a strange title which they had not heard, and there was a shrill note of excitement in Reena's voice. She moved so that they could all hear, and they crowded six to a bunk, to come as near as possible. Then she began.

The story of Kay and the northern cold which reached his heart unfolded slowly. Reena made the Snow Queen a rani of the Himalaya, and Kay a boy from the warm delta of Bengal. Like him, they were travelling north. Reena used all her powers to make the love story a haunting tale of travel, search and worry. She finished just as the train began to slow for a station, and her listeners applauded even more wildly than they had for the dance drama:

'Oh Ma, it is good. Are there many such good ones in the book?'

'Yes, though this is just a little book.'

'Do not worry, in every city there will be book stores. I will help you find more, but you must promise to tell my children the tales one day.' Ashin spoke warmly.

'A village crone must tell tales to city children? They will not listen for a moment.'

'They and all of Calcutta would listen if you would tell the tales as you do now.'

'Hush, let us step down. There is sunlight.'

They walked and drank tea. Jaydev tried to find the irrigation sprays, but failed. Arundati bought fresh pan. Ashin found newspapers. The cook had filled the teapot. Rhunu bought a stone doll for her grandson. When the train moved on she spent a long time wrapping the little rider on horseback to give to Harischandra for the post. Amiya, too, gave him a letter. He had watched her struggling with it most of the day. Ashin had written to Sundara-devi, Bankim had inscribed a prayer for his grandson, and Uma had paid the writer to write a letter to her sons. The packet was large as Harischandra tied it together. Night was drawing in. The cook passed the tea and some cold rice. Surendra teased him for

101

giving them only a village supper, but the cook would not laugh. He was cold and hungry and his burn was painful. When the talis were put away and the villagers were at ease, the cook huddled in the corner wondering how he could be free of this train and these stupid folk. He wanted a good city house, with rich people who slept late each morning and stayed in one place.

Sleep was disturbed often. Each small town seemed to have waited for just this train, and the clamour at each stop could not be ignored. Even Surendra lost his temper and shouted out at the crowd. No one understood his words, but his tone left no doubt of his anger. Vituperative Punjabi replied.

'Ignorant northerners,' grumbled Surendra.

'But Indians all the same,' replied Mitu. Surendra laughed and fell asleep.

Once they had to wait long for a connecting train. Ashin was called three times to show papers and tickets. By dawn they were grumpy and argumentative. Tea was welcome.

'When do we come to wherever we stop?'

'We stop in Hardwar. We should arrive there by noon if the second connection is not late.'

'It will be late.'

'Hardwar, birthplace of the Ganges, is it not, Ashin?'

'Yes. From there we will see the Himalaya.'

'When?'

'Tomorrow I would guess.'

'Tomorrow we see Himalaya?'

'Yes, and do not forget your shawls. It will be cold in the hills.'

The news that the home of the gods was so close subdued them. Surendra smoked and watched the horizon off to the north. The connection was late, and it was not until late afternoon that they entered Hardwar and the carriage was put in its berth.

'Look, all over the station. There are sadhus and priests everywhere.'

'Is there a festival?'

'No, they come to worship and pray in the hills.'

'Careful, they have staves. They are not like our priests, and not fat like the ones in Benares. Do not speak loudly.'

'Ai, see, each is different, yet they all have powers.'

'Keep back, keep back.' The voice of caution was Nirmal's and he claimed enough authority that at his words the villagers drew back from the windows out of direct sight of the flowing crowd of lean priests.

From all parts of India they had come. Some were old and wrinkled, stern from the long journey, but slow before the cold wind. Others were lithe, their long locks flowing out, their strides rhythmical, their gaze sharp. Many were wrapped only in dreams of the high hills, and wandered

102

here and there, not leading, not following, but keeping away from the crowded tracks of Hardwar.

Ashin and the station master conferred. A young boy was found to lead the villagers to the bathing ghats. The lad was delighted with his curious charges. He took them slowly, pausing at each shop to explain the wonders of carving, or images, or prayer shawls known only in Hardwar. Ashin was taxed to understand the boy. They did not reach the top of the main road until the wind was strong and the sun was setting. They rounded a corner where a souvenir seller was haranguing a group of tourists. There before them rolled the little Ganges. Narrow and grey with cold it foamed and protested against each dam. In it stood praying priests, men and women, sick children, each determined that this holy place should give them its blessing, despite the freezing temperatures. The villagers turned towards the wind and reeled back with surprise. There, to the north, loomed the high line of hills. These were no ordinary hills. They cut like scythes to harvest the adoration of the plains.

'This is Himalaya,' Surendra almost whispered.

'No, these are just the low hills. Behind them are the high hills and then beyond is Himalaya. If there is good weather, you will see Himalaya tomorrow.' The stranger addressed Surendra in Bengali. Turning, the cultivator saw that the speaker was a rich Bengali, perhaps from Calcutta. The two men exchanged greetings and asked each after their home place.

'I come now from Delhi where I work for the government. My family place is Mymensingh. We fled to Calcutta at the division and then to Delhi. If my eyes do not mislead me, you are one who ploughs the land. What brings you to this holy place in search of Himalaya?'

Surendra told the story of Uma Sen's will and the strange journey. The polished tourist looked over the group critically and offered Surendra his foreign cigarrettes. As he smoked he told Surendra that things would not be easy ahead:

'It will be a hard journey. There are many who will scorn you and try to drive you from the holy places or the places where there is power and wealth. Be careful. Be careful, brother, to bring the herd safely to shelter.' He was gone down the hill. Surendra turned back to the villagers still looking to the folds of the hills and the Ganges. For the first time the farmer saw his fellows as the stranger must have done. They were small, dark and shabby. The women had covered their heads with their saris. They huddled in their shawls, obviously chilled. Only the shawl of Reena seemed to give any warmth, and her frame was lost within it. Surendra looked again from one to another. They were tired, the pallor of one seemed to be shared by each. Ashin looked drawn, the easy sparkle which had greeted them was gone. Amiya stood tall in stately solitude, but the rigidity was banished from her bearing and Surendra wondered why she seemed so nervous in repose. Deepaka was smiling with wonder, but the tendrils of hair that blew across her forehead were whiter and the hand that brushed them back trembled a little. Nirmal and Bankim stood apart, frail in aged transparency, still rapt in their awe of the worshippers in Ganga. Jaydev and Uma stood together, Uma was now wizened, no longer just small, and Jaydev had lost the easy laughter which was his trademark in the village. There was tension on each face, a holding back which was also a straining of attention. Surendra looked and saw it even on the faces of those who slept most of the time. Mitu, intent upon sketching, had not changed, unless to have become happy and hopeful and confident in his bearing. Narend beside him stood tall, the shadowed eyes seeing far, the hands of work without a tremor in their unaccustomed idleness. Rhunu beside him shivered, but she looked unaffected by the tension of the others. Surendra thought her face had softened. She was wrapped in her own silence, apparently listening. Surendra looked again at the deep shadows on the faces and moved forward:

'Come, it is cold. Let us return to warm food. We can worship tomorrow.' His voice broke upon them and several were shocked by the familiarity in these surroundings. They turned and eagerly followed him down the road. The cook greeted them sharply and hurried them through the little meal. The wind roared in the shutters of the carriage. They were content to crawl into their blankets early. Still they shivered. Suddenly the flickering light of a lantern made them cling to one another in fear. Ashin went forward:

'Who is it?'

'It is I, your guide,' came the little boy's voice. Ashin opened the door and the boy jumped up into the carriage. Behind him came several servants carrying large bundles.

'What do you bring?'

'Blankets. They come from my uncle's hotel. He saw you standing by the river and asked me about you when I came back. He says you will need more blankets to keep warm. There are no guests now in his hotel so use them as long as you are here, I will collect them when you go.'

'Must we pay?'

'No, no. My uncle says you are his guests. He once worked on the railway in Bengal and he remembers your country. Now I must go, for my mother is angry,' and the boy led the bearers away. Ashin and Narend, Rhunu and Reena passed out the blankets. Surendra lay awake alone in the night.

Dawn did not bring warmth. The few who went to bath returned miserable and blue with the chill of the winter water.

'Silly Deepaka, this bath will not bless you. Drink the tea quickly.' Amiya scolded and fluttered around her serene friend, but seeing that the chill did not abate she stopped her scolding and wrapped Deepaka in four of the hotel's blankets, combed back the wet hair, and clucked in her anger. She ordered Jaydev and Ashin to do the same for Nirmal and Bankim whose chattering excitement at having bathed at Hardwar could not conceal the spasms with which they shook. Reena attended to her own care, but was grateful when Rhunu brought more blankets:

'It was cold, niece, but we are blessed for having done it.'

'Let us hope the gods protect the foolish among the devout,' was Rhunu's answer. Ashin left the carriage and did not return for a long time. The villagers grew impatient to be off. At least then they would be walking in the sun. Ashin returned, distracted and disappointed.

'There has been a telegram. We cannot go north because of the unrest in Kashmir. The officials do not think it wise to take us. We will stay longer here and longer in Delhi. The station master is getting a bus to take us along the river to the bridge of Lakshman. We will visit some ashrams and then go to a mountain village. Tomorrow they think we are to walk in the high hills so that you can see the true Himalaya. The bus will fetch us so that in three days we will return to the train. Take the extra blankets.'

After scurrying preparations, the villagers climbed into the bus. The sides of the vehicle were painted with flowers and pictures of the gods of the mountains giving blessing. The driver, jovial and adventurous, greeted them happily. He drove with abandon, singing prayers loudly, or yodelling a strange music all his own. He swerved and jolted his way up the winding road. Suddenly he stopped beside a flight of stone steps. His seasick passengers gratefully tumbled forth. A bowing figure waited above them, and gestured that they should mount the steps and follow her. They found themselves on a wide terrace which was bordered by low, spotless buildings. Everywhere there were cattle, sleek and combed, like none the villagers had ever seen. Among them walked men and women who were always smiling and stroking the cows. A murmur of a preaching voice came from one doorway. Before it the walkers always bowed before moving on to the next cow. Sometimes a woman would talk to a beast, addressing it in a combination of reverential speech and baby talk appropriate to a doting grandmother. The villagers did not know what to do. A priest came and welcomed them. This was the ashram of his master, and he said a name of no meaning to the villagers. Here people came to reach and know the absolute truth, and the priest described the daily routines by which this was done, he said. There were sermons and prayers, times for meditation and times for cleaning. Once in a great while each would take the darshan of the master who would give pertinent guidance for the individual's life.

'Who pays for the food?' asked Babla.

'Each devotee gives a sum to the ashram when first they come, and more later if they wish to stay longer. From that the ashram is able to buy food.'

'Ai, the savings of a life, or the first earnings of a grandson,' said Jaydev.

'Why do the cows look so fat? Why do they walk here and not in the fields?'

'They are our living god. We worship them since they bless us by their presence.'

'You feed them well.'

'Perhaps they would not stay away from fields if they were not fed.'

The priest was not amused. After the villagers had been invited to look at the great master, and had seen a man dressed in fine silk and wrapped with a magnificent Kashmiri shawl, they returned to the bus.

'It is a place for rich men who want to be comfortable and pious.'

'Did you see, all the women wore silk saris?'

'They were brushing the cow as if it were a bride!'

'The yogi looked like a hotel keeper. He was reading, not preaching.'

'Maybe those were prayers.'

'Or his accounts. It would not make much difference to the worshippers.'

'The lady said they came from Delhi and a few stay as long as a year. They are so rich they need not work for a year!'

'Look at us, we are not working.'

'That is different. We will have to bear our burdens when we return.'

'You speak like the priest, he only mentioned duties and burdens and the problems of being good.'

'The families of the rich must bear the extra load for the year.'

'Yes, if only to pay the bills of the ashram.'

'The people looked very happy, do you think they have found god?'

'Know that they are certainly told they must look happy. It is part of being good.'

'No doubt they have had a good life. Like the cows, they like to dwell in those ashrams.'

'If there are gods of cows and land, they do not visit such a place.'

'Hush, do not say such things.'

'My fate has almost finished with me and Uma Sen has given me a pilgrimage. Do not worry, I am surely saved from cursing in the next life.'

'Maybe all ways of worship, even those of rich men, are welcome to the gods.'

'The gods must be very lonely to need so much.'

'Hush, hush. This is another.'

'But there are foreigners. I told you the gods must be lonely.'

The chatter grew quiet as they climbed to the terrace of this ashram. Uma was reminded of the school in the big town. The villagers were startled to see the dung drying on the wall of the big building just as in the village. Young foreigners mingled with Indians on the terrace. They were waiting for something. A foreign boy was brought to the villagers. He addressed them in hesitant but clear Bengali.

'Welcome. It is almost time for our meal. Please will you join us. We eat there, in the hall.' The boy led them over to the others waiting and together they all walked along a dark corridor and into a low room. At one end there was a small dais. They were shown to places at the rows of benches. A procession of young people entered bearing the talis. The villagers were served first and stared at the beautifully presented meal before them. A man came into the room and bowed to the assembly from the dais. As soon as he began to read aloud, people began to eat. The villagers tried to turn from the sight of so many, but it was not possible. They ate little. The language the man was reading was not familiar. After a time the reading stopped, the assembled group rose. Each rinsed his tali at a tap before stacking it at the doorway. The villagers followed and imitated carefully. The boy joined them again at the door. He asked:

'Would you like to see where we grow our food?'

'Do you have fields?' The interest was at once hopeful for something familiar. The villagers walked carefully as he led them to another terrace. There were neat plots of vegetables and grains. The whole terrace was a garden. Young people were working at weeding or cultivating. Jaydev noticed that along the plots there were metal pipes:

'Is this your watering system?'

'Yes, it is a spray irrigation system. We must pump the water up to it because we are so high.'

'How do you pump it?' Several of the villagers shouted together.

'Come and see.' The boy led them to a shed. There were pipes everywhere.

'This is the pump. We keep it covered because the rains would damage it.'

'Does rain damage a pump?'

'It can. The parts can rust, and then the machine breaks.'

The men pressed forward to see, and the other squatted to wait. They were sheltered from the wind. The boy was having trouble keeping up with the excited questions of the cultivators. They explained that they had a pump which was broken, and that they had no system of irrigation but should like to build one. Carefully the boy explained everything, to their delight.

'How is it that your ashram is concerned with machines? Do you not worship the gods?'

'We learn through work and study.'

'Was studying Bengali part of your worship?'

'No, I studied Bengali in college in my country. Now I study meditation.'

'How do you study meditation?'

'First I had to learn to sit cross-legged.'

'Was that difficult?'

'It hurt terribly and my legs would go to sleep. Once I broke my ankle because I stood before my legs were awake. Then I had to begin again. Once I could sit without thinking of my legs I had to learn not to worry about sneezing or whether my stomach was rumbling like thunder.'

'You do not sound a very saintly student.'

'Oh, I am not a saint, that is too hard work.'

'Do you all work in the food places?'

'We must all work there and help with the cleaning and the cooking. We are our own servants.'

'Do you take the darshan of your yogi sometimes?' Nirmal echoed what he had just heard.

'That is easy, he is always around working and talking just as we are doing now.'

'Is he not a saint?'

'Oh, perhaps. But he is a saint who works for his students. Maybe he thinks our own efforts will not be enough.'

'How did you come to be in an ashram? Why did you leave your country?'

'This master came to my college and lectured. He was the most interesting teacher I had. When he was coming back, I came too. I wanted to learn more about living from him.'

'How long will you stay?'

'In this ashram, or in India?'

'Both.'

'I have been in the ashram two years. Now I must find work. I would like to stay in India three more years and come to the ashram each winter.'

'What is your work?'

'I teach at a school down at the refugee centre near Hyderabad.'

'Does your mother wish you to stay? Why should you stay in our country to teach?'

'My mother worries that I do not wear enough clothes and will catch cold. She knits me socks.' Here he paused and pulled his skirts up to show the heavy socks on his feet.

'Last year my mother came to see the refugee centre. She liked our work and my father liked the gardens. They say that as long as they know that what I am doing is useful to the people, they cannot feel anything but respect for what I am doing.'

'You are an unusual foreigner.' Reena looked the boy up and down. 'We saw others who pretend to be saints with the dreaming drugs, but know nothing of Sanskrit, and do not work for their dreams.'

'It is very sad. Many come here searching for some answer for their lives but they are not willing to work. The dreaming drugs are an easy way. I am sorry you were made angry by them, mother,' and the lad bowed to Reena. From the road the horn of the bus was calling them raucously. Ashin and the others thanked the boy, but he merely wished them a good journey. Deepaka drew close to him and asked:

'And have you found your god, or truth as you say?'

'What do you mean, mother?'

'I mean, do you know your god, see what is truth, within you?'

'Once I saw, and therefore I came to learn more.'

'But if you saw once, what need is there to try again? Is not the truth there for always?'

'I was very young, I do not think I understood as much as it would be possible to understand of that knowledge.'

'And you have no doubts that it was so?'

'No.'

'Does it make you happy?'

'In that moment when I knew it, I was more than happy, but there are many things around me that make me angry and that I want to change.'

'Is not anger insulting to the gods?'

'Surely if what men do is untrue and wicked, our anger at that is right and not an insult?'

'But is not the wickedness also part of the fates of those ones?'

'And all are part of god, are we not, mother?'

'Come Deepaka, we are waiting.'

'I do not know, I do not know,' and Deepaka moved away leaving the boy alone to watch the bus roll away up the valley.

'He is a son to be proud of,' Uma muttered.

'Yes, and he has shown us that we shall have a water sprayer, too. Mitu can you draw while the bus moves?' Jaydev watched Mitu struggle to put on paper what Babla and Narend had observed of the pump.

They were now travelling through a small village deep in a gorge. At the end of the line of houses the bus halted and the driver showed them a path ahead. They walked two by two and progress was slow, for the wind drove rain before it. At last they saw a frail structure high in the gorge ahead of them. Their pace quickened for they saw the goal—the bridge of Lakshman. They hurried, pulling the shawls closer, lengthening their old strides. At last they stood on the bridge and looked down. The sky and the water had turned to purple, and high on the edges of the forest above them the last rays of orange were caught and held a moment. The purple faded slowly while they talked. Darkness stalked up the gorge and embraced them on the bridge. When they could see no more Surendra led them slowly back along the path to the bus. They kept silent while the driver found the mountain road he needed and began the long grinding ascent of the first ridge of hills. Reena began to tell tales of Lakshman, one more exciting than another. Finally, when her throat was beginning to rasp, she began to tell of Jotayu, the great bird of valour much loved for his sacrifice for Lakshman and Ram. By the end of the story the villagers were weeping. They had forgotten the lurching of the bus until suddenly it stopped. The driver stood and stretched, happy that his work was done. They followed him into the night:

'Is there a village? I see no lights.'

'There above, there is a fire.'

'That is far off.'

'Can we be going there?'

'Here, do not forget your blankets.'

They loaded the bundles up on to each other's heads, and then stumbled up a steep path behind the driver. They could see nothing. Surendra and Narend dropped back and kept the last ones moving on. Most were panting from the effort and the cold and the fright at this strange end to their day. Just when Uma thought she could go no farther, they reached the crest of the hill and saw the driver taking a lantern from a stranger. He took them across a cobbled street to a long room. Here they would sleep.

It was not until well after dawn that Surendra awakened, and the others slept on until sunlight broke into the room from windows high near the ceiling. Deepaka and Nirmal were both coughing and Uma often gasped for air. Amiya found a tea pot warm at the door and soon she was soothing the three with tea. When they were all fed and ready, they stepped out into the sunshine and were astonished.

They stood on the top of a high hill, below them to the west was cloud, sometimes they could see Ganga shining up at them. Turning, they saw the plunging hills, stretching as far as they could see. Then Mitu grasped Surendra's arm.

'Look, brother. The line that dances on the edge of the world. Those are the snows of Himalaya.' Surendra stood riveted. Yes, they were peaks, and yes they were dancing under the morning sun. The snow was blue at this distance, and Surendra was not alone in thinking he saw the highest of the great line of mountains. The villagers pointed and laughed, and forgot the cold in their excitement. At last a short man with a great stick waved at them to follow him. Hour after hour they tried to keep him in sight. He did not pause long, nor did he explain who they were to the villages they passed. Past midday the villagers were so scattered along the track that the last could not see any but the next to last and so on through the forests and up the gorges. Many were panting heavily. Uma was leaning on Jaydev, Arundati on Babla. There was no complaint, there was no energy for that. Reena, who was to the front of the trek, sat down and waited when she saw the ones ahead had reached some sort of summit. She massaged her cold feet and thought how unsuitable sandals were for this climbing. After a long time a few caught up with her. They looked grey with strain. Reena took a second bundle of bedding to ease the struggles of Bankim. She moved up the track quickly until she found Ashin panting beside the guide. They were sitting on a gently sloping meadow, looking at the white snows:

'Ashin, you must stop this idiot from killing us all. Look, here are a few, all the others are out of sight behind. Who knows how sick they will be. We will have to go back to help.'

Ashin was too weakened himself to heed her scolding. Narend rose and looked back. He could see no one on the track. Ashin managed to find out from the guide that if they stayed on the track they could not miss the town where they were to sleep. Narend told Ashin and the guide to go on to the town and fetch lanterns. He made the guide carry Reena's two bundles, and bade another villager carry Ashin's, then he and Reena turned back to retrace their steps. The forerunners moved down the meadow and into the trees. Ashin often paused with the effort, or to help another.

Reena and Narend reached Jaydev and Uma and about ten others after only a short time. They told them to go on and rest in the sun on the meadow. Jaydev was carrying two bundles, but the others managed their own. Narend and Reena hurried on. One by one they found the stragglers. Most were sitting panting by the track, few were still moving forward. Arundati was asleep beside Babla and he bade Narend and Reena not to waken her.

'She will be refreshed by the rest. Then we will go on.'

'No, she will be chilled by this cold if she sleeps. Waken her and go on now. There is still sun above.'

'Where is Deepaka, and Amiya, and Nirmal?'

Again they moved back down the track. Soon they found Elder De leaning on Harischandra. They were moving, but very slowly.

'Are you ill, Elder De?'

'I do not know. My head is thumping like a drum at a sacrifice, and I cannot breathe. Harischandra is not much better but he gives me his shoulder.'

'Are there others behind yet?'

'Some have stopped to sleep to see if the head pain goes away. Deepaka coughs very much.'

'Reena, you stay here and carry the bundles. The sun is still on the hill, uncle. Try to get up and see Himalaya. Then you go down again to the next village to sleep. Perhaps the head pain will vanish when you go down. I'll go back to waken the others and to help Deepaka. Try to go on, and do not stop or you will become cold.'

'Go Narend. Here Harischandra, give me the bundles.' Reena soon had the men moving at a better pace, and Narend no longer looked back. His long strides took him over the track quickly. Whenever he met one of the villagers asleep or sitting in the cold he would waken the person, shake him, and send him forward again to see the mountains. At the news of the meadow and the village, their spirits would rise for the first

111

time in hours. Narend continued on alone. He was in no pain, his long legs were enjoying the hard walk and but for his worry he would have been excited by the challenge to his body. He often worked to exhaustion in the village just to feel his big frame tried. Now he could sense a pace which was his own, not hampered by paddies, and he liked the fine, thin air of these dark hills. He hurried towards the twilight of the valley. After a long time he saw a small group far ahead. They were moving, step by step, but the two figures in the centre were bent double. Narend could hear the lonely echo of their coughing long before he could see their faces. At last he recognized Amiya supporting Deepaka, Surendra supporting Nirmal. The two looked very ill. Narend began to run.

'How much further is it, Narend?' Amiya was bent with the weight of the two bundles as well as Deepaka.

'Much farther, but on the top of that ridge there is a fine view of Himalaya. Then it is just a short way down to the village where we sleep. The others should be there now.'

'We cannot reach the ridge. Hear how they cough, and Deepaka is dizzy and cannot walk.'

'And Nirmal?'

'He trembles so. Is Himalaya very beautiful?'

'You shall see.'

'Narend opened one bundle and wrapped Nirmal in one blanket and Deepaka in another.

'Amiya, you carry these two bundles. I shall carry Deepaka up to the ridge to see Himalaya. Surendra, you walk with Nirmal until I return. Do not stop. Can you manage?'

'He is warmer. It will be easier.'

The three set off, Narend at first unsteady with the weight, but then settling to the task. Deepaka did not protest, but slept against Narend. Amiya kept pace beside him, though she carried three bed rolls. By the time they reached the ridge the others had vanished from the meadow. The figures of Elder De and Harischandra with Reena slightly ahead could be seen vanishing into the darkness of the cleft. Deepaka roused as Narend laid her on the grass of the meadow:

'Are we come?'

'This is a ridge, Deepaka. See, there is Himalaya, golden in the sun. You will warm a little. When you feel better you must follow Reena, there, down to the village. I go back, Amiya, to bring Nirmal.' At once he was gone again down the trail. Amiya shook herself at the thought of his task, and then she turned to look at the mountains:

'Deepaka-didi, do you see the snows? Are they not beautiful?'

'They show their shadows even at this distance. They must be part of the heavens.' The two sat a long time, but there was no sign of Narend. When Himalaya was beginning to turn orange and pink and the sunlight was fading from the meadow, Amiya hoisted the bundles again. Deepaka rose.

'It is a pity. Perhaps Surendra will not see Himalaya after all,' she said, and the two women shuffled down into the darkness.

When the sky was deep purple and only the line of Himalaya shone gold, Narend reached the ridge carrying Nirmal. Surendra gasped to see the peaks:

'There they are, Narend.'

'Yes.'

'They have hung on to the light until we came. Oh Ma, that I should see the snows.' Surendra squatted and the three men watched the reflected sunset change to deep red, then sullen mauve, and finally the peaks were dark shadows in the night. Nirmal gasped without pause. Only the bright happiness in his eyes showed the others that he had marvelled. Again they set off down the hill. Narend was tired and the trail was unfamiliar. After he had stumbled several times, Surendra bade him pause.

'I will light a torch, Brother, then the way will be easier.' He scrounged at the edge of the forest and found a suitable brand. Soon they had enough light to see the way ahead. Once again Narend lifted Nirmal. When they reached a point when the trail was level Surendra lifted the brand high. There was no village. Above them, on another ridge, Narend saw a light.

'Oh Ma, we have been in error. There is more to climb.'

'I will get help. Nirmal, can you hold the torch?' The old man roused from his prayers and grasped the torch eagerly with both hands, hungry for the reassurance of the light. Surendra moved on quickly, and Narend watched him leave the circle of the light with relief, sure that they would soon be safe. Surendra had not gone far, however, when he found two figures huddled in the shadows. Deepaka only gasped now, she did not cough. Amiya was almost asleep with the exhaustion of long panic. Surendra added his bundles to the pile beside them and made a torch for Amiya. Then he lifted Deepaka. She was heavier than he had expected. He swayed a little and moved only very slowly forward, and upward. Narend below saw the flicker of a torch and knew that Surendra had found more trouble. His pace slowed until he thought of Rhunu above, then he moved on steadily. His arms ached and the back of his neck was numb. Half-way up the hill he stopped and put Nirmal down to rest. Above he could hear dogs, some shouts, then silence. He lifted Nirmal gently, for the old man murmured in pain, and step by step they ascended. Suddenly Jaydev and Babla were there with torches. Babla had a tea pot swinging and splashing. Narend again put down Nirmal and squatted beside him:

'It is all right now, old man, they have come.'

'Hail, Narend, where are the bundles?'

'There, just beyond the bend.'

'Drink the tea while I fetch them. The guide shall pay for this. He planned it all, I think.' Jaydev made an abusive gesture and trotted down the track. Babla poured tea, grinning from ear to ear in relief and terror at the strange night.

'How are the others?'

'Most are vomiting and have head pain. Deepaka sounds like the death rattle. Ashin cannot stand. Elder De and Harischandra were given some spirit by the villagers up there, and they sleep. Amiya is making tea. The village women have made the room very warm. The smell is very bad.' Jaydev and the bundles returned. They found that Narend alone was strong enough to carry Nirmal, so once again he lifted the sick man and the procession set off. They reached the top of the ridge and stumbled along a path until it opened into a cobbled court. For a moment dogs barked and jumped, and then they were inside the building. Bankim came forward and supported Nirmal as Narend lowered him. Jaydev and Babla moved down the crowded room to the stove where Amiya was busy. Narend stood stunned for a long moment, unable to focus on the figures moving in the light of the lanterns. Surendra called from somewhere:

'It is done, brother. All forty-five are here.'

Then Rhunu was on one side of him and Reena on the other. They led him to a mat near Amiya's fire and began to knead and massage his arms and back. Though they continued long, he was asleep before they had even removed his sandals.

The long terrible night drew out the full misery from each hour. When the first light of early morning filtered into the building the villagers lay drained of all struggle. Amiya slept with one hand on Deepaka's shoulder, Babla with Arundati cradled in his arms for warmth, Uma against Jaydev, neither daring to move for fear of disturbing the other. Narend wakened and found his arms and legs gripped with pain at each movement. He looked at the others. Clearly many had been sick most of the night. The breathing still rattled. They looked very old. Deepaka slept deeply, and Nirmal was rousing himself for prayer. Stealthily Narend tried not to waken Rhunu, but at his first step away from the blanket, she sat up and whispered,

'Whither, lord husband? Are you ill?'

'No, Rhunu, I go to make tea. It is cold and I see the others have been ill. Do you suffer?'

'No, only a little head pain.' The two bent together and lit the fire. Before the water was boiling Reena joined them. She did not speak but assembled the cups which had been brought by the village women. Narend filled them and the two women moved back and forth, up and down, until each of the villagers held a warm cup. With his own tea Narend moved to where Ashin lay:

'Does it go badly still, Ashin-dada?'

'Yes, Narend, there is much pain.'

'When will the bus come for us?'

'It was to be here in the night and we are to go at dawn. Surely we cannot travel now?'

'I shall go and see about the bus. I think the sickness will go if you go down. I will ask these people if it is not so.' Narend stepped out into the morning. Above them the sky was bright, but all around them was cloud. The route of the night before was hidden. Smoke was rising from a house not far away so Narend went towards it. In the courtyard was the bus, and inside it, shivering, and subdued, was their tempestuous driver. At the sight of Narend he rose and burst into an angry torrent of Hindi. He went into the house and came back, pulling their guide of the day before, pounding him about the head and shoulders and kicking him when possible. Jaydev had joined Narend and the two tried to understand. When the driver had finished he spoke slowly to the farmers:

'For the health of the others we must get down to the plains quickly. When the cloud goes, we must be ready.'

'May they wait in the bus? The room does not have good air.' Jaydev translated and the bus driver nodded emphatically and then strode with them towards the villagers.

'What was the fight about?'

'The guide is some cousin of the bus driver. When the driver got word that he would take tourists to the hills, he sent word to this cousin to be ready to guide tourists in the hills. The cousin thought that only rich people could make such a journey and that they would pay him more if he showed them the best view of the peaks. The bus driver drove all over the hills looking for us yesterday, he says we have come the hardest way of all. It is a walk only for mountain men and we might all have been killed. He says he will not pay the cousin one paisa.'

'Is the head pain and sickness from the mountain?'

'Yes, they say it is common. But we must get down soon.'

Other hillmen had joined them and waited while the rest of the villagers came out of the room. The clouds rose, hung, then disappeared, leaving the deep rifts of the hills naked below. The hardier villagers loaded the blankets on the bus and helped those who were still weak and dizzy to find their places. The headman of the village came to bid them farewell and made apologies on behalf of his people. His speech was long. Suddenly he bowed and presented Narend with the carefully carved walking stick he had been fondling.

'What is it?'

'Why does he give Narend that?'

'What must I do?' Narend faltered. The bus driver clapped him on the back, beaming:

'He says your feat of carrying the others makes you a true man of the hills. He salutes your courage and your strength. He gives you the hillman's stick to use wherever you go.' Ashin roused himself for the formalities but it was an effort to whisper the translation. Narend blushed.

He touched the headman's feet. He turned and saluted the ridges of Himalaya, once more visible, and swung up on to the bus.

'Let us go, quickly downward,' he said to the driver. None but Jaydev looked back to see the villagers waving. Narend found a place to sit, cradled the stick, and watched out of the window for another glimpse of the mountains. He did not see them again. All morning they twisted and turned, sometimes climbing, sometimes descending, the driver cursing the whole journey through. Often they had to stop while one or another was sick. Sometimes they stopped to fetch tea. Even Reena and the stalwart Rhunu were sick with the turning of the bus. At last the worst was over. In the afternoon the bus drove the last miles into Hardwar while the villagers slept. When they reached the station the driver sought out the station master and explained what had happened. The travellers had found their bunks and curled up on them, forgetting their bundles and blankets. Again Surendra, Narend and Jaydev unpacked the bundles and covered the sleepers. They carefully kept the hotel blankets to one side.

The station master arrived with two officials. He explained that these were doctors and that they would look at the travellers. The station master apologized for the trouble. The doctors went quickly through the carriage, gave Jaydev a handful of pills 'in case there was more trouble' and left, obviously disgusted with these patients. Narend wakened Ashin to hear what the station master had to say.

'The train will leave in an hour for Delhi. It is a long journey. The doctors said you must take great care of that woman, the old man, and the one with glasses.' Here he indicated Deepaka, Nirmal and Elder De. 'I have telegraphed and you will have a hot meal served when the train stops.'

'Can you tell us what has happened to our cook?'

'Has something happened to the cook?' Ashin was shocked.

'I am sorry. He was talking to some rich travellers who were here yesterday. I think they offered him a job in their house. He went with them to Delhi on the night train.'

'What are we to do, without a cook?'

'I have told you, there will be hot food tomorrow.'

'Please thank the hotel man for the blankets, they saved our lives in the hills.'

'He will be humbled to have been of service.'

'We have not thanked the bus driver.'

'He is too ashamed to come.'

'Tell him not to be ashamed. We will recover.'

'Ai, and we have seen Himalaya.'

The train whistled. They moved out, away from the hills.

5

The capital: Delhi

There was little interest among the villagers as the train arrived in Delhi station. They slept. They were sick. They were hungry. True, the station masters of two stations on the way down from Hardwar had sent hot meals for them, but only Surendra had eaten. The others had watched in horror as he ate the strange food cooked by strange hands. He sat smoking at the window. Occasionally someone eyed him surreptitiously. He was not yet sick. The food had not been poisoned, perhaps. Surendra had served the others tea during the night, explaining that someone had to stay active. Ashin lay on his bunk, sweating and coughing. He had not noticed the crisis over food. Amiya was grey and huddled beneath her blanket and shawl. Even after the shunting of the carriage the stillness did not provoke their interest. Surendra went alone to the station master's office.

'Go away, Beggar, this is a place of business.'

'I am not a beggar, I must see the station master.'

'You can only see the station master by appointment.'

'Has not Baroda House and the officer Mr De told the station master of the coming of the villagers from Srimati Sen's village in Bengal?'

'The station master does not attend to every stray villager who comes to Delhi station.'

'What was that about Bengal?'

'There is a beggar here who says he is not a beggar. He says that the great ones of Baroda House should have told you of villagers from Bengal. Is that not a new way to enter your office, sahib? A begger will stop at nothing. Now go.' The attendant spat towards Surendra, who grinned. Behind the guard there was a bustle and a portly man, immaculate even late in the day, pushed to the doorway.

'Do you come from Srimati Uma Sen's village in Bengal?'

'Yes, Sahib. The carriage is here. All are sick.' Surendra gestured behind.

'Where is Ashin Mukherjee who was to lead you?'

'Ashin-dada sleeps under fever and has need of a doctor. It was cold in the mountains, many have fallen ill. Our cook has run off and the

117

villagers will not eat the station foods. I ate them myself and can say it is good food.'

'What is your name?'

'I am Surendra, the cultivator. Can you help me by calling a cousin of my daughter-in-law? She will know how to cook Bengali food. The villagers have met her. They must soon eat. We must have a doctor, one who knows Bengali.'

'Old man, you bring me much trouble.' The station master led the way back into his office. The guard watched in astonishment and then ran down the platform to tell his colleagues. Surendra squatted on the floor beside the station master's desk and brought out from his shirt a small notebook. He thumbed the pages and then handed it, open, to the curious official:

'Here is the place. There is a Delhi phone number there, yes?'

'Yes, there is one, though badly written.'

'That is the number of the woman who must help us.'

'Here is the telephone. Why do you not call yourself?'

'I do not yet read, sir. The cousin will pay more attention if you call than if an old cultivator calls. Is that small machine the telephone, then? How does it work?'

'I do not know, but let me see if the woman answers before you praise it.'

In due course the cousin was found, the tale told, and she agreed to come at once. When the station master had told her she must cook for forty-five she had protested loudly and called Surendra many names for having remembered her. Then the men spent a long time trying to find a Bengali doctor, but finally one agreed to come to the station. Surendra relaxed to light a biri. The station master wanted to call Mr De, but the cultivator did not wish to notify the tourist officer until they were well again.

'Will your villagers not want to stop the journey?'

'Of course not, we have only begun.'

'But you say they are ill.'

'Old men and widows are often ill in the winters in the village. Now they have little to do and too much to think over. It always brings illness. When they eat, they will recover.'

'You have much trust in the cousin though she cursed you. She cannot make the journey with you.'

'From what I recall of that cousin and her city ways, the women will soon decide to cook themselves and we will travel in peace and feast the whole way.'

'You are a cunning politician.'

'What is a politician?'

'We have many here in Delhi. You will soon see.'

'How long do we stay?'

'Do you not know?'

'No, only Ashin-dada, the teacher, knows the plans of the travel.'

'That is not good, for now he is too ill to help you. It is lucky this has happened here. You were to stay one week in Delhi and at the end make a trip to Agra before going to Rajesthan.'

'In one week we must get them well, see the city and prepare to move on. It is little time.'

Surendra rose, saluted and left the office. Immediately the station master returned to his telephone and shortly was speaking with Mr De.

'Truly they are here, and ill. A ragged farmer seems to be in charge.

'He told me to get a Bengali doctor who will come this evening, and he had me call some cousin to come and cook Bengali food.'

'No, their cook ran away at Hardwar and they have refused to eat the food of the stations.'

'I do not know. The farmer said they had been cold.'

'The teacher is ill. The farmer knows nothing.'

'He said they would not wish to see you until they were well, but will you not end the journey now?'

'I see. You will come? Yes, I see. But I do not want to have forty-five sick ones here in my station. There could be a scandal. I am a busy man.'

A few moments more the station master listened before the conversation ended. He was greatly puzzled. Mr De had not panicked. The station master was annoyed. He scolded the attendant who brought his tea. Two hours went by before there was a clatter of pots tumbling on the platform in front of his office. He looked out and there were three small men, rather wizened, trying to assemble a bundle of pots and vegetables while a young plump matron, tightly wrapped in a nylon sari, scolded them in Bengali.

'You must be the lady for whom we wait. Do you come to feed the forty-five villagers? Have you brought enough food?' He looked at the parcels and thought to himself they would not go far.

'Old people do not eat much. They are on a pilgrimage you said? It is not good to eat heavily when worshipping. Why did no one write to warn me? Hurry up, I want to get this over quickly.'

The station master watched with amusement as she interfered with and harried the bearers. He laughed as he recalled Surendra's prediction.

'Come this way. We are very grateful to you for helping the old people. They are sick for lack of your good Bengali food.'

He led her through the confusing halls and tracks until they reached the siding where Surendra sat smoking by the carriage. There was no other sign of life from it. Surendra rose and grinned at the cook while the cousin bent and touched his feet.

'So, uncle, you are in a bad way they tell me. You look all right to me. Have you got me across this city for nothing?'

'No, there are forty-four sick and bad-tempered people who await your food. I am the forty-fifth and will eat as much as all the rest. We have eaten poor food since Lucknow, and many adventures make a man hungry I have found.'

'Hark, he is an adventurer now. Why do you not fetch your elephant and put on your finery? What is this nonsense, uncle?'

'Cook, and perhaps if the food is good I will tell you.'

The station master left them. The cook knelt on the ground unwrapping the vegetables and the pots. The lady stood a little apart, now fussing with her hair, now with her sari. Surendra helped the cook, fetched water, laughed to himself, and talked incessantly. There were stirrings inside the carriage. The station master glimpsed a face at a window. As he walked back along the siding he heard the chatter of women greeting one another, the haughty tones of one voice not in the least deterring the authoritative scoldings from the others. The station master watched the smoke of the cooking fire rise up within the station, and then hurried to his office. A young man was pacing up and down looking at his watch:

'You must be the station master. Do you not keep to your office? I have little time. Where is the patient you said needed me?'

'Are you the doctor?'

'Yes. Calcutta Medical School. First Class. Now I specialize here in Delhi. You have a patient?'

'Not one patient.'

'Then why do you call me across the city to your filthy station? Do you think doctors have nothing better to do? I came because you said someone was in need of care, and spoke only Bengali.'

'That is true. But, you see, we have not one patient, but perhaps forty-four. I am not quite sure how many are truly sick.'

'Have you been drinking?'

'No, sahib, but I think you should come and sit down while I explain.'

'But should I not see the patient first?'

'No, the patients will stay sick. They will eat a little. Then you will see them and make them well.' Slowly and carefully, in the most official phrasing he could manage the station master told the long story of the will and the journey. At first the young doctor kept looking at his watch, but as the station master told of their encounters and trials, of the cold in the Himalayas and of their fear of strange food, he became still and attended. Then the station master had to turn to other petitioners. The doctor asked quietly:

'Will they continue around India?'

'Yes, so the old cultivator said. You will find them like beggars, and they are all old. The elders of the village.'

Surendra grinned at the station master and climbed into the carriage, helping the doctor to ascend with his case. The cook and bearers were laughing and the station master smiled as he sat to eat. When he was licking the last rice from his fingers, a small, hesitant man came up behind him and waited until he had rinsed his mouth and washed. Then the stranger bowed to the station master and smiled:

'I am the tourist Officer, does it seem better now? What does the doctor say?'

The station master blustered in his embarrassment and it was some time before the two could converse sensibly about the villagers. The cook stayed busy near by, listening. Inside the carriage Surendra had led the doctor first to the side of Ashin. Ashin was breathing with difficulty. He rattled and winced with each inhalation. When Surendra spoke to him his eyes showed that pain and fear were distracting the schoolmaster from everything around him. Carefully the doctor examined him. Watching, the villagers grew calm. This was a doctor. He had come to make them well. They withdrew to their bunks when Surendra said that each would be seen. The doctor was unaware of this bustle behind him as he bent over Ashin. He turned back to Surendra:

'Who is there to take care of this man?'

'Why, all of us. Not all are so ill.'

'But is there no nurse, no one who knows anything of medicines?'

'Amiya and Deepaka and Reena and Rhunu have nursed many in the village. They are a little ill now. Perhaps if you ask their help they will be better more quickly.'

'Who knows the most?'

'Amiya, she is here.' Surendra turned into the compartment where Amiya lay stretched on her bunk. The skin of her cheeks sagged and she was pale, but her eyes sparkled with interest as the doctor came to her.

'This man says you know something about medicines.'

'A little. A doctor in Allahabad gave me medicines for the journey. I have been helping some, but nothing helps Ashin except the sleeping tonic. With that he slept a little better this night.'

'Show me the medicines, please.'

Amiya rose and tried to get down from the bunk but was convulsed with coughing. The doctor gently settled her back again and examined her. Then he asked:

'Which is the bundle of medicines?'

Amiya showed him and he lifted it up beside her. One by one she went through the medicines telling him what each was for and to whom she had given it. He listened with astonishment which turned rapidly to admiration. Amiya coughed now and then. She said she was very weak.

'That is because you scolded us so energetically for bringing the Delhi woman to cook. But look at you, now you are sitting up because of that food.'

'She is a fool. To dress like that before cooking for her elders is a disgrace. You are right, we needed her food. I wish there had been more of it.'

'Listen, didi, you know more of this medicine than Surendra here does.

I need help to give the medicines properly to all these people, and especially to Ashin. If Surendra supports you and you sit when you can, can you come with me to the travellers? You have bronchitis, which will soon mend with some pills I can give you. You need much good food. Others here need your care. Can you come?'

Amiya did not reply, but leaned forward and grasped Surendra's shoulder. She stepped down beside him. It took three hours to go from one to another. Twice the doctor left the two vigilant while he went to the office to telephone. Narend was up and making tea when the doctor returned the second time. Soon he had served all of those wakeful with a warm clay cup. The station master and Mr De had been waiting in silence and were grateful when Narend found them and pressed the cups into their hands. He bade them enter the carriage for warmth and was astonished when Mr De introduced himself. The tall cultivator bent, grimacing with the pains of his stiff muscles, and touched the young man's feet:

'You have given us much beauty and much that is new, sir. It is strange to us, but wonderful.'

Sensing that here was a man usually as reticent as himself, Mr De was moved by the gratitude. He turned shyly away to gesture the station master to a seat at the head of the carriage. Surendra had lit a lantern which they could see glowing at the other end of the corridor. There was a low ripple of talk as the villagers wondered about the doctor. Finally he was finished. He followed Amiya and Surendra back to Amiya's berth, where she collapsed with relief.

'No, do not go. I must rest, but we must also talk. Please go over again what must be done for these sick ones. For Ashin?' Amiya could command even while wheezing with bronchial pain and the doctor did not hesitate for a moment before obeying her.

'Ashin has infected lungs, pneumonia. I have sent for some drugs from the hospital and will give them to him when they come. I will stay here this night to be sure they work. Then at dawn I will show you how to give them to him with a needle. He must have them every four hours tomorrow and the next day. I will come again tomorrow evening and relieve you.'

'But you cannot stay up each night and work in a hospital each day.'

'When we are students we all must do so, it will be a good reminder to me to have to do it again.'

'Now to the others. Deepaka is also ill.'

'She has pneumonia, the infection of the lungs, though not as seriously as Ashin. So do the old men there.'

'Bankim and Nirmal.'

'They will all have the same medicine. The others, you, the lady in the hammock, the two men with glasses—'

'Elder De and Harischandra.'

'You all have bronchitis and must rest, but the medicine will work quickly. You must all have much good food.'

'Those who cough and are often sick?'

'It is partly that you all have colds, partly that you have been too long hungry and are weak, and partly some shock from which you have all suffered.'

'That would be the climb in the hills.'

'No,' Surendra interrupted, 'It is the whole journey. There has been too much to see.'

'I will get medicines. You must sleep. Thank you for helping me, mother, you would have been a fine doctor.'

The young man bowed and tried not to notice the tears which she let fall down her cheeks. He turned and approached a very tired Mr De. Surendra followed with the lantern.

'What do you think, doctor, must they end the journey?' Mr De spoke quietly, but the doctor did not reply. He motioned to someone waiting outside the carriage and a bearer climbed up to give him a package. The doctor carefully unwrapped the hypodermics and ampoules and again Surendra held the lantern high while he gave injections, capsules and tablets to the sick villagers. He watched while they swallowed the medicines, too, and Surendra was amused at his knowledge of their suspicion of him.

When they returned, Narend served tea and the five men sat together in the dark night.

'I do not know if you should stop the journey. I think perhaps the shock has been a beginning, but will not linger. Some are very ill, but the woman Amiya can care for them as well as any nurse once she knows what to do. How long will the carriage stay in Delhi?'

'A week.'

'Then most will be better in that time. Those who are truly ill will remain so whether they travel or stay among strangers. Perhaps you can change some of the travel so that they may have more time to rest and reflect?'

'Yes, I could eliminate parts of the journey, and change the arrangements.'

'That would be better Mr De, sir, for we need time to sit and talk of what we do not understand. To see too much with blind eyes is as bad as seeing nothing.' Surendra spoke seriously.

'What do you think?' Mr De turned to Narend.

'I agree that we need more time in some places. It is wearing for us not to be able to walk on the earth, or to sit around a fire. But do not eliminate the places which Uma-didi wished us to see. This is her journey, we will make it as best we can for her.'

'Uma-didi?' asked the doctor.

'The lady who gave the money, as I told you,' the station master interjected. He was tired and annoyed at being so late, more than a little worried by the charge upon him.

'She is there, above us, sharing the journey.' Surendra waved the lantern which shone feebly on the wilted garlands and the photograph.

'It is time we slept, there will be much to do later. You have not yet rubbed yourself with ointment,' said the doctor, handing a tube to Narend. Mr De and the station master rose to go.

'You will sleep here?' The station master was too astonished to object.

'Yes, they will need attention in the night. I must be on duty again just after dawn. Can you get a cook by then and buy some proper food? They must feast if they are to be well in a week.'

'Do not worry, sahib. I will cook. If those elder brothers can assist me in the dawn, I can bring back food from the markets for a feast.' The wizened cook who had accompanied the young cousin stood below them on a step into the carriage. He had waited and listened through long hours and his eagerness to help was obvious.

'We will help you, and some of the women will meddle, no doubt.'

'Let us fetch some blankets. It is cold and I see there are not enough here.' Mr De led the station master away. Surendra showed the doctor where to wash and then removed his bedding from his bunk into the corridor. Mr De and the station master returned with several porters bearing blankets. Narend and Surendra bade them good-night and then carefully gave each of the travellers another cover. Few were disturbed by their movements even enough to murmur or turn, but old Reena roused and blessed them softly before falling back into her uneasy sleep. Surendra made up a fresh bed on his bunk. When the doctor returned, Surendra bade him sleep.

'But that is your place.'

'I am more used to sleeping on floors than you, sahib, and you must work tomorrow.' Surendra saluted and was gone. Narend checked that Rhunu was breathing easily and then eased himself on to his bunk. The ointment had relieved the muscle pains, but still he could not understand the weakness which had gripped him. He tried to lie awake thinking but soon he too slept. Twice in the night the doctor roused himself and checked on Ashin and the others. Once Surendra appeared with the lantern, and once near dawn Amiya whispered as he passed:

'How are they?'

'Not much changed. Why do you not sleep?'

'I keep vigils over the sick in the village and I have slept all day.'

'Sleep again, mother.'

The days passed. At night the doctor returned, examined his patients, slept on Surendra's bunk. In the day more and more went out on excursions through the capital. Only a few remained under Amiya's care, and of them Ashin was the weakest. Deepaka was now up part of the day and able to help with the cooking. Bankim and Nirmal, for all their wheezing, were punctilious in their recitations of prayers. Harischandra had become Amiya's shadow, always present when needed, often ready with something of aid when it was wanted. Elder De read the newspaper slowly and awkwardly each morning to Ashin. One evening Surendra called a conclave and insisted that those who could rise and join him outside the carriage should do so. Only Ashin and Deepaka remained behind in the carriage. The others sensed that Surendra was willing them all to participate in something. When they had gathered he told them they must now decide about the food for the rest of the journey.

'This cook is acceptable to you because he is Bengali, though you know nothing about him except that he cooks well.'

'After this week have we not learned that nothing else matters?' Babla interrupted.

'I think that. I am glad to know that others do. But, listen, we cannot take the cook with us. We are not going to find another Bengali cook each time we stop. We can cook for ourselves when we are in one place long enough to go to market, but while the train moves we must have other food. The railway provides vegetarian and non-vegetarian food at every station. We can book ahead so that it is brought to us at the proper times.'

Amiya moved forward into the light of the fire. There was a silence as the others noticed that she was no longer grand in her bearing. There were shadows of thinness about her frame. She coughed and then spoke:

'We are making this journey because Uma-didi wished us to do so. Uma-didi also travelled around India and even to the great ocean and across to England. She did not take a cook with her.' Her audience nodded. 'It makes the journey more difficult not to have a cook. Even if the first grains of rice are hard to swallow we must eat the railway food, or whatever food is given when we need it.' She paused, seemed to wish to speak more, but then retreated from the fire. There was a shocked silence while the villagers absorbed what she had said. Amiya had always followed all the rules carefully. She had been the most bitter in scolding Surendra when he ate on the journey from Hardwar. Reena looked carefully from one face to another before she spoke.

'We are old. We are weak and some are sick. We need good warm food. If our place in the next life depends on what we eat now that we are old, then all this virtue and propriety we have been so proud to show has no meaning. I agree with Amiya. Let us stay healthy with Surendra by eating whatever we find. Tell me Surendra, have you yet tried one of the things called ice-cream cone?' The others spoke, Jaydev and Elder De took over the control of the assembly from Surendra. When the doctor arrived he found them laughing over Arundati's struggle to have a Delhi pan maker make a Bengali pan for Babla. Surendra told the doctor

they were celebrating that tomorrow they would see the parliament and
learn why India was a great democracy.

'Ah yes,' he grinned, 'we have decided to be lazy and to eat your
railway food on our travels. The women say they must keep in practice
so they will cook sometimes if we find a market. Come, Sahib, the two
within await you.' Surendra took the doctor's bag and led him off, while
the station master watched them go in amazement. He turned back to the
group around the fire:

'Do you truly wish to go on with the journey?'

'Yes.'

'Of course.'

'Truly.'

'It is so.'

'Why would we stop?'

'We have just begun.'

'The money has been paid.'

'There is still much to see.'

'Uma-didi wished it so.'

'We cannot deny the fate.'

The comments came quickly and the station master was bewildered,
then amused. The old farmer was right again.

'Then I must tell Mr De to send the telegrams tomorrow,' the station
master muttered.

'Now that we are well, may we meet Mr De and thank him?'

'He wants to come and see you in two days before you depart again.'

'Then we must cook a proper Bengali feast for him.'

'And his wife.'

'Yes, yes, with sweetmeats too.' At once the women were off in a
babble of plans and recipes. The station master interrupted them.

'Shall I invite him for you?'

'Of course, for the evening meal in two days' time. And you and your
wife must come too.'

'If my duties allow we will come with pleasure.'

With his departure the villagers began to return to the carriage. The
doctor was sitting talking with Ashin. Elder De shyly approached and
asked:

'Does it go better at last, nephew?'

'Yes, Uncle. I begin to learn that I have been a great trouble to you
all.'

'No, no. But, Doctor Sahib, will Ashin be able to travel with us? He
looks very weak.'

'Yes, he can travel, as long as he rests much and you feed him well.
He has carried too much on his shoulders I think.'

'That is now changed. We are going to eat the railway food, Ashin,
though the women will cook when we are in one place for a time.

Tomorrow some of us will have the station master explain the route and all that is ahead of us so that we can help. In two days we give a big feast to thank Mr De. Will you come too, doctor, and your wife?'

'Thank you, it will be a pleasure to see you all rejoicing.'

'We eat the railway food did you say, uncle?'

'Yes, it is all decided. Amiya said we had better not starve, and Reena said the kind of food we eat won't bring us to a better life if our lives have not already been good.'

'Truly, uncle?'

'Yes, Ashin, we talked it out properly as we do in the village. There was less cursing here than there, but even old Nirmal now knows he must have more than prayers in his stomach. You will have to persuade Deepaka. She was here with you and did not hear.'

'No, no. Deepaka-didi has already agreed and she says she will make the sweet for the feast. Now you go and let Ashin rest. You have not taken your medicine yet, Elder De, and the doctor must go home to his wife tonight since we are well.' Amiya smiled at them as she gave her orders, and they followed her without objection. Surendra led the doctor down the siding as usual, carrying the lantern high. At the gate the young man turned back to the old cultivator:

'What do you see tomorrow, Surendra?'

'The Assembly, and maybe we will learn what is government. It is hard, no one seems to be able to tell us.'

'Is it important to you?'

'Yes, because we do not yet know what is India. We go to see India but we feel we are Bengalis. These guides speak of India as democracy, and of India as the oldest culture in the world. We do not understand. Maybe if we see this assembly we will learn. It is not as important as seeing the great Himalaya.'

'No, it should not be.'

'Do you think this assembly is important?'

'Yes, it can do great harm and great good. But I do not think it will explain what is India.'

'What will explain that then, Doctor Sahib?'

'I do not know. Perhaps you carry what is important to know about India within yourselves.'

'That is a riddle worthy of Reena.'

'I am not a story-teller.'

'No, you are a healer, and a tired one. Amiya is right, you must rest at home tonight.'

'Thank you for your bed, brother.'

'With my blessings, Sahib.'

They bowed with folded hands and then the doctor took his bag from Surendra and turned to the waiting lines of taxis. Surendra watched him get into one and roar away into the lights of the city. He turned back with his lantern and followed the tracks. Sometimes he stopped to wave the light into a corner where a beggar was curled in sleep, sometimes he peered down the dim lines to watch an incoming train. When he reached the carriage all was quiet, there was no restless tossing and little coughing. The cook was asleep on the platform of the carriage and did not start when Surendra hung the lantern near him. Surendra stepped back to the tap and washed, scraped the embers of the fire together and lit a biri. As he squatted smoking, Narend joined him.

'The worst is over.'

'That we do not know. At least the crop has not withered before the rains came.'

'The food will help.'

'Yes, and our knowing enough to take some of the duties from Ashin.'

'He is still very weak.'

'Deepaka too.'

'She will weather it. It is old Nirmal who would live on prayers. Deepaka has more sense.'

'Come, I cannot live without sleep and this Delhi is cold.'

'To look at as well. There are no fires or groups talking as in Calcutta.'

'Ah, you have seen, too? It is not a friendly place.'

'Maybe tomorrow we will see its heart.'

'You become talkative, Narend.'

'Do you not miss the mud in your toes, Surendra?'

'Yes, brother, let us dream of it.'

The two were the last to sleep and first to waken. Not even the cook was stirring when they bathed and washed their clothes. Reena soon joined them and lit the fire. As dawn broke they served tea to the travellers within the carriage. Ashin, too, woke early and watched as they made ready to depart. Deepaka sat near him, silent but alert. Whenever Amiya looked towards them Deepaka smiled and reassured her. At last they were off to the bus, and Deepaka and Ashin retired to sleep away the morning. The cook bade them drink soup and managed to feed them four big meals that day. When Deepaka took him to task for wasting the food, he smiled and apologized that he would not be there much longer to cook for them. Ashin asked him where he would go.

'Why, back to the cousin-daughter of the old man who laughs. The lady who wears nylon saris and walks like this.' He mimicked her walk to perfection and the pair could not help but laugh, though they had been too sick to notice the cousin's visit.

'She released me to stay here this week, but now I must return to cooking sweets all the time.'

'Has it only been a week? I feel we have missed a month or more of the journey by being ill.' Ashin looked worried at the thought and Deepaka sought to distract him.

'Tell me of Delhi, Ashin-dada, for you have seen it and I not.'

The bus took the villagers to the square before the Lower House and solemnly they descended and walked behind their guides to the door. The guards would not let the tattered procession enter. The guide went off in embarrassment to find someone in authority who would help. The villagers squatted down on the steps in the sun as they watched the passers-by. The members of the Assembly were arriving slowly, some in Western suits, some in white cotton with Congress caps on their heads, and a fine shawl draped carelessly around them. At first the villagers watched the limousines driven up to deposit these figures at the bottom of the steps. Then the repetitive similarity of the motor-cars bored them and they turned their attention to the people entering the building. Most of the officials glanced briefly at the group of villagers, and as quickly away. They must have seemed to be just another group of beggars or petitioners come to plague some poor deputy. Some paused to ask the guard who they were. Others protested that they should be moved on, that they disgraced the Assembly. One pair of members stopped before the villagers and addressed one another about them:

'Look at that. That is India. That is what we have to change. It is any wonder nothing progresses in this country?'

'Do they not make you ashamed, sitting there like that. Where could you see such a sight in America or England, I ask you? They sit watching us like cows.'

'Yes, and we are supposed to think that their votes put us here. Lucky we know better. It is enough to drive a man to emigrate.'

'This is what we argue about, two children for each family, and new ploughs and irrigation systems, and what do they do? Sit like beggars on the steps and probably have fifteen children each.'

'Not that survive, sir,' Uma said in Hindi. The two men started and hurried away into the building. Uma was fuming. Not even Jaydev dared address her.

Several more deputies objected to the presence of the villagers. Many were rude and spat in their direction. The villagers huddled more closely together but stayed silent. A portly man descended from a car, and two lackeys who had been waiting for him loudly addressed him:

'Are these your constituents, honourable sir?'

'The guard says they come from Bengal. Did you pay two paisa per vote?'

'Surely they must be family servants. These could not be voters,' one laughed. The official surveyed the villagers and asked the guard about them.

'They are villagers from Bengal on a tour around India. I would not let them in. The guide has gone to get permission for them to see the assembly, sir, though why I do not know. They should not disgrace this place. Why should these people want to see the assembly, sahib?'

'Well you never know, perhaps they are hecklers in disguise.' His two companions cackled at this and the portly man beamed. He spat copiously:

'Oh Ma, how I am tried. As if we do not have enough to do with all these border fights. Now I suppose we will be expected to ask villagers what they want for India.' He rolled his eyes to the sky and again convulsed his companions as he sauntered over to the villagers. He looked them up and down with obvious disdain and amusement, blew his nose loudly while winking at the two companions behind him and then leaned back. To no one and nothing he said:

'And what do we have here? A village road has been flooded, maybe? Or perhaps you want more of the foreign trucks to come and dig a well? Or has someone died who deserves a monument, perhaps? How do you come to be here in the capital? Do you go on a last pilgrimage to the site of Krishna's frolics?' Here his wink was lascivious in the extreme. The villagers stared in silence.

'Not talking? The big city has frightened you? Well, do not worry. Some of us are not frightened and we will look after it for you. You just go back to the village and be sure the rice is good this year. It was not a good enough harvest last year. Perhaps you do not have enough land? Never mind, just go back to it and forget your fright in Delhi. When harvest comes think of all those who share in your work.'

Again silence. Babla, Jaydev, Narend and Surendra were still, tense, staring at the backs of those in front of them. Elder De was shaking with rage. He polished his glasses over and over.

'Did you come to see your great government? Here India, the greatest democracy in the world, is ruled. Here we make the plans for your crops, we make the arrangements with foreign countries to give us aid, and we preserve the ancient traditions of political wisdom which have been known in India for longer than anywhere else in the world. This is where everything you do is governed. This is the peoples' assembly.' He gestured grandly and his two companions were joined in their applause by several other deputies who had stopped to listen and were grinning. He bowed to the applause and continued:

'What has made us great? What has maintained our independence of all other cultures? What has brought you on a truly holy pilgrimage to this revered centre of all things? My children, I shall tell you. We follow the simple path of Gandhiji and the great Nehru himself. We are the one party which procured the independence from the British and which now leads you to leadership of all the world's peoples. We follow the ways of the spirit, not of the machine. We are trained to lead you from illiteracy to the brilliance of the true knowledge. We will turn this greatest unused resource, these millions of simple, spiritual people, into the greatest society the world has ever known. We do not know the shallowness of the West, we do not know the boring uniformity of the East. We know only unity amid diversity, the spiritual truth of India. We are the servants of India.'

The deputies on the steps behind applauded loudly. The two companions were openly laughing. Narend stood. His height and dignity, and the stern gaze he settled on the little fat man silenced the group:

'We are cultivators of India. We do not wish to soil our eyes with the sight of scavengers and gatherers of refuse.' He turned around and sat, and the villagers turned with him so that their backs were to the speaker. Narend's term was one of total insult, their gesture a time-honoured one of rejection and disgrace.

The portly man faltered, looked at them in shock and then rushed into the building, followed by his two companions. Some of the other deputies had not understood and clustered close to the few who had. They laughed nervously and looked again at the backs of the cultivators. Their shawls were worn and as grey as their hair. Their shoulders were bent with age. They had a strange power in that moment which none on the steps could mistake. A few moments passed before the student guide appeared with a tiny man hopping and jumping to keep up. The little person was a clerk in the offices which dealt with Bengal and he had agreed to accompany the student and show them the assembly. He ignored the turned backs by going around to face the villagers. He fairly bounced in his excitement:

'You come from my river. You come from the village of Uma Sen. Oh Ma. On the river have I grown up. Oh Ma, it is a beautiful land. Ai, how I remember the trees and the water. There is nothing so beautiful in all India. Oh Ma, tell me, tell me all. Is old Siv still the ferryman? Is there still a school in the town? Ai, the times we had. One time, do you know what we did to the mission lady who was so kind to us? Ai, we were bad boys. I will tell you.'

The tales the little man told and the questions he asked made the villagers laugh and relax. The clerk did not notice the student's grave look as he talked with the guard and learned what had happened. Soon the villagers rose to follow the little man. He did not stress the grandeur of the building. It was clear his heart was back with them along the river, enjoying the bending of the sugar-cane fronds in the wind from the water. The villagers walked with him, happy to have found him. Narend held Rhunu's arm for a moment and then they too moved into the building.

The group moved from one room to another, pausing here to be told about the duties of this office, there to see how the communications system was run. They lingered to look at a portrait described by the student, and hurried to catch up with the little clerk who chatted only of the childhood he missed and the beauty of life in a village as compared with that in the city. The student kept them hushed and motionless as they looked in the assembly hall and saw the representatives coming to their places. As yet, there was no debate. Again they moved on. This time they gathered in front of the student in a small hall which looked to the villagers like a luxurious school—there were desks with chairs and magnificent polished wood. The student then began to describe, carefully and with pains to expand each point, how the assembly functioned. He spoke of the elections, of voting procedure, of the essence of the vote being a choice, and of how that choice should be reflected in the assembly. He told them of the introduction of bills, of how bills became law, and of how the law was administered. He described the work of the members of the assembly and of the involvement of many with the special administrative tasks of the departments of government. He described the post of prime minister and told of her power within her own party. By this time most of his listeners were asleep. At last he finished and the tiny man clapped his hands so that the villagers could waken without embarrassment. The student asked if they had questions and at once Surendra spoke:

'Please tell us what is democracy and why is India the biggest democracy?'

'It is government by the people, and we have the most people who vote of any country in the world.'

'But you said voting was a choice?'

'Yes, of course.

'But we are always told by the money-lender where to put the mark on the paper. Where is the choice?'

'You should not be told by anyone.'

'Then how would we know where to put the mark?'

'You should put it by the man you think is the best, who will do what is right for you here in the assembly.'

'But why should any man in Delhi be concerned with our village? We have seen no one who knows our village.'

'Besides what could one from Delhi do for us anyway? It is we who must mend the ditches and plant the paddy and keep the pulse growing. No one here can do that for us. What can they do?'

'But I just explained about bills and the discussion of national issues and of the army and so on. All that is done here and is for you.'

'No, it is not for us. It is for the power and entertainment of those here, just as for the emperors before. We are not concerned with bills and laws. When a law is broken among us, it is we who suffer. We must find the culprit and judge him.'

'And usually we must pay the police to keep away and not come and take away our grain. What do we want with your Delhi laws?'

'But India needs laws to run as a nation. Without the laws you could not travel from Bengal to Delhi as freely as you have done.'

'That is true, but it needs railways not all these palaces to provide that.'

'Just a minute. You said government was by the people in democracy. Which people? Here you have only the rich, for only a rich man could leave his lands and come to live in this city all the time to do nothing but talk and flatter other rich men. Is democracy government by rich people?'

'No, democracy is all the people, the votes are equal.'

'How can my vote be equal to Elder De's vote? He can read the papers and knows what the men are saying, and I do not understand.'

'You still have choice, your view is just as worthy as his.'

'No, that is not true. His vote should count for more because he knows more. I can only do as the money-lender says, or nothing.'

'But no vote counts for more than another.'

'Yes it does. We have just told you that the rich alone are here, and that the money-lender directs the votes, so his vote counts for much more than ours alone. Surely, it is the same in other villages.'

'Then the democracy is not working.'

'What is government? Is it just another kind of ruler, as before?'

'Of course, of course, but now they refuse you seed money or put you in prison instead of killing you quickly or making you a slave. Nothing changes because men remain as evil as ever.' Reena spoke bitterly and the student was shocked by her interjection.

'You do not think this assembly is a wonderful thing, mother?'

'It could be wonderful, perhaps, if anyone could come and speak and be listened to, and if those who held power were wise as Buddha and as virtuous as Sati herself. But I am old, son, I have watched many money-lenders and many policemen come and go. It is always the same. He who has wealth and power wants more, and is ever more greedy and more vile. Government here is a strange monument to corruption if what we know to be true of our voting is true all over India.'

'But there are many fine and wonderful men here, mother. Some you would see in a moment to be saints.'

'Like the fat man who spoke to us more rudely even than Babla here speaks to his buffalo.'

'I am very good to my buffalo, Reena.'

'By comparison with that man, yes.' The villagers laughed. The student was distressed. The tiny man was dreaming, humming a Tagore song. Suddenly he sprang up:

'Come, come my friends. You must see the library here.'

'Ah, there is a library?'

'Yes, yes, and many records of all that goes on in India.' He was out of the door in an instant and the villagers had to run to catch up with him. As they did so passing dignitaries muttered disapproval. When they

reached the room where the small man waited gleefully they were all
excited, remembering the library in Benares. They followed through the
doors. Almost at once several officials descended on them and ordered
them away. The student and the clerk tried to explain, but they were
ignored.

'Out, out. This is a private place. We do not want beggars here or
thieves. Where are your passes? You have none, of course, so leave at
once. Go, go.'

'We are visitors, not beggars.'

'All the same. You have no passes. Go, go.'

The villagers retreated and found a door out of the building. They
gathered in the courtyard and again were scolded out of the way of a
limousine. The student and clerk joined them after a time. They had
failed to obtain permission to show the villagers anything of the library,
and they sensed their own disgrace in the withdrawn sadness of the
villagers.

'It is past midday. Let us walk back to the train.'

The villagers were forlorn as they walked up to the carriage. But the
food was ready, Ashin was eager to hear all that had happened and
Deepaka had hung a fresh garland over Uma-didi's picture. They talked
far into the night about government and power.

It was well after dawn when the cook roused them with a rattle of pots.
The young doctor surprised them as they ate. He looked stern and
impatient as he hurried up the siding, but when he saw them sitting in
the sun his face softened and his eyes conveyed his delight.

'Have you eaten, sahib? What brings you in the morning?'

'I come on my way to the hospital. I am sorry I missed you last night,
there was an emergency.'

The doctor watched the villagers while he listened and ate. He noted
wheezing here, a pallor there, a tremor beyond. He nodded as they told
him of the Assembly, and he grew still and attentive as they talked of
their discussion into the night, of the sadness they felt seeing the cold
arrogance of power. As an awkward boy unused to being watched by so
many, he rinsed his mouth and washed his hands in the traditional way.
Then he turned to Amiya:

'What does my assistant say of her charges?'

The old woman blushed, and then the two went from one to another.
The doctor examined each as he had done the first night. Amiya recounted
and remembered all that had been done and was yet to be done. Before
he left he gave Amiya a fresh array of medicine and heard her recite
flawlessly the disposition of each. As he hurried away Surendra called to
him:

'Doctor Sahib, do you feast with us tonight?'

'Yes, and my wife. We will come at sunset.'

The talis were cleared away and the last orders given to the cook. Clothes were washed and spread to dry. Ashin and Deepaka sat watching the activity. Rhunu was sharp once more as she ordered the carriage to be cleaned yet again by the station's sweepers. Elder De paced up and down. When the sun was high and the cooking occupied all the women, six of the men went together to the station master to hear the plans for the rest of the journey.

The day passed slowly for the women cooking and even slower for the men waiting for them to finish. At mid-afternoon Mitu said he wished to see again the Red Fort and soon a little group departed with him for some unguided sightseeing. Arundati and Babla went together to fetch the post which should have come from the village. Amiya spread out all the medicines and carefullly described each and its use to Harischandra, who wrote it all down. Amiya feared lest the others should not be able to use the precious gifts of the doctor if she herself fell ill again.

'Why do you not write it yourself?' asked Harischandra.

'It takes too much time, I have forgotten the ease of it.'

'But you used to read much, and write letters to your sister in the city.'

'True but after she died there was no reason to write, and you know as well as I how little there is to read.'

'Then let us take more books. See, Reena is reading now, and it would be good for the grandchildren to see that we old ones can study too.'

'What you say is true, Harischandra, but what we must ask Ashin to arrange when he is better is that a newspaper comes to the village. I like knowing what is happening in Calcutta while we sit here in Delhi.'

Reena waved the paper towards them to show that that was what she read. Surendra stood and took it from her:

'Is it not difficult for your eyes? The letters are too small.'

'Ah I have some magic. Remember the glass in the library at Benares? I found one here and bought it. See how easy it makes it.' Reena showed them the magnifying glass.

'Even I can see it. Mother Reena, I have a task for you,' Surendra bowed in mock formality. 'Teach me to read, you and Harischandra here, so that when we return to the village I too can read the paper and send letters to our friends in India.'

'What? You would change old bones? Well, Surendra, there are worse ways to be foolish with your time. Come, Harischandra, lend me some paper and let us see what the old dolt can put in that grey head.' The three sat down outside the carriage and began to work. Surendra was quick and eager and they soon had him recognizing the signs of the Bengali alphabet. But others were watching. The enthusiasm spread. Soon the little class had grown to seven, including Deepaka, who sat shyly near Reena and half-chanted the letters as they were taught. Rhunu, who had been out shopping alone, was surprised to see them so occupied. Her face clouded again with the pinched, sour look she had lost for so many days. She retreated within the carriage, and it was only much later, when Amiya climbed up to change her sari before the feast, that she was discovered.

'Oh Rhunu, how beautiful,' Amiya gasped. There across the end of the carriage on the floor beneath Uma Sen's picture, was a cascade of alpana. Rhunu had covered the whole floor with colour and made borders down the length of the corridor so that the portrait was the focus of a beam of colour. Rhunu now sat withdrawn on her bunk, turned away from the corridor, her fingers busy. Amiya saw that she wielded a paintbrush and withdrew, knowing it was best not to disturb the shy woman at whatever she made. For a time Amiya was able to distract the others from going into the carriage, but it was nearly sunset. The food was almost ready and they wished to change. There were shouts of praise and each villager who entered the carriage walked carefully, hallowing the unexpected beauty found there. When the tourists returned with Mitu, full of excitement and tales to tell, Amiya quickly bade Mitu to come with her and she led the potter into the carriage. He was overcome by the sight and bowed as the others had done, to the alpana, the portrait above it, and then suddenly, to the artist herself:

'Rhunu-didi, it is very beautiful. May I use your coloured chalks to draw it in my book?'

Rhunu turned and looked at him shyly. She saw Narend beaming with pride behind. She bowed her head, turned away again and said:

'The chalks are there, under my bedding.'

Mitu sat and sketched. The chalks were not as vibrant as the powders, but he managed to show the tunnel of the long corridor, the glow of colours along it, and then the beauty of Uma Sen at the end. Narend watched him and finally Rhunu was finished and ready to join the others. He summoned her softly:

'Come, the feast is nearly ready. The guests will be here soon. Let us find some flowers for your hair.'

He led her down the siding to the station and they bought jasmine and marigolds and returned laden to the carriage. Quickly Arundati and Uma joined Rhunu and the three wove a garland for the portrait, another for the door of the carriage, and a third for Mr De when he came. Narend plucked a coil of jasmine from them and awkwardly twisted it round Rhunu's bun. She blushed, but the others had no wish to tease her.

By mid-morning they were rolling again southward and east from Delhi on the way to Agra. At one station Narend filled the tea pot. Uma found a row of new tiffin carriers carefully wedged under a bunk. They were full of food so the villagers were soon feasting for the second time in two days, an unheard of luxury. There was a note from Mr De explaining that they would need the carriers often and to be careful to take them whenever they went on journeys away from the train. Again they blessed him. Ashin sat uneasily. He stretched out again on the bunk. Each jolt of the train trembled through his body and he had not the rhythm now to ease the long hours. Deepaka watched him and knew from her own weakness that he was in pain. Amiya sat fondling a book, a gift from the young doctor. Reena was reading. Surendra addressed the storyteller:

'My teacher, you neglect your student. If I am to learn to read you must hammer my head each day. Come down and let us work together while the train moves.'

The little class gathered and Harischandra and Reena worked hard to encourage the efforts of their pupils. Surendra could not remember all of the letters, but some of the lessons of his long-ago schooling were coming back to him. The others were eager and progress was quick.

Suddenly Arundati gave a cry: 'Oh Ma, Babla, we have forgotten. With the feast and all we have forgotten.'

'What is it, what is lost?'

'Nothing is lost, but we have forgotten the post. Here it is in my bundle. We forgot to give it to you.' She took out the pile of letters and Harischandra read out the names. There were several for Ashin, one for Amiya, two for Jaydev and Uma, and one for each of eleven others. Harischandra was kept busy reading the letters to the recipients.

The new thatch has been finished and looks strong. The earth is very dry and hard. The oil crop has withered. The baby of the Bose family was sick but has not yet died. The river is low and the fish very plentiful. There is to be a wedding up the river and many are invited. Two women had a fight at the well over an insult and now there will be a feud.

So it went on from letter to letter, each written in the same hand of the letter-writer who was used in Harischandra's absence. The news was talked of back and forth. Each item lit fires of nostalgia which soon kindled throughout the carriage.

The conductor came through the carriage and urged them to get ready, for the train was coming into Agra. There was little to prepare. They watched the train follow a wide river bed, now dry to the very centre. They were greeted briefly in the station and taken to a bus. They enjoyed the wide aspect of the town. Ashin talked little with the guide so Jaydev took over the burdens of conversation.

They visited the fort, built as a centre of administration and pleasure as well as defence. Mitu fingered the stone filigree and Jaydev puzzled over the masonry. Before they had had time to absorb the magnificence of it they were off again, herded to the bus and scolded for straggling.

This time they parked beside other buses and there were crowds of sellers of trinkets and tourists mingling together. Everywhere there were foreigners, all with cameras, and the villagers felt strange as they too were photographed walking towards the towering gate. Through it, before them was the Taj, glowing softly in the winter sun, a blue grey sky behind it. The guide showed them the patterns on the gate, led them down past the pool, and then up on to the platform before the tomb. The patterns in the marble astonished them, and Rhunu sat bent over her book drawing the arabesques of flowers until the guide grew impatient and shooed them forward into the building, where there were more wonders. At the end of the day, content and filled with beauty, they returned to the bus and the station, ate their first meal of the railway food and slept.

Early in the morning Uma and Amiya, Rhunu and Arundati carried the tiffin carriers to the cook in the station restaurant and watched as he filled them with rice and dal, vegetables and chapattis. Then it was time to board the bus. They went to see Fatehpur Sikri, the red city built and deserted by the great Akbar. In the astonishing hall of private audience, where the stone blossoms, and bridges arch to Akbar's throne, the villagers heard the tales of Akbar. It was he who built cities of amazing beauty, he who planned this capital because a sage had promised him a son; he who had wished India to live united in tolerant harmony; he who had brought foreigners to his court to learn of all things new and strange.

The villagers were awed as the guides took them from one building to another, each more wonderful than the last. They saw musicians practising under a marble canopy and wondered to learn that here Akbar's favourite musician had sung and played, and still four centuries later musicians came to study there to gain from the power inherent in the place. From gallery to palace they trod, until at last Ashin and Deepaka, Nirmal and Amiya, Bankim and Uma were worn to distraction. They sat in the shade of a tracery screen and watched the shadows shimmer and change while the others wandered on down the corridors and heard more of Akbar. At noon they were called to the bus, and again began their journey north, this time passing Agra and going on to Sikandra, to see the tomb of Akbar.

The shadows were long when they reached Brindaban. Here they walked in the sacred garden of Krishna and watched a group of village girls dancing, but the guide would not let them linger, and hurried them further south to Mathura. There they were taken from temple to temple until they found themselves on the Jumna where many worshippers were gathered and many priests were singing. As the sun set and darkness crept across the river the worshippers bent and launched on the water tiny lamps which sailed as a glittering flotilla across the dark water. Strangers standing near the villagers saw that they had no lamps and handed them some. Soon Deepaka and Mitu, Rhunu and Jaydev had bent and sent forth the little lights.

'Now back to Agra,' said the guide.

'No, wait. Let us eat here where the tea seller can warm the pot and our food will not spill.' Uma had begun to pass the tiffin carriers back along the bus. The villagers finished every scrap.

'This railway food is better than I expected.'

'Especially when it is the only meal of the day.'

'You will have to fall ill again, Ashin, so that we can give another feast and the women will cook.'

'Hush, man, what ill fortune do you utter?'

For a time as the bus moved they talked, but then they watched the rising moon intrude upon the villages they passed. In Agra they did not go to the station but to the Taj and stood before it as it glowed in the moonlight. Again they returned to the train too full of impressions to talk. Even Surendra slept past the dawn.

They tried to light the fire for tea in the morning but an angry station attendant scolded them and bade them mount the carriage again. He shouted and gestured, but it was long before the villagers realized that he was telling them the carriage was to be shunted to join another train. The return to Delhi was slower than the outbound journey and it was mid-afternoon before they wearily climbed down to the familiar siding.

It was cold when they boarded the same bus again, much later that night, and the villagers pulled their shawls closer about them. Through the wide avenues they journeyed, here and there passed by a taxi, but there was little traffic. The houses and official buildings loomed behind their gates and the villagers found them threatening in this darkness. Surendra suggested to the driver that he take them along the river so that they could pass the fort once more. Under the clouded sky the fort seemed immense. Here and there the villagers saw humped sleeping bodies, or a woman leaning against some support with children huddled against her. Then they left again for the station. Their carriage had been moved and joined to a train. The villagers found it, but they were refused entrance by the guards. Ashin and Elder De and Surendra went in search of the night supervisor but he was nowhere to be found and the attendants to the offices were even more unpleasant than the guards. A man sleeping on his luggage raised his head and told the villagers:

'Don't try, brothers. Just get some sleep before the train is due to leave and then you can find a place when no one is looking.'

'But it is our carriage. Our beds are there.'

'Ai, and it is my station and I tell you to stop disturbing my sleep like restless bhuts.'

'Come away, we must settle ourselves out of this wind,' Surendra said.

Ashin was grey with exhaustion and shaking with worry. He had not brought the tickets out of the carriage with him. They had nothing to show anyone to prove their claim. He had begun to cough dreadfully when they reached the others, and Reena wrapped him in her heavy shawl and held him like a babe until he slept. The villagers drew close together to share their warmth. Only the ones on the windward side watched the remainder of the night pass slowly and cursed the guards each time they shuffled along the platform.

At the first light Surendra rose and moved to the office of the station master. The attendant was asleep. The door stood ajar. Across his desk the night supervisor snored. Surendra wakened him by banging a kettle down on the stove, and was treated to a flow of curses which only Reena could have matched. Surendra grinned:

'Enjoy yourself, honourable one, for when the station master learns that you have kept the villagers of Srimati Uma Sen's village out of the carriage and cold on the platform, you will be a porter once again.'

'What is that? The station master's village? Get out, beggar.'

'No, no. You wake now. Here, drink this tea.' Surendra waited until the man looked at him more sensibly.

'Now, listen. We are the villagers of Srimati Uma Sen who paid Baroda House for a carriage to go around India. All week you have seen us here with the doctor coming and going and your master worried that one might die. The carriage has been moved to the train to Jaipur and your guards will not let us on board. We have sat the night in the cold while you slept by your stove. Your master will be pleased, I tell you.'

'Beggar, get out. Where is your ticket? How did you get into my office? Here, Police! Police!'

The station police came running. Surendra had often gambled with them and they greeted him warmly.

'Take this beggar away. He threatens me. Take him away.'

'He is no beggar. He is the Bengali cultivator who has been here all week. He is a friend of the station master.'

'Are you all fools?'

'From the special carriage, sir, where so many have been ill. It waits to leave for Jaipur after dawn.'

'Show me.'

The four moved into the station. The deputy passed them looking tired and harried, but he saluted Surendra as they went up the platform, and bowed to his superior. The police led the night officer to the platform where the villagers sat coughing, and where the guard leaned against the door of their carriage.

'Here is the special carriage. If you look in the window you can see the picture of the lady who gave the money. Did you not see the master come to a feast with these people three nights ago?'

'I have no time for feasts. Where are the tickets?'

'In the carriage, of course. All our belongings are there.'

'Guard, open the door. You, get the tickets. Watch that he steals nothing.'

Surendra mounted the steps and from instinct found a bundle of papers in Ashin's briefcase. He descended to the platform. The official snatched at the papers but Surendra did not part with them.

'Give me those. I will look at them in my office.'

'No, the station master and Mr De from Baroda House told me no one must ever take these from us. You may look, but you may not take these away.'

'I am in charge now, give me the tickets.'

'No, now you have seen that we have them we will get into the carriage. You have about half an hour to decide what you will tell the station master.' Surendra did not know what half an hour was, but he knew that the young doctor had said that to mean a short time. He saw the effect was right for the supervisor frowned. The policemen were grinning. Elder De was awake, watching. It was Reena who broke the moment of inactivity. She walked to the steps and climbed up. When the supervisor began to protest she turned to Surendra and said:

'You got this sweeper to clean it. Good. Thank the policeman for opening it. Come, we must get the others into bed or the doctor will be angry.' Surendra and Narend carried Ashin to his bunk. Stiffly the others tumbled up the steps. The night supervisor moved back down the platform quickly. The policemen went to their own office. When the station master arrived he found the deputy in charge, saying that the supervisor had gone off sick earlier. On his desk the station master found the report of the police and thus learned the story. By that time the carriage was on the way to Jaipur.

Amiya was awake attending to Ashin. When the train stopped, Narend fetched tea. The conductor told the villagers of the grey hills and the proud men of Rajesthan.

6

Some problems of destiny

In the winter dawn the dry hills of Rajesthan were desolate to Narend's eyes. He watched as they gradually turned to brown and wondered how the farmers could grow crops on such hills. There were no crops to be seen. Sometimes he saw a stone wall high on a hill and traced it carefully from one crest to another, as if he were watching a boat slowly retreat from sight on the Bay of Bengal. Sometimes there were sentinels of cedar trees marching along the railway, sometimes he saw a camel caravan moving sedately south. Silence, but for the chatter of the train to its tracks, enveloped both the hills and Narend. Surendra did not disturb him when he wakened and came to the window to watch. They sat together wondering at the desert until the surprise of Jaipur wakened the others and alerted them to prepare for the stop. Shortly, they had eaten the breakfast provided and went out to tour the strange city. Everywhere there were palaces, façades or sweeping balconies, one burdening another with filigree and carvings in red stone. Despite all the fascination of the empty halls of rulers, the villagers could not attend to anything but the new people around them.

These were tall, bronzed folk; they walked with the lope of those used to pacing caravans; they squinted at the far hills like warriors awaiting an attack or preparing an advance; their women jingled with jewels and bracelets. The little Bengalis were like minnows suddenly caught in a school of shark: they darted here and there, close together, sometimes brushed aside by the bigger school, sometimes isolated in an eddy and suspended for a moment to watch. Even Narend felt small, or rather diminished, as he walked beside the hall of winds and listened to the echoes of the street noises blown back and forth among the towering galleries. Their guide was a haughty lady who had once been to the Loreto school in Calcutta. She gestured casually to the harems, the observatory, the displays of jewels in shops, and it was clear that she thought these symbols of power and richness were the due of her people. Arundati paused to watch some women passing; they were proud, each carried a large brass pot on her head, each wore the swinging skirt and blouse of the Rajesthani peasants. Around their ankles they wore large silver bands, and their arms were laden with bracelets of silver. Each had a nose jewel or ring, and their head coverings flowed out behind them like magnificent tails of birds in flight. They swayed and jingled as they walked. Arundati stared. She did not hear the peasant behind them shouting at her, or paid no heed, and jumped back just as a camel snorted above her. She cowered as the beast passed by, realizing that it blocked her view of the other villagers. They were waiting for her, watching the procession of women pass up the street.

'Come along. We go into this shop, the owner is my friend and he will let you see the Jaipur jewels which are famous.' The guide bustled ahead not waiting for her charges to follow. The forty-five found their way up a steep stairway and crowded into a jewel shop. They passed two huge men, each with a rifle. Babla wondered to Ashin if they were soldiers.

'No, just guards I think, probably hired by the shop owner to guard the jewels.'

'Do they need guns for that?'

'I do not know, they seem to think so.'

'Hush, hush, show some respect for this maker of fine jewels. He will tell you about the things in his shop'. The lady guide bowed to a small man, swollen big with rich living, and retired to a corner where she sat drinking coffee and talking with another lady. The proprietor led them into a large hall where hundreds of pieces of jewellry glittered from the glass cases. He stopped in front of the first and told them of the process of workmanship. Slowly he led them from one case to another, pointing out a ruby necklace here, a pendant of diamonds, a bracelet of sapphires. The villagers were stunned. By the time the day was finished and they descended the stairway into the bustle of the evening, they were cast into loneliness for the familiar poverty of the village, just as the stones they had seen were cast in gold.

'Did you see? The woman bought the necklace of blue stones? Did you see the pile of rupee notes she gave? No one in the village, not even Uma-didi, not even the money-lender, has had so many notes.'

'Did you see that the guard had to carry it for her? The man said she must bring it back and keep it in his guarded place, not in her house. What is the pleasure of having riches which must be locked away?'

'Did you hear the mother tell the man to make a necklace of rubies for a wedding? She said it must be worth one quarter of the dowry. They have so much money!'

'They were Bengalis, too. They are here as traders.'

'But the hills are dry, where can they get wealth when the land is poor?'

'It is not rice land, they grow other crops here, and they must dig the jewel stones.'

'Look, there's a bride in that limousine. Her head is bent from the gold. Look at the rings on her hands.'

In front of the station a crowd had gathered around some acrobats and jugglers. The villagers laughed at the antics of the small troupe. The people around them were bigger than they, but they wore only heavy anklets, and were as gnarled as Surendra himself from long days of work. Soon they passed cones of hot spiced grains to the strangers, and the group was united in the pleasures of the entertainment. Then came a storyteller. The villagers looked for their guide but she had gone. They crouched and listened anyway, Reena swaying with the cadence of the storyteller's art. Not one of them knew what tale was told. They reached the carriage in twilight and settled down to their meal at peace. Fighting dogs kept some awake but the deep night lulled their restlessness. Ashin coughed frequently and dreamt of Sundara-devi.

The bus took them through morning crowds out to a beautiful summer palace made for a queen who had come from Kashmir and was homesick for her high, green hills and lakes. The white building floated suspended over the shimmering lake and all the man-made delights of this foreign nature pleased the villagers, who understood the lady's homesickness for greenery. They wanted to linger but once again they were herded away by their guide and the bus took a smaller road away from Jaipur. Up along the hills to their right a high wall curved with crests and furrows, and far ahead to the left the outlines of a fortress became evident. The guide was talking about the Rajput warriors and their battles. The villagers could not hear above the sounds of the bus. When they stopped below the fort they saw that its position gave it great beauty. This was more a palace than a fort, terraces and archways were high above another lake, then there were balconies, domes, and above, the hard desert sky. It was a grim sight, the beauty one of awe rather than engagement, so the villagers stayed close together as they walked up through the first gateway and began to ascend the steep road to the rooms of the palace. Now they understood from the guide that this was Amber, once the capital of Rajesthan. They recognized the name of Akbar and learned that these rulers had served him well and honourably. The villagers were passed by two decorated elephants taking other tourists up to the palace. They stared at the beasts and did not notice that the riding tourists were taking pictures of the wondering Bengalis. The guide took them first to an extraordinary chamber of mirrors where the villagers were transformed into a multitude, and stared and laughed at the mirror mosaics now showing themselves. Reena and Surendra clowned and laughed to see themselves in the ceiling as well. Mitu was sketching furiously but Rhunu did not take out her sketchbook. Deepaka and Bankim withdrew from the room and wished to leave before the others were ready, they did not like mirrors. The guide came out and asked them why they did not admire the wonderful room.

145

'There are mirrors.'

'Of course. It is a great treasure made of mirrors. There is no other like it in India.'

'They reflect our faces.'

'Do we not all want mirrors just for that purpose?'

'No, it shows our death.'

'What?' The lady guide cracked her knuckles, 'Mirrors do no such thing, they show us our faces.'

'The gods did not intend us to see them.' The guide walked away, glancing back disdainfully at the quiet pair. Eventually the others came out, and they began a long day of seeing the rooms of the fort. To them all, the best was a place of celebration of victory where there were panels of alabaster inlaid with motifs of flowers and birds. Rhunu took out her pastels and sat beside Mitu, the two of them murmuring with amazement at the delicacy of the work. In the harem they sat in the lacy shadows of the marble filigree at the windows and smoked and talked in the quiet out of sight of the many other tourists. The guide found them and asked if they would like to see the temple of Kali.

'What? You have a temple to our Kali-Ma?'

'Come, tell us, show us.'

'We have not bathed.'

'Wait there is a flower seller.'

The excitement grew as they approached the sanctuary of the goddess. It was a fervour well fed by the distance they had come from Calcutta. The men joined their wives in making the gestures of homage before the image. Surendra stood behind the others to watch. He asked the guide about the temple.

'It is known as a place especially beneficial to women wanting sons. You see over there, those are mothers-in-law with their young daughters-in-law who have not yet borne an heir. Each must wait her turn, for the goats are only given at the auspicious hour. It is all very foolish.'

'That you cannot say.'

'Belief helps in bringing children after troubles.'

'Certainly a trust that there has been a cure helps'. Amiya spoke quietly but with authority and the guide looked at this woman in her dirty sari, frayed at the hem, her head covered, her eyes confident, and then walked away and left them. The others joined Amiya and Surendra. Arundati had prayed for a husband for her granddaughter and a cure for her grandson. Babla had asked to return safely to his lands. Bankim and Nirmal had given their devotion with only an appendixed petition for release and transcendence in the next life, though neither was sure whether release meant salvation or comfort. Uma had prayed for the happiness and fertility of the coming marriage of her son. Jaydev had not known what to pray for so had thought of Uma herself and that she was very peaceful as she prayed. Rhunu had uttered prayers for her children and grandchildren and then had asked that the goddess might let her fingers show her devotion. One by one they came, bowed, and asked for aid. One by one the priest marked them with sandalwood. They sat with radiance at this spiritual homecoming and watched the preparations for the sacrifices of the goats. Amiya told what the guide had said of the blessings conveyed here and the women turned to watch the crowd of nervous women beyond them.

Most of the older women wore saris of raw silk, traditional prayer saris among the rich of the north. There were rich and a few poor, nervous and at ease, some watching every movement of the priests, others bending now and then to say a word to the younger woman beside them. The younger ones were hunched, feeling disgraced at having to make this major petition. One or two were crying. They kept their eyes downcast, fingering the water pots and garlands before them. A drum sounded, a goat was brought forward squealing its protest. The priest gestured to a fat old woman and her wisp of a daughter-in-law. They came forward. Each made the proper gestures, the daughter-in-law standing alone before the image. Then the knife dropped, the blood spurted forth, a cup was filled and poured on the image, and the priest blessed the girl. The pair departed, followed at once by others. All the time the drum beat a staccato and the smell of the blood and incense rose and permeated the courtyard. The carcases of the goats were pulled off to one side.

The villagers were about to leave when they noticed a strange pair of women behind the others. The older woman was richly dressed, her hair short and curled in the Western manner. Her ringed fingers were deeply stained from cigarettes. Her face was hard, her eyes not those with which one would wish to bargain, her gestures those often made in asserting power. She sat on a chair and fanned herself. Beside her on the ground sat the young daughter-in-law. She was like one of the stone figures of Khajuraho, the rich but gentle curves conveying a perfection of sensual form. She wore a prayer sari. Her long hair was hung at the back of her neck in a bun. She wore little jewellry, but what was there was exceedingly beautiful, unlike the ostentatious rings which flashed with the fan above her. She sat bent, one hand playing with some pebbles on the ground. She did not glance about her, nor speak to her mother-in-law. There seemed to emanate from her an aura of calm determination, a serene strength and alertness which caught the attention of the villagers.

'Who are they?'

'Rich and powerful. The priest has given her a chair.'

'Why does the girl seem calm, if she has failed?'

'Why does the woman seem so cold?'

'If they are rich and powerful then the son will be important. The girl looks healthy and well able to have sons, not like some of the others here.'

'She is not happy'.

'With such a sari and such jewels how can she not be happy, Deepaka?'

'Let us watch.'

Two more pairs of women worshipped and departed before the priest bowed in the direction of the strange pair. Two goats were brought forward. The mother-in-law tossed gold at the image. The girl stood proudly, a pot of ghee in one hand, a garland in the other. Her eyes were watching every movement of the priest. The worship was conducted simply until the priest lifted the bowl of blood to pour over the image. The girl suddenly raised her hand, knocking the bowl to the ground and spilling the blood. The priest and her mother-in-law gasped and jumped back in horror. The girl merely wiped some of the blood off her foot as she stepped down and away, without being blessed. The others waiting covered their heads and hurried away from the temple and the horror of the moment. The mother-in-law screamed invective at the girl, and then grew cold and walked away. The villagers, stunned, began to whisper. They followed the girl out of the temple.

'It will not work, she will remain barren.'

'Truly, truly.'

'What has she done? The goddess will curse her.'

'There will be no children now.'

'I hope that is your blessing for me,' the girl spoke in Bengali.

'Hush, hush.'

'Did you hear what she said?'

'Do not wish upon yourself such a fate.'

'Why do you know Bengali?'

'How could you do it?'

The bus alone was waiting down in the courtyard. The guide had gone with those who fled. The girl looked around. Still the villagers watched her.

'May I travel back with you to Jaipur? My Mother-in-law has taken the car in anger. Is there room for me in your bus?'

'No, no, she will bring the curse with her.'

'There is no room.'

'Ai, we must not share in the curse.'

Amiya looked at the girl slowly. Then she took her arm and led her into the bus despite the protests of the majority. The rest crowded behind them and carefully left an insulating space near Amiya and the dangerous beauty. A few of the others allowed their curiosity to lead them to seats near by. The girl asked how they came to be in Amber. The story took long to tell and the girl asked many astute questions and showed much sympathy for their feelings of the journey. Amiya questioned the stranger:

'Where did you learn Bengali?'

'In Calcutta. I was a student of medicine there. It was a happy time.'

'Of medicine?'

149

'Yes, it is the best school of medicine in India.'

'You are not Bengali.

'No, my family is from south of here. I went first to the university in Delhi, where I studied biochemistry.'

'What is that?'

The girl explained. She told of her family, of being the only daughter. She had a brother in the military school at Ajmer. He was now a diplomat. She told of growing up under the eye of an uncle who believed that all should be educated according to their ability. As she was the brightest child, she was to have the best education. She told the villagers of the excitement of going to Delhi, of working hard and always coming first in her classes. She had won a scholarship to go to Calcutta and her uncle was very proud of her success and had seen her well settled in her studies. She spoke with love of the sprawling city and the villagers listened with surprise to her reminiscences of the places they had seen. Amiya broke them off:

'How did you come to be worshipping for the sake of a son?'

'There my story really begins. You see, in my third year of medical studies my uncle died, thus leaving my mother as my sole guardian. My brother was across the sea. My mother had always thought it wrong to let me study. She began at once to try to persuade me to come back. She had many troubles, for her younger brother asked her for help. He is a landowner with two sons, both of them gamblers. Both sons had fallen into debt to a very rich and powerful man here in the north, also a gambler. To this man my mother was also under bonds, for he had been my father's commander in the army, and that is something the Rajputs hold sacred. This man has only one son, and for reasons which my family did not investigate they had not got him a wife though they were rich and he was over thirty. They are not educated people. This family agreed with my maternal uncle and my mother that they would cancel the debts of my cousins if my mother would give me in marriage to their son.'

'Ai, a good match.'

'The right solution.'

'Hush. You had to give up your studies?' The agony of Amiya's memories was obvious.

'I protested. My professors protested. Even the professor from the University of Delhi came down and begged my mother not to do it. The bethrothal was done without my knowledge, then my uncle and cousins came to Calcutta to collect me. I tried to run away, but they brought me here as a prisoner. The wedding was grand, with much jewellery.'

'We have seen.'

'None have jewels as we do in Jaipur. It was terrible, tali after tali of necklaces given to women who already had no interest in such things because they had so many.'

'Were you not pleased by this joy and the sight of the lord husband?'

150

'He was garlanded and kept away the three days. I did not see him until the night of the flowers.' She stopped and looked out of the window.

'I am sorry you are so pained.' Deepka spoke in the moment of tears.

'You see, he is an idiot. Something happened at his birth which means he did not grow in awareness, only in body. He is very big, but he behaves like a beast, or a small baby, because he has no thought. He will never have.' Her audience was silent with shock. Arundati and Babla were weeping openly. It was Narend who spoke at last:

'Then you do not want children because the idiocy may come again, as with flawed beasts.'

The girl looked at the fine farmer and thanked him with respectful eyes for his understanding:

'That is the reason, but there is another.'

'What can it be?'

'By the Rajput law, if a woman is not fertile for five years of marriage then she can be divorced without having to return the dowry. If I can avoid having children for five years, then the family will lose nothing which it gained, and I can leave and go back to my studies. My mother will not have to pay anything, for the disgrace will be mine alone.'

'How long have you been married?'

'Two years.'

'Then you must endure three more years.'

'Amiya, you cannot wish that she succeeds. To be divorced for infertility is a disgrace! She will be nothing but a slave to her mother-in-law.'

'She is that now, I think.'

'I massage her feet each night.'

'It is not done.'

'None have done it since my grandmother's time.'

'It cannot be so.'

'Hush, it is right and proper if she has not had children.'

'She must show her obedience.'

'Will you be able to go back to your studies after five years?'

'I still have my books, and sometimes my professors send me books. No one else in the family reads and I am often beaten for idleness.'

'Oh Ma.'

'If there is work, she must do it.'

'It cannot be so.'

'You must be sure not to have children.' Amiya spoke firmly and the others stared at her in shock.

'It is not easy, my mother-in-law is very watchful and my husband very eager.' The girl smiled and the cultivators shared her amusement. The bus pulled in at the station and they descended. The girl explained that she must take a taxi and do penance before her mother-in-law. A few of the villagers—Deepaka, Narend, Harischandra—wished her well before they entered the station, but most of them fled from her, talking fearfully of her disobedience and the curse upon her fate. Amiya held Ashin back and spoke again to the girl:

'Do you sometimes go to Delhi?'

'Yes. We go next month again.'

'Then take an address. This is a young Bengali doctor who treated us when we were ill. Tell him your story and ask him to give you one of the contraceptive coils. Have you seen the posters?'

'Yes. No doctor in Jaipur would give one without telling my family. I dare not ask.'

'This doctor will help. Tell him that Amiya has sent you.' Ashin wrote a note and Amiya signed it. They gave it to the girl, who stood amazed before them.

'Memorize the address and the name so that you do not have to have a paper. The note says only that you are a friend and need his attention and help.'

'The others do not read Bengali.'

'Then take the note and go to him when you can.'

'Thank you, mother. I pray that it works.'

'And I pray that you have this courage as long as you need it. It may be very long and very hard, child, but you will succeed one day.' Amiya turned away to the station. Ashin stood beside the young stranger.

'They are odd, your villagers. They are shocked when women smoke and study, but they understand that idiocy remains in the family. That one now wishes me to divorce. My mother-in-law is not so modern.'

'Yes, they are strange. If you see the doctor, tell him we are all well.'

'But you are not well, dada. I hear you breathing with pain, and you are weak.'

'You would have been a good doctor, you see much.'

'Wish that I may still be, life is not yet over.'

'No, it is not. I do wish you that.' The schoolteacher called a taxi for the heiress. Then he walked alone back to the carriage under the evening lights.

'It is wrong not to want children. If she is married, even against her will, she must have children.'

'You know, it is in animals just as in families. Once there is idiocy or a failure of growth, it stays in each generation. It would be wrong to have such children.'

'How can it be wrong when we do not know who is blessed by the gods?'

'There are too many children. They die. We cannot feed them. We cannot, do not, send them to schools. How can it be right to have half-formed ones if it can be avoided?'

'But it is the will of the gods. We must depend on Lakshmi, and the girl must obey her mother-in-law.'

'No, we must worship Saraswati by showing that we can judge what we must do. The girl knows there is no life for her in this family. It is a disgrace upon her mother to have married her to an idiot.'

'You are stern. We too have an idiot grandson, and we try to marry the sister. Do you think she too can have only idiots?' It had taken Babla a long time to find the courage to speak.

'I do not know, but I would ask a doctor and find out, since your granddaughter does not wish to marry.'

'Perhaps she is afraid that this will happen.'

'I had not thought of that.'

'This girl, this beauty. Will she endure these three years? One has children by fate and she is healthy. She cannot toss the blood of goats away always.'

'What matters is not the blood of goats but the mother-in-law. Will she learn that the girl tries not to have children?'

'The girl seemed a good fighter.'

'But the old one is used to having her way. She is cunning, and cruel too.'

'But she must obey. It is wrong. It is against all duty.'

'Truly. She must accept her fate.'

So the talk went on far into the night. Ashin fell asleep listening to it. Amiya was never part of it. Rhunu and Narend sat silent, at peace with their understanding of each other. Reena hushed the conversation at last:

'It is the business of gods, not men. We can only help her by our prayers.'

Mitu made sketch after sketch of the beautiful figure standing before the image of Kali-Ma, but he could not capture the moment and abandoned the effort. It was a drawing for Rhunu's hand. He would ask her.

By dawn the carriage was moving south, the dry brown hills emerging reluctantly from the night. Surendra watched a dust storm rise from the sand and whirl off, a moving tunnel between earth and sky. Narend squatted beside him, the two of them watching the dry land, the tents of the nomads in search of water, and sometimes a marker of a place of grandeur and power. Reena joined them, avoiding waking the others, restless now as the light reached the carriage.

'Can they farm this desert?'

'They must.'

'It is fighting land, not land for villagers like us.'

'There are palaces and many cars. We do not have those.'

'Here, perhaps, they do not have much change to worry about. We have floods and drought, the big waves and the cholera. Here I think little has changed since the time of those palaces.'

'The girl of yesterday lives in our time, the mother in the time of those forts.'

'Who can say, Reena? We are cruel, also,' Surendra thought aloud.

153

'Is it so, Surendra? I thought you married your children well.'

'Who is to say what is the joy of another? When life seems to be orderly and the children survive, so we say a couple is happy. Perhaps Babla and Arundati know each other better from their constant fighting than those who bow their heads and go on each day. There are many sorrowing daughters-in-law, maybe mine is as well.'

'Why has Amiya helped her? She would not have done in the village.'

'It was her own fate she saw written again.'

'Truly, the girl wanted to study medicine and that was Amiya's sorrow. But I think we are all like the girl, forced to do one thing when what is right for us is something quite different.'

'Do you see yourself as massaging a mother-in-law's feet, Narend?'

'No, but Rhunu gave up her drawing. We ask too much and expect too little from those we marry.'

'How so? Are not we always disappointed with our neighbours and pleased with the cattle?'

'Yes. If we tell the beasts we need their best work, they give it. We only tell each other what we do not want and what they must not do. Who has ever asked you to read, Surendra? There you sit with a book as able as Ashin himself to read if you wish.'

'I see your thought. Surendra, I have neglected your lessons. Let us prove to Narend that he is right and you can read.'

The company relaxed into the now familiar rhythms of the travel. Amiya was alone by a window, avoided by the others. Deepaka and Ashin with a small group of singers were remembering the old village songs which Harischandra wrote as soon as the words were ordered. Elder De was discussing crops with Jaydev. The incessant card game was under way. The women were mending and gossiping about the letters from the village. Mitu spoke softly to Rhunu:

'Didi, I have tried to sketch the girl, but my hand fails. I think it is your task. Will you try? We must have a picture to show the ones at home.'

'How have you failed, Mitu?'

'Look at this one. There is grace and youth, but none of the dignity or strength. In this one the mother-in-law must not be just indifferent, she must be cold with power too.'

Together they leafed through the pages Mitu had filled with his attempts. Rhunu looked earnestly at Mitu.

'Do you think our hands can show this on paper?'

'Of course. Remember how we wept at the pictures of sorrow in the museum in Delhi?'

'But those pictures were made by men of long training.'

'We must try Rhunu, only we have seen it.'

154

'You could do it in clay.'

'I might. It would be good to feel the clay again. But please, you try with the colours?'

'Do I hear right, does our potter say he has forgotten clay? Mitu, Uma-didi did not wish us to forget our gifts on this journey.'

'It is true, Ashin-dada, though you tease me. I had forgotten the feel of the clay. These sticks seem to fit my hand well.'

'Why do we forget, Ashin? I have been forgetting the feel of the pestle, though I have ground grains since I was a tiny child.'

'And I forget what it is like to rise early.'

'We are no longer as we were. Each of us is more because we have seen more.'

'Then by the time we are finished this journey we will be grown to the great gods themselves, I suppose,' Nirmal spoke angrily.

'No, but we will be better than we were, I think.'

'I would remain a simple, pious man.'

'That you shall always be, uncle.'

'This talk of becoming more than what we are is dangerous. All that is happening is given by the gods, and known to them. What we suffer, we suffer because of our faults. Let us not forget that the gods can strike us low and they are easily angered by those who go too far from the path to the temple.' Nirmal had the attention even of the card players.

'But we go to many temples, new and grander ones each time. Surely the gods hear our prayers from these too, uncle?' Arundati spoke up.

'It is not good, this travelling. It is giving us strange dreams and we dare to speak of them. Better to be silent as in the village and go about humbly before our fate which has cast us so far from that village.'

'In the village, uncle, you tell us to be more earnest in our prayers. Are we not now making the biggest pilgrimage any of the village has ever made?'

'It could be a pilgrimage if we prayed and kept control of our thoughts. These blasphemies of pride have led us astray. We no longer think of this as a pilgrimage, but as our travels.' The scorn subdued all but Deepaka:

'What blasphemies do you mean, Nirmal? Do you fear my worship in strange temples?'

'No, simple one, you bring your own fate on your own head, not on mine. This business of telling women not to have children and to try to leave their husbands and disobey, this is against all order. We shall be cursed if we do not give honour to our parents, whatever they may do.'

'That is so, that is so,' came the echo.

'What we do is from our own fates, as you say, we do not injure others.'

'That is not so. Good villagers now think about whether men can pass on the idiocy from generation to generation just as with beasts. Good

155

women who have raised proper families go and tell strangers how to arrange their destinies, as if you are Saraswati, or Lakshmi, or Kali-ma herself. Do you know what is wise, what is worthy, what is to be destroyed?'

'There is truth in what you say. We do know nothing of those we meet, but we dare to help, just as strangers have helped us while we travel. Do you not think it wrong that we do not help each other in the village, too?' Deepaka watched as the old man shuffled away from her, but she knew that the majority opinion was with him. She returned to the window.

'You speak now as well as you sing, Deepaka. Thank you for fighting my battle,' Amiya's voice was uncertain. Deepaka did not look at her old friend. Had she done she alone might have glimpsed the fear in Amiya's eyes. Eyes which had not shown fear since the night of her betrothal when she had vowed to herself never to expose her feelings again.

'Reena, you must not give Surendra private lessons, others are waiting. Come, Harischandra, bring the newspaper and show us its secrets.'

They arrived in the quiet station at Ajmer and tumbled out to see more palaces and schools, dusty streets, and the deserted town. The town was as spacious and open and windswept as their own village was hidden, verdant, and concealing. Some of the great houses were walled. The hesitant guide told them that behind the walls lived princes and sons of rajas.

'Where are the people?'

'The women are within. The men away in the army.'

'The army?'

'We go to see the camp now.'

In the midday brightness the tanks and guns, the rows of trucks, the barracks, and the hordes of supplies were incomprehensible to the villagers. The officers explained what each machine was for, how many men it took to operate, and how those men were trained. Only Ashin tried to make conversation, but his own dislike of this violence and pity for the men who were proud of it prevented him from being talkative. And he was having difficulty breathing. The officer led them to something called the Mess and offered the villagers tea. The break was welcome and slowly the group relaxed and began to question the tall officer with his sad eyes. This time it was the card players and the gossipers who led the conversation:

'The army you say is to defend India. But against what? There are no dacoits who attack all of India. They only come to little villages and no army comes to defend us then.'

'The army is to defend India against our enemies, those who want to rule us only in their way.'

'What enemies?'

'The Chinese attacked our borders.'

'The Muslims would fight us.'

'No, you know that is untrue, only soldiers fight soldiers now.'

'All these machines must sit and wait for years just in case some Chinese attack the mountain passes? It is a waste of much work.'

'It would not be a waste if they did attack, for we would be ready. If we are not ready then perhaps your village would be a battlefield.'

'No, none have interest to fight in Bengal. Here on your deserts there might be battles, but not in our paddy.'

'Perhaps you are right, but Bengal is closer to the mountains than we are here, and if the religious wars start, your Bengal would be the centre.'

'I hope you are wrong,' Ashin spoke softly, 'but tell me how do the men of your army justify planning to kill other men? We are all taught that it is evil and will cause our rebirths, though we are not as strict as the Jainas. How do you speak to yourselves when you train to kill other men?'

'Ashin, that is a question for a mother to ask her son, I hope the officer will not be insulted by it. Though I would like to hear his answer,' Reena bowed slightly in apology for them all.

'I cannot speak for the others, only for myself and how I feel when I try to teach the newcomers. I turn to the Lord Krishna in the *Gita*: it is the duty of the soldier to fight, and as each fulfils his fate, there is no escape. But more than that, too, though I am a soldier by choice and must do that duty well, I can only do the duty if it is for India. I can only train men to fight for India to preserve us within our land so that we may follow our destinies. I could not fight for another land. If that were my duty, then I would fail.'

'Indian soldiers fought for the English against the wicked ones even when the followers of Gandhiji were fighting the English here.'

'Yes, and they were right to fight. But I can only defend the land where my children are growing, not another's land.'

'Sir, I see a mist only. If each obeys the *Gita* then there will be no order, and no duty, only fate. If each soldier fights for his family, then he will lose all, and still will have fulfilled no duty.'

'I must do my own duty, what is another's I know not.'

'One moment. You speak in Bengali though you are not from Bengal. You say you would fight for our village if Bengal were attacked because we are part of India. If we had war within India, where would your duty lie? To us, because we are nearer the borders with other lands? Or to your desert where your children are growing?'

'My place is to fight as a soldier for India. I pray that I may never be asked to fight against others of India. But if it came to that I think it would not be a fight of soldiers but of you in the villages. Each place would have a common madness and would be able to see only his own paddy. India would be in the mist.'

'For many of us, though we travel, we do not understand what is India.

We are strangers to all who do not speak our language, yet we are friends to those we can help and to those who help us, be they rich or poor, Indian or foreign.'

'When you see foreigners, do you not fear them, and scorn them for their dirty ways?'

'Yes, yes.'

'Truly.'

'It is right.'

'No,' said Deepaka, 'they also think we are dirty and foolish and sometimes they fear us too. We met a boy in the mountains who was a son to be proud of and he was not fearful, nor angry.'

'That is true. He was a good boy. He was not as the others in their bazaar clothes.'

'Do you feel the same to those we call Indians, who also wear bazaar clothes?'

'That is strange, sometimes we fear them, sometimes we do not. We have met good people, and others who behaved worse than the foreigners.'

'Then who would you defend if there was a war between Indians and foreigners?'

No one spoke.

'Would you send help to other villagers in India if they were attacked and you were safe and well-fed?'

'What help can we give? Only on this journey have we been well fed, we are not so in the village.'

'Your sons to fight in battle, your grain and rice to feed the soldiers, your daughters to be nurses—'

'No, no, stop.'

'It would be wrong.'

'Our sons do not fight, except with one another.'

'We have no grain and no rice to send away. What we do not eat is taken by the tax. If we send our children away, what is left of the village, what would be remaining to fight for? Too many of them leave as it is.'

'But another ruler might come, India might be made slave to others.'

'India has survived many rulers.'

'Perhaps we have survived because there were soldiers to fight.'

'No. We have survived because each has done his duty, the soldier to fight, the cultivator to stay by his plough, the holy man to pray. Thus have the gods granted India survival.' Nirmal nodded to the officer.

'If one day each village must guard itself against the next, where will be India?'

'In the hearts of our children if we teach them that India is better than just the village. I do not know if it is.'

The officer was called away and the villagers returned to the bus.

'Show us a place of the gods, O giver of light, for we are weary of places of men,' Reena teased the guide.

At a fort the villagers learned of the coming of Akbar. They heard of battles, of the arrival of the English, of the legends of miracles associated with the fortress. Before a famous mosque they were jostled by Muslims coming to pray. Then they were taken to the artifical lake of Anasagar. The dusty villagers were tired when they stepped down to the parapet along the water. The lake was painted gold by the slow sunset. Perfumes from the gardens lingered near the marble paths and pavilions. The villagers scattered and singly began to replenish themselves with the secluded beauty of the lake. Ashin sat and wrote a long letter to Sundaradevi. When he had finished he found he was humming. Someone near by joined him. It was Deepaka, sitting watching the water, harmonizing with the well-known melody. Ashin began to sing and together their voices drifted out across the waters to be echoed back, and back again, by the dry hills. The villagers listened with pleasure. Tourists paused for a moment to stare and then to listen. Torches were lit when finally they were summoned to the bus. The white of the marble, the lonely cypresses were reflected in the lake. The last bird songs stopped. The twittering of bats above the water was the only movement. As the bus journeyed back to the train an argument broke out among the villagers about the dangers of bats. By the time they reached the carriage they were irritated and the absence of food made tempers flare. Groups began name-calling back and forth, children were insulted, and the general incompetence of one and all was proclaimed to the workers of the station. No one was to blame. The cook had assumed that like other pilgrims they would not wish to eat after sunset. They went to bed ready for bad dreams, and were satisfied, but still irritated when the guide wakened them before dawn.

'Where do you want to take us now?'

'To the holy lake of Pushkar. Do you not wish to bathe in the dawn light?'

'I never heard of a lake called Pushkar.'

'What nonsense is this?'

'The lotus of Brahma fell here.'

'Truly?'

'And did he bend to pick it up?'

The guide scolded them for their scandalous ignorance and a strange calm descended. Nirmal spoke of miracles in holy places and the gods moving to bring them to reason. Bankim tried to recite all the names of families and students for whom he had promised to pray at each holy place. Arundati fussed again about praying for a husband for the granddaughter. Ashin fell to coughing. Deepaka was stupefied by nausea at the rolling of the bus. The others continued the arguments of the night before, quietly. Narend and Surendra smoked.

At the lake there were many priests. When the villagers stood before a Brahma temple, priests of every shape and distinction came to ask for their fees or to tell them that they were not of the castes allowed to worship there. Deepaka and Arundati did not wait for a priest, but went inside and performed the puja just as they would have done in their homes. The priests were horrified and at last drove the villagers away. Surendra sensed the bitter mood and began to herd the villagers towards a place which smelled of cooking food.

'The gods have not yet fed us today. Let us ask the cook to replenish our boxes.' After long bickering as to whether the food was acceptable, the villagers boarded the bus, belching and uncomfortable from the strangeness of a meal at midday.

'Why do we go north?'

'We must meet the train at the junction of Sambhar. Then we go south to the holy mountain of the Jainas.'

'And from there?'

'To the cities of Gujerat. Then down the coast to Bombay.'

'Shall we see Bombay?'

'Not for some days.'

The connection with the train was made without incident. Narend wakened and realized that the carriage was being shunted to a siding. He knew that he would not sleep again so went out into the night of the unknown city of Jodhpur. There was a smell he did not know in the air, a dry freshness which increased as he walked along the rails. The ground was hard, and when Narend bent to remove a thorn from his foot he found the scent was very strong. He picked some leaves from the plant he had just stepped on. Yes, this was the source. Quickly he gathered some of the plants and tied them in a knot in a corner of his shawl. Then he swung away from the tracks and up the slope of the bank. Above him there seemed to be a high hill, but for the moment Narend was interested to look back at the way the tracks had come into the city. All he could see, for as far as he could see, was the night sky lying against a deserted land. There were no fires, no lights, and Narend felt he had intruded into an intimacy of the desert. He began to follow the wall. After a time he became used to the patterns of buildings and began to attend to the people sleeping and moving about the city. Once he almost collided with a peasant carrying a load of wood. The man heaved down his load, struck a brand and held it high so that he could look at Narend. They were equally tall. The Rajput sinewy and wrinkled, Narend taut and smooth. The Rajput's gaze saw all and told all, while Narend's eyes missed nothing and gave nothing away. Deciding that this stranger without a turban was harmless, the Rajput offered Narend a biri. Narend accepted. The two crouched, cupping the warmth, not speaking. The Rajput stood, hoisted the wood upon his head, saluted and was gone. Narend moved on. He returned to the carriage as dawn broke upon it and made tea for the others.

Rhunu came to him and he knew she had wakened and worried. He told her of his walk and asked what she had done through the hours. She showed him her sketchbook. Page after page had been filled with pictures of the girl at the temple. There were the other groups waiting before the priest. The villagers themselves, curious and intent. The mother-in-law, truly caught. There was the lonely, lovely figure, watching the priest. A single hand knocking a bowl of blood and, behind, the horror of the priest's face. Shadowed figures hurrying away. The girl alone, watching them go, her beauty even more isolating than her lack of fear. Here was the crowd of villagers listening to her tale: the awe of Deepaka, the hard anger of Amiya, the fear of Arundati, the sorrow of Ashin. There was a picture of the girl looking at Narend, and on his face Narend saw all the sorrow and sympathy and respect he had felt for the girl. The pictures were the best Rhunu had done, some just lines in black, others shaded and detailed with quiet colours, still others dazzling, bright, alive. Narend bent and touched the feet of his wife. Reena, who was coming down to wash, saw and withdrew. Narend and Rhunu walked away alone far up the track and did not return until the others were waiting to go to the city.

The next days of sightseeing and travel passed as the others had done. There were too many sights, a few adventures and much talk. By the time they reached Abu Road they were sated with tales of grandeur and pride. A student had been hired to guide them and he wished to spend the evening telling of the history of the carving and the benefactors of the great temples. Ashin tried to be polite. Elder De intervened:

'We would like very much to learn from you tomorrow. Now we need refreshment from the reeds that blow along the banks of our village. Reena, make us laugh again with your tales. Tell us of fools, not princes.'

The invitation was met with shouts of agreement and Reena rocked with delight. The carriage was too cramped so they moved out around the cooking fire. For long hours Reena conjured the great tales out of the fire. Her words had rarely been so mesmerizing, her eyes never so transfixing. She talked until her voice had become a whisper, though none noticed. She talked until all those who had long feared her magic had drawn close and would for the rest of their lives tell of the wonder of that night. She talked until the green warning of dawn brought the station policemen out on their rounds to scold the villagers back into the carriage. They had laughed and cried and listened so fully, that now, in the few hours that they slept, there was no need to dream. They were spent, like babes, and lay still in the early morning, deeply breathing the fresh cool air. Reena's hammock did not swing, but cupped like a bird's nest around the tiny, tired occupant. Surendra lay grinning in his sleep. Amiya's face had lost the strain of recent days. Deepaka curled like one of her grandchildren, her grey hair resting against her neck. Ashin's pallor remained, but for once he had not huddled against the wall to cough, but lay facing the others. His kind, shy face was a younger and more frail reflection of his uncle's. Elder De lay across the corridor, one hand clutching his glasses, the lines of worry smoothed away by the night. Uma and Jaydev lay together, their joined hands stretching across from bunk to bunk. Mitu and Rhunu slept on their sketch books, both smudged with charcoal and colour, both at peace. Narend's long legs were the first touched by the sun, but even he drew them away and continued to rest. Down the corridor Arundati lay wrapped in her shawl. In sleep she looked like a querulous child, for the fear had gone, as had the sorrow from Babla, as he snored below. The conductor found them this way when he swung aboard with the duty officer to check their plans and tell them of the buses going up to the temples.

'I smell no liquor, but they all look drunken.'

'Let us have some fun.'

'What are you doing?' Before the conductor could stop him, the officer had rung the clanging, shrill alarm bell, and was shouting 'Fire,' 'Fire' into the megaphone.

The terror of what followed caused the conductor to rush down the track to be sick while the officer lay convulsed with howling laughter. The villagers broke and pushed through the windows of the carriage and fell to the cinders below. Then they tried to run, blinded by the bright sun and clutching at their clothes and bruised selves. Surendra dived at once through the door, ran to the siding, filled a bucket, and ran back through the confusion of the escaping villagers to throw the water in the carriage door. When he turned to go back for more water he saw the officer, now joined by guards, rolling with laughter. In a voice that could have carried across all the paddy of the village Surendra called the villagers to stop and shouted that there was no fire. He stood sagged, an old man, watching a tattered and very bloody group of equally withered men and women slowly come towards him in pain and puzzlement. Surendra's face showed nothing but the furrows ploughed by the long years of his toil. There was no merriment, no trust, no wonder at the adventures of his destiny. Narend came, supporting Rhunu and Reena, both of whom were bleeding. Surendra jerked his head towards the trio, still convulsed. Narend looked, then looked into the carriage, then looked at the villagers around him. When at last Harischandra, Jaydev, Babla and Surendra managed to pull Narend off the officer, the two guards had to carry the young man away. At the moment when they needed quiet, a doctor, warm food and privacy, the conductor dared to return and tell them that the bus was waiting. He fled into the station. Surendra's water had only soaked his own bedding and bundle, which allowed him to laugh and brought the others a little out of their shock. He mourned his biris, destroyed by the water, and spread his map carefully in the sun, wiping away the stains of the running ink as gently as he could with his old shawl. He was suddenly sobbing over the map, cursing himself as he would his buffalo. Little Uma brought him tea and said:

'We must go to the temples and forget this quickly.'

Immediately Surendra was himself. He carried the medicine chest for Amiya and Deepaka, and urged the others to dress and come away to the bus. Nirmal and Bankim clung to each other, a great gash on Nirmal's head bathing them both in blood. It took Deepaka a long time to calm them and persuade them to let her touch the cut. They would not let Amiya near and raved in a babble of fury about this being a punishment of the gods brought on by her pride. At last Ashin, more pale, coughing and now limping, led them to the bus. The station master spent the morning marshalling a work party to mend the carriage.

Somehow they got through that day, and even remembered the splendour of the carved marble and the ceilings of the temples. On the way back to the station in the evening they stole glances at the bruises and cuts and caked blood, and they realized what a peculiar sight they must have made at the luxurious temples. When at last they found their carriage, the broken windows had been removed and boarded up, it had been scrubbed, their bundles were in order. A servant was making tea for them on the siding, even though a train was hissing near by and they knew they were to join it. That night they went south into Gujerat, but they slept fitfully. They ached and their dreams were fraught with flames and alarms. From the moment of their arrival in Ahmedabad until deep in the following night when they were brought back to the carriage, the villagers were harried and rushed from one mosque to another, from one gateway to a splendid tomb, from one point where Gandhi had spoken to another where he had worked. None of the several guides could distract the villagers from their exhaustion and their pains. None could prevent Surendra from squatting down to share a biri with a ricksha puller. None could drive away the crowd which gathered to watch Mitu and Rhunu sketch.

'What do you wish to do tomorrow? Please tell me and I will arrange it' asked the conductor.

'Sleep.'

'Yes, yes, now you must sleep. But what do you wish me to do with you tomorrow?'

'Are there no letters?'

'The letters have gone to Bombay.'

One by one they retreated to the carriage. A few, like Rhunu and Narend, walked a little to shake off the smell of the bus, but failing, they too climbed up to their bunks and slept. The next day they were taken to the Gandhi ashram and heard many descriptions of the fights of the early days. Constantly the guides chivvied them. At last they had seen the cotton mills for which the city was famous and the guide delivered them back to the train. Once again they found themselves rocking along the cradle of the tracks, soothed at last by the solitude.

'Where do we go?'

'To Baroda.'

'When do we come to Bombay?'

'The day after tomorrow.'

'Will there be news from the village?'

'I think so.'

'Hush, do you not see my nephew is tired?' Elder De shushed them and the few that glanced back saw that Ashin's face had a grey look to it and heard him rattle with each breath. Elder De turned to Amiya:

'Have you still the medicines?'

'Yes, they are here.'

'Bring them out, you have patients and must attend to them.'

Amiya busied herself with the medicine box and was appalled to find so many with infected cuts, large bruises, and weakness. As she moved and muttered Surendra kept close with the lantern, steadied her when the train rocked, and watched as he had done in Delhi. When they were finished and Amiya was packing away the box, Surendra surprised her with a cup of hot tea.

'Where did you get this?'

'On these trains which go so fast there is always a car where the cook works and where the train staff eats. Sometimes in the night I find their place and play cards with them. They always have tea.'

'Have you no fear to move from the carriage?'

'No, it is like fetching tea on the boat we use on the river. Sometimes I spill more than I drink, but usually not.'

'Thank you, you cannot have fetched tea for many.'

'Do not console yourself that way, Amiya. I have had many cups from his hand, and so have those old praying madmen down the way. At least they cannot pray when drinking tea,' Reena grumbled, irritated by the constant drone from Nirmal and Bankim. The two had paid attention to nothing since the fire alarm sent them plunging into the sun. As the others tried to sleep, they prayed in marked dissonance, one faster and more shrill than the other, neither listening to the meaning of the words. Surendra had disappeared and soon passed the old women with two big cups of tea steaming in his hands. There was silence and even Surendra curled to sleep on the bunk near Ashin.

The train parked in Baroda station during the night. Before dawn Mitu and Surendra stepped off to explore. They returned in excitment as the others were bathing:

'Come, we must all go and see. There are places with grass and much water and trees. They call them gardens and anyone can sit there. It is like the village. Come'

'We cannot, we must go to see ruins and two palaces. It has been arranged.'

'But we have not sat under trees and watched water for days and days.'

'You can do that when we reach the village. You will not come to Baroda again.'

'It is senseless for us all to make ourselves ill with seeing too much. We said that to Mr De and the doctor, now is the time to rest. If we do not rest, there will be trouble.'

'Has the cultivator turned astrologer? Do not grieve, Surendra, there will be other trees.'

Again the day was spent chasing the limping ones and the coughing few from place to place. Again there was no time to sit. Again there were too many things to see. When they assembled at the train for the evening meal, they were tired and angry. The food pleased no one. They noticed that Mitu and Surendra were missing.

'They are probably walking back to Bengal, just to feel the mud on their feet.'

'Who would not envy them that?'

'Mitu was at the museum, have any seen him since then?'

'Not even a potter can have been so stupid as to leave us now. Surendra always brings in the slow ones so he must be here somewhere. Perhaps he has found some more beggar friends.'

'I must go and tell the station master.' Ashin rose and started to cough. At once Elder De pulled Deepaka forward and cautioned her to look after Ashin.

'Come, Narend, we will find the others. The rest of you stay here. I shall tell the station master we do not wish to travel now. Then there will be no danger that we shall miss Mitu and Surendra.'

'Look to Nirmal. He is wandering there, he will have an accident with a train.'

Amiya went over to the old man. Seeing her he screamed and, pointing his finger at her, shouted, 'Witch, Witch, Witch'. Amiya ran in terror and shame back to the carriage while he screamed his reproaches across the echoing station. Rhunu took Deepaka's place beside Ashin and the singer went down to Nirmal. After a long time she drew him across the twilight into the carriage where Bankim was waiting. Deepaka settled the two against each other and moved back up the carriage, noticing that many were nodding and murmuring about the accusation of Amiya. Ashin was sleeping. Rhunu and Reena were massaging him. Amiya sat alone by the window.

'Amiya, does the medicine book say anything about wounds of the head?'

'How is it with Nirmal, Deepaka? Could you examine it?' Reena looked keenly at the singer and knew what the answer would be.

'No, he would not let me touch it. I think he must have fallen on his head and there is so much pain that he cannot think or see who we are. He calls Bankim his mother, and his prayers are disturbed by shivers and then he cries.'

'Get the book, Amiya, and let us hear what it says.'

'It is my present from the young doctor.'

'We will not harm it. He gave it knowing that you could use it to help us if we needed it.'

Reluctantly Amiya unfolded the book from the wrapping she had given it. Slowly she found the index, and even more slowly she sought the right entry. At last she turned deep within the book. There were many drawings of skulls and wounds to the skull. Reena tried to read but could not. Amiya's finger moved from one word to the next. After a long time she gave up:

'I cannot understand it.'

'Let us waken Harischandra and get his help.' Reena moved and shook the scribe awake.

'Harischandra, Nirmal is ill from the head wound, Deepaka thinks he cannot think properly because of the pain. Amiya has the book but we cannot understand it. Can you read it?'

Harischandra tried, and after a long wait the others could not refrain from interrupting.

'What does it say?'

'What should we do for Nirmal?'

'I cannot understand it all. It says he must lie down and should be looked after by a doctor. He is not supposed to sit or walk about and should not be fed much—'

'He vomits everything anyway, so there is no point in feeding him.'

'That is bad. If he vomits and cannot walk properly he may have an injury inside the head. It says not to give any medicine, to keep waking him after he sleeps, about every two hours, to be sure he is not un . . . I cannot read the word.'

'Unconscious. It means no longer aware of things. The book is telling you he may have caused bleeding inside his head which would give great pain and might kill him. We must get a doctor,' Ashin had interrupted, and now raised himself despite the protests of the others.

'Amiya, you come with me. Deepaka, you stay with Nirmal, and, Rhunu, when she is tired, you sit with him. Make Bankim sleep in his own bed. We will go out and find a doctor. When Narend and my uncle come, tell them to waken the station master and have the carriage put to the side.'

'Are you well enough? Shall I go in your place?' Harischandra asked shyly.

'No, please. Read that book, as much as you can, and tell Deepaka all that it says about head wounds. If she needs you to get anything you will be here. Do not wake the others.' With this last whispered admonition Ashin made his way down the steps followed by Amiya. He began coughing and lost his balance. She took his arm. Together they moved towards the lines of tongas.

'Now let us get that pair settled before Bankim makes Nirmal a divine madman,' muttered Reena and she padded down to the keening men. She disentangled them and pushed Bankim to his own bed, tucking him in with an appropriate scolding. Deepaka and Rhunu had tried to ease Nirmal but he only became more shrill, and there were restless, angry murmurs down the carriage.

'Sing to him, sing the night prayers to the river,' Reena hissed to Deepaka. The old woman began to sing softly and Nirmal turned and looked at her. The staring eyes lost something of their glaze and the lines of strain softened. He reached out a trembling hand and stroked her old, wrinkled cheek.

'Mother,' he said, and sagged to his bed. Reena at once checked that he lay still breathing, and she covered him. Humming, Deepaka stroked the hair away from the cut on Nirmal's head and Reena delicately felt it. Suddenly she stopped, and stared at Deepaka and Rhunu:

'There is a piece of glass from the window in the cut.'

'How can there be, he has been walking about these two days?'

'And only the great gods know with what pain.'

'But what can we do? We cannot open the cut and take out the glass.'

'We cannot leave him like this. Ashin has only just left and is weak. It will take him long to fetch a doctor.'

'Not so long, mother, Narend has gone in my place.' Ashin spoke in a whisper so that he would not disturb anyone, but he startled the women almost to shrieking. Beside him was Elder De, with Mitu and Surendra behind.

'What is it, what have you found?'

'There is a piece of glass in the wound on Nirmal's head. It must come out, and quickly, for you see how he tosses and turns with the pain.'

'Could Amiya take it out? She has gone to tell the doctor what is needed.'

'Amiya could, or I,' Surendra spoke in his ordinary tone.

'You?'

'I have taken out pieces of glass from the other cuts, my hand is more steady than Amiya's. We often cut out things from our beasts.'

'It must be done cleanly, Surendra, or the glass will break and injure more of Nirmal than it has already.' Reena had little doubt that Surendra could do it.

'Should we not wait for the doctor?'

'We must.'

'Look, the wound bleeds again. The glass is cutting more.'

'Is it deep, Reena?'

'No, it is there by the ear.'

'Where is the medicine box?'

'Here.'

'You must hold him still, Mitu.'

'But, Surendra, you must wait for the doctor. What is the paint?' Elder De's panic might easily have been caught by the others had not Ashin started to cough. The uncle led his nephew to his bunk.

'I saw the doctor paint his hands thus, he said it kills the dirt.'

'Amiya does not do it.'

'I would be better to try to do as the doctor did.'

Deftly Surendra felt the cut. Nirmal stirred and Mitu lay down on the bunk and locked him in a paralyzing embrace. Surendra opened the gash and after a moment's search with the tweezers pulled out a long sliver of glass and dropped it in the top of the medicine box. Then he sprinkled some of the powder he had seen Amiya put into other wounds, held the skin close and taped the wound closed. He was astonishingly gentle, whistling softly as he worked. When he stood back at last, Nirmal's eyes were open, staring at him. Surendra showed him the glass.

'This was in the cut, uncle. I took it out so that you will not have the pain now.'

'It is better. Bless you Surendra.' Mitu rose and drew up the covers. Deepaka bathed the old face and slowly the others grew calm. They saw Amiya and Narend leading a small man up into the carriage. He was protesting at having to come to a railway carriage, at this time of night, and in a tonga of all things. When they reached the bed Deepaka and Mitu tumbled the tale out in a confusion of pride and excitement and relief. They showed the man the piece of glass. Amiya stared at Surendra and realized that he was carefully cleaning the tweezers in the bottle of paint. The doctor pushed them out of the way.

'Just a piece of glass near the surface you say. Let us see.' He ripped the bandage and tape off the old head, ignored Nirmal's screams, and poked his finger along the deep gash. Surendra and Mitu held the old man as the blood spurted forth. The little man stalked away, shouting at Narend:

'You did not need to wake me. It is just a cut. He will be well in a month if you keep him lying down. Otherwise he will die. You had no business bringing me here.'

For a moment Nirmal fainted and Mitu sprang away from the limp body in horror, but then Nirmal's eyes opened once again and as he sobbed Surendra and Amiya dressed the wound and settled the old man into sleep. The others sat shaken for a long time after; except to reassure

Ashin that all was over, they did not speak. Narend's hands trembled as he clasped and unclasped them. Reena disappeared. She was grinning from wrinkle to wrinkle when she returned:

'Look Surendra, I found the cook's carriage in the big train over there. They have given a whole pot of tea, and biris for you too.' For a time they sat in easy communion, drinking the tea and glancing from Nirmal to the very restless Ashin. Then they slept fitfully, waking to the shout of the station master.

'Here, you Bengalis. You get ready. I cannot keep you in Baroda for ever. You are going down to Bombay today. The train will be shunted there, do not miss it.'

Breakfast was fetched, bundles repacked. Deepaka managed to keep Ashin in bed.

'I shall say the thanks, Ashin, it is my duty as village elder,' and Elder De walked down the platform with unaccustomed speed.

Surendra bathed and changed Nirmal, who was calm and slept easily. Bankim watched Surendra as he worked from where he sat at the end of Nirmal's bunk.

'Can I not do that for him?'

'It is not necessary for a time, but you can see that he rests easily. I think his head should not move, so I have put his bundle here and yours here to keep him still. When he is awake perhaps he will want tea.'

'Surendra, he cannot travel long like this on the train. The doctor said that for a full month he must lie still.'

'You were awake?'

'But too frightened to help. What are we going to do?'

'I do not know. Ashin is too ill, he has the look of a calf born too soon about his eyes.'

'You must tell them to send us back to Bengal. The rest of you go on, for Uma-didi, and make prayers for me. But we must go back. Otherwise others will become ill for caring for us.'

'I will see what is to be done. Now rest. The train will soon move.'

In the shunting of the carriage there were many jolts. Nirmal moaned, but Ashin was tossed and banged against the wall. Gradually his coughing deepened until his whole frame convulsed and each breath brought a grimace to his once placid face. Reena watched and to her self muttered:

'There will be an end to this and Sundara-devi will wear white before we reach Calcutta.'

'Say it not, aunt, though our thoughts are one,' said Narend as he passed up breakfast. Their eyes met and held in that sadness of knowledge and understanding which few share. They were interrupted by a shout at the door.

'Here is the train about to leave for Bombay. You cannot delay them.' The station master tried to block the way of a gentleman in a Western suit, who was too quick and climbed up into the carriage:

'I must be paid, I must be paid. Here is the bill from the doctor you called from the hospital last night. You cannot leave until you pay it.' He thrust the paper into Surendra's hands, the cultivator's form conveniently blocking the corridor into the carriage.

'What is it? Pass it to Harischandra.'

'It says 200 rupees. I can read that if not the words.'

The gasping echo went down the corridor: 'Two hundred rupees.' The sum was phenomenal.

'Yes, yes, the doctor is a very famous man, and to treat a head wound is no small thing. You must pay now, cash, before you leave.'

'The doctor did not treat the man, he came too late and left after causing more pain.'

'It says this is a bill for a specialist. When we asked at the hospital he was the doctor on duty, no one said he was a specialist.' Narend looked shrewdly at the clerk and recognized the unease of fraud.

'Ah, but to come out in the night, to a dirty railway station. This is no small thing.'

'Hear, there is the whistle, the train will go. You must get down.'

'But the money, I want the money. The doctor told me to get 200 rupees. He will beat me if I do not return with them.' The station master pulled the man down the steps, as Surendra pushed. Narend tossed a coin to the clerk as the train began to move.

'Tell the specialist that his services were worth five paisa to us.'

Long out of the station they could hear the shouts of the clerk. Their laughter and the jokes they made did not mask the discomfort and strain of that seven hour journey down to Bombay. Sometimes it was Nirmal who caused concern, more often Ashin, whose weakness suddenly seemed to abandon all effort and resistance to the illness. Amiya would not help; she shivered against her corner watching the others with wide, staring eyes. Narend, Jaydev and Harischandra engaged the men in the project of listing all the things to do with farming which they had so far seen and thought they could use in the village. The list grew unexpectedly long as the men recalled even simple tools which were unknown to them. Mitu and Rhunu tried to distract the women by making drawings of all the sari designs and motifs they had liked and wished to copy. It was slow work, but it meant that few noticed when Ashin retched blood and Deepaka stifled a scream, or when Nirmal fainted and then wakened to clasp Bankim's terrified hands. When at last they pulled into the dusk of the station in Bombay it was difficult for them to summon any excitement. Arundati suddenly exclaimed like a child:

'I want to see the sunset over the western sea. Who will come and watch?'

Most of the villagers joined her and went off in a little procession to find the sunset. Elder De went in search of the station master. Deepaka and Reena bathed Ashin, who was lost in fever. Surendra begged Amiya

170

to help him change the bandage for Nirmal. Night slowly embraced the carriage on its lonely siding. When the night supervisor returned with Elder De he brought no relief but said it would take many hours to find a doctor willing to come out in the night. They would have to go through the proper channels and first contact the tourist officer here, who was responsible for them, and would not wish to be disturbed at his home. Elder De spoke sternly and for a moment Amiya recaptured her spirit and lashed out at the bureaucrat. He went away promising to do as bid. Surendra followed him, telling the others that someone must goad him or he would forget the duty. Reena and Elder De with Amiya took the tiffin carriers off in search of food. So it was the friend of his childhood, Deepaka, who held Ashin's hand as he died. Nirmal was awake and watched her tears flow silently when Ashin lay no longer struggling for breath:

'Deepaka, he taught us well. I was never such a good teacher. Now you must cover him, and draw the curtains so that the others do not see. Then when his uncle and Surendra return they can find a burning ghat.' Silently Deepaka obeyed and before she could compose herself the sunset tour had returned and obeyed her shaken request that they eat out on the platform where Elder De and the others were bringing the food. At last Surendra stepped up into the carriage, followed by Elder De bringing a bowl of soup. They merely glanced at Deepaka's face and turned directly to Ashin's bunk. Nirmal weakly cautioned them to keep silent in their shock. They went to him.

'It is our loss, but you must not let this destroy the others. We must tell them simply, and then you must call Sundara-devi and tell her. Do not waste time before you go to the station master. You will need wood and his help if you are to burn Ashin with the dawn.' Elder De could not contain his weeping. His panic and sobs reached the others. Surendra stepped down, told them of the death, and what must be done. There was much wailing, but the tasks were accomplished with speed, and in the latest darkness of the night Ashin's body lay garlanded. The villagers were ready to accompany him to the ghat. The station master rushed with a doctor to them and the doctor examined Ashin and asked Deepaka and the others many questions before going to see Nirmal. When he descended he looked at Surendra and Narend, composed, dignified, and spoke to them rather than to Elder De, crouched and broken before the body:

'The old man cannot travel on the train more. He must rest quietly and be peaceful. This man died of pneumonia. He should not have travelled after Delhi. I am sorry I cannot help you. Keep the old man very still, and find him a place to rest.'

There was a pause as they watched the doctor depart. Then Surendra lifted Elder De and, pulling the station master along, said:

'Now you must call Sundara-devi and ask her if she wishes us to say

171

special prayers at the ghat. The telephone is quick. This man can arrange it.'

'What shall I say?'

'Wait until you hear her voice.'

The connection took less time than Surendra expected and suddenly the station master was saying:

'Srimati Mukherjee? This is the night supervisor of Bombay station. Your uncle wishes to speak with you.'

'Sundara-devi?' Elder De held the telephone away from his face in fear, so Surendra could hear the woman's voice clearly.

'Uncle? I wakened some hours ago feeling that my lord Ashin had died, and I broke my bangles. Was I right?'

'Yes, devi, he died in the night of pneumonia. The doctor says he should not have travelled after Delhi.'

'Ai, uncle, he was right. He wrote me that he could see his father every time he closed his eyes, and so felt death was very near.'

'What are we to do, what are we to do?' The old man wept across the telephone.

'Will you burn him at dawn for me? And say the prayers in Bengali? By the western sea?'

'Yes, yes.'

'Ask Deepaka-ma to sing for him. He would like that. And bring back some ashes for our Adi-Ganga?'

'Yes, but what are we to do?' Elder De collapsed sobbing on the desk. Surendra took the telephone.

'Sundara-devi, this is Surendra the cultivator. Your uncle has collapsed.'

'Yes, Ashin wrote to me about you, Surendra. You will see that it is done with beauty.'

'Yes.'

'And will you make sure that you all go on as Uma-didi wished? My lord Ashin would not want you to end the journey now.'

'That will be difficult.'

'Uma-didi knew there would be difficulties, and in my heart I think my Ashin knew he would not see the end.'

'Devi, it is nearly dawn, and we go to the ghat for you.'

'Bring my uncle safely home, Surendra.'

'If it is in my power.'

'Blessings upon you all.'

The voice was gone. Surendra supported Elder De and they beckoned up the siding to the others, who brought the garlanded corpse down to them. Elder De took one of the poles upon his shoulder, three others joined him, and they moved off through the strange city towards the ghat. The funeral was over by noon and the sad crowd walked slowly back, noticing little but the pot of ashes under Elder De's arm. When they were again inside the carriage the women let go with their sorrow and the men joined them. Surendra and Narend sat outside with Reena, smoking and trying not to listen. Surendra spoke:

'How are we to get Nirmal home to the village?'

'He cannot go by train, it shakes so much.'

'He cannot go alone, someone must be there to care for him.'

'The others wish to go home, too.'

'We must go on. This is part of the journey, not the end of it.'

'Can you convince the others of that?'

'No, but Reena could with a tale.'

'Not now. In a day or two after this city seems more than only a ghat.'

'How will we get the money? Ashin was to go to the bank here to get money and directions for the next part of the journey, and again in Madras.'

'We must call Mr De. He will tell us what to do.'

'First we must have a discussion with the others and find their feelings.'

'Better wait until the weeping stops.'

The discussion which took place that noon on the siding in Bombay would have staggered many of the people who had met the villagers. Surendra put the problems to the group:

'We have lost our guide. Nirmal is too ill to travel and must be sent back with one of us to care for him. We cannot get the money for the rest of the journey until we tell Mr De. I do not know if we can make the journey Uma-didi intended without Ashin-dada. Now you must decide what is to be done so that Elder De can call the office in Delhi and ask for help.'

'We cannot go on. You see where our pride has brought us. We have meddled in destinies from ignorance and Ashin lies dead because of it. We must go back and try to live honourably,' Amiya said, speaking for the first time that day.

'No. Uma-didi wanted us to see all of India, not just the first part. Ashin-dada would have wished us to go on. It is for the benefit of the others at home that we travel and learn, not just for our own fates,' Reena countered.

'But we only become ill and tired and fight. We forget to pray at the temples and know nothing about the sights we see. It is no use to go on. Others will become ill.'

'If there is no money we cannot go, anyway. Soon it will be the planting time and we should be back to help.'

'If there is no money, how can we go back?'

'We have seen Himalaya, now we must see the end. It would be an insult to Uma-didi not to try.'

'We have become proud, as Amiya says. Better to go back to our familiar walls.'

'Sundara-devi wished that we go on.'

'She sits in her house in Calcutta. She does not know how hard it is and how often we are troubled. She would not believe we are cut and hurt because someone made a joke.'

'But maybe she would, and maybe we should try to learn from that. It is not good to push and run when there is a fire, but we all did it.'

'Even Ashin. And you, Elder De, who tell us to keep calm.'

'I feel empty of all. Ashin was like a son on this journey. I feel I must try to do as Sundara-devi wishes and go on. Will you all not also try?'

'That is foolishness. How many more must die before we see how wrong it is to wander?' Amiya turned away, and when Deepaka tried to calm her shook her off and huddled against the wall.

'We are not half-way on the journey. We have lost one to death and one to injury. If one goes to help, that makes three. Will we lose more than three in the next weeks?'

'Look what we have learned. How many crops can we save if we use what we have seen with the irrigation and the ploughs? How much more can we help our children now that we know of the work available if they go to schools?'

'It is uncomfortable. We do not sleep. We do not eat properly.' Again and again the same points were made, until finally it was Babla who turned the argument:

'Look, the money has been given. We cannot get it back, we can only use it on this journey. That is our fate. Now we have lost our only helper, which is a good way of showing us that we must now prove ourselves. We are old, we are being given one last chance before death. Before we began I said this was madness, I still think it was madness, but now I want to see it to the end. I want to know if I Babla, cultivator of Uma-didi's village, truly am a fearful man, or if I can endure the sufferings and see the wonders that make up this strange journey of fate. We should all pray to Lakshmi-ma and Saraswati, then go on.'

'Who will lead us? Babla, you say you look to see if you are a fearful man. I know I am one, and I want to know who will lead us and do all this work of programmes and telegrams which kept my nephew so tired?' Elder De would have been the obvious choice for leader so his statement was startling. It was Nirmal who broke the silence. He was propped on one elbow and spoke with none of the bombast he had always shown:

'Surendra will lead you because he watches and learns from all and does not forget and does not fear trouble. Narend will lead you because he sees far and does not waver when he knows things are right. Reena will lead you because she knows you better than you yourselves and she will teach you of the new places. You will lead each other as the time and day show it to be needed. There is no question, you must go on.'

'Are we agreed, we go on?'

'We go on.'

'There is no other way.'

'It is our fate.'

'It would be a pity to waste the money.'

'Who goes back with Nirmal?'

'I do,' said Bankim promptly. 'I am too frightened to go on and I can keep my friend at ease. But how will we go?'

'I do not know. We will ask Mr De.'

'Elder De, remember to ask about the money.'

'I do not call, Surendra does, he has no fear of the telephone.'

While the two went off to the office, Narend and Harischandra led the villagers to the Gateway of India and thence to Colaba market. The river-dwellers watched the butterfly fishing boats on the sea and their hearts yearned back to the little village on the river.

'Baroda House,' an impersonal voice replied across the telephone.

'With Mr De, Tourist Officer, please. This is the station master in Bombay and I call in emergency over the villagers of Uma Sen's village.'

'One moment, please.' There was a long wait and the station master was called away. Surendra took the instrument.

'Hello. Mr De speaking, Tourist Information Office.'

'Mr De, sir. This is Surendra, the cultivator of Uma Sen's village.'

'Yes, Surendra, you carried the lantern. What is wrong? Can I help?'

'Our Ashin-dada, Ashin Mukherjee the teacher, died in the night of pneumonia, just after we reached Bombay.'

'Oh Ma. No. That is terrible.'

'Yes. We have been to the burning ghat and have his ashes to take back to Sundara-devi in Calcutta. I talked to her this morning and she says she wishes us to go on. We have had a talk and the others say they will go on as well, but we need money to pay for food. We need to know the route. Old Nirmal has cut his head in a fall and the doctor says he must go back, the train rocks him too much. Bankim says he will go with him to care for him. But how are they to go if not by train? And how will I pay for it?'

'Surendra, who else is there?'

'Elder De, Ashin's uncle, is here but he is afraid of the telephone, sir, and too full of weeping to help much just now.'

'There is no one else, someone who can read and write?'

'I can read now, Reena has taught me. Harischandra can write well, but he is not here. Narend has taken them all to see the sea and the market so that they do not sit weeping.'

'That is wise. Surendra, this is too fast for me. I must have time to arrange things and talk to you again. Tell the station master I will call tomorrow at eight o'clock and to go and fetch you so that you are there.'

'Would a wrist clock tell me that?'

'Yes, yes of course.'

'Then I shall buy one. If I am to get this herd to water, I must have something to tell me when the trains run.'

'You will manage, Surendra. I will talk to you tomorrow at eight. Tell the others I, too, weep for Ashin. He was a good and gentle man.'

'Truly, Mr De. He thought that of you. Goodbye.'

For the next many hours Mr De worked in Baroda House and around Delhi in a frenzy. When he called Bombay the next morning, Surendra was sitting at the desk of the station master, his new watch registering three minutes past eight. Harischandra sat beside him, pencils and note-book ready. Elder De and Reena squatted behind, and the station master paced up and down staring at the bizarre assembly.

'Hello, this is Mr De. Is Surendra there?'

'This is Surendra. My watch says you are three minutes late Mr De.'

'Good, you bought it. Now, Surendra, will someone write down what you say?'

'Harischandra will copy down all that I say.'

'Then, first point. Do you know what an aeroplane is, Surendra?'

'Aeroplane? One of the metal birds that men make to fly quickly from city to city?'

'Yes. Your doctor friend says that Nirmal can fly with Bankim back to Calcutta. We will send word there and have someone meet them. You must go to the airport at Bombay and buy a ticket for each of them to Calcutta. You must tell the stewardess, that is the lady who looks after people, what is wrong with Nirmal and ask her to make him a bed on the aeroplane. Can you do that?'

'Buy a ticket on the aeroplane for Calcutta for Nirmal and Bankim. Tell the stewardess lady he must have a bed and how to look after him. That is simple, but how do I persuade Nirmal to get into a metal bird?'

'Surendra, ask Reena.'

'Yes, ask Reena,' and he gave her a wondering, relieved look which would have caused Mr De to laugh could he have seen it.

'Now, about the money. You must go to the bank in the Mercantile Bank Building and tell the manager who you are, the station master is to go with you. I have sent a telegram to tell them to give you the money for the journey, and when you reach Madras you will get more. Take Elder De, too.'

'Mercantile Bank Building with station master, to manager of bank and ask for money from your telegram.'

'Now, you will sit with the station master tomorrow and he will show you the route and Harischandra will write down all the names of the people you are to meet in the towns and stops. I will send the extra telegrams from here.'

'Tomorrow station master to tell us route and names of people in places we stop.'

'Good. Now, are there any more problems?'

'Yes, some of the windows of the carriage have been boarded up and we get very little light or air.'

'Why are they boarded up?'

'We broke some when we thought there was a fire and some jumped through the windows. That is how Nirmal cut his head. Others have many cuts and bruises.'

'I will tell the station master to have the windows replaced. Now your friend the doctor wants to talk to you.'

'Hello, Surendra, my bearer of light.'

'Greetings, Doctor Sahib. Is not this telephone a wonderful mystery?'

'Listen. You must keep Nirmal from moving about. You need to take him in a taxi to the aeroplane. Then you must go on the metal bird yourself and see that he has small bags of sand beside his head.'

'I thought his head should not move, I wedged it with bundles. He sits up now about once each day and says he is only a little dizzy. He now drinks a little soup and eats curd, but he has not started saying his prayers again, so maybe he is still very sick.'

'Surendra, you are always irreverent.'

'What is that?'

'Never mind. You must tell Bankim to be careful that when Nirmal is on the aeroplane if he has difficulty breathing he must ask the stewardess to give him oxygen. And be sure to buy a ticket that goes without stopping between Bombay and Calcutta.'

'If Nirmal struggles with air in the metal bird, Bankim must ask the lady for o-x-y-g-en, and I must buy a direct ticket, no stops.'

'Yes, how are the others?'

'Tired, and we have not had much good food.'

'Get the women to cook another feast.'

'Another feast would be good for us all.'

'How is Amiya?'

'Not well. She mutters about all our troubles being brought by her pride. Nirmal called her a witch when he was mad with the pain of glass in his head.'

'He had glass in his head?'

'Just a little piece. I took it out because Amiya's hands are no longer steady. It was like taking out things from the buffalo.'

'You must look after Amiya, she was once very strong.'

'Now she is not. She has seen her fate, I think.'

'I go. Blessings upon you. Here is Mr De.'

'Surendra, get the women to buy fruit and carry it with you.'

'They need to be more firmly driven. I will tell them.'

'Now give me the station master. Call me whenever you wish, Surendra, and please send me a telegram when Nirmal is on his way.'

'Good-bye Mr De.'

Once he had the telephone the station master spoke very rapidly in Hindi so the villagers lingered only a short time and then walked back to the carriage, where they talked of all that must be done. Surendra went off to the bank. Reena spent the rest of the morning talking with Nirmal about the aeroplane. At first he only stared at her, but after a short time he said:

'If it is the quickest way, then I will go and Bankim with me. The best medicine for us both will be the sight of the ferry come to get us at the river.' At that moment a stranger climbed up into the carriage and told them in hesitant Bengali that Surendra had gone from the bank to the office of the metal birds and would be back later. The rest of the villagers returned excited by the sights in the market. They heard the tale of the aeroplane with wonder and they all wished to see Nirmal and Bankim off. Reena gathered the women and told them they must give Nirmal a farewell feast. The cooking was well under way in the late afternoon when Surendra returned. He paused only long enough to tell Bankim to be sure all was packed for their journey and to collect Narend and Harischandra, before he hurried off again to the office. The station master tried to protest at yet another call but Surendra brushed him away and soon heard Mr De's voice.

'Hello, Mr De, this is Surendra. I call to say that Nirmal goes on the great bird this evening.'

'This evening?'

'Yes. There was a cancellation of a big group of tourists, so the plane to Calcutta is almost empty. The lady is making a bed and we will all take them out at sundown. Can they be met in Dumdum about nine this evening?'

'Yes, Surendra. This is wonderful.'

'It takes only three hours. That is very little time by my watch.'

'Have you the money?'

'All went well. I have half in cash and half in the papers which are cashed in the banks when I sign them.'

'You will sign them?'

'Yes, maybe by the time I call you from Madras I will keep a journal like Harischandra.'

'I would no longer be surprised.'

'Look after Nirmal in Calcutta, Mr De. I must go to our feast.'

'Goodbye.'

As soon as he had hung up Surendra explained to the station master that they must have a bus within the hour to take them to the airport. He told Narend that Nirmal must be carried so that there was no chance of his head moving, and he gave the tickets to Harischandra and asked him to read them carefully and memorize the numbers and what they said. They returned, ate with speed, and led the others to the bus. Nirmal lay on the floor listening to the others describe the sights of the wealthy city at this time of the promenade. When they came to the airport the villagers became subdued. A shuddering whine cowed them all when they realized it was an aeroplane landing. Surendra would let no panic take over the group. He insisted it took eight men to carry Nirmal, and at least eight women to carry the luggage, so that soon each felt he had a job to do and followed along dutifully in a strange procession. The home-made stretcher with the gaunt old man drew many glances from the other travellers in the terminal. Nirmal thoroughly enjoyed his moment at centre stage. Surendra found the proper desk and Narend spoke to the clerk who checked the tickets and then realized, with astonishment, that the passenger was the supine figure grinning up from the floor. A number of officials gathered near and tried to protest, but in the face of the villagers' strength they decided that the safest course was to conduct the two passengers and their guardians to the aeroplane forthwith.

The villagers wound down the corridors enjoying the strange sights and attention. When they caught sight of the plane they grew silent and Bankim found his prayer beads and began reciting loudly. Nirmal told him to hush. Suddenly the villagers stood alone at a window as Surendra and Narend and two uniformed officials carried Nirmal on to the plane. Bankim followed, measuring each step with a backward glance at the others. They eased Nirmal on to the bed, found the straps which would hold him in place. He protested that they had pulled them so tight he could not breathe. Bankim was seated at the window near Nirmal. Surendra pressed the tickets into Bankim's hand and nodded to the steward that they were there. Then he and Narend touched Nirmal's feet and bade him a safe journey.

'No, I am the one who must wish you well. I shall be in the village by tomorrow's sunset, you have many miles yet to go. May Lakshmi-ma herself go with you.' The two farmers withdrew down the corridor. As soon as they joined the others there were many questions:

'What is the bird like inside?'

'Does he have a proper charpoy to sleep on?'

'Why does it not fall out of the air?'

'How much were the tickets?'

'Why does it go so quickly?'

Surendra could only say, 'There was good wool cloth along the floor, to walk upon.'

They watched as the door was closed and the machine moved slowly away from the building. There was a whine and they saw it race down the road and rise up into the golden evening. The carriage seemed dark and empty when they finally reached it. Reena lit a candle and told them the most bawdy of wedding tales so that they went to sleep laughing. Surendra sat long at the door, smoking biri after biri.

The next morning they did their laundry before going out to see the caves of Elephanta. They wondered at the Trimurti, the lingams, the Lord of Yogis, and the destruction of the demons. When they finally returned the sea was smooth and the journey back in the boats had them waving gaily to other pilgrims. A bus took them on a brief tour of the city and then north to the dairy farms, where they ate ice cream and marvelled that even the insides of the barns were painted. Harischandra again was kept busy writing notes of all they had remarked as the bus journeyed on to the caves of Kanheri. They heard more tales of the Buddha and admired the stern images, but they were happy to see the ring of lights on the coast, the necklace of Bombay, when they returned in the night. The next day they were out again to tour the Towers of Silence of the Parsees, and see all the famous places of the city. Surendra had stayed behind to work with the station master and was in no mood to listen to the shrill talk when they returned. He and Narend walked barefoot along the coast with the wealthy promenaders of the evening. Talk was unnecessary until they came to two young foreigners squatting beneath the lamps of the street and trying to sell their belongings. Narend watched and then spoke to Surendra:

'Are those not the sacks the foreigners carry on their backs?'

'Yes, they put clothes and food in them and still have their hands free. It makes their travelling easy.'

'Let us see if they will sell them to us. We could carry the maps and our tickets more safely than tied in the ends of our shawls.'

'That is so, and we have far to go.'

Narend crouched down beside the boys while Surendra looked over the two rucksacks. After a time a crowd of Bombay citizens gathered to watch two scruffy Bengali cultivators pay two young foreign students a sum of money which, in the village, represented a feast or a new plough. Then Surendra and Narend helped each other into the rucksacks and turned back to the station. They were pleased with their purchases. Later on the journey they would look a strange sight as the rucksacks sprouted water bottles, umbrellas, bedding rolls, and all the extras that none of the others would carry but which all wanted.

Early in the morning the station master brought a telegram to the carriage. Harischandra read it out slowly:

Arrived home safely. All in village well and send blessings. Garuda very noisy. Nirmal.

'Imagine, Nirmal sent a telegram.'

'He too has travelled now.'

'They are all well as of yesterday, that is better than letters.'

'How does the telegram work?'

Each one handled the paper and each thought of more questions. Before they realized, the morning was bright and the train whistle was warning them that they were about to be off. There was a last rush to load the tiffin carriers and fruit up into the carriage, then another rush to say formal thanks. The gate was locked, the door swung to, they had all been counted. Surendra sat against the metal watching the roof of the station change to a morning sky broken by the buildings of Bombay.

'Come, Surendra, you must tell us where we go and what we shall see. You cannot sit alone out there any longer.'

'We go to Aurangabad. See, to the north and east. Here are three new maps, pass them down so everyone can see. There it is, Aurangabad.'

The train moved on.

7
Journeys from Aurangabad station

The wind from the Deccan blew constantly through the tawny corridors
of Aurangabad station. The villagers tried to shield themselves from it
as they hurried about their various tasks. During the journey they had
divided the labours, and the working groups had scattered to collect food,
interview their guides, and so forth. Deepaka sat watching the others
discuss their adventures as they ate the evening meal. To her the food
tasted of the sand blown everywhere. She pushed her tali aside. What
were the people in the village doing now? Probably still pestering Nirmal
with questions, who needed rest. Perhaps some would go down to fetch
Sundara-devi home to the village. She would not want to stay alone in
Calcutta, of that Deepaka was sure. Ai, Ashin, Ashin, now there is no
one to sing with an old lady. Deepaka wiped her eyes and looked at the
villagers.

Surendra was himself again, joking and teasing, then silent. Now that
they each had a task and would do it, he did not look bothered as he had
for a time in Bombay. Narend was talking with Reena. Strange that they
talked now more than ever in the village. He was playing with the little
horse of his grandson as he talked and Deepaka glanced at Rhunu as she
thought, 'he is truly a fine grandfather'. Rhunu was smiling serenely as
she watched Mitu shape a lump of clay. The brown hands were kneading
the grey stuff with love—why just the way I make chappatis, thought
Deepaka. Harischandra was reading from his history book, and many
others were listening to tales of the caves of Ajanta and Ellora which
they would now see. Then Deepaka saw Amiya. She was sitting hunched,
collapsed in upon herself, her tali untouched before her. Arundati was
urging her to eat, without effect. Deepaka saw that Amiya's eyes were
focused on something far beyond the carriage, and they conveyed a
harshness which Deepaka did not understand. She turned around to see
what had caught Amiya's attention and saw a young foreign couple sitting
on their bedding on the next platform.

They were dressed in kurtas and both had hair below their shoulders.
The boy was bent listening to the girl. Deepaka realized at once that she
was in great pain. Her face was drawn, there were grey shadows around

her eyes and mouth, and as often as a snake's, her tongue tried to moisten her dried, split lips. The flickering movement Deepaka recognized as weak and fearful. The boy moved away and the girl tried to find a comfortable position. As often as she moved, her face contorted with a grimace and one hand moved to her side. Deepaka looked back at Amiya and saw that she now looked at the cement of the platform. Her hand jerkily stroked the filthy floor. A noise from across the way made Deepaka turn again and she saw that the boy had tried to help the girl to walk. She had cried out with the pain and now was collapsed again against him. Deepaka moved toward Amiya:

'Amiya-didi, the girl is sick. Have you nothing in the medicine box to help her?'

'I am no doctor.'

'She is ill, Didi, and you are skilled in healing.'

'She is foreign.'

'And young as your granddaughter. See how her face constricts with pain.' Amiya did not look up.

'Please, let us get out the medicine box and go to them and see if we can help.'

'It is my medicine box.'

'It is for those who are sick, not to keep as a treasure.'

'It is my medicine box, not for foreigners.'

'Let me take it and see if I can help.'

'No, it is my medicine box. You are Simple Deepaka.'

'You could help if you would come.'

'Healing is for the gods, she must give an offering. There is no help in medicines, only among the gods.'

Amiya rose and clambered up into the carriage, where Deepaka found her a moment later stretched upon her bunk pretending sleep. Deepaka turned back and spoke to Reena about the girl. The story-teller had been watching the couple and agreed with Deepaka that they needed medicine. Deepaka told her of Amiya and Reena's eyes darkened and withdrew inwards. Harischandra interrupted:

'I have listened, Deepaka-didi. I see that we must go to them and offer help. I do not know what we can do, but they are as children. The boy looks blankly to the girl, then to his bundles, then at the station. The girl looks at nothing. I will go with you if you wish to help.'

'Come then, let us see what is to be done, though I wish they had washed and visited a barber.' Reena spat as she rose. Then the scribe, the story-teller and the old grandmother walked down the length of their own platform and back up the one next until they came to the huddled pair. Harischandra addressed them and the villagers watching from across the track wondered that the talk went on so long before the three retraced their route.

'What is it? What do they say?'

'Where do they come from?'

'Why do they sit like beggars and not sleep in a hotel?'

'Why does he not fetch help for the girl?'

The questions came from all sides. Reena was about to enjoy telling the tale when Deepaka burst forth:

'She is sick with pains of the belly which cause her legs to ache and her head to pound. She has not eaten in four days and she says she cannot walk to the taxis. The boy is weak and does not urge her to try. He says if she does not want to move, they will not move. He says a doctor told them she must go to a hospital and have an operation for there is an infection within, he says that will spoil their journey, so they will wait until she grows better.'

'And if she does not grow better?'

'He says it was just an Indian doctor, so he does not know if it was true counsel.'

'What do you think?'

'Her belly is rigid, hard. The doctor was probably right. She must not sleep on the stone, it is cold and she will become weaker.'

'What is to be done?'

'We must ask the station master to fetch a doctor.'

'First we must move her to one of our beds. We can bathe her and give her the tea which gives sleep.' Deepaka waited for the expected onslaught.

'Bring a foreigner into the carriage?'

'We are no doctors.'

'Amiya gives no help.'

'We cannot move her if the boy wishes to do nothing?'

'They are rich, they should get help. They can pay for it.'

'They are dirty, we do not want them in the carriage.'

'Deepaka, they are perhaps sick on the dreaming drugs.'

'Look, she vomits on her clothes. Shall she vomit on our bedding?'

'She is sick. She is the same age as our grandchildren. We would help each of them, now we must help her. We can make a stretcher as we did for Nirmal and carry her across the iron rails. It is not far. She can lie in warmth until the doctor comes.' Deepaka rose and entered the carriage while the others talked of her determination and the horrifying suggestion she was making.

She returned with the blankets which had been used to carry Ashin. She merely nodded to Narend, Mitu, Surendra and Harischandra. They did not hesitate, but followed the old lady as she struggled down on to the cinders, across the tracks and up the other wall. Reena followed, clucking, and the others drew themselves closer to the carriage. It took no time at all for Deepaka to explain what she wanted. Soon the girl was cradled in the blankets as the four men lowered her tenderly down the wall and up again to their own platform. It was clear she was ill, young and frightened. The men acted as they would with a calf in a similar situation. No gesture was wasted, no strength withheld; each murmured the singsong words of comfort and soothing reassurance he would have used for his beasts or his grandchildren. The boy followed, numbed, and Reena had to goad him several times not to fall against his suffering companion. Deepaka led the procession into the carriage and cleared the maps and papers off Ashin's bunk. They laid the girl there, and as Deepaka tucked blankets around her the boy threw himself on to Surendra's bunk and was asleep before Reena had even begun to make tea.

'He is exhausted. While she has been ill he has been sleepless, and now that he knows there is help, he sleeps.'

'Come, Amiya, come and heal the sick child.' Amiya rose and accompanied Reena into the next compartment, where Deepaka and Harischandra stood beside the girl. The healer froze and then began to laugh shrilly, which shocked the villagers even more than the sight of the stranger in their carriage. At last Amiya spoke:

'The death bed for a foreigner. That is right. With the village simpleton and the letter-writer to help her on her way. Surely the gods are just. Now we will watch a foreign tourist die to balance our own death.' She turned and went to her bunk, drawing the blankets around her and holding the medicine box firmly.

Surendra and Harischandra withdrew and went in search of the station master, whose help they soon enlisted. The other villagers padded softly to their beds, stealing frightened glances at Amiya and wondering if the terrible words would again bring death in the night. Reena and Deepaka bathed the girl and managed to get her to swallow a cupful of tea. Narend and Rhunu ran errands for them. The boy did not stir throughout the long hours. Early morning brought the doctor, who stepped up quickly, examined the girl, and stared in puzzlement at the occupants of the carriage. In a short time the men again carried the girl down the platform. This time the boy was alert and anxious, awed by the help which had come. A strange vehicle which the station master called an ambulance took the foreigners and the doctor away. That was all. The villagers straggled back to the carriage only to be told that they must hurry to the bus. As Narend urged Amiya to hurry away from the train, Amiya passed Deepaka shuffling slowly with weariness. The healer hissed at her old friend:

'You have disgraced and polluted us all. You with your prayers to strange gods and your talk with foreigners. You are a bringer of evil.'

Deepaka halted. Narend took her arm to draw her along.

'Ignore her, aunt, she is still ill from the shock of Ashin's death. She will return to herself after we have seen more wonders.'

'But she was my friend and she called me evil.'

'And how many times at the well have you women shouted and pulled hair over nothing?'

'You are right, we are too fond of cursing. But look at her eyes. Narend, I am frightened.'

Narend looked and he too felt glad when they were seated on the bus and he could not see Amiya. Most of the villagers slept during the hours of the journey. Deepaka sat and wondered. Only when they were nearing Ajanta did her old body slump into sleep. She was wakened by a blast from a microphone as a Bengali voice greeted them and told of the wonders of Ajanta. Mitu was unable to sit still as the guide talked of the paintings they would see. Rhunu's eyes shone with anticipation. Reena grinned as the guide tried to tell some of the tales of the Buddha but lost his audience by keeping to the dry details. Harischandra thought of the English hunters climbing and finding the caves, a century ago, and shared their excitement. Then the time for thought was over and they were climbing up the long dusty path with other tourists, each stepping carefully, each trying to look ahead to see the horseshoe of caves and the gorge beneath. From one cave to another their interest grew, for here was a life much like their own portrayed in colour and movement. When at sunset the villagers had seen the last monastery, had squinted up at the last goddess flying across the ceiling of a cave, had bowed before the last statue, they watched the shadows of the gorge, listened to the murmurs of those ahead in the descending queue, and drew themselves up with pride. Babla paused at the souvenir stand, untied some coins from his shawl and bought a book with the coloured pictures reproduced. Arundati stared at him!

'What is that for?'

'For the girl at home to see.'

'What will she care about these paintings?'

'She will care, we have seen them now.' And he thrust the book into his belt and smiled at his strange extravagance.

'So, Rhunu, there were artists who could make caves alive. Do you not feel happy to be one with them?'

'To be able to make even one picture as lively would be a great gift to my old hands, husband.'

'Let us catch Reena and sit near her while we journey home.'

'Home?'

'Yes, to the carriage.'

'I feel it home, too, and will be glad to put a new garland over Uma-didi for her gift of seeing these caves.' Deepaka turned and bowed in farewell to the hill above them.

'So it is you, aunt, who puts the flowers over the picture?'

'It is a puja, for I am grateful to be part of this pilgrimage.'

'Even though you are sometimes mocked, my gentle aunt?'

'Even though. It is right, I am simple, and what matters it if some call others evil if we know in our hearts that what we do is right?'

'You are the closest we have to a saint among us.'

'Do not tease me, I am tired and saints are supposed to rise above such feelings. I want only to sink into my bed.'

'Hark, now she is making jokes about the great ones.'

'Tease us all, Reena, with a tale.'

It was sixty miles back to the railway carriage, but the journey went quickly as Reena wove patterns and pictures for all the villagers. When they were walking up the platform Harischandra spoke to her:

'You have been telling us tales we never heard in the village. Where have you learned them?'

'You wish to learn my secrets?'

'Yes, mother, I think the tales should be written, so that they remain for our children to know after we are gone.'

'Then I agree and will tell you. The new tales come from the books I bought in Delhi and Bombay. I am trying to buy a book of tales from each of the regions we pass. It is difficult, there are few in Bengali.'

'Let me help you to read the English, and you tell me the tales which are only in your head and let me write them.'

'It is a bargain, Harischandra, though I did not think I would be a teacher of reading and telling you the old tales before the end of this journey.'

The following day passed in Aurangabad with tours of a mill and gardens made by one of the Moslem rulers. Within it was the tomb of a Moslem saint, and when Deeepaka went to make her offering she was sent away by the guard. The old woman merely sighed and placed her flowers beside a waterfall.

Late that night as they were sleeping in the carriage, the villagers were roused by an engine arriving on the track beside them. They opened the shutters and looked out to see the station brightly lit, and a pushing crowd pouring along the platform. Each person carried bundles, and each was driven by a panic that the train might depart. The leaders were running, trying to get to the last of the third-class carriages before the others. Before long the area between the trains was a turbulent sea, the crowd clawing, shrieking, pushing and being pushed back. The doors of the train remained closed, for the officials could not get through to open them. The villagers leaned out the windows to watch. They saw, coming slowly through the frenzied crowd, an official leading a tall foreign girl who was struggling with a suitcase. Every time the suitcase became entangled in the crowd, people would push forward between the official and the stranger, shouting that there would not be enough room. The official would batter his way back to the girl and lead her forward. At last they were opposite the villagers' carriage, before the door of another third-class carriage. The villagers saw that there were no steps to the other train. Each passenger would have to haul himself up the several feet by grasping the hand rails above head height. From the far end of the train came the sounds of slamming doors and the villagers could see the pushing throng climbing up into the last two carriages. Then they saw the official working his way back down the platform. The foreigner stood alone before the closed door of the third-class carriage. The door was opened. The girl raised her suitcase above her head to hoist it up on to the doorway. The crowd began to shout and to surge. For a moment everything seemed suspended and still. Then a shout went up:

'The foreigner is too slow.' The crowd pushed forward. The girl fell beneath the train and was lost from the view of the villagers. The throng did not pause but flowed up into the train, though the villagers were shouting at them to get the girl out. No one heard. Deepaka and Rhunu, Arundati and Uma were weeping. Reena and Surendra, Narend and Babla were cursing, Elder De was pummelling the side of the carriage, screaming at the crowd. Amiya was laughing.

Suddenly a young man blocked the doorway. He jumped down and drew up the girl, tossing her like a light child on to the high step of the carriage before he drew himself up beside her. The villagers saw that she was bruised by the cinders, her clothes torn, one sandal gone, her hair which had been braided like a schoolgirl's loose in disarray. The man pushed her inside the carriage and returned to the doorway, where he shouted at the crowd.

'What does he say?'

'What does he say?'

Jaydev tried to translate the Hindi:

'He says they should ask themselves if it is worth killing a student come to learn about our country just for the price of a third-class ticket. He says there are places enough or the station master would have put on another train. He says they are more stupid than buffalo, more clumsy than cows, more selfish than scavenger dogs. He says he spits on them. He says once he was proud to be Indian, now he is ashamed. He says the girl is a stranger to him too, but he feels she is as a sister to be protected from the filth of the crowd.'

The young man jumped down from the carriage. The crowd began to mount again, slowly now. From somewhere the battered suitcase of the stranger was lifted up and passed into the carriage. Then the platform was empty again. A few families clustered near the windows. Elder De hailed the young man. He strode over and they saw that he was still very angry. Narend spoke in hesitant English:

'Is the girl safe?'

'Yes, she is in the ladies' compartment, weeping a little. I have locked the door. She will clean her bruises herself and now they have given the suitcase to her, so she can change clothes.'

'Who is she?'

'I do not know. The station master says she is a student of our history come from England and that he had word from Baroda House to care for her since she is a girl and travels alone.'

'You have saved her life. Blessings upon you.' The young man went away.

'Baroda House told them to look after her.'

'She comes all the way across the sea to study our history.'

'He says he was proud to be Indian but now he is ashamed.'

'There are others sent to see India who are not tourists, just as we are sent.'

The talk went on. After a time Reena brought up the big pot of tea and they settled themselves by the window to watch until the other train departed. Harischandra asked an official when the train would depart. The answer was not for an hour or more.

'So all that was for nothing. They have more than an hour to wait and all have found places.'

It was Uma who noticed that Elder De was crossing the platform from their train to the other. She called the others back to the window to watch the old man's desertion. They saw him work his way slowly along the track until he came to some shutters. Then he paused, listening. Stretching, the elder reached up and banged on the shutters. After a moment the metal grate was wound up and the villagers saw the face of the foreign girl at the window. Elder De reached up again and handed the girl his cup of tea. Then he pressed his hands together and bowed, and the stranger bowed to him. The shutters were wound down again. Elder De returned to the carriage, polishing his glasses and shuffling his slippers along the cement.

'Why did you do that?'

'Now you have no cup for tea.'

'Who are you to give things to rich foreigners who pay to come across the sea?'

'Hush, all of you. She is our guest, in our land.' Elder De turned his back to them all and curled in sleep. Soon he was snoring. The others stopped muttering about his strange action and went to sleep themselves. They did not see the other train pull out of Aurangabad station, but in the morning Siv found a tattered sandal lying crushed at the side of the rail, and showed it to the others.

When the station master greeted them after they had bathed he was apologetic to Surendra and Elder De. The bus which was to have taken them to Ellora had been hired by another group. The station master could only repeat what a pity it was that they would not see this greatest of all wonders. Surendra asked if there was not a regular bus which made the short journey.

'Yes, it goes from the market square.'

'Then we shall take that bus.'

'You are too many, and you have no tickets.'

'We shall see.'

Surendra cautioned the others to stay close to him and walked out of the station in the direction indicated by the station master. Everywhere the loud music of films was amplified into the din of traffic, shouting tradesmen and the factory whistles. At the square there were rows of buses, each with a community of squatting people, chickens, luggage, goats and a tossing babble of children. Surendra found a ticket office and approached the seller:

'Ellora caves, ticket please.' The villagers giggled behind to hear him speak in English.

'How many?'

'Forty-two' said Surendra. He wrote the figures on the paper of the counter, proud to hold a pen in public view. The seller lost all calm and started speaking rapidly in a language Surendra could not understand. Surendra waited until there was a pause in the flow and then repeated:

'Forty-two tickets, Ellora caves.'

'Forty-two not go. No room. Small bus.' The man tried to make his point. Surendra grinned.

'Make another bus go. Two buses for many people.' A man moved in behind the ticket seller and the two shouted for a long time before turning back to Surendra:

'No room. No Bus.'

Surendra was jostled by a small man festooned with cameras who pushed up to the wicket and demanded.

'Ten tickets on next bus to Ellora caves, quick please.'

'How many?'

'Ten. Quick now.'

'Why ten?'

'I need ten for my staff. I am photographer from a tourist agency in Delhi. I come to photograph the caves. I need bearers for my equipment. Quick, tickets for the next bus.' The little man shook himself and tapped a coin on the counter. The ticket seller shouted louder at the official in the office, then slammed down the shutter and left the little man and Surendra staring at the wood. The man began to pound on the shutter and shout. Surendra lit a biri and waited. The villagers behind squatted to watch the bustle of the square. After Surendra's third biri, when the photographer was wiping his head with a soaking handkerchief and explaining to everyone how important the light was for photographing the caves, the shutter was flung open. A triumphant, if flustered, ticket seller shouted, 'Two buses for Ellora caves.' Surendra stood and purchased forty-two tickets while the photographer gazed in impatience, anger, amusement and wonder to see the cultivator act as businessman. After a while they were packed in with the chickens and cameras on the two buses. Surendra and Jaydev sat up on the roof with two boys who were minding a goat tied down to the bundles. After an hour of driving through fields of cotton and up into the hills—at every swaying turn the goat bleated since the boys clung to it very tightly—the buses drew to a thunderous halt and the travellers tumbled out, laughing with the excitement of the public bus. Surendra arranged that the drivers would both return in the evening to take them back. The tourists were already climbing the hill to the caves, but Surendra was content to stretch and remove his shoes. Then he joined Elder De on the slope.

When the villagers arrived back at the station and sought their beds that night, there was pandemonium. Surendra, walking up the siding barefoot, heard the conductor shouting at the villagers. They had joined all the other passengers in the crowd which passed the guards and now they pushed and fought with all the ferocity of the crowd they had watched before. When at last they were in the carriage, there was panic. Elder De was trying to count heads. One of the compartments had been occupied by a Muslim lady, her sister, her large family, and a lone, but wealthy, widow. The bundles of the villagers had been thrown up into Reena's hammock, their bedding pushed to the floor, and now the strangers refused to answer or even recognize any of the shouted pleas and admonitions of the villagers. The conductor came and joined in the fray by telling the Bengalis to be seated, that there were still bunks free, and to quiet down before he sent for the guards. With a jerk and a hiss the train moved out of the station. The villagers were thrown one upon another with the unexpected movement. Soon all but Reena had left the commandeered compartment and were grumbling and protesting all down the carriage. Surendra was already asleep when Elder De went to urge him to deal with the strangers. Elder De shook his head and returned to the door of the compartment. He was immediately told to go away and many gestures of insult were made by the women. Reena had climbed to her hammock and sat among the bundles and retrieved bedding. At last she, too, told Elder De that he could do nothing so to go and get some sleep. Arguments and bickering had begun. Narend covered his head with the blanket. Jaydev shouted. A few slept. Most would pad up the corridor from time to time to look at the strangers, and ask Reena if she was safe. Some shouted at the strangers and were shouted at in return for waking the baby. They went away in anger at the strangers and their effrontery.

The Muslim lady was tall and heavy, her dark velvet tunic not able to hide the rolls of flesh. She wore much jewellery, and even her toes were ringed and painted. Beside her sat a slightly younger but just as heavy version of herself, also in a velvet tunic. Around them and above them on the bunks crouched and lay seven children, sticky with sweets and smelling of perfume. A small baby tried to snuggle against its mother's thigh but was pushed away. At last it found the small lap of an older sibling. The two women talked and ate fruit, dropping the peel on the floor to join the sweets spat there by the children. Across from them the widow had spread a heavy blanket along the bunk. Then she stretched out and pulled an equally heavy one over her. The two women reached out to feel the richness of the fabric only to be slapped and scolded roundly in their own tongue by the widow. She wore a white sari, but of imported nylon, and the gold bangles up her arms jingled with every movement. Her hair was grey, but cut and curled. As long as the women talked she leafed through women's magazines which lay in a wrapped bundle by her side. Every so often she would spit her pan juice and after a while there was a red puddle just inside the door of the compartment. One of the children roused from sleep and was sent down the corridor to the toilet. He came back whimpering that the place was awash with filth for the drain had stopped. Promptly the mother took down his trousers and a puddle of urine joined the puddle of pan. One after another the seven children rose to the same need. The compartment reeked of urine and perfume. Reena rasped out a protest. She was told to keep quiet for the baby was crying and vomiting. She settled back among the bundles.

For hours it seemed that at least one of the children was crying or being sick, and the widow and sister too were vomiting. Finally when all but the baby had at last fallen asleep, Reena crept down and gently lifted the restless child up to her hammock. There she softly sang the lullabies which had soothed all the children of the village, and the baby nestled against her old body and slept. When Rhunu rose to check on her aunt she saw them thus, both with open mouths breathing deeply. The grey head was supported by a bundle, the baby asleep in the thin arms. The hammock rocked with the motion of the train so Rhunu closed the door and went back to her own bunk. When dawn came the Muslim mother awoke and cried out to find her baby gone. The rich widow pointed up to the sleeping pair. They smiled and did not rouse them. Once again they all slept until the morning heat made the smell of the compartment too strong to bear. They opened the door and the shutters.

When the villagers came to see they recoiled even from entering to ask Reena how she fared. Reena enjoyed a breakfast such as she had rarely eaten, for the Muslim lady shared her food generously. Reena licked each finger clean with delight. When the sun was high and they had stopped in a small station, Reena climbed down and fetched a sweeper. The women were appalled that she would send such a person in to see their privacy, but the sweeper kept his eyes to the floor as he washed. Reena sent him back with the disinfectant used for the lavatory, which Reena thought was an unpleasant but effective deodorizer. Reena joined Rhunu and Narend and was plied with tea and questions about the strangers:

'How can they be so filthy and be so rich?'

'It costs no gold to bathe. Why should a rich man be more clean than a poor one?'

'But they put food upon the floor and fouled it with the urine and sickness of the children.'

'Do we not also cast our food upon the floors of the buses when we travel? What use is the latrine when it is stopped?'

'You ate their food, aunt.'

'What is the greater danger, eating their food, or holding a restless child until it sleeps?'

'You held one of the children?'

'She did, I saw her. It was the infant who did not sleep except for Reena.'

'Did you use one of the sleeping drugs from Amiya's box?'

'Fool, only the songs that put you to sleep when you were toothless and fat.'

'What does the widow do?'

'Did you see her hair and her bangles? She has the yellow stain on her fingers.'

'She has picture books of women from across the sea, women who show their legs. If she can look at those, she can stay with such a smell.'

'Why have they taken our wagon? There is room in the other carriages. This is ours from Uma-didi.'

'Where is the sign which declares it so?'

'True, there is no sign.'

'Is not the picture of Uma-didi enough?'

They turned to look at the portrait at the end of the carriage. Around it the garlands were wilted, the petals sat shrivelled among the incense burners. Without a word Deepaka rose and went to it. She removed the garland and cleaned away the petals. She was ashamed to have neglected it. Her movements reminded the others of their own tasks and once again they worked quietly in separate ways. At last Reena began to tell a story. The children from the compartment hesitated but a moment and then ran and threw themselves on the floor in front of Reena. Their attentions moved her to act, since she knew they did not understand her words. The villagers laughed to see Reena strut as a peacock, writhe as a snake, command when a prince, and flirt like a courtesan. By the end of the tale the children were cuddled by six of the lonely grandmothers and hidden stores of sweets were exposed and given away. It was a surprise when the conductor shouted that they must be ready to get off at Hyderabad. Babla stood by suspiciously watching the strangers pack up and waiting for any moment when one of their own small possessions might disappear amid the strangers' luggage. The wealthy widow handed him her suitcase. He dropped it immediately, realizing that she thought him a porter. She was furious and tried to blame him for a scratch along one side of the case, but he walked away down the carriage. The widow screamed and turned to her neighbour and accused the children of making the mark. Their mother defended them well. At the station when they left the strangers were sullen, even the children looked sickened again. The Bengalis watched as the strangers were met by many people, and the lone widow by one young man who shook her hand and took the case.

'He must be her son.'

'Why did he not touch her feet?'

'The rich do not do that.'

'Nor do foreigners.'

'What do foreigners do when they greet their parents?'

'They shake hands.'

'Maybe that is only the way of the rich ones.'

'Why do the women cut their hair like men?'

'Maybe they mourn, or do it from pilgrimage.'

'They do not mourn, even the tourists in Delhi who wore bright colours had short hair.'

'Perhaps they wear bright colours in mourning.'

'Hush you. We want no more talk of foreigners. Is not the pollution of the carriage by those ones, and by the dying children enough?' The villagers recoiled from Amiya's anger. She had been sitting collapsed in a corner. Now she retreated there again and paid no attention to the station or to Deepaka's urging that she join the others when they went to explore the city. Deepaka spoke with Narend and then went on with the others. Narend swung up into the carriage and sat down opposite Amiya:

'Aunt, we are going to see the city. Do you wish to come?'

'They talk of foreigners and filthy Muslims.'

'What would you have us speak of, aunt?' There was a long time of silence and Narend waited patiently. When slow tears began to find their way down Amiya's face he did not look away, but waited, unmoving. At last, when there were no more voices to be heard outside the carriage, and when the drumming of the station had become an accepted part of their enclosed silence, Amiya said:

'Of the village.'

'What of the village, aunt?' Again the silence.

'I try to remember it all, but I cannot. It keeps fading and all these new places push in.'

'What do you try to remember?'

'The ordinary things. What the river looks like in this season when I rise in the morning. Where my books are kept. What stories my grandson liked to hear as he lay dying. It is all gone. I can remember none of it.' The woman wept and rocked. Narend stood, then sat again, then stood and watched the business of the station.

'Go, go away with the others and leave me.'

'No, it is not good for you to stay alone.'

'I want no part of the others.'

'You will forgive me for my words, I am not Reena.'

'She ate of the stranger's food.' Amiya hissed at him, but Narend went on:

'But I too miss the village. Sometimes when we are walking on the hard streets of cities my legs tell me I am a foolish man for my feet belong in damp earth. It is long since my feet did not ache, and too long since we looked upon green.'

'Here there is only one green, a hard one of tall trees.'

'I like the soft green of the rice when it first comes forth, and the grey mist on old thatch which is green in the dawn.'

'The thatch is best in the early afternoon when everyone sleeps. Then it is gold and deep and the waves along the edge are like the waves of the river.'

'I like the smell of thatch after rain, and the warm, dusty smell of the dung cakes burning when we come from the fields at evening. But mostly now I miss my grandson, who used to twine his fingers between two of mine and try to hold the plough. He will be big when we return. Perhaps he will have forgotten me.' Amiya looked at the tall man, usually so silent. Then she spoke:

'Narend, I wrote a letter to my granddaughter to take the examinations for a scholarship to the big college in Calcutta. I wanted her to be a doctor since I could not be. So I wrote to my son and said I would give all that remains to me of the dowry to pay for her housing in Calcutta if they would let her try. Then we met the girl of Jaipur and tried to meddle in her fate. The gods showed me there is no help from doctoring with the death of Ashin. I have tried to turn the hand of destiny. Narend, if I do not reach the village again, see that the girl has a chance to go if she wishes? I have longed for it, now perhaps my blood in her will do it. But then it may be foolishness and wicked. Maybe I have now damned her to dreaming as I have done. I do not know.' Again Amiya wept. This time Narend reached out and took her hand:

'It is not foolish, aunt. But it is foolish to speak of your not seeing the village again. Come, before the light fades let us walk together and see what of this city reminds us of our childhood.' Narend drew Amiya up and slowly they left the carriage and the station and moved into the city of Hyderabad. At first Amiya hung back, but Narend took her arm and she who had always walked with her head high leaned on him.

They walked down the avenue in the crowd. Sometimes they looked at fruit and vegetables, or Narend would point out a child playing a game of cat's cradle or trying to cast gambling sticks. They joined the promenade to Char Minar, a memorial gateway which marked a central crossroads. Narend realized that the press of the crowds was because it was time for prayer, and that those around him were Muslims going towards a mosque. He asked Amiya:

'What is the strange odour? I smell hot spices and food, but much more.'

'There is wet wool, and dyes, and musk, roses and jasmine, and hair oil.' They stopped and tried to identify the sources of all the smells. Above all there was a pall of human odours: sweat and soap, tobacco and feet. As they listened to the din they gradually distinguished individual sounds. The bellicose lowing of the taxis and bicycle bells interrupted all else, but often there was a shrill whine of a whistle, tinkling bells on a tea cart, shouts back and forth in Urdu, a low murmur and metallic clanging from the restaurants, and everywhere the soft jingling of jewels, bracelets, anklets, and the tiny silver bells worn by the women. Some were heavily concealed in dark burkahs, most were dressed as the women had been on the train: in tight tunics of velvet, with wide pants, embroidered slippers and a lace shawl draping the head. Narend and Amiya were forced on again by the crowd. Overhead hung carpets, gold-embroidered bed covers, saris, cloth pieces, more carpets. Everywhere there were sellers of sweet coloured waters, of strongly aromatic teas, of spiced gram and hot pulses. On a whim Narend reached out, gave a small coin and was given a paper cornet of pulses. He held them out to Amiya, who hesitated but tried the treat. It was good and they now ate as they walked. Before long they were in front of an enormous building where the press of the crowd was too much to pass. Narend turned Amiya and they walked down another street.

'What was that?'

'I think the mosque. It is time for sunset prayers.'

'These are Muslims?'

'Yes, I think so.'

'Ai,' blind with fright and anger Amiya started to rush down the street against the crowd. For a moment Narend lost her and stood high trying to see her through the other heads. This was a tall population and Narend could see nothing. He pushed on, hindered at every step by the people now converging towards the mosque and the great arch. He comforted himself with the thought that she could not go faster than he in this press, but then he wondered if she had turned back to look for him and now had passed unnoticed. He paused, and in that hesitation a man plucked his sleeve and pointed further down the street. Narend did not understand, but then he caught the word 'Bengali', bowed to the man and hurried on. There, braced against the wall of a shop, staring in terror, was Amiya. Narend was at once before her, but she did not lose that look of fright until at last they were alone along a river. Narend had spoken often, commenting on the sights, but Amiya remained silent. On the river bank they sat to rest and watched the sky and water join in the night. Amiya put her head on her knees and shook. With difficulty Narend got her to rise. Then they began a nightmarish journey back to the station. Amiya covered her head and face and would not look where she was going. Narend had to attend to her confusion and to his own doubt of the route. By the time they saw the rows of buses before the station Narend was weary to his core, and Amiya swayed with every step. Rhunu and Deepaka, Elder De and Jaydev were squatting at the doors of the station. The two women took Amiya and supported her back to the carriage. Narend said nothing. Elder De began to get angry:

'Narend, you cannot go off like this. It is too dangerous. We all worried. It is too much for us to endure.'

'Where did you go?' said Jaydev.

'Is Amiya ill?' asked Elder De.

The questions went on and on but at last they were at the carriage. Narend saw a tap with a bucket of water near it. He lifted the bucket and doused himself. As soon as he was washed Rhunu appeared with a tali of food. Narend had almost finished when he suddenly looked up and spoke to Rhunu:

'Have you waited to eat?'

'Yes, but finish, you are hungry.'

'No, you eat now.' Narend passed over the tali and Rhunu finished the food, though it made a meagre meal. Narend brought her tea and they sat in the darkness. Deepaka and Reena came down to them to question.

'Is Amiya sick? She sleeps, after only taking tea. She breathes like a child that has cried a long time. She has not slept so for many days.'

'What has happened? Have you found what troubles her?'

'She is tired. I lost her for a moment in the crowd near the mosque. The sleep will do her good. Let us rest.'

'So you saw the mosque, too? Did you see the rugs and the cloth? Never have I seen such colour, or smelt such a city.' Reena watched Narend carefully as she chattered. She saw that he would say no more of Amiya. She retired with Deepaka to the carriage. Elder De rose to go to his bed:

'Tomorrow you must stay with us, Narend.'

'Where is Surendra?'

'Ai, he is off somewhere gambling with the beggar boys, or smoking, or walking. I do not know. When he had brought us back here and eaten he said he would go out alone to clear his head of all the women chatter.'

'Do not blame him, Elder De. He is just as I am, a cultivator who does not like the weight of the village upon his shoulders.'

'Does not the plough know its furrow? Would you bend old bones? That is what Deepaka said to me. Ai, why was Ashin taken?' Elder De went off into the carriage.

'Let us walk, wife. Or are you too tired from the waiting?'

'No, let us walk.'

Silently they went up the tracks of the siding until the night hum of the city was far away. Narend stopped and Rhunu waited for him to speak. She prodded:

'What worries you, lord husband? You did not tell all of Amiya.'

'She says she will not return to the village. She says she tries but cannot remember it, though when I spoke she could. She wants us to see that her granddaughter has the chance to go to college in Calcutta. She has written that what remains of her dowry is to be put to the cost.'

Rhunu gasped.

'She is in terror that she has tried to change the writing of destiny and is now to be punished. I think she feels she has failed with Ashin and has failed in her life. There must be a sickness within her. I do not understand.'

'What must be done?'

'We must watch her and keep her close to us. The others must not know or there will be great fear. Nirmal called her a witch and they will remember.'

'Are you not afraid, Husband?'

'No, I feel a great sadness upon me.'

'You are tired, let us go back.'

'Not for a time. Surendra is right. We need to clear ourselves of that chatter.'

'You speak more than ever in the village, my lord.'

'You tease me, but it is true. There is more to say.'

'Perhaps not.'

'Would you have a babbling mate?'

'I do not know.'

The two laughed, loved, and slept covered by their shawls. Surendra stumbled upon them as he came back down the track in the deep night.

'Here, you two. Do not hide so that a poor clumsy cultivator may break his neck upon you. Get up before you are chilled and help my old bones on their way back to our metal house.'

'Surendra, you have been taking lessons from your bullocks. Your feet are too big.' Rhunu laughed as she stood. They began the walk back. Narend paused:

'Surendra, you smell of fish.'

'I thought you had forgotten that smell since you did not speak before. Here, look.' He held up a string of many small fish. The others stared.

'Yes, fish. I caught them on the river. There were others fishing, too, so they must be good to eat. We shall feast at breakfast.'

'How did you catch them, you had no nets?'

'Here they have hooks, with lines and sticks. I bought three hooks and had three lines going all at the same time. The others thought me greedy.' Surendra laughed, but grew quiet as they neared the railway yards.

'Did you take Amiya on a tour of the city, brother?'

'Yes.'

'He says we must watch her, Surendra, there may be the sickness of madness within her.'

'But I said-'

'Surendra must know.'

'Rhunu is right, Narend. If one of the herd is about to go wild, all of the herdsmen must be warned. That will not make sleep easier.'

'Think of your fish.'

'Ah yes.' With that the three were in the station and made their way to their beds in silence. Reena watched them come and chortled to herself:

'Like a pair of newlyweds those two. Always have been. And now their grandson is big enough to hold a plough.' She glanced about, saw that Deepaka slept snoring and Amiya breathed deeply.

'She will be better for having slept well,' Reena nodded and then slept.

In the half-wakefulness of dawn Deepaka heard Amiya muttering:

'I smell fish cooking.'

'No, didi, there is only fish in the village, not here. Go back to sleep.'

'But I do smell fish.'

'You cannot, we are far from the river and the sea.'

'Waken then, and tell me what is cooking.'

'Oh Ma, I smell fish.'

Reena was down from her hammock and out of the carriage as quickly as she could move. Amiya was before her. Along the carriage the villagers were stirring and rising with the same cry:

'Fish, where is the fish? Who is cooking fish?'

Amiya saw Surendra bent over a fire, with the large cooking pots spread about him. He was cursing and laughing to himself and looked up happily when the women rushed to him:

'Now I shall have help. I have made the rice from last night hot again, and there are fish. I have only two in the pot, for I do not know how you cook them.'

'Man, man, move away. How many fish are there? Where did you get them?'

'I caught them with hooks in the night. There are seventeen, we can each eat some.'

'Quickly, call the others to hurry.' Amiya and Reena took over and the villagers eagerly watched the feast being prepared.

'Fetch the talis.'

'Bring the spice box.'

'Don't block the fire.'

'Be ready, we shall serve them hot.'

'Don't let that one burn, Reena.'

The excitement of the food distracted many from the fact that it was Amiya who was giving orders again. Amiya of the flashing eyes. When they were all eating, Surendra was asked by Babla, 'Will we see the palace of the Nizam? He is said to be the richest of all men in India.'

'I do not think they let visitors into the place where he lives. We go to see old palaces.' It was Elder De who answered, for Surendra attended only to the food before him.

'How can you think of gold when we have fish, Babla?'

'Ai, this is the best food I have eaten. Surendra, you are blessed among farmers and fishermen.' Jaydev sat back with delight and began to pick the last shreds of the delicacy out of his teeth.

'It is said we go to the museum.' Mitu spoke shyly.

'Only if you promise not to hide within it.' The potter ignored the joke and went to fetch his pads and pencils. Narend turned to Rhunu but she was gone after Mitu. Deepaka collected the talis. She and Uma sang and the other women joined in as they washed them, Arundati off tune, but with greater volume than the others. As they walked to the bus Surendra told Amiya of how he had caught the fish. The villagers listened to the drone of the guide's voice as they passed large houses and official buildings. They admired Golconda fort and learned of the diamond market often held there. They were taken to see the tombs of the kings who had ruled the Deccan, but many recoiled from the cold alleys where small mosques and minarets marked the burial places of the wealthy dead. Others, like Uma and Jaydev, Harischandra and Mitu, were intrigued and followed the guide closely from tomb to tomb through the gardens. When they joined the small group which remained outside, Uma said to Arundati:

'You should have seen it. There were even carvings and pictures for the bodies. Imagine putting so much work into a burial place!'

'Did you not feel the ghosts?'

'What ghosts?'

'The ghosts of the unburned. It is a bad place.'

'You are silly. There are no ghosts here. The Muslims do not believe in burning.'

'You are not afraid even in the village. I could feel the ghosts.'

'Why do they not believe in burning?'

'They think the dead will go to some place in their same bodies and there they shall enjoy good rice and harvests for all time,' the guide responded.

'You mean, for all the lives of the gods, they think each man must stay in the same body?'

'No, they do not have many gods and creations, only one and only this world.'

'But even so, for all the time of this world, a man must stay in the same body?'

'Yes, though there would be no sickness and no one would be old.'

'Oh Ma, how terrible.'

'Why is it terrible?'

'Imagine staying as you are always. Do you not want to change? I do. That is terrible. They should burn the dead and free the soul from the old body.'

'How would you change yourself, aunt?'

'Do not be foolish, I am not of the gods to say.'

'Why would it be so dreadful as to remain as Deepaka?'

'Maybe in the next life she plans not to be Deepaka.'

'Oh, it is all right to be simple, but maybe I could one day not be so plump.' They laughed until the tears came, and even Amiya had to stop and embrace Deepaka to stop her laughter.

'Perhaps the gods like you as you are. You have made all your family happy and proud. I who am thin, have not done that,' Mitu grinned.

'You mock me for a small thing. I still think it would be dreadful to be condemned to stay the same for ever. I like to think of us all as starting anew with each death.'

'It is not starting anew, the soul is learning the teachers say.'

'That I know, but we have a chance to live more kindly as the soul learns. We are not condemned to remain as foolish and selfish as one day, just as children learn not to be so as they grow.'

'I understand Deepaka,' Babla interrupted. 'You think that our lives are like this pilgrimage from Uma-didi, a gift to learn again and prove to the gods our worth. But the Muslims have only one chance and that depends on only one god.'

'Yes, that is what I mean.'

'Then you are right, our way is better. I liked the tombs, though, for they are reminders and we have no reminders of our dead. Once we burn those who die they are gone, we give away all so that nothing remains. I like the way these tombs tell of the great men. Do you not remember the wonder of the tomb of Akbar?'

'I liked that too, Babla,' said Elder De. 'But you would have it both ways. You want to have souls reborn at each death for a chance to learn and you would have us reminded of each life by a tomb. I think there would be too many tombs.'

'No, we would only need reminders of good men, like Ashin. We would not want reminders of all.'

'Then it would quickly become reminders of only the rich and not the poor, as with everything,' said Reena.

'Could we not have a memorial, not a tomb, of Ashin? Could you not make one?' Deepaka turned to Mitu.

'Yes, Mitu, you could make a figure for us to put in the temple when we return home. Then we could see it each time we go to make puja.'

'That is a good plan.'

'Mitu, make him look as he did in Calcutta, not when he was ill.'

'Make it big, so that we do not have to enter the temple to see it.'

'Surendra would you not even enter the temple for that?'

'I do not know if I could make a memorial which would last. The clay carvings must be renewed each year after the rains.'

'Then you must have some hard rock, or marble.' Jaydev kicked at the stones and danced with the pain of the blow. In front of the mosque near Char Minar the guide told them to get down, but the villagers were afraid of the thick crowds. Amiya tried to stay in the bus but the driver pushed her out. She was trembling. Rhunu stepped up to her and took her arm:

'Come, aunt, we must see if Deepaka is right and if these Muslims are all too ugly to stay the same for all eternity.'

'I did not say that.'

'But it is true,' Amiya joined in the banter. The villagers were turned away from the mosque. The guide led them away to the gardens. The villagers, relieved, questioned him as they walked:

'Where do you come from in Bengal?'

'From the north.'

'How did you come here?'

'I joined the railways. When word came from Baroda House that you were coming, I was given leave to guide you.'

'Do you have family here?'

'My wife and four sons.'

'Ai, he is blessed. Did you hear? Four sons, living.'

'Do you like living here or would you come back to Bengal?'

'Bengal is the home of my heart, but here life is good. There is work, a house for my family, good food. Now there are riots and troubles, so perhaps our good fortune will not last.'

'Why are there riots?'

'People fight over language, and whether we should become a separate state away from India.'

'There have been riots in Calcutta since the time of my grandfather. It is nothing.' Elder De waved away the problem.

'Do you think not? Here there is much bitterness. South by Madras way it is worse. I fear much trouble.'

'What is your solution?'

'The same as the solution to all things, education.'

'How can that be a solution for all things?'

'Surely you have seen on your travels. We must teach the young that there is India and that villagers suffer in all places if the villagers in one place fight.'

'But we have not yet seen that the success of the harvest helps any but the rich.'

'That is what my sons say. I do not know, but I think education must be our hope. I want my sons to be drillers of wells so that they can bring water to this desert.'

'And who is to fix the well when it is broken?'

'The villagers, that is why each must be schooled. If we were all educated we would not be afraid and always vote for the rich man. We would know enough to vote for the honest and true man.'

'What honest and true man would want to be part of the government?'

'If all were educated, perhaps some would think it worth trying.'

'You have not explained the riots. Is not religion part of it?'

'Yes, and no. Not for the sake of who is right about the gods, but about rights to govern and language, yes the religious differences are part of the problem.'

'You said it was worse to the south, why?'

'There it is the language issue.'

'What is the language issue?'

'All those who speak one language wish to have their own state where only that language must be used.'

'Ai, what foolishness. If there is one thing clear about India, it is that we have too many languages. Ai, that is nonsense.' Jaydev was horrified by the guide's explanation and did not notice that they were about to cross a large square to the station. The guide turned to Elder De:

'You are the leader of the village?'

'No.'

'But are you the leader of the pilgrimage?'

'No, our leader died in Bombay. We share the duties now.'

'I must give you a warning. The station is not safe from gangs of thieves. You should hide well any money you carry and you should not carry much in the city.'

'Is the carriage not safe?'

'No, I hope you can warn the others.'

'Yes, it must be done.'

Cautiously they crossed the square. Uma led some of the women to the kitchens of the station to see if their meal was ready. The place was empty of staff and only an old porter appeared to explain that they had all gone off on strike. That night the villagers went to bed dreaming of their fish.

Next day the on the bus the guide urged them to leave that night for Bangalore.

'We must go to market, for we have had no food.'

'No, now there is a concert at the university.'

'What is this concert?'

'Two singers, a man and a woman. It should be fine. They sing ghazals.'

Unsure, the villagers followed the guide reluctantly into the hall. The sad melodies of the love songs moved many in the audience to tears, but Elder De slept and Babla grew impatient. Midway through the concert he made his way across the legs and passed the annoyed students until he found a door. An hour later the villagers found him there, half-asleep.

'That was good for me no doubt, but I would rather listen to Reena any day,' Jaydev said as he stretched.

'Do not mock the beauty because it is strange. We were honoured to be taken.'

'Ai, and my head is honoured to ache. I am a simple man, leave me at home with the beasts next time.'

'Did the rulers have singers like this?'

'Yes, and poets too. There were many competitions and music was performed each day.'

'Then I am glad I am a poor man.'

'Why do they always make love into something sad?'

'But the songs are beautiful, they are sung all over India.'

'Bah.'

One group went to the market. Those who waited sang their own lively songs of fishing and harvest. They were in fine spirits when the others returned, and joked and teased all the way to the station. But there was no time for a feast. Officials pushed them along the platform and stopped Elder De from making a speech. The train left with a hiss and a rush before the villagers had had time to pack their bundles.

'What is the matter?'

'We will ask when the conductor comes.'

'Don't spill the curd, put it in a pot.'

'Don't sit on the bananas.'

'Let me put the pulses down .'

'Is there no tea?'

'No, none.'

'No tea, no pan, no food since Surendra's fish. It is like a year without harvest.'

'Hush, do not say such things. It is a bad omen.'

'It is worse to spill salt.'

'Get off my bundle, my feet hurt.'

'Move your bundle to the other side.'

'Come, Mitu, and draw the fighters. They can be the first of your village pictures.'

'Is Mitu going to make pictures of the village?'

'Draw my compound first, Mitu. My family has always been good to yours.'

'No, let him draw the temple first, that is most important.'

'He must draw the well and the tree at the centre.'

'What is it, what does he draw?'

'I see, it is the river. There are the trees of the village. What are those things?'

'Boats, fool. Can you not tell they are going across to the village?'

For a long time the villagers crowded and watched as Mitu drew sketch after sketch of the familiar sights. Though no one saw how she came, Amiya sat at Mitu's elbow watching every stroke. When Mitu grew tired he turned to Rhunu:

'Will you bring your chalks? My hand cramps.'

'Before the others?'

'Does Rhunu draw too?'

'Who would have thought it?'

'Come, Rhunu, draw for the women. The sights Mitu does not see.'

'Yes, show us our kitchens and how we pound the grains.'

Rhunu withdrew to her compartment and Narend followed. He drew out the chalks and handed them to her:

'Do it for Amiya and the others who are sick with loneliness.'

'But they will laugh at me.'

'No, they will wonder that you can do it.'

'You wish me to?'

'Yes.'

'Then only out of obedience to you.' Rhunu moved back along the corridor and Narend saw that she was rigid with anger and fear. She first made some upright lines, then some sweeping curved ones. Narend could not see what it was to be. Those nearer cried out:

'It is Deepaka's compound. The thatch only curves like that at her house.'

'Hush.'

In silence the villagers watched as Rhunu drew the compound, the cooking fire, the pats of dung on one wall, a chicken scratching, some cooking pots, and finally the shape of a woman squatting over the fire. Her hands were slower than Mitu's, but the villagers gazed with wonder at the picture:

'It is truly as it is.'

'Look, there is even the design that Deepaka made for the last feast.'

'Deepaka, see, your house.'

'Is it magic?'

'No, we watched Rhunu make the picture.'

'Draw the women drawing water.'

For as long as she could Rhunu drew. Mitu and Narend sat behind her, proud and attentive. Amiya would not move from her side as the colours took on form and the village appeared before her. At last Rhunu's hand ached and she closed the box. The sketch pad was passed from hand to hand and the hours of the journey went quickly. Just after nightfall the conductor came.

'Why did we leave in such a hurry?'

'Some rioters said they would bomb the bridge as the evening train crossed, so we left early. I think the police caught the rioters.'

'Is it as bad as that?'

'Every day something is burnt. You should talk to the girls in the next carriage. They are going south to an aunt. Many years ago their father was killed trying to defend his village. All these years his widow has kept the village safe. Now the girls have been threatened at college, so she sends them away.'

'Is it not just feuding, as before?'

'When the methods are of violence and fear what is the difference between a feud and a political raid? If the rioters and the police both kill and attack villagers, what is the difference?'

'Are the police attacking, too?'

'Of course. They do not know who are the rioters, so all are beaten.'

'Do you want a stronger government?'

'Stronger with more beatings, no, for what is that but more terror in the night? Stronger if made of better people, yes, but how are we to get it?'

'The guide said it would come with education.'

'Maybe he is right, but people are afraid to send their children to school and teachers are attacked and disappear. I hate this fear. We are worse than a bunch of brothers the way we destroy ourselves.'

'Then you think it is we who must change things?'

'Of course, India is only a country of poor people. The rich do not matter, they care little. Those who kill because they have power will be killed by others who want it in their turn. It is only those who work long for their rice who can change this.'

'How can a poor man change a rich one?'

'I do not know, ask the gods to tell us the fates.' The conductor spat and moved away.

In the morning the city of Bangalore welcomed them with sun and sobriety. The villagers were taken out of the city to see a young saint, said to be an incarnation of one of the great gods. They saw a beaming boy and were not ready to bow before him. The next day they went west and north to the baroque temples of Halebid and Belur. One more intricate than the other, but Halebid struck a more homey chord with the villagers for it was decorated for the new year, with fresh green leaves and new patterns drying in clay beside the walkways. One of the guards of the temple came to address them in English:

'Where do you come from?'

'From Bengal.'

'No, I do not know.'

'From Calcutta.'

'No, I do not know.'

'From the eastern sea.'

'No, I do not know.'

'From Benares and the Mother Ganga.'

'No, I do not know.'

'He does not know of Ganga and Varanasi.'

'Please, from where do you come?'

'From Delhi, the capital of India.'

'Ahhhh. Delhi. Where the Lord Siva lives.' The man looked at them in puzzlement, for Lord Siva was great and wealthy, with many powers, and these were dirty, old and poor people like himself.

'Not where Lord Siva lives. Where the government of India is.'

'Delhi, yes, I hear the voices on the magic box. Where Lord Siva lives.'

'No, that is the radio, and those are men speaking not gods.'

'It is great magic to have a box that speaks. He—that one—my cousin who runs the shop of drinks, he has such a magic box. I have heard the gods.'

'We also have heard the box. Those are the voices of men. Delhi is not the home of Lord Siva. He lives in Himalaya and we have seen that, too.'

'If those are not the voices of the gods then how do they come in the air and stay in the box?'

'I do not know, but I tell you they are the voices of men.'

'You see, you do not know. Why should I believe that you have seen the home of Lord Siva? You tell me they are not gods in the magic box. I am a man of schooling. I can speak English. I know. Delhi is where Lord Siva lives, and you are too poor to come from there.'

'You may speak English, but you are a fool. Delhi is not where Lord Siva lives. Delhi is where the government of India is.'

'What is India?'

'India is our country.'

'It is your country maybe, but my country is Mysore. That I know. Oh yes.'

'No, your country is India. Mysore is only a small part of India.'

'That is foolishness. Mysore goes one way to the sea, and one way to the mountains and there the world ends. Those who depart do not come back, unless they return bewitched. Like my cousin's son who came with a wife with yellow hair. Ai, how we shrieked. They went away again. My cousin's son will not return. He has been bewitched.'

'You are a silly man. Mysore is not the world. First there is your village. Then there is Mysore. Then there are all the other parts of India, then there is India. Then there are the lands beyond like Persia where the emperors came from and England of the Queen. Some of those countries are across the sea. The world does not end at Mysore.'

'You are not English?'

'No, we have told you. We come from Bengal, also a part of India.'

'You speak in riddles. I wish the English would come back to Mysore from wherever they have gone.'

'Why do you wish that?'

'Because the English do not have prohibition. Now we have prohibition, and I would like the English back.'

'You are a strange man.'

The conversation was cut short by a policeman who came to the temple compound and addressed them. They did not understand him. The guard spoke to the policeman and for a long time the villagers tried to catch what he was telling the officer about them. Then the officer grinned:

'You come from Bengal?' He spoke hesitant Bengali.

'How do you come to speak our language?'

'Once long ago I was a student in Calcutta.'

'Oh Ma, the whole of India has studied in Calcutta.'

'So I thought when I was there.'

'Your guard says there is no India and that Delhi is where Lord Siva lives.'

'That is what the people here believe.'

'Where has he learned English?'

'From the traders, when he was very young. There are many tourists here so he speaks it often.'

'Sir, what is the wealth of this land? I am used to paddy and water. How can a man farm this hard earth?'

'You see our sorrow. The earth should not be as you see it. The rains have failed for several years. Sometimes they come but it is too little. Once the lands were green and soft, now the farmers fight with the gods for every grain of rice.'

'Are there no rivers?'

'Once they were great, now they are small. When there is no water farmers become angry and there is fighting. If one builds a canal there then the other says it takes water away from him here. Then there is fighting.'

'Only fighting?'

'Some have been killed and now there are few children.'

'Why are there few children?'

'The mothers are too thin when the child grows, and then the baby dies soon after it is born. Or maybe it lives for a year until the rains fail and there is nothing to drink. Then it dies with the old ones.'

Babla asked: 'Do your villagers not keep grain and rice aside for planting? Then they could plant again.'

'Who will stop the thieves, or the ants? I and my assistant? No, for my wife must live, and if I attack the robbers then surely my family will starve. There is no life here for a widow with children.'

'Can you not get help?'

'It is all as bad or worse. Only in the hills is it better, there live the hill men and the foreign saints. Beyond the hills it is worse. Do you go south?'

'Yes, to Mysore and across the hills to see the end of India.'

'Then you will see. How do you go?'

209

'We have a special train.'

'No train goes south over the hills.'

'We have our own carriage, how else can we travel?'

'How did you come here?'

'By bus.'

'Then a bus will take you south.'

'What will happen to our train?'

'I do not know. Look, there is the dust of your bus coming. No other is expected this day.'

The villagers rushed to pack away the remains of the picnic and then hailed the bus. The driver spoke rapidly to them but they did not understand. The policeman translated:

'He says your train is in Mysore where you are to unpack it. Then you must go on by bus. The train will go to Madras and you will meet it again.'

'Must we take everything with us?'

'Do you wish to leave it for the gondas?'

'When will we come to Mysore?'

'He will get you there by morning.'

'Thank you. Good-bye.'

'May you come back safely to Calcutta.'

'May you have good rains.'

'That would be a blessing from Lakshmi-ma herself.'

Reena was the last to board the bus.

'What curse are you muttering now, Reena?'

'Do you not like the bus?'

'Is there a tale to tell?'

'Hush. I was saying that here I am in a dry desert too far from the village to be of use to anyone and I am counting myself lucky in my life.'

'Ah, but that is because you have seen Delhi where Lord Siva lives.'

They were off, leaving the guard and the policeman saluting in the dust.

'What did they mean when they said they came from Bengal, and that Lord Siva lives in Himalaya not in Delhi?'

'Lakshman, their country is far away. I do not know why they come. People who travel much speak strangely to those of us who stay in one place. Go now and fetch me something from your cousin. I am tired of talk.'

'Sir, to me they looked just like beggars.'

'Don't we all, Lakshman?'

The guard ran off down the street. The policeman was left alone. He watched the cloud of dust settling, kicked a beetle away from his feet, scratched, and stretched out on the temple balustrade to sleep.

8

A rest in Ootacamund

The pink buildings of the main square in Mysore looked like the painted illustration to one of Reena's tales. Everywhere, from arches and door-ways, windows and balconies, green leaves hung in garlands and fluttered in greeting to the new year. The square was a hullabaloo of taxis, rickshas, market sellers, fortune tellers and shouting gamblers. Even at this hour the villagers saw tribal groups dancing in small circles, whooping and giggling in tune with the city. Then they were led across the square to their carriage in the station.

'Hurry, hurry. This train goes north at noon and the carriage must be empty by then. Clean it all out. Hurry ladies. The shops are closed in Mysore so there is no reason to be slow. Come along, come along!' The guard kept up his shouts until all the villagers were busy inside the carriage. The station master came to address them but contented himself with telling the guard to be sure nothing was left in the carriage. He indicated the bus which was to be loaded, and then hurried away, anxious to be free of these charges so that he could enjoy the festival.

The sorting took a long time. Every few minutes an argument would erupt as to whose bundle this was, who had taken that parcel. At last Reena, her books tied up in one sari, her purple shawl hung around her shoulders and her bedding bundle on her head, went down the platform to the bus. She began to stow things away. Elder De went after her carrying the jar of Ashin's ashes:

'Where shall we put this, it must not be broken?'

'Leave it here. I shall find a place.'

'Yes, I must bring my other things.'

'Wait, leave room there for my bedding.'

The villagers began to fill the bus. They made several journeys back and forth cursing the difficulty of keeping track of their possessions, though those few possessions would not have filled a small suitcase. Surendra found a lone seat behind the driver and installed his rolls of maps, then spread his bedding in a neat pad on the seat. Deepaka moved her own things first and then realized that Amiya was sitting silent again.

211

She began to move the bedding for Amiya. Amiya started and looked suspiciously at Deepaka:

'What are you doing?'

'Didi, we must move everything from the carriage to the bus. The carriage does not go south.'

'This is our carriage.'

'It cannot go south. There are no tracks of this size over the hills. We go down the coast to Comorin with the southern trains. Where are your bundles and the medicine box? We must move them.'

'Uma-didi gave us this carriage. This is our carriage. We must travel in it. Not in the dirty bus.'

'No. This will be a special bus and we will keep it clean. Ah, here is your book, now where is the medicine box?'

'Give me my book. The doctor gave it to me.'

'Yes, yes, now stand up and let me roll your bedding. Where is that medicine box?'

Deepaka bent and searched, then knelt and looked under the bench. She only found a few paper parcels. These were quickly claimed by their owners, and once again the old lady scrabbled about the floor looking for the box. Suddenly she realized that Amiya was laughing. It was not an ordinary laugh, but a high, shrill cackling. Deepaka leaned back on her heels to look at Amiya:

'What is it?,

'You are a great fat frog. A fat frog hopping on the floor. And there is no medicine box. None.'

Deepaka searched the face now contorted with laughter for some sense she could recognize:

'What do you mean there is no medicine box?'

'None, none. All gone,' Amiya drew out the last words like a child mourning the last of a sweet. Rhunu came to see what was the matter.

'Where is it Amiya? We will pack it in the bus.'

'Hurry up, ladies. It is time to shift this carriage.'

'What is it, aunt?'

'Rhunu, I do not understand. Amiya will not pack her things and now I cannot find the medicine box. She tells me it is all gone.'

'Amiya, be quiet. You sound like your silly cousin.' At this insult Amiya stopped laughing and stared angrily at Rhunu:

'I am not Arundati. I am Amiya. She is a fool.'

'Good. Now where are your saris and bundles. We must get them to the bus.'

'There, in the hammock.'

'Deepaka, you check it. Now, Amiya, where is the medicine box?'

'Gone, all gone. They were my medicines.'

Again the laughter. Deepaka stared at Amiya. Rhunu frowned. Deepaka picked up the bundles and went down the platform quickly in search of

Narend. When she reached the bus it took but a moment before he was striding back to the carriage. He swung up beside his wife, who was ignoring the shrieking figure as she searched all the bunks and hammocks. Rhunu turned to Amiya and said sharply:

'See didi, here is my husband and you laugh before him with your hair hanging down.'

'Tch, tch, shame, shame,' Amiya giggled coyly as she turned away from Narend and rolled the long hair up into a bun and covered her head with her sari. When she turned back, her lips quivered with the laughter she could not well restrain.

'Now tell Narend where is the medicine box so he can carry it to the bus.'

'Stupid woman. I told you. It is gone, all gone.'

'Where is it gone then, didi?'

'It was a box of death. I gave it to the Muslim selling medicines at Hyderabad station. Let him kill his own people with it. Now there will be more prayers and no more playing with fate here.' Again the laughter. Narend took Amiya's arm:

'Come. It does not matter. We must go to the bus so that you can check that all your things are there.'

'Yes, that fat frog might have stolen from me.'

'The fat frog?'

'Deepaka, she hops like a fat frog. Hurry, hurry, we must see if she has stolen my book.' Half-running, Amiya led Narend up the platform to the bus. She patted her bundles, lay back and was at once asleep, to the complete consternation of Deepaka:

'What is it? What has she done with the medicine box? Why does she laugh?'

'She has given the box away to a street vendor in Hyderabad.'

'Then we have no medicines?'

'None.'

'What if we are ill again? Those were special medicines from the hospital? What is to be done?'

'Nothing. Do you have everything?'

'Yes, I have counted. All is here. Let us hope Amiya sleeps long.'

The bus was filled to capacity with all the villagers and their ill-packed belongings. The driver scolded them in a language they could not understand and went from one to another repacking things himself. Even so, when they moved several things fell off the first time the bus turned a corner. Soon the floor was a tumbled confusion of rolling pots and possessions and villagers trying to catch them. The bus stopped and the driver waited while order was established. Again with a jerk, a cough, and many bumps they were off.

'Where do we go?'

'To see the palace of the ruler and then to the temple of Chamundi.'

'Where do we sleep tonight?'

'In some hotel.'

'Oh Ma, real tourists we have become. A hotel! Now that is something we have not done yet.'

'Will it be clean?'

'Will there be one room for all?'

'It would be better to stay in the open, there are thieves in hotels.'

'Let us stay on the bus.'

'It will be just as safe as the carriage.'

'Strangers can steal from a sleeping man.'

'Surendra, we will not go to a hotel.'

'No.'

'Certainly not.'

There was a loud pulse of talk as the villagers discussed this new unknown. They were off the bus before the discussion had ended. During the hour that they were shown the palace the villagers tried to attend but always they were distracted by a murmured voice:

'Hotels are dirty.'

'Perhaps it will be a Bengali hotel.'

'There are no Bengalis here.'

The bus took them out of the city and up Chamundi hill. When they arrived at the temple where a massive Nandi stood carved in the rock, the discussion of the hotel quieted for a short time. The cultivators patted the stone and criticised the shape of the forelegs as not appropriate to a good ploughing bull. They moved up the hill to the goddess and her monster Mahishasura. The monster was brilliantly painted, made of mortar, and the villagers gladly turned away from him to bow before the victorious goddess.

Next, the villagers were taken to a dam in some magnificent gardens. They did not follow the guide but sat beneath a tree and watched as first one fountain and then another were illuminated. Uma and Jaydev produced the tiffin carriers and they fed happily on the scraps of the last meal. It was Amiya who noticed, shrieked, and turned away from the cameras. The other villagers then noticed that above them was a group of foreigners from the near-by hotel. They were taking pictures of the villagers as they chatted and enjoyed the evening. One by one the villagers rose on some pretence, dusted themselves off, turned away and drew together. A shout of laughter from the foreigners and a few dared to glance back.

'Oh Ma, some of them are coming to us.'

'What for?'

'Harischandra come. They will speak English.'

The strangers were close now and the villagers stared. One was a lady, her short skirt drawing all eyes, which only slowly crept up the sun dress to see her short grey hair, and the bright blue around her eyes. The two others were men, both wearing jackets and ties, both with cameras, both with grey hair. The lady spoke first:

'Do you speak English?'

Harischandra bowed shyly and murmured that he would try. Most of the villagers pressed close around him out of curiosity, but the leaders formed a protective circle around Amiya. The lady spoke again:

'You turned away when we were taking your pictures.'

'Yes, madam.'

'How much do you want for letting us take your pictures?'

'How much what, sir?'

'Listen to that. Simple eh?'

'Money, you know, like good dollars.'

'What is dollars, please?'

'Hear that?'

'Dollars, the best money, you know, coins, gold.'

'Excuse me, I do not understand.'

'No, I'll say you don't. You're the funniest beggars I've seen this whole trip. You don't hold out your hands. You don't yell at me. You don't even know what dollars are. What kind of beggars are you, anyway?'

'We are not beggars.'

'Why sure you are. Look at your clothes, and look at that little bit of food you just shared among the whole lot of you. I can tell beggars now.'

'No, we are tourists, like yourself.'

'Tourists. Did you hear that? He says they are tourists just like us.'

'What do you mean you are tourists?'

'We come from Bengal. We travel around India to see the great cities and the places of the gods.'

'Oh, you are pilgrims. Oh, yeah, well that makes it a bit different.'

'No, we are not pilgrims if you think we go only to worship. We have been seeing many things, great farms, industries and many schools. We are tourists.'

'Well how does a bunch of beggars like you get to be tourists? Find a pot of gold or something?'

'No, it is a gift.' Slowly, with great care, Harischandra told their story. While he did so the villagers had a chance to examine the three in detail. Some even dared to touch the bright cloth of the lady's dress, wondering that she pulled away from them in fear. When Harischandra finished, one of the men spoke:

'Well that beats anything I've heard about in this weird country. A rich lady giving all her money so that some simple farmers can go around and look at factories and schools and temples. How many rich folks back home would do that? None, eh? Well, sir, you and your friends here should forgive us for calling you beggars. We are getting kind of used to being asked for money by beggars when we take their pictures.'

'They bother us, too, even though we have no cameras.'

'Beggars ask you for money?'

'They think we must be rich if we can travel. And it is true we are richer than many.'

'You mean beggars bother Indians, too, not just foreign tourists?'

'Of course. There are beggars everywhere and there are Indians everywhere, but there are few foreign tourists. They would not live if they only begged from you.'

'Well I never.'

'Now. Look. Why don't you all come up on the terrace there where our group is waiting for us and have food with us. Then there will be two groups of tourists making world friendship, eh? Not just some farmers making friends with other Indians.'

'But we could not come into the hotel.'

'Of course you could. You come as my guests. The hotel is for tourists, so we will all be tourists together. Come there, little lady, you look too old to walk up those steps.'

'I have walked around India.'

'Hey, she speaks English too.'

'Only a little.'

'Where did you learn to speak English?'

'From the English traders and missionaries who were up the river when I was a child.'

'You mean when you were a colony.'

'A colony?'

'You know, when England owned India.'

'England never owned India.'

'Oh. Sorry. Well, when the English were still here.'

'Yes.'

'Well, you tell your friends to come on up with us and let us give them a feast so that all our friends can hear this story about the wonderful rich lady who paid for your trip.' The obvious good will and good humour of the strangers was infectious. When Harischandra told the others what had been suggested, the villagers were eager, and it was the ones who normally led who shrank back. At last the majority won and moved off with the three foreigners. Reena urged the others to follow:

'We must be sure no harm comes to them. They do not understand.' After a short walk the two groups met on the terrace of the hotel. The villagers cringed at the bright lights, the chandeliers, the carpets, and most of all from the eyes of the elegant crowd. At once a number of waiters and a man dressed in a black suit came towards them speaking strange words whose meaning was clear. The villagers would have obeyed, but one of the two men addressed the waiters sternly:

'Now just a minute. These are my guests. I want lots of food, fruit, rice, whatever they will eat, and I want lots of chairs. These people are very special tourists and they have a wonderful story to tell. Now all of you from our group gather round here and listen. You won't ever hear anything so fantastic again, believe me.'

After a moment of embarrassment the foreigners did assemble and sit down in a semi-circle around the frightened villagers. After a moment the Bengalis sat on the carpet.

'Here, don't you want chairs?'

'No, sir, they hurt our legs.'

'Well, sitting like that hurts my legs.'

'Yes, I understand.'

Surendra pulled out a biri but at once several foreigners offered him their strange white cigarettes. He took one, bowed in thanks and offered his biri to the foreigner, who accepted it graciously. The two men then smoked slowly, holding out the strange tobacco from time to time to look at it, smiling across at each other hesitantly. The host pulled Harischandra forward, and beckoned Reena to join him. She did so reluctantly.

'Do any of the rest of you speak English?'

'Only a little.'

'Well, let's hear that story again and don't leave anything out.'

Harischandra began softly and was told to speak up. Gradually the solemn attention of the foreigners and Reena's interruptions and cues overcame his shyness and he told the tale with a richness almost worthy of Reena herself. The audience was wide-eyed and tired with listening, and the speakers spent. When Harischandra concluded by saying that then they had come to Mysore, the foreigners clapped and clapped. The host pounded Harischandra and Elder De and Surandra on the back in turn. Deepaka found that she was weeping.

'Isn't that the greatest thing? Now in our country any group of people who looked like these people and tried to go around would be rounded up by the police. But here they are taken on tours of factories, shown into the libraries of universities, and given real first-class treatment at all the places. They say the East has a lot to teach the West, but this really is the best. I never heard anything like it.'

'You must understand us. We also never thought that foreigners would ask us to be their guests in a hotel, just to hear our story. We thought foreigners were all dirty and unmannered.'

'You did?'

'Yes. You see we do not understand why you take our pictures when we are worshipping in temples, or eating, which to us are very private things to do. We do not know if you take pictures of your own people when they are at prayer. To us many things are strange.'

'We take pictures in order to show the folks back home what we see over here, we don't mean to offend you. Is that why you turned your backs?'

'Yes.'

'Then we apologize. To us eating is like a party, we do it together. Why is that lady crying?'

'Ah. That is Deepaka. She is happy I think. She has been kind to the foreign children who wander our country, and we told her she was wrong. Now I think she cries because we all see that you are good.'

'She was kind to hippies, you mean?'

'Hippies?'

'The long-haired kids that go around in dirty clothes and sing and stuff.'

'Yes.'

'Well she is better than I am. I have no time for hippies myself.'

'Sometimes they are lonely, or sick, or in need of their mothers, and Deepaka sees this and tells us. Few are as good as she.'

'Yeah, well I can see that any foreign kid here might need help, but it beats me how they can behave like that.'

'Many are taking the dreaming drugs.'

'Pot? Sure. They'd be in jail in our country if they were caught. Here they can get it cheap.'

'Is that why they come?'

'Not just that. A lot of them want more than what we offer them at home. You know kids, they want to do better than everyone else and be wiser faster. I guess we all do sometime. Now they come here because they think India is a country of saints, and because they think you will let them get away with more than we would, and because all the other kids are doing it too.'

'India is not a country of saints.'

'It must be to put up with the way you live.'

'Why do you come?'

'Boredom at home, I guess. We want to see something new, do something different, escape for a little while from what we know.'

'So about the same as the hippies?'

'Maybe, though the saints I see are the ones like your rich lady who give the money and do something, not these dirty types wandering around half-naked.'

'Some of those that you see are false, few are true holy men. The real ones you do not see because they are alone somewhere, or are scholars studying, or like our Uma-didi, they are only important to one village.'

Near the villagers some of the foreigners were standing looking at two tables laden with fruit, sweets and hot titbits. The host drew the villagers forward with many kind words, and at last, very shyly, the villagers ate a pinch of this, a handful of that, a slice from here, a sweet from there. The foreigners carefully watched how they ate and then tried the food, as gingerly as the Bengalis had done, urging one another on to more daring. Soon the trays were empty, even the fruit had been pressed upon the villagers, who tied it up in their shawls and saris for another day. The foreigners scattered suddenly and the villagers wondered if they were now to go without farewells. Elder De stood forth and declaimed a magnificent speech, the Bengali lilting and echoing like soft music in the large room. Harischandra translated uneasily:

'He says he is the elder of our village. He is sorry he cannot speak to you in your language. He says you should be our guests, for you are in our country, but you have shown us how the great ones give hospitality to the humble. He says if you would come to our village we could give you a real feast, too hot for you to eat, but you would have to sit on mats and sleep under our thatch so perhaps it is better that you do not come. He says we have learned to look at foreigners as good and ordinary people, not to be feared. He hopes you have learned to look on Indians as not beggars. We are proud to be tourists, and proud to have shared your food. But we are old. We are tired. We must sleep. The blessings of our gods be on you all. He thanks you for all of us.'

Rhunu murmured to Narend: 'Look, they are weeping. What is it? Why do they cry?'

'Have we offended you? Why do you weep?'

'It is so beautiful.'

'It is just like Thanksgiving at home.'

The villagers, uncomprehending, turned to go. They were suddenly engulfed by the foreigners, embraced, kissed, their hands shaken, their backs thumped. After a moment the villagers fled, but not before each had been pressed with some gift—a pen, a scarf, some money, a wrapped parcel. By the time they reached the bus they were chatting incessantly over these strange gifts, wondering what they were, urging the others forward to the light of the bus. Back and forth the gifts were compared and touched. Again and again there was surprise that there had been money concealed in the gift. The villagers were astonished, then ashamed.

'Why give us money, we said we are not beggars?'

'So much, here are twenty rupees. Who can give so much?'

'We must take it back. They have erred. They could not mean to give so much.'

'Think a moment. They did intend it, for it was done secretly to not offend. See they have even pushed a bill into Amiya's hand though she has not noticed.'

'Another twenty rupees.'

'This must be wrong. It feels like thievery to me.'

'Fools. Can you not see? They had no other way to help us. There is no other way for them to show the friendship they feel. Do you not remember the tales of travellers who were showered with gifts by strangers whom they saw but once?'

'Maybe you are right, Reena, but why money? Money is for beggars.'

'Do you carry gifts for all the world in your bundles? Recall that they also travel far, what can they give but money?'

'They have given Deepaka a sweater. Why do you not put it on?'

'It is so soft. It is for a rich woman's skin, not for mine.'

'Deepaka, it is even white, you need have no shame.'

'Perhaps it has been worn by the foreigner.'

'Arundati, you would take the pleasure out of the bed of flowers if you could. Pay no attention to her, Deepaka. See there are paper things hanging from the buttons as in the shops. It cannot have been worn.'

'No, I believe not. It still smells of the perfumes of a shop.'

'Then put it on and let us see you.'

'There, Deepaka, you are a queen. Is it warm?'

'Yes, very.'

'Then bless the woman who gave it.'

'Yes, bless them all. I have not seen so much money given since the English traders said good-bye.'

The excited babble quieted and the villagers sat turning over their gifts and examining the money. For many weeks to come the gifts of the foreigners would be a frequent topic of conversation, and for most of the villagers the extra money meant that a small souvenir reminder of their adventures could be bought. Rhunu turned to Amiya, who had sat with eyes closed throughout the time in the hotel. Rhunu spoke gently:

'Amiya, you ought to put the money away where it will be safe.'

'Money? I have no money. Only a few jewels given me by my father. No one would sell them for me, they will not sell them for her. There is no money.'

Rhunu bent towards Amiya to hear better and realized that the old woman was far away. She took the crumpled note out of the wrinkled hand and tucked it into Amiya's purse at her belt.

When the bus lumbered to a stop the driver waved them out. The sleepy villagers would have gone with nothing, but he shouted that they must take their belongings and began throwing down the parcels. The scramble which followed wakened Amiya enough to make her carry her bedding down to the dirt with the others. The driver started the bus but Deepaka mounted again. She removed the picture of Uma Sen and the ashes of Ashin. Then the bus was away and the villagers were alone, coughing, their possessions around them. There was no light in the dark street. The shutters were drawn and the doors of the houses barred from within. A stray dog came skulking down the lane and sniffed at them, but ran on quickly. Gradually the villagers became aware that they were alone and no one was greeting them. Panic mounted quickly. Only when shutters above them were thrown open and a wakened sleeper shouted at them did they realize that they had been crying out. Surendra looked at Narend, who shrugged his shoulders and looked at Elder De. The officious elder was slumped on the cold ground, asleep. Harischandra turned to the stranger who still scolded them from the balcony and called up in English.

'Sir, where is the hotel?'

The man paused, spoke again in a rush and banged his shutters closed. The villagers sat down and began to argue as to what was to be done. Amiya was asleep, as were many others. Then the doors at the bottom of the house of the shouter opened uneasily. The sleeper held a lantern out and examined them slowly. He emerged, naked to the waist, clutching his pyjamas, but holding the lantern steady and high. First he waved it over the huddled assembly, then he brought it close and looked first into Narend's and then Surendra's face. Again he moved to the assembly and stood a long time, his lips moving as he looked from one to another. Surendra realized he was counting and said as much to Narend. The man turned to them and asked something which they understood to mean Bengali.

'*Han. Han-ji, Bengali, Bengali,*' they repeated anxiously.

The stranger nodded, finished his counting, and then looked at the two men again. He turned his back on them, crossed the street away from his house and banged a large door with his foot. A dog barked. The man banged again and shouted. The dog replied. The man put down the lantern, hitched his pyjamas and banged the door with both fists. Then he shouted so piercingly that even Elder De shook himself awake. There was an angry mutter from behind the door. Another harangue from the stranger. The door opened. A small man looked out. The stranger held his lantern high and showed him the villagers, speaking the while at a pace which the small man was clearly having difficulty following. The little occupant of the house mumbled and closed the door. The stranger turned back to Narend and Surendra and smiled, sat down against the door and warmed his nakedness with his lantern. At last, after Arundati had nearly stampeded them all by asking if they had been captured by bhuts, there was a thump. The stranger rose. The door opened. Holding it was a man as tall as Narend, his skin deep black. Around his hips a brilliant orange lungi, the skirt of the men of the south, was draped elegantly. He smiled at the villagers, bowed, and like a dancer beckoned with his torso that they come in. The stranger held the lantern high so that they could see into the dim courtyard beyond. No one made a move. The lantern lit the body of the dark man with mystery. The southerner bowed. The stranger yelled. The villagers recoiled.

Harischandra asked 'Where is the hotel?'

Both townsmen smiled and pointed into the courtyard. Narend and Surendra explained to the others that this must be the hotel. No one moved. They tried again. The two strangers stood grinning. At last they stood, gathered their bundles, and crowded to look in at the door. They could see only shadows, an unfriendly dog, a wooden staircase rising abruptly just inside the door. They drew back. Elder De spoke firmly.

'Come, Babla, we are men of the world and true travellers. Let us show these country folk how to behave in a hotel.' The two confirmed cowards crossed the threshold. They clutched all that they could close to them and gave the smiling proprietor a wide berth. Jaydev and Uma followed, and behind the others pressed, drawing courage from sharing the common doom. At last Surendra and Narend half-dragged Amiya and Arundati in across the door, and the barrier slammed closed behind them. The shouting stranger had gone. With magnificent grace the hotel keeper eased his way through the crowd and disappeared through a small doorway. There were shouts, protests, more shouting. He was waking the servants. The man rippled back again, smiled and pointed to the steps, urging them to climb. A servant emerged with three lanterns, and handed one each to Narend and Surendra. Then the proprietor led the way up.

The stairs were constructed of remnants of lumber so that no two were the same shape, length or height. Perhaps the carpenter had suffered from an eye ailment, for each step had found an angle unique to itself among its fellows. The supports defied the old iron nails which struggled to hold wood to wood and step to step. In some places old ropes bound the staircase to iron hooks placed in the wall for some other purpose. The ropes were frayed and with each step the staircase shook, swayed and sang. Despite the proprietor's efforts, the effect was not enticing. Narend told the villagers to leave the bundles below to be fetched afterwards, and to climb now in the light. Elder De made no move. It was Babla who first set foot on the stairs.

'Why should we sleep above ground? I am not a bird, nor a night cat like that one above. I am just an old cultivator in search of my fate. Oh Ma. Oh Ma.' He climbed as Arundati shrieked without pause below. Reena was behind him urging him to go faster.

'Man, I have always fancied myself to be an angel, now we shall both fly.'

'Ai, and if we make it to the top I shall tell you you have always looked like one, too.'

'Hold on to the wood, not the rope, dolt.'

Jaydev followed, leading Uma, and they mounted without pausing to look at the strain on the ropes. Reena was hopping at the top and the proprietor was trying to quiet her. Babla was grinning. In a rush, the villagers overcame their fears and began to climb, Surendra in their midst holding his lantern high. Narend waited below and watched as they all made the ascent. Rhunu led Amiya. Deepaka crawled up, as did many others. When the staircase was empty, Narend mounted carrying the first load of bedding. He hung his lantern on a hook half-way up and continued to the top in darkness. He was on his tenth trip when Surendra came and joined him. At last the courtyard was cleared of bundles. They had been given seven rooms where there were beds and doors which locked. Narend guarded the pile of bundles while Surendra called the others. At once the thunder of the bare feet on old boards set the balcony shaking. Narend watched as clouds of dust and insects fell down from the roof and out of the cracks in the boards. When the last parcels were gone, a caravan of servants came running up the stairs as if they had been made of marble. Each one carried a bucket of steaming water. Not a drop spilled. The proprietor appeared in the halo of his light and returned below with the servants.

'Lord husband, lord husband, where are you?'

'Here by the stair. I come.'

'We are in the third room. We have six rope beds so there is room only to climb across the end. There is hot water for washing.'

'I cannot see. Who is with us?'

'Amiya and Deepaka, Reena and Harischandra. He sleeps by the window, and you are to sleep by the door.'

'Do they all sleep?'

'Only Amiya sleeps. We are all awake.'

'Do you think it is safe, Narend?'

'Yes, but for the stair.'

'Will there be thieves?'

'No, the courtyard is guarded.'

'It is good that we come in the dark. We cannot see the dirt.'

'Do not wake Amiya.'

'She has slept all the day. Will she sleep all night?'

'Let us hope so.'

'Have you all bathed?'

'Yes.'

'I shall wash my feet as well.'

'What sort of a cultivator is that who speaks?'

'Hush, Reena.'

'Have you bolted the door?'

'Any who pass it must brush my legs, the bed is too short.'

'Do not pull them up then.'

'Sleep in peace.'

No one passing in the corridor would have known that few of the villagers slept. Occasionally someone would whisper about the smell, or the lack of air, or the strange habit of sleeping on beds. By dawn even Arundati had fallen into restless slumber, twitching and whispering with her dreams. A gong was struck and the villagers rose to the noise of running feet and shouting along the corridor. They searched to see if their bundles had been disturbed and reassured, dared to open the doors. The servants were cleaning and shouting. When the Bengalis looked out they hallooed a greeting and thundered down the steps. The villagers carefully rolled up their own bedding and retrieved that of the hotel, which they had all suspiciously stowed under the beds. Then the women combed their hair and tried to send the men in search of food, but Jaydev said he would not descend the stairs more than once, not even for her. There came another thunderous ascent of the stairs and the servants

appeared bringing a feast and fresh banana leaves to act as talis. The food
was strange but welcome. For the first time the villagers ate searing-hot
coconut gruel and dipped the crisp iddlis in it. When they had finished
the proprietor appeared and pointed to a gaily painted bus waiting in the
street. The villagers began their careful descent. It was slowed by their
curiosity for the sights offered by the hotel. Each villager had time to
notice the cockroaches running along the wall, the chickens feeding
under the balcony, and the dark, oily cave which was the kitchen. Elder
De was among the last to appear from his room, having taken the time
to rearrange each of his small parcels. The proprietor was clearly relieved
by the sight of the blue jacket flapping over the shirt and dhoti. Elder De
stopped before him, confused by the effusive greeting of the southerner,
and once again rearranged his parcels. The proprietor handed him a sheet
of paper. Each of the parcels was put down. Then Elder De tried to read
it at arm's length, then against his glasses. Finally he resorted to removing
his spectacles and cleaning them. He tried again. The proprietor, who
lounged sinuously against a pillar of the balcony, thought this magnificent
theatre and applauded as he laughed. Elder De looked at him solemnly,
picked up his parcels again, and, edging round the proprietor, scuttled
down the stairs squeaking for help. The proprietor followed closely and
jumped from the last stair, setting the staircase swinging. Surendra and
Harischandra came into the courtyard from the bus and Elder De gave
them the strange paper. Surendra tried and failed. The proprietor was
now sitting on the ground rocking with laughter at the comic ability of
these visitors. Harischandra took it:

'It is the bill for our rooms and the food. I cannot read the words, but
the numbers say that it is a total of 61.20 rupees for all of us.'

'That is very much.'

'No, it is little. Quickly, get the money and let us be gone.'

Surendra produced the notes, added five, which he took over and thrust
into a hand in the darkness of the kitchen, and gave the rest to the
proprietor. With a flourish the man discovered a pen hidden in a hole in
the wall just for that purpose, and signed the bill. Surendra did not
understand but Harischandra explained that this meant that the man
agreed they had paid it properly. They boarded the bus and the hotelkeeper
gesticulated and laughed with their bus driver. At last they were away,
and soon were moving slowly through the festival crowds of the happy
city. By mid-morning they were on the dusty road going straight, as far
as they could see, towards a line of blue hills. The country was brown
after the winter, little whirlwinds of dust here and there telling the
villagers how parched the fields were. Sometimes they passed another
vehicle coming away from the hills, but they were lonely travellers that
morning. Deepaka sang the morning prayers and then all of them joined
in song after song. Even Amiya beat time on the window frame. She did
not speak until the bus began to slow. Then she said:

'It is good that we leave school now, before the Muslims come to take us. I am glad we go home to my father's village.' And she began a gay song of harvest and happiness. Only Narend noted that Rhunu was pale with strain. The bus stopped by the side of the road and the driver opened the door to a man and his daughter, both fancily dressed, both carrying baskets of flowers. The driver shouted and the man argued until at last the driver waved him aboard. The two strangers crouched on the floor in front, watching that their flowers did not spill. They looked at the villagers curiously, but were met with only silence and suspicious glances. The driver talked with the man for a while and Jaydev leaned forward and offered the stranger a biri. This was accepted. The girl bent and gave Uma a red flower. The silence eased and once again the villagers sang and talked of the hotel. When they reached the next village the driver stopped near a temple where a crowd was gathering. Before the flower sellers could go, Amiya rose and strode forward. She bent and plucked a blossom from the basket, turned back to her seat, and shouted:

'All the schoolgirls will wear flowers in their hair.' She pushed the flower into her untidy mass of grey hair and sat down, unaware of the shock and fear which now rippled from one end of the bus to the other.

As they left the village the country began to change, becoming more rolling and less bare. By noon they were climbing steadily, the forest thick and lush around them. It was a forest different from any they knew in Bengal, for here vines and ferns and flowering creepers made the lower trunks a mass of colour, while high above the branches cut off the light. The bus crawled along in a green mist. At mid-afternoon the driver turned and shouted something back to them. The bus came up, round a bend, and was in the town of Ootacamund. The houses, each withdrawn in its own large garden, were set in a semicircle along the curve of the hill. Below in the cup of the valley was the town square. The driver pulled the bus to a halt and leaned on the horn for some long minutes. The villagers emerged slowly into the mountain air, returning to the bus several times for their bundles. Running across the square towards them came a fat little person, a briefcase in one hand and an umbrella in the other. He started talking in Bengali when he was still fifty paces from them:

'Welcome, welcome. You will be tired, and hungry for there is no good food on the plains. The bus was terrible? Yes, terrible, terrible. Never mind, all is peaceful here, we will restore your health. Oh Yes, Ooty is the best medicine. You will have no need of doctors, the air and the quiet mend everything. Now how many are you? Let me see? Thirty perhaps? That many we can lodge with us, good Bengali cooking and the whole day Tagore songs, no extra charge. My wife and daughters sing better than all other families in Ooty. You will be lulled to sleep by their songs, you will arise eager for the day with their songs. Never will you be far from their songs. Oh Ma. Now you will stay a week at least, two would be better, yes?'

The villagers listened to him come, too bewildered to laugh, too amused to be frightened. When he came close to them he put down his briefcase, retrieved from it a pair of exceedingly thick glasses and peered out at them:

'But what is this? These are beggars. There was talk in the railway station of Bengali tourists. Where are the Bengali tourists? Here, you driver, when do we give rides for beggars to Ooty? Where is your load of tourists? I am an honest hotel keeper, I have come to welcome them and give them the comfort of my lodgings. I was told they speak the best of all languages, my own. Ah, we would make poetry together, of the green and the gold and the river. We would speak of the wise men of our land. Where are they? Where are they?'

'We are here, the beggars you see before you. The bus driver speaks no Bengali. We are the tourists from Bengal.'

'You are the tourists? You cannot be, cannot be.'

'Has the south taught you to disbelieve in miracles? Truly it is a miracle, but we are tourists.'

'Oh Ma, oh Ma, what has befallen me. How will I find the dowry for my eldest daughter? How will I find the dowry for my second daughter? How will I find any dowry for my ugly daughters? I have a bad fate written on my forehead to see before me beggars who claim to be tourists. Oh Ma, oh Ma.'

'Does the station master not come?'

'No, he cannot come. He moves in a roll chair. There is only one train each day which goes from Ooty. If you wish to speak with him you must go there, to that building where he sits.'

'Did he send you to us?'

'No, he sends no one. I heard him speak with the clerk that there were many Bengali tourists coming with the bus, so I hurried to find them and welcome them to my hotel. It is good to see those who come from the river of one's youth when one is far from home. I know even a great sage who always laughs like a child when he can eat sandesh, though the southerners think that he eats only dried grain. But my heart is broken. You do not cheer me, for you say there are no tourists with you. To my eyes it is obvious that you have not even five rupees among you.'

'How much is your hotel?'

'Oh, it is very cheap, very, very cheap. Only one rupee fifty per person per night.'

'Does the air cost so much? We paid only one rupee in the city of Mysore.'

'Oh Ma, what is a poor man with bad fate and nothing but four ugly daughters to do? With one rupee I would starve, I tell you, starve,' and he smacked his fat belly to emphasize his anxiety.

'We shall see what the station master has arranged, for as you say we have few rupees and they are not to be paid into the dowries of your daughters.'

'Oh Ma. But let us talk of the river. Do you come from the river?'

'Yes.'

Elder De and Surendra moved into the dim station while the Bengalis wallowed in nostalgia with the hotel keeper. At the other side of the hall a door was ajar and through it Surendra saw a man sitting in a wicker chair with wheels on either side. He beckoned to Surendra and seemed eager that the villagers come to him. This they did, hesitantly, bowing at the entrance to his office. Beside him another man was standing. Elder De jumped to realize that this was a foreigner, burnt brown by many years in the sun, but with deep blue eyes and red hair. He wore a black dress, a round stiff collar at his neck. Surendra wondered what kind of railway official he might be. Surely there were no foreigners working for the railways, but why should the man wear such strange clothes if he was not in the service of some company which kept its servants in uniform?

'He says he welcomes you with all his heart. Mr De in Delhi is his very good friend. He has looked forward to your coming since the first letter. He is very sorry that you have lost your helper to death. He hopes your sorrows have not wearied you. It was first planned that you would not stay at all, but since you have had to flee the troubles in Hyderabad you have gained time so he urges you to stay at least two days.' Surendra stared as the stranger translated the unfamiliar language into beautiful, perfect Bengali. Elder De shifted nervously from foot to foot. He could not bring himself to look at this stranger who spoke his language so exquisitely. The station master watched with growing amusement and said something to the man in black which caused him to smile. He spoke again:

'The station master says I should tell you I am not a demon but a priest. I am in charge of the hostel for priests and nuns and workers who come here to rest. You are to stay in my hostel these nights.'

'There is a Bengali outside who wants us to go to his hotel.'

'Sengupta? There is room in his hotel for no more than twenty and he would ask money which you should not have to pay.'

'You will not ask for money?'

'There is no need.'

'Where does the food come from?'

'We grow much of it. Do not worry. You will not be abused.'

The station master spoke again.

'He asks if you have messages to send to Mr De? He says you look very tired, and should rest.'

Elder De whispered to Surendra, bowed and went away to the villagers. Surendra squatted on the floor, grinned and began to speak:

'Elder De prepares them for the shock that we stay in the house of a foreign priest.'

'Will there be trouble?'

'No, though many will be unwilling to come at first. Perhaps one woman will give trouble, but she is ill and her fears are greater than when she is well.'

'Should we get a doctor?'

'No doctor can help her. It is not a sickness of the body.'

'You speak as though she is possessed, brother?'

'Arre. I am a simple man. I have seen many buffalo and many bullocks grow old and die. I have seen good harvests and bad. Never have I seen anyone possessed. I have seen some lazy girls pretend to be, but they only wished to get free of their mothers-in-law. I have seen the poor idiot boy who writhes on the ground in the pains of stupidity. Never have I seen any possessed.'

'What ails the woman?'

'She grieves for Ashin and for her skills of healing which could not save him. She once wished to be educated and not a village woman, and this journey shows her that both ways are hard. She worries that perhaps all is written on the forehead after all, though she has long said it untrue.'

'You sound like a teller of fortunes.'

'I am Surendra, a cultivator of Uma Sen's village.' The two men acknowledged this formal introduction.

'What is it that you wish to ask?'

'Now is not the time, but may I return with my map and mark where next we go and in what places we shall stay? The station master of Hyderabad did not tell us that we would leave the train in Mysore so we are burdened. Can you show me what lies ahead so that I can make better plans?'

'Come tomorrow in the morning. Now you must bathe and eat.' The station master's kindness, though conveyed by another, was obvious as he motioned Surendra to leave with the priest. The two found that they were of equal height and stride as they went out of the station. Surendra was surprised that the stranger walked so silently. They found the villagers sitting questioning Mr Sengupta. When they saw Surendra, they rose and gathered their bundles.

Jaydev called, 'Surendra, we go now to sleep in the house of a foreign priest. Must we bow before his temple? He does not look as if he eats well and I am hungry.'

'The same could be said of you, my friend. The food is good in the hostel and there is enough. Come let us go, the sisters wait to greet you.'

Jaydev and the others gaped to hear the priest speak Bengali and watched as he bent, picked up a bundle and two of the tiffin carriers, and began to move across the square to the forest. The hotel keeper looked not at all disappointed that the villagers were going elsewhere, but accompanied them, asking about the crops, the festivals and the evening promenade as he remembered it. The villagers answered him eagerly, glad to talk about home, but they told nothing of themselves. The procession crossed the square and followed the priest between small houses with carefully tended gardens and on up a woodland path. They thought they were out of the town, but they had entered the grounds of the church and almost before they realized that the forest was becoming darker they stood in a bright compound where several nuns were sweeping and tending the flower beds. Some of the nuns were foreign, some Indian, and they all shared the menial work. The villagers stared and went no further. The priest went through a far gate and called to them. Arundati edged past her companions until she stood at the front of the group. She looked only for a moment at the nuns. Smiling as the others had never seen her smile, she turned back and said:

'Come, they are as the ladies in Benares who cared for me when I was lost. Come, we will be at ease here,' and the little waddling woman for the only time in her life led others into an unknown courtyard.

Along three sides were low white buildings, each with several doors. On the fourth side was an iron grating through which were visible other buildings, a tall one, and flower beds. As the villagers assembled in the square they stared at the neatness around them. Nowhere was there dung drying, nowhere were there tools or cooking pots stacked against the wall, and nowhere was there dust. Beneath their feet was grass, prickly and tickling. They often shifted their positions to look down at it seriously with the searching eyes of those in the habit of seeing natural mysteries. Narend and Surendra unshouldered their heavy rucksacks and stretched. Deepaka put down the heavy load of her own and Amiya's bundles. Rhunu bade Amiya to sit. Sit she did, without the grace of the woman she had once been, but with all the awkward, sudden obedience of the child she now was. She looked at her hands and chanted some singsong. Reena circled the courtyard like a newly caged beast, sniffing at everything, starting back here and there from something unknown, then going forward to learn what it was. Mitu sat against the gateway, sketching the scene. He was so in the habit that he dropped on his haunches and drew out his pad before he looked about the square. Now, sketching the others, he saw more than those who stared, and was unaware that the priest was behind him watching the swift strokes turn into villagers, their pathetic hillock of possessions, the clean courtyard, the forest in evening beyond. The priest called out to the others.:

'Take your bundles to your beds, beyond each door is a small room. In some there are two beds, in others four. You will find basins and towels. The sisters will bring hot water. Then food will come. Do any wish to eat before the sun sets?'

'Yes, please, and Amiya will eat with me.'

'Then I shall join you, Deepaka, for though the widow's rules are not to my liking, you must have help.'

'Take that corner room and food will be brought at once. The sun goes quickly in the mountains.' The priest went away and timidly the villagers explored the little houses. Gradually they sorted out the bundles and withdrew into the darkness of the sleeping cabins. Suddenly the bare light bulbs which hung from each room were illuminated and the villagers shrieked and then laughed at their own surprise. Deepaka and Reena were eating eagerly of the rice, dal and vegetables which had been brought. They kept urging Amiya to eat, but she continued to mutter at her hands, hands which were now ever fluttering, never still. When Reena finished her own meal she moved over, sat in front of Amiya and began to croon one of the songs sung to children in the river villages. She picked up a spoon and, singing, fed the grey old woman. Amiya opened her mouth, chewed and swallowed obediently and swayed a little with the old song. Her eyes followed the spoon back and forth from tali to her own mouth, and not once did she look to Reena. Deepaka grew alarmed and would have cried, but Reena bade her to block the door so that the others might not see. Deepaka did so and began the slow cadences of the evening puja. From around the courtyard the others emerged, refreshed, silhouetted by the lights behind them. They joined in the song and sat content when it was done. Then the soft swish and chink of the nuns and their keys drew all eyes to the gate where the nuns brought their food. Uma asked one sister if the priest would return and the sister shook her head, smiling. After the meal and after cleaning the talis, the villagers gathered and began to talk of the days past. At first the talk ranged over things seen and visited, hovered a moment around the foreigners and the gifts of money, then moved on to the things ahead. There was silence. Arundati spoke for them all, asking:

'What has changed Amiya? Why does she act like a child?'

'Often she is sharp, and has seen and heard all that we say.'

'Then be careful she may hear now.'

'No, she sleeps.'

'I fear a bhut has taken away her mind.'

'Silly woman.'

'Do not curse her. I fear that something strange has befallen Amiya.'

'How can she have been cursed? She has always been with us. No spirit or witch could have attacked her.'

'Or it could have attacked all and we will follow the same way.'

'Hush, do not speak of things in darkness.'

'Do you think it so?'

'No, Amiya has always been the strongest of all, she will soon be scolding again. She mourns for Ashin and the children who died before him.'

'When we mourn we do not act like schoolgirls and put flowers in our hair.'

'You are right.'

'There is a curse upon her.'

'She brought it upon herself by meddling with the Jaipur wife.'

'Aye, but so did we all, for we spoke against the duty to the parents.'

'Only Amiya and Ashin spoke of ways not to have children.'

'And one is dead and the other . . .?' There was silence.

'Mad. Yes, I shall say it. We have seen the beasts who drool and attack their masters. You have seen my boy when he writhes and knows nothing of what he does. Amiya is the same, she knows no longer what she does. I do not know if it is sickness or curse, but I know that as with my boy we must care for her carefully.' The villagers looked at Babla in horror. Arundati whispered:

'When they do not know what they do they can harm others. My grandson has cut us with cooking knives and bears many scars he has given himself.'

The silence emphasized the embarrassment the villagers felt for the old couple, but Rhunu broke in sharply:

'With Amiya it is different. Her power was once in words, her power to hurt is also in words. Her sickness is not that of the drooling beasts, she has chased words around in her head until they no longer mean what they should mean. We can only help her by asking her to share her usual burdens and duties, they will help her grasp hold again of all that is trustworthy and helpful to her.'

'That is true, if we make her do her duty she will see that she can do it, just as a mother teaches a new bride.'

'Oh Ma, let us not be as cruel as that.'

'We have all crept away from her and Deepaka has carried her loads. We must show her we expect her to be as once she was.'

'She is not, she is accursed.'

'That you cannot say. We only know she is changed.'

'I say she is cursed and we must guard ourselves against her.'

'You will only guard yourself, for she is ours and we are among strangers. We must bring her home safely. She will lead us again.'

'No, she will never lead us. She has a twisted fate, so it was said by her husband.'

'Her husband was a cruel and selfish goat and all know it. She would have been better had he died young, but he had too little goodness to think of that.'

'Even those who have a twisted fate need our care. She is little more than a child, but when we bring children to age do we guard ourselves against them? No, and shame to think of it. She will come again to herself if we give care to attend to her sense. She does not speak foolishly all the time. These moments before sleep she spoke of the sari of the nuns of

Benares which Arundati was given. She knows where we are, but there is a pain within her which is like the pain of giving birth—she can think on nothing else for the moment.'

'But, Reena, to what does she give birth? To another curse, or a bhut?'

'Foolish one. Listen to Deepaka then, if not to me.'

'Reena is right. There is a pain within her which she cannot neglect, but her eyes see truly none the less. I sorrow to see her stripped of her pride, for there is no comfort we can give since we know not the pain. Wait and watch and do not fear her. She will never cause us injury, her training is to heal. But she is tired of being called on to care for our wounds. The wound within her is very old.'

'It is possible then to have a twisted fate and still be of worth to others?' The villagers started at the strange voice of the priest who had joined them unremarked.

'What is written on our foreheads as our fate has little to do with how we live, only with the good and bad that is put before us. How we act towards the good and bad makes the fate of the next life.'

'You are a philosopher, for I have heard many say that because all is written on the forehead what is done in this life is of no matter, and I have heard many say that what is done determines the next life, and that nothing is written. You would have both?'

'Oh Ma. of course. The chance of our birth, just as the chances of death or good marriage, or bad land, or droughts, or floods, or no sons, that must be in the hands of the gods, to whom we pray. But whether we do our duty to our parents, or live in honesty, or treat our beasts wisely, or even pray, that gives the gods the evidence on which to judge how to cast our fate for the next life.'

'So there is always a chance to improve, to gain the grace of the gods?'

'Yes, in every life, in every age. And a chance for disgrace as well.'

'Halt, Uma. You are a priest, and from over the great waters. When there were missionaries visiting the English traders they always told us there were not gods, nor fate, nor rebirth for each of us. Yet you sit with us and do not scold. Are you not of the same belief as others who wear the black skirts?'

'My name in entered in the books of the same faith, but I think the work of a man shapes his own road to the gods. You are farmers, you women are mothers of children, cooks, healers. You pray for rain, for an end to flood, for health for the children, for food in the pot, and mercy from the goddesses of pestilence. Is it not so?'

'It is so.'

'As you say.'

'To all gods.'

'I am a comforter. My work is to see that the nuns and priests stay strong in their bodies and their service, that orphans learn to laugh and grow tall, that wanderers find peace within my walls. Therefore I pray for those who come and for my own wisdom, to a God whom I must view as a giver of the graces of wisdom and of comfort. But I cannot say you are wrong to pray as you as you do, for your work is not mine. I can believe in one wise god, but I cannot say that you must as well. Perhaps I can pray that that god will grant you wisdom and comfort too, and perhaps you will pray that your gods will keep me from disease and my gardens safe from drought. It is not my charge to scold.'

'But sir, would not those across the sea be angered to hear you speak this way?'

'Perhaps some who are a little foolish might. But would not your pujaris, even some sadhus, scold you for staying with a foreign priest?'

'That depends on how much they had been paid, or how good the last meal was.'

'A money-lender's greed and a priest's hunger, both are endless.'

'Know you of no good priests?'

'One perhaps, or maybe a sadhu or two. But those of the village are ordinary fools like the rest of us.'

'Elder De, speak carefully. Even priests can curse.'

'How do you tell a good from a bad priest? Are the good sadhus the sannyasis who frighten my nuns?'

'Oh Ma, no.'

'You lock the door and keep your nuns away from those men. They are wild with dreaming drugs, and vicious from having no home. You be careful.' Reena shook her finger at the priest and he smiled:

'Some sannyasis are not wild and they do not come to frighten others. They stay alone and speak with the gods, those who pass by leave food. They are good men.'

'Or lazy ones who run away from their duties.'

'Babla, hush.'

'But a man who sits alone does no kindness for others. Does he not sit for himself alone?'

'That depends on the man. Some sit for themselves to become great spirits and powerful. Some sit to learn what to teach others. But I do not know where they find the faith to make the first step beyond this world of duties.'

'Is that a bitter wonder, brother?' The priest tried to see Harischandra's face, but could not in the dark. There was no answer and Reena spoke again:

'You tell a good priest the same way that you find a good neighbour—by what he does, and how he holds himself before your troubles. But how to tell a man's holiness, is that not a sight kept and given rarely by the gods? We have among us a woman who worships before all temples, who gives her devotion to each of the roads to the gods. Some say she will bring the wrath of all upon us, some say she brings us much blessing. But who of us can judge what the gods think of her homage? We can only see that she is a good neighbour who never turns away. If a priest is that to his fellows, then he is a good priest. If not, then no more than a bad neighbour can he be a good man. Where is the difference?'

'I do not know, mother. A priest among us is one who feels summoned to be good, but among you is he not the son of another priest?'

'It is so.'

'Then among us there is a duty we place upon ourselves, while for your priests of the village there is that which has been given by the fathers?'

'Yes, and they pass on only greed and cunning.'

'I see a difference, for we are trained to think of ourselves as examples and guardians of what is good, but for your priests they are guardians of their own heritage?'

'No, that is not right, for some try to be guardians of the village, and some are teachers who try to show us what is right.'

'Do they oppose changes in the village?'

'Oh Ma, you should have heard them screaming when the well drillers came, and they do not want the teachers from the colleges to come, but the children to be kept on the temple platform. It is not good.'

'But, Jaydev, is that so only with us, or in other villages?'

'Of course it is so with others. Did I not tell you of what I was told at the market, that the priest of the village to the north of the river's bend has driven away the young teacher by burning his thatch?'

'Oh Ma, what fools.'

'Is it the same with you? Do you priests oppose change?'

'Bad priests do, and many who know no better. I think it is because they misunderstand the duty of the priest.'

'And what is that duty?'

'To comfort our neighbours. Whether the problems are new or old, whether the sorrows are brought by change or constancy. Simply to stand in comfort steadily, for all, and no matter for whom.'

'But what man or woman is strong enough to do that? We are all reeds.'

'Only those given the gifts of the gods could stand that way. There are too many sorrows that bend us, and too few ways to find joy.'

'Then you must be blessed by Saraswati, for only she with her music could give you peace if you stood to comfort all.'

'I did not say I was one given the gift. I said that is the duty as I see it.'

'Are the Muslims to be given comfort too?'

'They have their sorrows.'

'And their babes do not sleep well on trains, is it not so, Reena?'

'What does it matter?'

'We must sleep well on these good beds. Deepaka is dreaming now though we talk of gifts from the gods.'

'I am sorry, I have kept you.' He rose and left them.

'Deepaka, come to bed. The priest goes too.'

'Ai, have I slept while he talked? Oh Ma, what a shame. My old bones fail me too often.'

'Then come and give them rest.'

'See how big the stars are, we are closer to them.'

'What was that wailing?'

'Only a dog in the forest.'

'Sleep, dog, we old ones startle to your call.'

'Simple one, southern dogs do not understand Bengali.'

'How can you tell? Now it is quiet.'

'Oh Ma, how they will laugh in the village when I tell them that Deepaka has started talking to forest dogs.'

'No more than when she tells them you had not enough sense to go to bed in deepest night.'

'Ah, wife, I feel young again. Had I a flute I would play it. This is not a night for sleeping, but for talk and music and good dreams.'

'Then dream at least in silence so that those of us with sense can sleep as well.'

'Woman you are not a true Bengali, you have no feeling for beauty,'

'Hush. Argue in the dawn, not now.'

'Good-night, good-night. Even in the house of a sad foreigner we are at peace. Uma-didi sent us a great gift.'

'Aye, but a tiring one.'

Amiya had watched Reena and Deepaka leave her:

'They think I sleep and it is better so. Maybe they will leave me alone. Always I must eat, come, carry bundles, help us here, heal this one, show that one how, tell us what to do. Ai, I am tired. Reena feeds me like a baby and it is easily done. My hands do not stay still. Strange, Surendra saw on the train, after we broke the windows. No longer are they healing hands. No, they never were, never were. It is too late to learn, always too late. Ai, so many have died that I wished to heal. Ashin, the boy babe, my own sons, so many, so many. One day the girl in Jaipur will heal. She will change all this stupidity of marrying girls off. No, fool, that is not true. She will be caught by her mother-in-law and caged as I was, and she will bear idiot after idiot to please the family down all the generations. It is written. It is always written. Why, why does it hurt so? I feel the writing hurting. Reena does not. No, but Reena reads, Reena does not feel the hurting. Maybe she does, her eyes have seen much, too. No, she has not tried to heal the others as I have. She has not wronged the gods. I am as a wife who has slept with her husband's brothers in secret—given a gift I have misused it and blasphemed. Ai, ai. It hurts so always to think. Even the fool Arundati thinks. They talk now of me and if they should fear me. No more, no more. My doctoring of fates is done. There is no need to fear those who cannot heal. Perhaps I should go out and tell them? No, no, they would fear the more. Poor children, poor children, playing their way to death, and always with the eyes of all the others upon them. Always the eyes, and the hands that cannot help. Always the eyes asking me. Always the hands. Too late, too late. Poor, poor children.' At last Amiya fell into the clutches of her terrible dreams.

With the morning the nuns brought more hot water and the women had a happy time washing all the clothing and bedding and spreading it out on the sharp grass. Some of the men had gone with Surendra to speak with the station master, Mr Sengupta, translating for them. The nuns took the women out, first showing them the convent, the church and rest hostel, then the orphanage, and at last the rest of the town. Before going they had put away all their possessions, so when Mitu returned to the courtyard he found it empty. He searched his own bundles, found the old clay, moistened it and tried to knead it. He sat bent forward, his long legs before him, his white head watching his hands work the clay between his legs. After a long time he tried to shape it, but it crumbled and would not obey his fingers. The priest was watching.

'It is not good clay. I have some better. Would you try it?'

'If it is to spare.'

'I will bring it.'

Mitu continued working the clay. When he saw that indeed the priest was bringing him well-prepared wet clay, he pushed his own lump aside and reached up eagerly: 'Are you, too, a potter? How comes it that a priest has clay, moist, to hand?'

'There is a kiln and a little school back there. Sometimes the potter tries to show me, but my hands are not skilled.'

'I thank you. It is many weeks since I had clay in my fingers.'

'But you draw. I watched you last night.'

'It is not the same, though both keep my hands happier than emptiness.'

'What do you draw?'

'What we see, what we do, how the others look as we travel. Sometimes, the scenes of the village which the others wish to remember.'

'May I see?'

'They are not good. You will have seen many better.'

'I would like to see.'

'A moment.' Mitu returned with a small cloth bundle. He untied the knots and pushed the six exercise books towards the priest, returning at once to the clay. The two sat in silence, one working, the other examining each of the pictures. Sometimes the priest paused and watched Mitu, trying to see his face bent in shadow to the work. Mitu did not look up.

His whole form was at ease, his silence was that of the craftsman engaged in his work, not of shyness. Shadows lengthened. At last Mitu pushed the little board out from under his leg. The wet clay glistened. Mitu turned the board around to examine the statue from all sides.

'It will do,' he said. Then he stretched and began to wash.

'Who are they?'

'The man who sings is Ashin, our guide who died in Bombay. The woman is Deepaka, the one with hair that is almost white whom some call simple. When they were young, they would sing together and we would gather to listen and dream. Ashin became a teacher. Deepaka a wife, mother of sons, now a widow. She was with Ashin when he died. She is the one who worships all images. She asked me to make an image of Ashin, like the Muslim tombstones, so that we could remember him as he was when happy. I only knew him to be happy singing, so this I have made.'

'It is very beautiful. She bends towards him, but they both are lifted with the music, high, to where his eyes go.'

'It will be hard to take it back on the train, perhaps it will be broken.'

'Shall we bake it? It is hot at the kiln at the moment, for the potter worked today.'

'I shall be much in your debt.'

'No, brother, I ask you to make me another image, something of your choice, that I may keep here when you return to the village.'

'You want to hold one of my statues?'

'Yes, anything you wish to make. The pictures are rare, but they must stay together as you made them. I would be grateful to have something from your gifted hands.'

'I am too honoured. I cannot.'

'Of course you can. Now is a good time, you still have clay. I will go quickly with this to the kiln.'

Mitu sat watching the retreating priest carrying the statue most carefully. Then his fingers from habit sought the clay again and he began to work. When the others returned it was past sunset and they found Mitu smoothing a curve on a small figure, another complete beside him. The finished one was of a woman cradling a child in her arms as she bent towards a cooking pot. There was a rare grace and dignity about the figure and the villagers gathered around, pointing with excitement. The other was a sleek, elegant portrait of a man and a woman embracing, she folded in his arms, her head nestled toward his face. In each of the two statues the faces had been drawn in the wet clay with exacting care. The embracing couple in peace, the woman and child with a tense solicitude which conveyed a sense of great tragedy.

'See, he has made Amiya, when she cared for the grandchild who died last harvest. She bends just as Amiya does and there is none other whose face looks like that when she holds an infant.'

'Mitu, you have never made anything like this in the village.

'Now I have seen the pictures with faces drawn more carefully. I am learning.'

'And these, are they not our own Narend and Rhunu? No other is a full head taller than his wife, no other wife becomes a beauty only when her lord husband is about.'

'You must hide them, Mitu, before they return. They will be angry.'

'Do you think so?'

'If they see the others looking, yes. If you show them alone, no.'

'She is right, Mitu, hide them quickly.'

'Here they are with the food and the priest.'

The beautiful clay pieces were taken into the darkness and those who had seen pretended to busy themselves but talked of Mitu's craft. Mitu himself squatted a long time before the tap, working the clay from his arms and hands. When he returned to the courtyard, his tali alone was full, the others were eating and talking with the priest. Some had seen a dance recital, others had stayed in the market, and a number of men had gone up the mountain. They told of the flowers, of the height of the trees, of the luxuriant foliage. The talk was light and happy and Amiya joined with the other women in chatter about the skill of the children in the strange masked dances of the south. At last night cloaked them all and even Reena admitted she wished to sleep. When the courtyard was empty the priest spoke softly to Mitu.

'The kiln is still hot.'

'Come then, two are ready and all the clay used. But we must not show them to the others.'

They made a hesitant parade carrying the boards across the court, along a walk, through a darkened door and down many silent passages which smelled strangly to Mitu. The smell was floor wax. At last they emerged from the building and went across two more courtyards and a garden before entering a barn where a lean black man was sweating before the kiln. All around him were trays of small cups, quickly shaped water jugs, and tiny oil lamps. On one table were recently fired clay crucifixes, eyes cut identically to slant the way the pujari's do as he chants. Alone at one end of the table was Mitu's statue of Ashin and Deepaka, warm but whole. Perfect now in its completeness. The potter looked with admiration at the two new images and the priest bent over them astonished. At last the potter eased them into the kiln and closed the door. He spoke to the priest, pointing to Mitu at the same time.

'He says this will be his last firing. Would you like some tea? He says he thinks you are a great artist.'

Mitu bowed and, though they could not see, blushed. Then he accepted the tea and they crouched together by the lantern. The potter asked Mitu many questions through the priest so it was not until the pot was empty that the priest himself asked:

239

'The figures in the two new statues, are they people with you?'

'Yes. The woman with the child is Amiya, who is sick now, but was once a fine healer. She wished to be a doctor but was pulled from school and married badly by her parents. The child is her grandchild who died last harvest. The couple is Narend, the tall one, and Rhunu, the woman of the very sharp face who draws better than I do but with colours, not black and white. Her book is a wonder. They are silent people, but since she came as a bride they have always smiled their best only for each other when none could see. Their family is whole, and all are strong neighbours. Narend is as good a farmer as Surendra, but he longs for more than the village. It is too small for him. He liked the Himalaya very much. Rhunu is a good housekeeper and can heal as well as Amiya, but for her the village is also too small. Sometimes when a potter is very lonely, he can go and find talk in that house.'

'You speak as one who sees much that is often kept hidden.'

'The potter is asked to all houses to mend and bring pots. They have known me since I was a child and made my first lamp, like that one there. But a potter is not the same as a farmer.'

'Is the village too small for most, brother?'

'Not before this journey. We did not know anything was beyond. A few like Amiya, or Narend and Rhunu, or Harischandra the writer, always yearned to cross the river and go beyond. The others, like Jaydev and Babla, and most of the women, for them all they could do in the village was more than enough.'

'And now?'

'Things will be changed.'

'For you?'

'For me it must now always be too small. I have seen museums and the ways of great artists, and I wish to see more.'

'Then come and see what few pictures we hold here.'

The priest led the two potters back into the buildings to the chapel and showed them paintings, statues and crucifixes. Mitu thought they were the finest he had seen. The priest scolded:

'No, they are far poorer than those in the museums of Calcutta and Delhi. You see them here by candlelight in a place where they are loved, thus do they look better.'

'What will you do with my statue and which will you keep?'

'If I may I will keep the one of Amiya which shows how hard it is to give comfort when it is needed. And I shall keep it on my desk where I can see it each day.'

'May I see the place?'

The priest led the two men along a corridor and up some stairs. At last they entered a dark room. The priest lit a lamp and Mitu realized he was in a room lined with books. Only the window remained without shelves before it. Everywhere there were papers, small statues or trinkets. Mitu stood astonished. The priest sat and watched him. The other potter squatted against the door jamb and waited. Mitu let his eyes wander from shelf to shelf and sometimes even stepped forward to something exceptional. He dared not touch anything. When the priest motioned him to open the books if he wished, Mitu cringed at the suggestion. Then he saw two white statues on a shelf and moved to them. Both were carved in ivory about the length of Mitu's palm. One he recognized as Saraswati, but a goddess of wisdom far more sorrowful and beautiful than any he had seen before. The other was a woman holding a child, her head draped as if by a sari, the whole shaped with a grace which Mitu longed to caress. He turned towards the priest.

'Whose are these?'

'Mine, I suppose.'

'You have made them?'

'No, they come from across the sea. They were made by one who was here long ago. See, I have his tools.' The priest opened a drawer in his cupboard and put before Mitu an array of chisels and knives more expertly made than any Mitu had seen. The potter handled then with respect as the priest tried to explain the purpose of each. The drawer was closed again. Mitu looked again at the ivory. He was silent. At last he moved towards the door. The other potter stood and the priest bent to blow out the lamp. As he did so Mitu said:

'I am ashamed that you have seen my clay.'

'Do not be ashamed, yours are pieces of true art. We could make many things together, I think, if you did not have to move on. Perhaps you will return one day and make a long line of images around our church as I hear you still do in Bengal.'

'Yes, I do it each year after the rains for the temple of the village.'

'Ah, then my heart will be even heavier at parting, for it is a skill I would very much like to watch. Come. You have worked all day and you are tired.

In the morning the women went early to market and filled all the carriers with fresh foods. Surendra had a last consultation at the station which did not seem to calm him. He was subdued as he walked back to the courtyard. Narend and Rhunu were explaining the pastels of Rhunu's book to the priest. Mitu looked on with obvious pride. The priest was called away and did not return until they were assembled to leave. He came bearing a large box with a braided rope holding it suspended from his shoulder. He swung the rope over to Mitu and the potter was surprised that is was not a greater burden.

'I have wrapped the images well, they will not break. Have a care that they do not get wet, for the short time in the fire will not protect them.

'What of this fine box?'

'Someday bring it back to me when you come to show me how to make the figures on the wall. Keep your tools in it safe from your grandchildren.'

The priest bowed to Mitu but the potter had bent and his hands were fluttering over the priest's feet. The others looked on astonished as the priest raised Mitu and then touched the potter's feet.'

'We are the followers of the same craft.'

'I am honoured.' Mitu turned and rapidly led the way down the hill to the station while the others followed slowly. At the station a small crowd waited and Mitu recognized two nuns. They smiled and he realized they were also leaving the town. They turned away and Mitu gently lowered the box and shifted his bedding.

The train was a strange miniature of those steam engines the villagers had seen before. The carriages were open, the roof a brightly painted wooden canopy. The engine, though not as tall as Narend, bore a chimney which seemed unlikely to withstand the journey. When at last the staff was aboard a musical burp told the passengers they were to mount. They did so laughing, with none of the frenzy of the people of the lowlands. The villagers themselves were scattered, but able to look over the backs of the benches into the other compartments of the carriage. There were many strangers among them and a busy time was required before all the parcels, bedding and suitcases were stowed away with common consent. The priest was there on the platform, bowing. The train began to roll forward easily and did not sound its ridiculous whistle until they rounded a bend and left the town behind. There the sound was not so incongruous and the echo sounded like the gulp of a wistful child after crying for a long time.

'We have been made young again by that rest, I think!' Uma turned to Deepaka. They were sitting with Amiya and Rhuna along one bench while opposite were the two nuns and a young girl nursing a baby. The girl was poor, though flashily dressed, and wore a bright brooch at her shoulder—a coloured piece of glass mounted in a wire flower and fastened by a very large pin. She seemed to be known to the nuns, who nodded to her and smiled at the baby but at the same time moved away on the bench until they were squeezed into the corner of the compartment. Rhunu and Amiya were watching the deep greens of the forest change to lighter shades as the train wove its way downward. Uma kept popping up and down to look at the other villagers and reported back each time to Deepaka. Soon they were all wiping cinders from their eyes and faces, for the engine was on a curve and the smoke was blown into the open compartments. Beyond the curve they could see the brown plain far below, stretching out to the horizon.

'It looks very hot,' murmured Amiya.

'Yes and dry. This is a beautiful mountain,' Rhunu answered. The nuns passed out some dried banana which the Bengalis tried and liked. Then suddenly the baby screamed and they all looked at it.

'She is caught. Her eye is caught on the brooch. Hold still girl. Do not move,' Deepaka and Amiya shrieked the last together as the girl twisted round to see what was the matter with the child. The nuns spoke to her softly and began to move towards her but she angrily shouted at them and they retired. The screams of the baby were causing others to bend over the benches to see what was the matter. The mother had lifted the child up to her shoulder and there, in turning its head, it had caught the outer edge of an eyelid in the pin of the brooch. Deepaka and Amiya stood, balanced, and bent to detach the child gently. Before they had touched the baby the mother simply wrenched it with force from the pin, causing a shattering scream unlike all the others. Blood streamed everywhere and Deepaka held her sari against the wound while the young mother adjusted her dress.

'Perhaps she has blinded it, perhaps she has blinded it!' Amiya screamed. Rhunu clasped her and pulled her down to the bench. They sat taut, bending forward to try and see. The mother said something and Deepaka sat down suddenly—she had been pushed away. The baby was silenced when the mother forced the nipple in to its mouth. The infant lay gasping, sucking, horrified by the pain. Blood rolled down into its ear and began to dry. The women could see now that the eye was unhurt, but there was ragged flap of skin which had once been the eyelid and was now just the beginning of a long gash which reached high on the child's temple.

Uma felt Deepaka's cold hand clutch her as the older woman saw the wound and realized what the child must be suffering. Then Deepaka put her head out of the window and was violently sick. Over and over she retched until the nuns saw that she weakened and pulled her in. Amiya sat staring at the mother. Sometimes she let her hands loose from each other and they would move towards the child before she caught them and started plucking at them again. Uma asked the nuns:

'Does she not know that she might have blinded the baby?'

The girl replied to the Hindi:

'Better to be blind as a beggar. She will have to beg one day, better to do it more easily.'

'She is such a beautiful child. Now she is marred by this terrible wound. You must have a doctor care for it so that there is no great scar.'

'What? Pay a doctor for such a thing? What use is beauty? As soon as it can earn some food, it vanishes. Better that she has a good big scar to make the rich look twice. This blood will help us tonight and tomorrow to earn a little.'

'But you have caused her much pain. Do you not care for her screams?'

'I hear nothing but her screams all day and all night, why should one more be different? She will sleep if you are quiet.'

'You are a cruel, foolish girl.'

'And you are a meddling snake of a mother-in-law whose only virtue comes from the alms you give to those who beg at your door.' Rhunu asked what had been said and Uma translated. When she finished the girl, who had been watching carefully, shot out her hand and began the high sing-song wheedle of the beggars. Deepaka retched again. Rhunu's mouth grew thin and she sat hard against the bench looking only at the scenery, but not seeing at all. Amiya abruptly turned to her and said:

'Draw her.'

'What, Amiya-didi?'

'Take out your coloured sticks and draw her. And draw the blood.'

'But it is terrible. Why, didi?'

'This is also part of the journey. You draw the journey. You have drawn me. Now draw her. It must not be forgotten.'

'It is too terrible for me to draw.'

'No. She is pretty, and so was the baby. Make her so, but draw what we see. The train comes to the plain soon. There is little time.'

'It is not a good memory.'

'Few memories are good. Do not be a fool. This is important for us. We must attend, for she is right. Now draw.' Rhunu obeyed and began to sketch. Uma asked Amiya:

'Why is she right?'

'It is better for a beggar to be scarred or blind. And we who give make it so. We are guilty, just as she is. She is right. For this child what use is beauty. Ask the nuns if she is a woman of the brothels?'

Uma shuddered at the word but obeyed and the nuns replied, eyes downcast, that the girl was herself the daughter of such a one, that though she had been to their schools she had taken to the streets as soon as a man had asked her to come. She had returned to them to have the child and they had kept her until disgrace forced them to send her away. She was going back to the city and the child would grow up watching and waiting to become as the mother.

'And what better life is there for it? Shut up with you in your shining prisons, never to laugh and only to tell others what they do wrong? No, she is scarred now, but she will at least have pretty things one day.'

'And when she is old?'

'Who begs better than an old one, whose grey hairs gain pity from all, or have you not found that adds to your skill, grandma?' said the girl, glaring at Uma. Uma translated. They spent the rest of the journey in silence, but for the constant thrumming wail of the child.

9

Cape Comorin

A bridge had been blown up in the plains so the villagers walked along beside the empty train in an evening which was bright and warm. The other passengers were chatting as if on a picnic. No one seemed to know why the bridge had been attacked. Those who could communicate with the villagers brushed it aside as a common occurrence. The villagers did not know where they were going, or where they would find food and a bed for the night. Amiya had begun to sway again just before they left the tiny hill train for the main line express. Deepaka and Rhunu struggled to lead Amiya forward at the pace of the procession. Sometimes, when strangers were passing, they took fright at the sight of the dishevelled woman and ran quickly beyond, pointing and calling to the others to avoid the trio. Uma and Arundati dropped farther and farther behind. Reena came back in the dusk to urge them forward and managed to bring them back to their companions only by taking both bedrolls. When dark was closing and most of the other passengers were out of sight, the villagers stopped as if by command.

'Where are we going?'

'Are there robbers here?'

'What is the light ahead?'

'This tiffin carrier is heavy. Why don't you carry it?'

'Where is Arundati?'

'Where do we cross the river?'

'What river?'

'Why, the river where the bridge has fallen. The train would have crossed it so we must as well.'

'Do you hear those dogs?'

'There must be a village near.'

'We won't keep dogs away without fire.'

'Where are we going?'

'Where is Surendra?'

'Is he not here?'

'He has gone ahead to find out if there is lodging.'

'Alone, in the dark?'

'Does he not walk so in the village?'

'He does not know this place.'

'The road is safe. The ones ahead must have reached their homes.'

'Is there a town?'

'See that glow, that is a town.'

'Is there any food?'

'It is dark, man, you cannot eat in strange places in the dark.'

'I can eat from my wife's hands anywhere.'

'You are blessed. What of those whose wives are long dead or whose husbands have returned to wish us ill?'

'Hush such talk.'

'Come, it is better to eat than to grow cold with waiting. What is there left?'

'I do not know.'

'Let me see. Open those carriers. There is cold tea in the pot.'

They ate quickly, often looking around them in the dark to see if something was about to spring at them. They did not watch the road so when Surendra shouted they jumped.

'Here, why are you stopped? I told the nuns you might stop to sleep, but I did not think I would find you feasting in the night. Is there a mouthful left?'

'More than a mouthful. But tell us what you have found.'

'The nuns from the priest's house in the mountains have gone ahead to their nun's house in the town to make us beds and warn the others that we come. They were told by the priest to care for us.'

'Did you find the town?'

'It is not far. You do not see the lights because there are few and we must go down a little hill first.'

'Was there no station master?'

'Ah yes, swinging his lantern and calling out to those who came along the road. He has time now only for those who blew up the bridge. When I asked him where we were to sleep he said on the road. It is all right, the nuns are good.'

'Let us hurry. Uma's leg is aching. Amiya and Arundati are taking strength from others.'

'Give me a moment to eat. Harischandra, have you matches?'

'Do you want to smoke?'

'No, but let us gather some grasses and make a torch.'

'There are no grasses by the road. I have searched. The whole land is nothing but cracks and dust.'

'The policeman said it was worse beyond the hills.'

'Surely there must be something to make a torch.'

'My old newspapers.'

'They will burn too quickly.'

'Let those who smoke all light a biri, even the glow from those will help us to keep together.'

'Give me two tiffin carriers. You, Jaydev, take one from Uma.'

They entered Coimbatore and were met by the two nuns trembling with the excitement of being out in the night. After a walk along silent streets, the villagers were shown through a gate. Ahead of them they could see lights and white figures moving quickly. The nuns asked them to wait; the villagers, understanding the expression but not the words, hunkered down and stayed quiet. Amiya's whimpering began again. Narend and Surendra shifted their rucksacks to the ground and were alarmed by the clatter they made. In a short time a new nun came to them. She spoke in English and Harischandra had to strain to hear her.

'Welcome. Have you eaten? Do you wish to bath? Are any ill?'

'Yes, mistress, we have eaten on the road. We are very dirty, but we will wash in cold water, please do not trouble to make hot. One is in pain from an old wound.'

'Let that one come to me.'

Harischandra explained to Uma, who was taken away by another nun. Jaydev spoke sharply to Harischandra but before the writer could translate the nun spoke again:

'That must be the woman's husband. Tell him she goes to see the doctor, who is here now. This is a hospital and an orphanage.'

'An orphanage?'

'A home for children whose parents cannot care for them or whose parents are dead. We are very crowded but there is room for you on the veranda of the school and in the schoolroom if you have bedding.'

'We have bedding.'

'Then come quietly, please. The children and the sick are asleep.'

Harischandra told the others what had been said and they gathered their bundles together and began to follow the nun along the courtyard. The paucity of their speech belied their exhaustion and the nun turned to Harischandra:

'As we go under the light you must count to see that none have been missed in the dark.'

The last to pass was Reena, almost hidden by all the rolls and bundles she carried. Harischandra relieved her of two.

'What are you doing?'

'Counting to see that no one is lost.'

'Do you think so little of my eyes that you would expect me to lose some on a straight road?'

'The mistress bade me count.'

'It was rightly done, but we are all here.'

'Uma comes back to join us.'

The villagers were in a large schoolroom. The nun motioned that they should spread their bedding. A basin was brought and several pitchers of water. The villagers waited for the nun to leave.

'Rest here or on the porch. None will disturb you and there is a watchman at the gate. Food will be brought in the morning.' She was gone and there was a short burst of chatter while the villagers disposed themselves in the space of the room.

'Where did you go, Uma?'

'To the office of a doctor. The doctor was a woman. She looked at my leg and has given me something to rub on it which makes it very hot. She says she will come and see us all in the morning. There are many beds, with many sick.'

'The nun says it is a hospital and a place for children without families. In Bengal there is always a place with someone for a child. I do not understand.'

'We will learn in the morning.'

'Where shall I throw this water?'

'In the courtyard.'

'No, look for one of those pipes as at the priest's house. These people do not throw water upon the earth.'

'That is too much for me. Where should water be except upon the earth? Pipes and holes in houses just for water are a waste of money.'

'Watch out. Do not make a mess of the school.'

'Hurry, others must wash.'

Deepaka washed Amiya while the others tried to avoid staring at the strange sight. Rhunu had told Narend of Amiya's command to her to draw and wondered now why she was again helpless. Reena told a short story. Long before she had finished they were asleep, but she kept on with the rhythms to the end, sighed, and pulled her blanket higher. Across the darkness came Amiya's whisper:

'Thank you Reena, I shall sleep now.' But Amiya did not sleep, unless sleep be a terror more alert than any wakeful state. She saw before her eyes as a dream all the failures and attempts she had made in her long life, each distorted now and horrible as the judgment Amiya felt it to be. Somewhere here there was a lady doctor. Uma had said so. She would rise and find her and be cured. The lady doctor would understand. Perhaps it was not too late.

Reena was awakened suddenly by a chill of apprehension. She sat up, taking care not to touch the figures close on either side. She looked about her, aware that something was wrong, something had called her from sleep. A movement on the verandah caught her eye and she rose to move towards it. A person was there, moving quickly and silently in the darkness. Reena crept across the sleeping limbs, touching no one, trying to match the speed of the figure. When she reached the door of the schoolroom Reena could see that the person was about to step out of the shadow into the half-light cast from the hospital windows. She waited.

It was Amiya. She was naked. As Reena watched, Amiya moved along the courtyard, going towards the wall and then the gate to the town. She was stepping with stealth and with a speed which Reena found very hard to match, but in her alarm the bent storyteller summoned some unknown reserve and reached Amiya just before the gate. With a twist she unwound her sari and draped half of it around Amiya. The tall woman started just a fraction at the sudden touch then looked at Reena and smiled. They did not speak as they walked back into the room, nor while Reena dressed Amiya, who stayed helplessly rigid throughout. Reena passed her hand gently down the still-smiling face from brow to chin and whispered

'Sleep, didi, we are all here. It is safe.'

Amiya cackled harshly and then just as suddenly began to breathe as deeply as if she sobbed. Reena watched for a long time and felt the body sink into sleep. She moved her own bedding over to the doorway and sat, wrapped in her purple shawl, guarding the darkness against the indiscretions of her companions. About an hour before dawn when there was a green tinge to the night, Narend awoke and moved towards Reena:

'What is it, aunt?'

'Someone must watch. Amiya tried to leave. She was without clothes.'

'Sleep. I shall sit.'

They needed no more words. Reena rolled away and was asleep before Narend had found a position of comfort for his long legs. A bell rang somewhere. Narend heard, but did not see, a rustle of stiff skirts hurrying somewhere. Close by a baby cried. Then another. A cock crowed. Narend smiled at the thought that it was late. Above him he heard the light, gurgling laughter of a child just awake. Then little feet thumped running down bare boards. More laughter. Another bell. Running feet above. A sudden bang, followed by a wail. An older voice just murmuring. The wail quieted to a hiccup, then a whimper, then more laughter. The babies behind were still crying. Suddenly they stopped. Narend strained to hear the excited gasps which punctuated the sucking of milk. Someone stirred in the schoolroom. Surendra was beside Narend, wriggling himself awake:

'Why do you sit by the door?'

Narend told him. Above there was another thump, another wail. This time the older voice scolded and the wail was stifled. Narend grinned and stood to look over the garden. He was just in time to see three nuns coming towards the school. Each carried two water buckets. Narend drew Surendra forward so that the two cultivators relieved the first nuns of their buckets. The nuns seemed surprised to see them awake. As soon as they put down the water the panic of the morning began. There was little quiet until food was finished, bundles repacked, and the mistress nun of the night before appeared at the door. She was greeted by a happy chorus of gratitude. For a long time she answered their questions, telling them of the drought in the area which had caused so much suffering.

They asked after the children and she spoke of mothers bringing their babies to the nuns because there was no milk, no water, nothing to feed them. She told of the circuits made by the nuns to find the children abandoned when they were sick, and too weak for the family to care for them. When the villagers asked where the nuns came from and how they obtained their money for the hospital and the food for the children, she described the mother house in Madras and the missions across the sea who supported the work. They had a short time to wait before they would go to the train.

'Surendra, Elder De, you must give the nun money for our shelter and for our food.' Arundati spoke firmly.

'But it is not a hotel, why must we pay?'

'They depend on gifts of money to work here for the children.'

'Uma-didi would have wished it.'

'But we are not rich men.'

'How much do you want us to pay?'

'We have had three nights in the priest's house and this house of the nuns. We should pay as much as a hotel would have cost.'

'But that would be 200 rupees, or more. In the bad hotel we paid more than 60 rupees for one night.'

'So much?'

'No, no, you must not pay so much.'

'Arundati is right, we must give the money.'

'But they have money from the foreigners. Who are we to give money to foreigners?'

'They look after the children from this land.'

'That is for them to decide. Let us not waste Uma-didi's funds. Surendra, pay no attention to this talk. Elder De you are a sensible man.'

'Wait a moment. Some feel we should give money. Some feel we should not. How did they tell us in Delhi we should decide? By voting. Let us have a vote.'

'Yes a vote.'

'Those who wish to give money raise hands.'

'Now those who don't wish it.'

'So those who wish to give are more. How much shall we give?'

'Same as for a hotel.'

'No less.'

'Much more.'

'Why not just 100 rupees?'

'Listen to Surendra say *just* 100 rupees.'

'Oh Ma, what a journey this is.'

Thus Elder De presented the mother superior with 100 rupees 'for the children' as the villagers left for the station. Rhunu gave her grandchild's horse to a boy who had clung to her hand all morning. The nun watched them go down the dusty road and then locked the gate.

They boarded the train to Cochin without incident, finding places amongst all the other passengers. When the train began to move, they settled to the rocking with something close to relief. Mitu and Rhunu began to draw, the men got out their cards, the women analysed the days past. Some nodded and smiled at the strangers who were fellow passengers, others got out Surendra's maps and watched him draw the way they had come and seek out where they were bound. Reena and Harischandra held their reading class and were astonished to find Surendra had leapt ahead. He would only say that he had been practising. Amiya slept in Deepaka's arms. Narend sat alone with Rhunu and talked of many things. The train slowed to enter a town and paused briefly at a small station. At once the carriage was filled with noise though there were no new passengers. The train pulled on again and the villagers craned to see where the noise originated. A wrestling group of children tumbled in from the passage-way. There were shrieks, curses, yells of pain, and the villagers realized that the children were fighting in earnest. Suddenly one boy broke out from under the group, darted to the end of the passage and stood glaring at the rest of the children. A very small girl pulling a toddler joined him.

There were seven children in the large group. For a while they sat talking about the passengers in the carriage. They merely glanced over the villagers once and then focused on the other passengers: a plump lady wearing many rings, a foreign student, and an Indian woman wearing Western dress. Elder De with his spectacles and jacket was also examined. Suddenly their apparent leader, a wizened boy with more energy than the others, stood and sang a little song, did a somersault down the aisle and held out his hand to beg from the four he had decided were of consequence. The other six imitated his begging but he scolded them. Then they did a little dance, holding hands and bumping often against the metal wall of the carriage before gaining a nod from the leader and beginning to beg. The woman of the rings and the student both gave small coins to the children, who retired and sat in a huddle examining their funds. Elder De said, 'Give to one and you get one hundred,' and looked out of the window. The other villagers watched the three children who sat alone. At the sight of the coins the little girl tugged at the sleeve of the boy, but he shook his head and she watched greedily as the others counted their coins over and over again. The toddler ferreted in their clothing and gurgled with glee when he found on the floor beside them half a chapatti. He nibbled it, held it out and gazed at it, turned it over and over in his hands, ran his fingers along the curve, then cautiously took another nibble. His sister reached out and tore off a corner which she stuffed in her mouth and sucked but did not chew. The baby did not wail, just puckered with sorrow and fingered the torn angle where the curve now ended.

When the train slowed at a small town the large group of children scuttled from one carriage to the next, the leader calling to each to run past the swinging door until they had made the traverse. The three did not move. The boy's eyes moved slowly from one detail of the carriage to another, first along the floor at the level of the bundles and the water pots, then up to the clothing of the passengers, then to their faces, finally above to the luggage racks. As the train rocked and the baby worried the girl, the boy reached over and lifted the child on his lap, bringing out from his ragged shirt a small wooden flute. The baby was delighted, sticking his fingers in the holes, looking into the end, and sucking on the mouthpiece. When he tired of this examination he tried diligently to put the flute into the mouth of the older boy. He was brushed away, gently but repeatedly. At last he began to cry. The older boy looked nervously around the carriage. He saw the girl had fallen asleep. He turned his back on the passengers, put the baby before him and began to play. The music was barely audible, but it was a sad, repetitive tune which might once have been a lullaby. The passengers strained to listen. Over and over again he played, and the baby boy smiled and patted his entertainer's knees. From two seats beyond him, Deepaka began to sing with the flute. The boy turned slightly, his eyes showing surprise, though he missed not a note. He let the volume increase a little and she sang sweetly, the two voices blending and defining each other until even the strangers were wiping away tears. The song was from a film and was the lament of a child for its dead father. 'Where has he gone? Where has he gone?' ended the refrain. After they had sung it twice Deepaka and the boy stopped and looked at each other. The baby was impatient. He rose, clung to the seats and clothes of the passengers, and made his way to Deepaka. Once beside her he would not quiet but repeated over and over some word which Deepaka did not know, but which was emphasized with an infant's insistence which turned rapidly into a shriek. The woman in Western clothes said in English:

'He wants you to sing again.' Harischandra translated.

Deepaka let the baby play with her fingers while she thought for a moment. Then she began a lively song which was a children's game in the village. The boy with the flute listened, put the instrument up to his lips and began to accompany her, tracing a pattern around Deepaka's old voice which made the whole melody into a concert piece. At the end the villagers clapped and called out praises to the boy. He put the flute away and called the baby back. The girl was urging him to do something, but he refused and she became sulky. Deepaka asked Harischandra to ask the woman to learn the tale of the trio and find out why they did not join the others. The woman spoke roughly to the boy, who would not look at her. Her tone became commanding, but the boy returned only silence. Deepaka asked kindly in Bengali. The woman with the rings urged him to answer. At last he did so:

'My name is Hassan. My village is past Coimbatore. I do not know who my father was. He has been dead many years. My mother has seven to feed. When I was six I saw that the five of us that then were, were too many. I went south to Coimbatore. There I found many like me who could earn food by carrying packages or begging on the trains. I began to travel on the trains. I cannot beg. I carry parcels, or clean the platform. There are many scraps, travellers are careless. We eat well. In a good month I can take one full rupee back to my mother. Two more babies have come since I left so all I get goes back to my mother. Somewhere, one brother of mine is on the trains. I do not know where. These are not my sister and brother. The baby was left by the mother in a station. I guess the mother must have been a whore. The girl was left to die when she was ill for there is no food for sickly girls in the drought. I fought with the others. I had earned some paisa from the station master for running messages in the night because of the bridge. The others said we must share, but I said no, I had done the work. The coins were to get milk for the baby and take back something to my mother. They took the coins from me. They will gamble them away with the porters in the big town. They do not go back to their mothers, they do not know who their mothers were.'

'Who cares for the baby? There was one as young with the others, too.'

'We care for each other. Most were left when they were smaller than this one, and have been fed by older ones who have gone on.'

'Where do the older ones go?'

'Those who live sometimes get work in the big town. Those who are injured, and there are many, for it is easy to fall from a train, become beggars in the city. Many die.'

'Have you trouble from the police?'

'There is always trouble, that is why we catch the trains in the small sections, and why we sometimes jump when the train moves, before the police can catch us.'

'What do the police do to you?'

'Take our money, beat us, put us to work as servants in the jail. But we escape unless the beating is hard. Then it is easier to die.'

'I come from Madras,' said the woman with rings. 'My husband has a good shop. Why do you not come with me and work as an apprentice in his shop? Then you could learn, earn money regularly, and be safe from the police?'

'No, no,' said the woman in Western clothes. 'He must come with me and go to our mission school. We will also teach him a trade, but he will learn to read and write and then be able to earn better money. Or here is a foreigner, why not go back to her country, where all are rich, and make a fortune to bring back to your mother?' The foreigner spoke and the shopkeeper's wife translated: 'She says you must understand this is not possible. She has no money to take you. It is a long journey. Not all across the seas are rich.'

'What will you do?' pressed the missionary. 'Will you be an apprentice, will you go to England to become a rich man, or will you come to our mission school and learn to read and write?'

Hassan thought a long time. The girl was watching him intently with fear in her eyes. The baby understood that something strange was happening and whimpered close against Hassan. Harischandra relayed it all to the villagers. They were at once animated with interest and watched anxiously as the boy's face worked. At last he spoke:

'If I go with you to Madras, I become your servant. Always I must work for you and stay by you. I cannot go to my mother when I wish and when there is need, and there will be little money to take her for I think you will ask me to pay for food and a bed. Now I pay no one for my food and my beds, and I go to my mother whenever I wish.

'If I go to your school,' he said to the missionary, 'you will make me into a Christian and I will no longer be one of my family. They will not want my help. There would be no place for me with you, for I would be a servant again, the lowest in the mission. Who among the missionaries would give a monied place to one who had been a beggar on the trains? None I think, though it is good to read and write. But what use is it to me? If I can be of no help to my family what use is my life? You say I should go to England across the waters, with the girl who says she has no money for my ticket. I believe her that all are not rich there. Even if I could go, what then? For many years I would have to learn the language, and only then could I get a job. What job? A servant's post, and I would be too far and too imprisoned to help my mother. Even if I became a rich man, by that time my family would have starved for I would not have known of their need. They could not write to tell me even if I could read the news. It is better for me to stay as I am. Now I am free to help where I can. No one is my master. What would happen to these two if I went away with you?' Hassan indicated the girl and the baby and remained quiet while the translations were accomplished. The missionary pouted a little over the rebuke:

'You are sure you will not die? What will happen to them, anyway, if you are injured or you die, as you say happens often?'

'Someone will help them, or they will die too. But I am not yet dead. Now it is better to help the baby. Maybe he will one day get a job.'

'You are a wise boy,' said the Madrasi, 'but you need a wash and a new shirt. Go there, and wash, and when you come out I will have a shirt for you.'

'I am no beggar. I have nothing to pay you with for something as fine as a shirt.'

'You have given me a concert of music, and you have made my journey pass quickly. Take the others and wash.'

'Look, the foreigner gives you soap.' The missionary passed the bar of soap to Hassan, who examined it with delight and bowed to the foreigner.

For a long time the three stayed in the lavatory. The villagers chattered about all that had been said:

'The nuns said there were many children alone, but I thought they were all in the orphanage, not out begging.'

'Maybe some have run away from the nuns.'

'From such kindness and such food?'

'As he says, it is a kind of prison.'

'We have seen many children on the stations, perhaps they were all like these.'

'What will become of him? How can a girl of that size and a boy raise a baby?'

'They will raise it just as we would. Did you not see how he played just for it? What matters if the bed is a rope one or a mat, or a piece of ground, if the eyes are clear and the heart is good?'

'It is a hard life. They may fall ill and there would be no help.'

'That is true for us as well.'

'Hush, he comes.'

The children were dripping and shining. Their damp clothes clung to them. Their gaunt pallor was more obvious. They went towards the Madrasi, pausing to return the soap, but the foreigner would not accept it. Hassan said quickly:

'Tell her I can sell small pieces of soap to the others for good paisa, and we will be clean for many months. It is a fine gift.' The missionary translated and added bitter comments of her own about the waste of good soap, foreign at that, on such children.

'Here, take off that shirt,' the Madrasi held out a clean cotton one. 'This is one of my son's, but he will not miss it.'

Hassan put on the shirt modestly, trying to hide his embarrassment by turning to the girl and putting the old one over her head. She in turn slipped out of her ragged dress, pulled down the shirt, and put the dress on the baby after removing the poncho-like cloth which had been his only garment. The train was slowing at the outskirts of Cochin. Hassan bent to look forward and spoke in a rush to the girl. They began to move up the carriage to the door. Some of the villagers pushed food towards them and Uma even found an orange for the baby. He cooed over it as he walked behind the girl, one hand clutching the skirt of her garment, one hand locked around the orange. In a moment they were gone. The villagers watched them skipping over the tracks, Hassan carrying the baby, the girl picking her way behind. They dodged between trains and were out of sight. As the train moved into Cochin, Deepaka noticed that Elder De was crying.

'What is it, brother?'

'Ah Deepaka, I wish I had given good coins to the boy. We are all taught not to give to beggars, but what use is money to an old man? He could have bought milk for the baby.'

'Never mind. You will want the money for a souvenir sometime, and remember to bring a sari for your daughter.'

'That is foolishness for me. I am an old man, I have a warm house with new thatch, and I have refused to give a few paisa to a wise boy. Ah, the gods will be angry.'

'No, they will understand. You are not rich like others, you are just a villager. What paisa you have have been saved in hardship.'

'But perhaps the boy will only live another year, or maybe two. He will never have a house, or a wife, and no child other than those he cares for now. Perhaps my few paisa would have made him proud once.'

'No, I think that he never would be proud of money. Did you not think him like Surendra?'

'Truly, the writing of the foreheads is the same, but the boy's life will be short.'

'There is no worth in worry over Surendra, for none will land as surely as he in the lap of the gods, so let us not worry over money for the boy.'

'But he looked so old and he played the flute like Krishna himself.'

'Then he is blessed.'

'Would that I knew in the moments of my life what to do. It is always so. I know when it is too late, or I never know. Alas, alas, why was I born a fool and a coward as well?'

'You were born with a conscientious heart. Quiet your thoughts. There will be much to do when we reach the station.'

Deepaka wakened Amiya and told her where they were. Amiya looked out of the window with interest but did not help as Deepaka counted and retied the bundles. The others were busy and only Rhunu noticed that Amiya had pulled the skin away from her finger nails and her hands were bleeding on to her sari. Rhunu wiped the blood away from the useless hands again and again. She and Amiya were the last to dismount and the others had already followed the officials. Narend was waiting. He did not speak, but took in what had happened and Rhunu's alarm. He gave her a load to carry and placed Amiya beside him. They walked at a good pace, but were far behind the others. Once Amiya asked, 'When will my wedding be, uncle?' but nothing else broke their silence. At last they reached a busy quay where the villagers were being loaded into boats to cross to the main city. Jaydev and the others were wading, pushing the boats off, and Narend could tell no one of their need of help. Reena hopped from a boat, to the anger of the boatman, but she was too far to be retrieved. She joined Narend and Rhunu, taking her place beside Amiya. They travelled in the last dinghy and twice they had to hold Amiya down when she suddenly stood as if to step out of the boat. At the far shore the others led a gay caravan to a small hostel in the ancient city.

That day and the next passed easily, filled with riches and sights of strange churches and schools. Each night Narend and Rhunu took turns with Reena and Surendra at the watch. Each night Amiya tried to leave, becoming more devious with each attempt.

The journey south through Kerala to Cape Comorin is one of the most beautiful in India. The dense forest is lit by beneficent sunshine. Villages of golden thatch, often on stilts, appear out of purple shadows and are gone. Elephants work pulling logs and the forest workers dip and sway as they fasten the chains or strip the great trees. Flowers garland every grove. Reeds rippling with the waves of the many ponds only conceal for a moment the coverlets of lotus blossoms floating on the water. The train of the villagers moved slowly and they sat pressed to the windows unable to turn away to miss a single sight. Little canoe boats skimmed along, parallel to the train. The Bengalis shouted over the speed and skill of these craft. Twice they saw the gossamer butterfly fish nets spread to dry. Often monkeys swung chattering away from the train and the villagers laughed to see them wild and free among the trees. Mitu sat in an ecstasy of despair, his charcoal idle. When they pulled in at the station of Trivandrum the villagers were more excited than tired. The night supervisor welcomed them without enthusiasm and sent a servant to lead them to their rooms above. At the top of a staircase of alarming pretensions, the servant handed Elder De four foot-long iron keys and vanished. Elder De looked at the keys. Babla stepped forward and moved to the nearest door, bearing the key like a bayonet. He tried the key without success and a voice within cried out in alarm. Undismayed, Babla moved on to the next door. This one opened. A quick survey showed that it contained ten beds and a shower, so the first group was deployed. The next three doors opened as easily and soon the villagers had sent out a foraging party. On one side of the rooms came the noise of the shunting yards and departing trains. On the other side was the din of the town, popular film songs, taxis arguing by car horn, fights among men and dogs carried on deep into the night. It was suddenly still. In the kindly silence the villagers slept.

In the morning Amiya's hands were bleeding again, but she was quiet and submitted to Rhunu without protest. Deepaka was haggard. In the square waiting for the bus she fell asleep. They had thought they would again have a special bus, but two other people were waiting with them. One was a sannyasi, his staff resting against one shoulder, his eyes half closed against the morning sun. He carried a shawl and a water pot. His legs were corded and scarred. He pushed up the aisle and sat immediately beside the driver, ignoring the bustle of the villagers. At no time did he speak.

The other stranger was a girl, tall, thin, wearing the kurta and trousers of the Indian girl; but the plait of hair was brown. The villagers realized that this was the foreigner of Aurangabad station who had been pushed below the train and to whom Elder De had given tea. She was the last to board the bus and stood alone as the station master asked if it was acceptable that a foreigner travelled with them. Harischandra replied that it was, they knew this girl from Aurangabad. Reena pushed Arundati over and beckoned to the girl to come and sit beside her. Soon they were all calling out that she was welcome, that they remembered her from Aurangabad, and where had she been since then? Carefully the girl tried to answer their questions in Bengali. As soon as they heard her speak their language they exploded with questions, one trying to shout down the other. The girl laughed helplessly and they joined her. Throughout the morning drive through the sand dunes of the coast the villagers compared impressions of the south with the girl and she questioned them about what they had seen. The driver paused for a visit with friends in a village and the villagers started to teach the girl to sing their songs.

After an hour or more Deepaka said they now must learn a song from the stranger's people. Some time later the bus pulled to a stop at Cape Comorin while the villagers finished the last strains of the 'Skye Boat Song'. The sannyasi strode off towards the sea. The villagers were greeted officially. The girl eased away. Along the sea front there were large guest houses, each with a windblown garden and steps to the beach. To one of these the villagers were led. They were sent to an early supper while their hosts cautioned them not to miss the sunset. When the meal was finished they went out into the wind and walked the high dunes in silence, watching and listening to the roar of the breakers below them. Reena could not be persuaded to tell a tale when they were back at the guest house, so they went to sleep uneasily whispering that from now on they would be going homewards.

Morning and sunshine brought the villagers out to see the small temple to Gandhi, and to look at the several shrines among the rocks at the official point of the cape. Few of the others followed Deepaka as she made her rounds doing puja. They walked along the sand watching the sea. On a little bank where some gypsies were stringing shell necklaces, they found their foreign companion. She was crouched in the sand with the gypsies, watching their work, and they were trying to question her. The villagers called out and came up to the bank. The gypsies moved back rapidly, alarmed. The girl tried to calm them, but they would not come close again. She sat between the two groups while each tried to question her about the other. Eventually the villagers bought a few of the necklaces and the gypsies were well pleased. Reena bade the girl come back with them to the guest house to eat, and so they moved up the sand, chattering:

'You are much too thin.'

'All say so.'

'Does your mother not feed you?'

'Yes, and well, but I have not lived near my mother's food for many years.'

'Ai, that is why she is thin.'

'Where do you live, then, with your husband's family?'

'I am not yet married.'

'So old and not married!'

'Engaged now. We will perhaps be married in the summer.'

'Better the spring.'

'It is more auspicious.'

'I will not have finished my studies by spring.'

'Does your husband pay for the studies?'

'No, I have a scholarship.'

'Do you hear, Amiya? She has a scholarship.'

'Will you be married in red, in a red sari?'

'No, we wear white at marriage.'

'Such foolishness. White is the colour of death.'

'Better to buy a good red sari, then there will be strong sons.'

'I have a Daccai sari. I shall wear that.'

'Oh Ma, I have not seen a Daccai sari for years.'

'Do you hear, she will wear a Daccai sari.'

'Is your husband rich?'

'No, he is also a student.'

'What does he study?'

'Mathematics.'

'Surely he is rich. No father would arrange that a daughter marry a clever man who was not also rich.'

'My father did not arrange the match.'

'What? Is it by choice?'

'Yes.'

'Well, then, how much money does the boy earn?'

'I do not know, for now he has a scholarship too.'

'Where will you live?'

'In London for a time, I think.'

'London is a big city, like Calcutta. You will need much money.'

'London is not as friendly as Calcutta.'

'Do you know Calcutta, too?'

'I live there while I study here.'

'Then you must come with us and we will teach you what you need to know to make a clever man rich.'

'As you see we have all made our clever husbands rich.'

At the guest house they spent a long meal pressing food on the girl. Even Babla joined in the effort to make her eat more than any of them would normally eat in three days. When the men took out their biris, the girl took out a pouch of supari from her bag and gave it to the astonished women.

'It is good Bengali supari. Here, try some.' They enjoyed the treat and stored a little away for the rest of the day. Then the girl began to ask them of the village and they answered eagerly. Hour after hour they talked of all they had left, they showed her the sketches made by Mitu and Rhunu, then they spoke of the journey. Mitu brought his box and for the first time unpacked it. The villagers applauded his sculpture of Ashin and Deepaka, though Deepaka wept and was ashamed that Mitu had included her. They told the tale of Ashin and were silent. Mitu unwrapped the other figure, revealing the Purush-Prakriti, or Narend and Rhunu, embracing. The villagers stared. Some glanced shyly at Narend and Rhunu, then at the foreigner. A few of the women would have spoken but Narend reached down, took the little figure, caressed it from base to head and slowly down again. He smiled at Rhunu and then said to the foreigner:

'It is beautiful, yes?'

'Yes, very beautiful.'

'In your country what would you do with such a figure?'

'If it belonged to me then I would put it in a special place in the house where all could see it and know the love that made it.'

'Ah, but this does not belong to me.' Narend turned to Mitu: 'What money must I pay you to own this, Mitu-brother?'

'You need not pay me, Narend. I give it as a gift. It is only the work of my hands.'

'Yes, but you are a potter and an artist. By the craft of your hands you must eat. We have paid you for your water pots, now I see you must be paid for these. What would you charge for this?'

'I do not know.'

'Who buys the other?' Uma asked.

'No one. That is the memorial to Ashin-dada which you asked me to make at the Muslim tombs. You said it should go in the temple.'

'So it shall. It is a fine memorial, Mitu, and the village should pay you for that, too,' Elder De's voice surprised the others.

'No Elder De, that I give. I can offer nothing more in memory of him.'

'Mitu, I must ask you to carry this for me in your box. We shall find out what the prices are in the cities. There is no other souvenir I want as much as this.'

'I will carry it, Narend, but please let us not speak of money.'

'What is the other bundle in the box?'

'I do not know.'

Mitu began to unwrap the cloths. He gasped. There, lying in the cotton bindings was a tiny wooden carving, the replica of the ivory Madonna and Child seen in the priest's study in Ootacamund. This figure had the same delicacy, but the red lights of the wood gave it a sombre quality which the other had lacked.

'What is it?'

'Where does it come from?'

'Who made it?'

'A priest of the hostel, now gone across the sea, made it. The red-haired one must have packed it with the clay.'

'It is the goddess of the foreigners.' Smash it, smash it! It will bring the anger of the gods!' Amiya's scream interrupted Mitu and astonished the others. She tried to take the carving but the villagers held her back and Mitu hurried away to pack the statues safely. Once the box was closed, Amiya's wail stopped and she slumped forward, weeping, against Rhunu.

'Take her to bed. We will bring food later.'

'Thank you for showing me your pictures. Now I must leave you. Soon there will be the summons to the sunset.' The bustle of bidding the foreigner to return, of asking if they could meet as they walked to see the sun, let the villagers lose their embarrassment over Amiya. Once the girl was gone, walking across the blowing sand, the villagers looked at one another. Mitu was forgotten. Only the terror of Amiya's state compelled their attention. When Reena tried to distract them with a tale, for the first time her audience moved away and did not listen. Each went to his own tasks. Each ate hastily, stealing a glance to see if Amiya ate. She did so, unaided, and even scolded the waiter for clumsiness and the poor quality of the food.

'Never mind, it is food. There have been many times in the village when we have dreamed of such a feast while we sucked on the seed grain and watched the babies shrivel and die.'

'True, true. Do you remember the time the British police came to see if we were eating dogs, or our own children?'

'Some Muslim must have spread that story. The dogs had all died, and most of the babies. But at least he brought food with him. My children lived because of that powder, I am sure.'

'You used the powder as food?'

'Of course. I mixed it with water from the river and we all ate it. There was nothing else.'

'We did not touch it. It was from the foreigners, so we did not touch it.'

'Ai, it tasted better than all the sweets at Parvati's wedding in those times.'

As they walked towards the sunset over the dunes the villagers remembered the times of disaster. When the colours faded, Elder De climbed the bank and fetched the foreign girl:

'You must learn some more songs, and hear a tale told by a real storyteller.'

Late into the night Reena talked, the others sang, the girl listened and watched. The watchman arrived to lock the doors and was chased away. Reena asked the girl:

'What will you do with what you have seen?'

'I do not know. What will you do? What will you tell the ones at home?'

'Oh Ma, won't they be astonished?'

The villagers laughed and argued back and forth about what they would say and how they would teach the ones behind about wells and canals, schools and scholarships. Mitu said he would tell of the foreign priest and of all the museums. Arundati spoke of the saris and the way the women of the south did not cover their heads but walked proudly, displaying their brilliant colours with striking grace. Jaydev and Babla spoke of the factories, of how the men worked together and did a task in order, instead of each working alone. Surendra remembered railway porters, Hassan and the children, and the other wanderers they had met. Amiya bent to the foreigner:

'Will you tell of me?'

'I do not know what or when I will tell, mother.'

'You must tell of me, and of women.'

'Of women?'

'Yes. You must tell of those of us, like me, or Uma, or Rhunu, or Reena, or all the nameless others in all the villages, who could have been something. But they were married off by their fathers and brothers and then kept foolish and useless by their husbands.'

'Hush now, it is not foolish and useless to raise children.'

'We did not, we do not keep you useless, didi. It is the way that each is bound to another and all are bound to our duties. I have given Uma her way and educated the sons. So they are useless to my fields. Is that not compensation for her, who left off her schooling?' Jaydev did not have his usual assurance.

'Do you hear?' Amiya drummed a finger against the girl. 'You must tell that. How can there be any compensation for a lost life? You must tell of Surendra who has only now learned to read, though any can see he could have been as good as any professor from cleverness. All his life he has followed buffalo, smoked, kept his own thoughts, until now when it is too late for anything but the funeral pyre.'

'I prefer the company of buffalo to that of the professors I have met. Do not wish upon me an unhappy fate.'

'Listen, child, listen,' Amiya's intensity had stilled them all. She again prodded the foreigner. 'We answer one another with that word 'fate,' and we say we prefer things as they are. But what could we have been had our parents not spoken of fate? We have also thrust it upon our children and what will become of them because of it? You listen, you must listen, and know that we could have been better than we are.'

'I think you are rather wonderful now.'

The slaps that Amiya gave the girl echoed around the circle. No one spoke until Amiya screamed again:

'Then your eyes are blind. You must see this is as nothing. This is failure and slavery. We are ignorant, poor, no better than the beggars whom others think we are. It could have been otherwise. It must for each life be otherwise. It could have been that some of us would have risen so that no one would again speak of what is written on the forehead. Now it is too late, too late. But attend to it, attend.' Amiya wept and allowed herself to be taken to bed. The girl rose to go and the others fussed and clucked. Narend took a lantern to see the girl safely to her lodging. Surendra said he would come for the air. There was much blessing in farewell. The three were out in the wind, walking along the beach.

'You will forgive Amiya for hitting you?'

'Of course.'

'Oh Ma. Even as a new bride she wanted things to be better. Now that we travel she sees things are not better even for those with riches and power. She is frightened for the children.'

'Is she right?'

'Yes. Because she is wise and strong the others are afraid to see her desperate. They think she sees some truth that they do not.'

'Does she?'

'Perhaps she sees that no matter what we tell those at home, the village will stay the same. The children and the old will die when there is famine. Girls will be married badly and not sent to school. Sons will be called to the land before they have been trained. Or they will drift away to the cities to be paid money, and there die alone, a part of nothing.'

'Has the journey not changed some things for you?'

'Each of us is changed. But whether we are all changed, I do not know. It is easier to return to the old ways than to bring the new with us and try to work together when we return. I do not know. It is Amiya who shows us that hands which could heal but will never heal as well as trained hands, are now torn, shaken, helpless.'

'In this you are wrong, Surendra', said Narend. 'Look, my Rhunu will never again be angry over her drawing. You will never again pass a notice or a newspaper without trying to read it. Harischandra will not again sit idly dreaming. He will keep Reena talking until she is floating down the river and even then he may wade after her, notebook in hand. Amiya's pain is her own, others of us are made more whole.'

'Ai, you are right, Narend. And you will not be thought of as the silent one. Many will come to you for help and good talk.'

'Save me from it.'

'And the others, the ones who smile, and sleep, and speak only of the food?'

'I think for each of those something will not be the same again. Whether we can show it to the others, I do not know.'

'Do not all of the village travel? Was not the will made so that one day all will go? But I think this journey will be soon forgotten, as soon as we are dead.'

'Yes, that is so. Many will refuse because Ashin has died, and others will refuse from fear, or laziness. Maybe someday some who are now young will go as elders.'

'Surendra, the young must sleep. Good-night, daughter. Travel with us in the morning.'

'Good-night, good-night,' and they parted.

After dawn there were cries and angry bellowing from the buses. In a rush of bundles and pots the villagers ran to the bus and scrambled into it. As they were starting they saw their watchman come running through the scrub with the foreign girl, her sari billowing as she ran. Surendra hopped with delight, paid the watchman, and pulled the girl on to the bus. He explained to Elder De:

'I told the watchman to bring her, no matter when we left. Come, child, sit. Have you left anything behind in the hostel?'

'No. Where do you go?'

'Up to see the temple of these southerners. To Madurai, and then to the sea at Rameswaram.'

'Hush Surendra, let us dream again. The sea is just turning to grey, it is too early for talk.'

'Why, Babla, in the village you would follow me to the fields in this light.'

'True, but a bus and too much talk weary an old man more than a plough.'

They slept until the morning sun was strong. The bus was following a route through villages and fields where sun-blackened people were busy. Some would pause and watch the bus, others would not glance away from the soil. The villagers remarked on the bright colours of the clothing, and exclaimed over the early spring greenery. By noon they had reached a town and were taken to the temple. When the guide had finished his introduction they removed their sandals and stepped up to cross the courtyard and enter the temple. The guide protested. The villagers did not understand what was wrong. Again the guide shouted and waved. At last the villagers understood that he was telling the foreigner to go away and that she might not enter the temple. She went back to the compound where souvenir sellers surrounded her.

'It is not right to leave her alone.'

'Why do they not let her in?'

'She is not of caste.'

'Neither are we.' [1]

'She is foreign, we are Indian.'

'Do they not all praise light skins?'

'Would you want a Muslim in our village temple?'

'She is not Muslim. She is clean and treats us with respect.'

'Would those in her country let us into their churches?'

'Ask her.'

'It is wrong that he should be so rude. Why not just let her come with us, as a daughter?'

'If one comes in they think the place is polluted, and then the others, the rich tourists with cameras will want to come too.'

'What makes us respectable? We look no better than when we have been turned away from other places?'

'Now by contrast we belong and the foreigner does not.'

'It is foolish.'

'We would behave in the same way in the village.'

'That is foolish, too.'

'Hush, we must give offerings.'

The slow procedures were repeated for each of the worshippers, so by the time they left the temple the villagers were tired and irritable. They found the foreigner near the bus. Beside her was a small mountain of green coconuts and beside them a youth with a huge knife was grinning. The bus driver and the boy were chatting and smoking, eyeing the girl. In front of her, children were showing her a game. The driver hailed the villagers and made a long speech which none of them understood.

'What does he say?' asked Deepaka.

'He says the foreigner has bought all these coconuts. All that he brought to sell in the station. She wants you to refresh yourselves with them. The boy will split them. Who is she that you take food from her?' a priest translated.

'What matters if the food is good fresh coconut?'

Thud, crack, thud, crack, one by one the tough fruit were opened and the villagers drank. They boarded the bus carrying the broken pieces to scrape as they travelled. The girl waved farewell to the children.

'Daughter, we have a question for you.'

'Ask then.'

'We wonder if in your country strangers would be turned away from your temples as you were turned away here?'

'That would depend on the church. Some are always open and any can enter at any time. Some are locked whenever there is no priest within. From some you would be turned away because of your colour. From some I would be turned away because I would be a stranger to them.'

'But we are told there is no caste across the seas. Why should any be turned away from one and not another?'

'There is not caste in terms of blood ties, but there are barriers for those of one colour against another, or those of wealth against the poor, or those of one tradition or custom against those who do not know it, or are not born to it.'

'Are any viewed as unclean, as we view the Muslims and they us?'

'It would vary from place to place. The town where I was born was a small one, but there a man of different colour became a leading singer in one church though he was a stranger. The city where I first studied was a place of many colours and languages, but I have been turned away from churches there because no one could say I was a member.'

'Then it is just as with us. A foolishness of each place.'

'But we know the Muslims are unclean and dangerous, that is no foolishness.'

'Even though you have sat and listened to Muslim teachers you can still say that?'

'One wise man does not erase the memory of the blood.'

'Was it terrible, then?'

'Child, it is not for your ears. Not even the worst famines have been as bad.'

'Could it happen again?'

'No, never.'

'Of course not.'

'We have learned.'

'Yes, child, it could. But only in the east where we are and the land is good and the people are not of the same habits as their rulers. Those who work the delta and fish are not like the Muslims of the west who take the tax. If they fight, there would be blood. I hope it will not come.'

'Let us not speak of terrors. Child, tell us of the wedding. How will it be made? Will there be music and much food?'

For the rest of the afternoon the villagers spoke of feasts and weddings, festivals and births. They told of the jatra groups, the travelling actors who came sometimes for a great festival at the trader's house when entertainers would come and perform on the big verandah while all the villagers for miles around sat and cheered the night away. They remembered Uma Sen's wedding and Surendra even described the platters of sweets which were brought down to the well. They spoke of their own weddings, Uma telling of being carried on the backs of her brothers across the fields, Arundati of her terror in the boat as they crossed the river. Rhunu drew as they talked and showed the girl the excitement of those days. The foreigner questioned, they answered and remembered, and so the hours passed. Now and again Amiya would stop pulling at her hands and watch the girl, but she stayed silent. In the evening they reached Madurai. The bus pulled up to the station and an official climbed in:

'Tonight your train will go to Rameswaram, then in two days you will return to see the goddess Menakshi. Please be sure to have all your possessions when you go to the train. Follow me, please.'

The rush, the calls, the search for extra bundles. Chiding of one by another. The loss of a water pot. A bundle broken and spilled on the platform. At last, the carriage. Reena looked about for the girl and saw that Amiya had her by the arm and was pulling her along the platform.

'You must eat with us. You are too thin, you must eat. Then we shall see to your bed.'

There was no refusing Amiya, though the officer was shadowing them and calling out.

'It is not allowed. She must not go. This wagon is only for villagers from Bengal.'

Suddenly it was quiet. They were within their own carriage, food was served, and Deepaka had managed to put up the portrait of Uma Sen. Amiya whispered to Deepaka that they would just keep the girl with them and the officers would not know, but there was a banging on the door and an important looking man, followed by two guards, demanded, 'Tickets, show your tickets.' He looked at each, carefully avoiding the foreigner until the last. Then he took hers, held it to the light and spoke.

'This is a third-class ticket.'

'Yes, tourist's circular ticket, issued at Baroda House.'

'It is not fit for foreigners to buy third-class tickets.'

'How else would we meet the others who travel?'

'Only beggars or poor farmers can use third-class tickets. Foreigners must pay more. It is not in order.'

'It is paid for and issued at Baroda House.'

'So was this carriage, we also travel from Baroda House.'

'I tell you it is not in order. No foreigner should travel third-class. That is why they will only tell others that India is a dirty and backward country. We want them to travel first-class, there are good soft chairs in first-class. Then you can have good servants and drinks, and see that the country is beautiful and has many industries. I tell you it is very bad of Baroda House to give you a third-class ticket.'

'Most people travel third-class.'

'It is not my affair that most people are fools and good-for-nothings who can only pay for a third-class ticket. Those who work go second-class and foreigners always go first-class.'

'The ticket is good. May I have it back, please?'

'The ticket is badly written. You must come to my office while I examine it. You cannot travel with these people. They have a special pass. You have no special pass. You have only one badly written third-class ticket. Come to my office.'

'You cannot take her away.'

'This ticket is not in order. You have no business in this matter.'

'Child, do not go with him, he is a bad man.'

'He has my ticket.'

There was nothing for it. The farewells were quick. The girl touched the feet of some and was blessed. The officer shouted that she must hurry. Surendra cursed him. Amiya clenched the girl and said:

'You will not forget us? You will not forget what I said? You will attend to what we could have been?'

'I will not forget.'

'Amiya, give her your blessing. She must go. He can destroy the ticket if she does not watch.'

'What blessings have I to give to one who is able to walk alone so far from her home? Is that not blessing enough?' Amiya turned away, crying, so Reena pressed forward as the girl was helped down by Surendra, Elder De and Narend, each of whom got in the others' way.

'Watch for us on the stations, child. We go north to Madras and then to Orissa and home to Calcutta. Watch for us.'

'I shall, mother.'

'Hurry, I do not wait for someone with a third-class ticket.'

'He is a fool.'

'True, but he has power.'

'Go safely, remember that we shall want to see you if you see the carriage again.'

'Farewell, farewell.'

'Wait, she must drink some water. Then we shall meet again.'

'Yes, she must drink some water.'

'Fetch a glass.'

'Good'

'It is settled.'

'We shall meet again. She has had the water.'

'She drank the water.'

'Then we shall meet.'

'No, it is too late, too late. She will forget. She is young, they always forget the old.'

They travelled again through the night. In Rameswaram they examined the pillars, the carved horses, and the pilgrims in the long galleries and felt very tired. They walked in the sea. They slept against the warm rocks. By the time they were on the way back to Madurai they were dour with the strains of exhaustion. Tempers were short, fights broke out often, and not even Surendra felt eager to see the unpleasant station master again. He was spared the trouble, for a different official met them and arranged for their comfort. When they wound their way in a timid crocodile up through the streets towards Menakshi's temple, the day seemed brighter, and they began to take an interest in the confusion. The city was intensely busy. Above them, terrifying in size, were the painted towers of the temple, each figure distinct and staring down at them. The other towers they had seen were dull red or grey stone and had seemed just ordinary temples. This one stretched its fantasy up to the sky with a commanding drama which drew all eyes. Not even the long walk in sight of it prepared the villagers for the temple within and beneath it.

For half the day the priest led them about the temple, pausing to let them worship at one of the banks of goddesses, hurrying that they might see some wonder in the best light. When he left them at last they followed the homebound crowds through the convoys of bicycles and the angry traffic to the sanctuary of the carriage. Before the guide came next morning they managed to wash their clothes of the previous day and spread them along the siding to dry, then they were off again through the city to a bus and then out to a painted pavilion in the middle of a pond. It looked like a moated wedding cake. The villagers listened as the guide told them that this was the summer holiday house of the goddess. She was brought here with her consort, in a grand procession, and spent her days merry-making in this pavilion. He described the feasts, the lights for her pleasure, the marvel of the procession itself. He spoke of the return of the goddess to her home in the temple and the resumption of the routines of her year there. He told them of new robes, jewels, crowns brought for use in the holiday. The crowds were so great that many had been crushed and some killed, he said.

'And does all this please your goddess?' Elder De asked dryly.

'Of course. She gives us her blessings each year. Without her holiday she would become tired and angry.'

'Then she must be a goddess of the rich and leisured peoples?'

'No, she is goddess of all. All worship the great Menakshi, not only those who have riches to give her.'

'Who among the poor farmers here takes a holiday? Is it a general custom?'

'No, there are feast days and festivals, but farmers must stay near the soil, and the workers of the town must stay at their tasks for there are others who would take the work if they were idle.'

'Then why does your goddess give them a cruel example?'

'I do not understand.'

'It seems to me that the goddess shows little mercy towards her worshippers if she does what they cannot do at their expense. You say she must have a holiday. You say she must have new clothes. You say there is a procession in which many are injured and some are killed. You say that without all this the goddess could not fulfil the routines of her year in the temple listening to the prayers of her worshippers. But the farmer who comes to worship, the mother who gives her only money to ask for a son, these cannot have a holiday. They must pay for the goddess's holiday and then watch her leisure and the wonder of it. I say it is cruel, and thought out not by the poor who beg her favour.'

'No, sir. You are wrong. A poor man likes to see things he cannot have. He likes to see riches and beauty and the power of the great ones.

When he sees that they have so much more than he can ever have, he gives more willingly his worship. It is a blessing to see the goddess on her procession. It is a blessing to know that she is enjoying her holiday. It is a blessing to give a coin, a sack of rice, or a piece of cloth which will enrich her pleasures.'

'Or enrich the priests and their pleasures.'

'There would be no priests were there no worshippers.'

'But the worshippers are kept dutiful by the priests.'

'We are a nation of faithful men. Do you not think we will obey our duty without our priests?'

'Priests have little to do with the faith of a man. No, I think that such a temple as this is built by and for the priests, not for the faith of men. We see it, we give it our wonder and fear, but our faith we keep for the gods who understand our sorrows.'

'Hush, you must not speak so. The goddess can be angry.'

'I am an old man. The goddesses of the heavens have had many chances to show me their mercy and their anger. I go now to the river on my own legs and will be reborn because of my own faith and my own duties. Not because any goddess feels she must curse an insignificant elder of a village far away who thinks her holiday is foolish.'

'You will bring misfortune upon all who hear you.'

'Speak not so, for fear has little to do with this place. Come, Uma. Let us eat our food on these banks and think of the goddess being feasted here in the nights of the summer.'

'Surely it is not wise to do so. It is a place of power.'

'And a place to eat and enjoy the spring. Come, let us think of our own river and how the waters play with the sun on a morning like this.'

'Elder De,' said Uma, later that day, 'we have now seen many temples to many gods and many goddesses. But I am puzzled. Are they all the same goddess, having the same power but answering different prayers in different languages from different men? Or are they different too, each with a separate power? Must we pray to each to gain the grace of all?'

'What say the stories, Reena?'

'Too many things to answer a question clearly. For my part I think they are all part of the same power, just as the gods are all of one. We people are different, lead different lives, and thus we say different prayers to powers we think we need.'

'Ah, then, you see it as what we think we need, not as what is truly there?'

'I did not say so.'

'No, but it may be so, and if it is, then the fate of each is in the hands of each, not written by some hand of power.'

'That I would not say. For we are not able to make the crops grow well each year, nor make all the children we bear survive to a wedding day. Could we do so, would our fates be in our own hands?'

271

'Perhaps we can do so.'

'That is a great danger, and not to be thought of. One would try to make his fate one way, and another another, and the result would be injury and chaos, without duty or compassion.'

'I think it is not so, the gods and goddesses have each their own power, and because of the different ways that prayers are said to them we must pray to each in that way to gain the blessings each can give. The gods and goddesses have been here beyond the lives of men, they are not made by the thoughts and wishes of men.'

'No, didi, that is not so. For this and all other temples have been built, and the goddess within brought to it, by the hands of men. True, it was long ago, and some that we have seen, longer ago than writing will tell us. But you have watched Mitu fix our temple. You yourself before marriage helped in the washing of the image. All are made by men, in their own ways. That is why they differ from place to place and craftsman to craftsman.'

'But we speak not of the piece of wood, but of the power behind the eyes.'

'There is no power but that we have faith in it.'

'Oh Ma, then our faith must be true and strong or there will be no power for our grandchildren by the time they learn faith.'

'What, didi, would you deny that the gods gain their powers from our faith and yet say that faith must be learned? Is not faith a gift of those gods? Are not some born faithful and others foolish?'

'Of course faith must be learned, just as we must learn our duties. One gives heart and mind to faith in the powers of the gods, and others give heart and mind to the order of keeping the duties.'

'Cannot the two be joined?'

'For some, perhaps, at times. But one is more the song and the other the harmony about it. Singers must be taught to sing and to obey the order of music, though all are given voices.'

'Didi, what of me? I have no patience with puja, though I stop none from making it and hope they make it well. I have no patience with the forms of saying that this folly is due to that forgetfulness of some strange god. I have even less patience with the screams and giggles over the stories of bhuts and other unpleasantness which cause you women so much trouble. And I am a happy man, not one of the long faces suitable to holy men. Have I then no place before the gods, as a man without faith or duties?' Surendra grinned, curious to see how Deepaka would answer him.

'You live your life as the gods would wish it and you do no harm to your neighbours and companions. The gods find no fault with that.'

'But we cannot know what pleases the gods. To say that or this is what they wish is to bring them down to the level of the tax collector in the next town.'

'Then you show that you are a faithful man.'

'No, only one who would have justice done, to gods as well as men.'

'Justice, justice? What have the gods to do with justice? Are they not all women with tempers to be placated, or forgetful men who tread on many because they cannot notice us? There is no place for justice among the gods, Surendra, and none among us either. Each must guard his own fortune, and no other, god or man, can do it for him.'

'It would be easy to think you believed what you say, Babla, but your long life has betrayed you. You are as careful as any to help your neighbour mend his dikes, to join in the digging of the ditches to the fields, and to see that no disease goes from your beasts to mine. If you have guarded your own fortune, then you have kept good watch over mine as well.'

'That is true but it does not answer Babla's question. If we join faith and duty as Deepaka says we can, then surely the result of the union will be justice among us. That is enough for my hope. The gods can take care of themselves.'

'Uma, you do not speak as cautiously as one should when the marriage of a son approaches. Let us hope the gods take care of the young as well.'

'Ai, I will still light the lamps before the goddess, if the young like the old must walk to the river on their own legs, and if we have made her from our own thoughts and dreams.'

'Why do you do it?'

'It is a comforting habit.'

'Come, we must go to that uncomfortable bus.'

When, after seeing more temples, they returned to the carriage the station master was waiting for them. He was apologetic but brief. A group of beggars had passed through the station when the guard was sleeping. All the clothing which had been drying was stolen. He was very sorry. There was nothing he could do.

'But I have only one other sari.'

'And I only one other dhoti.'

'Who needs more than two? We will all be the better with less to carry.'

'Ai, ai, that was my best one. The only one with a red border.'

'It does not matter.'

'We must go at once and buy more.'

'Why? We need no more.'

'That was a new one from my daughter-in-law.'

'Why should beggars steal from pilgrims?'

'We are not pilgrims but rich tourists, remember?'

'If the harvest is good there will be new cloth pieces, do not bother now.'

'That is well said. You do not live with an ill-tempered daughter-in-law. She will scold me.'

'Then you must say the beggars must have needed the cloth more than we do. Perhaps they were children like Hassan.'

'You have an answer for all.'

They were taken to a women's college next morning. The principal told them how hard it was to persuade the girls to finish their courses.

'All this is just for girls?' said Jaydev.

'Do not say "all this". There are few colleges where education is good, most are just a way of filling in the time before marriage. It is difficult to train the girls to think for themselves and judge what is right within their lives. And it is difficult to teach the families that it is right that the girls be trained to judge.'

Back on the bus Babla said 'I do not think it good to teach girls to think and judge for themselves. Then all marriages will have to be by choice, and all the men will have to leave the land to make money for the bangles of the city.'

'No, I think they teach other things than the wish for bangles. They must work hard against it, though, for mothers and aunts teach the wish for bangles for years before and after the girl is in college.'

'What good will come of it? These girls live away from their families. They are taught by women. They learn only those things viewed as fit for women. They cannot help make the land more fertile, or stop the fires in the thatch. It is just a more complicated kind of sewing and painting and talking of poetry. The same as women have always praised in idleness.'

'That principal was not idle, and she talked of training doctors and lawyers and more teachers.'

'But why train the teachers to teach the same things over and over again? If a girl spends four years in college telling her teachers exactly what they have said so that she may pass their examinations and have a certificate, what is the difference between that and standing four years before a priest and being hit each time there is an error in the recitation?'

'The teacher said they try to teach the girls to judge for themselves.'

'I'll bet it comes to giving the wanted answer, anyway, that is the whole way of schooling. You have two sons, grown now to manhood but still in school. Can they do anything as well as you, let alone better? No, for I have seen them trying to thresh last harvest and it was as if Narend's grandson, who is but five harvests old, had done it. So why do you pay for the years in school? What can they do? What can a girl do? Only throw away all your money.'

'It is true they can do nothing on the land. It is true I am sorry they have only studied poetry. One day they will be teachers like Ashin. They will earn money and support a family.'

'In the city.'

'True, in the city.'

'Then what becomes of your land?'

'They will ask others to till it.'

'You mean they will stay in the city and let others work your land, and take the rents, as a tax collector?'

'Probably.'

'That is an evil thing to wish upon the village, Jaydev.'

'It is not as I would wish it. But they are now college men. They can recite Tagore and talk of great problems. I am still a simple man whose interest is in pumps. It was their mother's wish that both should study.'

'I do not know which is more evil. To have two sons in school, or one daughter who wishes to study.'

'No harm can come to their own lives if they study.'

'There are too many who know only reciting of Tagore and not enough who know about pumps, that I can say after our travels.'

'We must be quiet, Babla. Uma will be angry if she hears me say our sons are of no use on the land.'

'That is the trouble. She is educated, so you fear her anger. My wife is not educated so I ignore her anger and hit her when she bothers me and she thinks it is the right way for a husband to behave.'

'And who can say if either of us are as happy as Narend and Rhunu?'

'Ah, those ones! Now if all our sons could grow to be cultivators as good as Narend and all our daughters housewives as sensible as Rhunu, we would need no education.'

'And Narend says he has cost Rhunu her life, first her youth, then her training as an artist, and last her hopes that all would come right before she was old.'

'But what can a woman do as an artist, or without a man to show her her duties and give her her place?'

'I do not know, but I think Narend will try to find out.'

'Those two were born with good fates.'

'Or they have worked to make their lives full, who can say which?'

They spent the days shopping and seeing the sights of Trichinopoly and Tanjore. Steadily the villagers moved north along the flat coastal plain. They watched the work in the fields and missed their own. Often they spoke of how fine the rice was. Once in the night Amiya woke them with a soaring scream which echoed down the train like the cry of the whistle. Another morning they stopped to watch the planting and Narend and Surendra disappeared. When they returned they were bent with the weight of their rucksacks, and the others were shocked to see that they had bought seed rice.

'Why not, it is better rice here.'

'But will it grow in our paddy?'

'Of course.'

'We will treat it well.'

'The soil does not like strange things done to it.'

'What is strange to our soil about rice?'

'This is southern rice.'

'You only want to worry us. It will be well.'

At last they arrived in Madras. The station master handed Elder De their mail and said they were to go on to Tirupati and would see the city on their return from the hill of pilgrimage.

'Then we must call Mr De in New Delhi.'

'Are you the villager named Surendra?'

'Yes, how do you know of me?'

'I have a letter for you from Baroda House.'

'Ai, a letter for me?'

'Yes, must I read it for you?'

'No, he can read. He has learned since we began the journey.'

'One so old has just learned to read?'

'Never have I had a letter before. See, brother, there is a picture on it.'

'That is the stamp.'

'Why have you not learned to read in school?'

'I have been too busy in my life for such idleness.'

'Never would I call reading idleness. It is work. Now I must go, for a station master must read many papers. Just work, I say.'

Elder De handed out the letters and Harischandra and Reena were called often to read for the others. Surendra was a long time over his own, but when he had finished Arundati came shyly to him and asked if he would read her letter since the others were busy.

'I do not know if I can. It has taken me a long time to read this from Baroda House.'

'It is but a short letter. Babla says that news can wait, but it is long since we saw the children. Please read.'

'I will try. It begins "Most Respected Aunt".'

'Then from whom does it come?'

'It says Sundara, widow of Ashin, written in our village in the home of Elder De.'

'Why would Ashin's widow write to me?'

'It is good that she is in the village. Can any of your family write?'

'No, none.'

'Then perhaps she was asked. Let us see. It is very clearly written. It says "I write not to grieve you".'

'Something has happened. Oh Ma. Babla, Babla, come! Something has happened to the children!' Arundati screamed down the carriage and the others paused to watch Babla move reluctantly towards Surendra.

'There is no hurry, wife. Harischandra will read it later. You do not need to bother now.'

'It comes from the widow of Ashin and she says she does not wish to grieve us.'

'Why would Ashin's widow write to us?'

'Let us hear, let us hear. Harischandra must read for many. Surendra can read this one. It is not long. He says it is clearly written.'

'I should hope that the wife of the schoolteacher would write well. Read, Surendra, if you can. There is no hope of quiet until you do.'

'I will try. "I will not grieve you but having had my own sorrow so recently, I know that to hear of bad news is better than to worry".'

'I told you something has happened, I know it, I know it.'

'Then hush and let us hear.'

' "Two days ago-"'

'When was it written, when would that be?'

'It was written on the sixth day of the last moon, let me reckon. That would be about nine days ago, so what happened took place eleven days ago.'

'So long?'

'It is very quick, think how far the news has come.'

' "Two days ago before the dawn-" '

'Bad things always happen in the dark. It is ever so.'

'Hush, Fool. Read, Surendra.'

' "Two days before the dawn, your granddaughter, who is a sensible girl-" '

'Ai something has happened to my granddaughter, my own! Ai! Ai!'

'Hush or I shall have to hit you. Nothing has been said about anything happening to her, only that she is sensible which none has ever thought or said before.'

'She is sensible, so have I always said.'

'Now, for the first time. Go on and ignore this woman, Surendra.'

' " ... girl wakened to a strange noise. She called across the wall for us to come and went back to her brother's sleeping place. She found him choking in one of his fits".'

'Ai, he has not had one in a long time. It is our absence.'

'He has them every week and often each day, do not speak nonsense. All know it.'

'You have never paid attention to his pain.'

'Have I not? Is not my only heir an idiot? Do I not watch him every day and wonder who will say the prayers for me when I am dead?'

'But you care not for his pain.'

'Shall I finish it?'

'Yes, finish it.'

' " . . . in one of his fits. He was already blue, and when I reached him with the lantern he was dead. His sister found he had swallowed his tongue and thus the spirit left him. We took him to the river yesterday and all was said properly. Your granddaughter stays with me now. I hope you will send her to school when the term begins. We care for the house and beasts until your return. I weep for you and hope you must still for me." I am sorry Babla, Arundati, it is not good to hear of the death of a son's son.

Babla slid down the wall of the carriage, stared at his hands resting on his knees and then began to weep, silently, covering his head with his shawl. Arundati was screaming, 'My son is dead, My son is dead!' pulling her hair as she ran back the length of the corridor to their place. Rhunu looked at Surendra, who told her what had happened and she at once went to Arundati. Elder De came and sat beside Babla, his arm around the miser, his own tears for Ashin coming again. Surendra moved out to the siding to smoke. His own son lived. He is good enough, for a son. He speaks little to me and I little to him, thought Surendra. When it is his turn, he will do things well. The children, too, are strong enough and calm. They will stay true to the land. Ai, that one was just an idiot, but the pain must be the same as when my daughter died. Reading is not good when it brings such pain to others. Narend joined him:

'Does Babla still weep?'

'He has gone to Arundati.'

'It is not good to have such news on paper.'

'It is better to have it here than to have slept while he died in the same house.'

'True.'

'Amiya, too, weeps.'

'She had a letter.'

'The granddaughter has taken the examinations and won a scholarship to the college of nuns in Calcutta.'

'That should please Amiya.'

'No, she says she has meddled with the fates and only despair will come of it. She says it is too late.'

'And the others?'

'Insects destroyed the seed grain at Deepaka's house so it is good that I have extra. Ashin's wife lives at Elder De's house. The boatmen lost one boat in a storm and want the villagers to help in the building of another. Nirmal is well again and has started his school once more. My grandson goes and is a good pupil. Bankim still will not go to the temple for he thinks he is polluted by the aeroplane but Nirmal says this is foolishness. The other news I have not heard.'

'What is to be done for Babla and Arundati?'

'Nothing. She will stop screaming and try to comfort Babla. Then they will pay some priest to say prayers and it will be over.'

'The silence after is worse than the screaming now.'

'You are remembering.'

'Yes.'

'Rhunu and I are the lucky ones, all of ours have lived.'

'Is it luck, or Rhunu's skill and watchfulness?'

'Who can tell?'

Reena came out to join them:

'Amiya sleeps. She would have been proud at the beginning of the journey if the news of the scholarship had come then.'

'Is it the journey, then, which causes her sorrow?'

'No, it might have come in the village. She sees education is no more a way to happiness than being a village fool. To what shall she turn? She has no gods.'

'I thought I was the only godless one among us?'

'No, Amiya too. She believes in the skills of men's hands and minds. It is hard to face the failure and pain those can cause if there is nothing more.'

'But she has always made the pujas and sung the prayers.'

'She has been dutiful. She has not believed it.'

'Perhaps she feels it is too late to find a way to a god, not just to teach her hands a skill.'

'Who knows? Her mind is closed to us. Perhaps Deepaka knows, but she is grown very quiet.'

'Is Arundati resting?'

'She sleeps against Babla. It is better so. Had the boy lived beyond his grandparents the girl's life would have been destroyed. Now there is a chance for her.'

'It will be long before they see it so, Reena.'

'No. They know that the girl wants to work and that she fears to have children. There will be no pleasure to them in forcing her to bring another such a one into this world.'

'Babla will not give money for schooling for a girl.'

'Too much wearies me. It must be that the station master is right and reading is work. I feel as if I had harvested all fields in this one day.'

'I, too, brother. There is another pilgrimage tomorrow.'

The station master roused them in twilight and sent them fasting on the ride to the hill of Tirupati. The crowd of other pilgrims flowed slowly up the mountain to the rich temple at the summit. For a long time the villagers climbed with them, showing a strength and endurance that the others envied. Coming down the steps were women with shaven heads, men with sandalwood paste clinging between their eyes. As the villagers walked they did not talk but wondered who would show the way at this new devotion. Arundati, a step behind Babla, spoke to him often. They were pale and alone in their grief, separated from the others by a barrier of loss which made their usual loneliness all the more acute. Elder De tried to stay close to them for he was frail again with the reminders of Ashin. Inwardly he rejoiced that he would be going home to Sundara-devi and her children instead of to the lonely niece who had served him since his wife's death. Reena hung back to watch, but she found the sight unpleasant. At last they were at the summit and the temple soared glittering above them. From every side the barbers called, the priests shouted devotions on behalf of clients and the excitement of the crowd was shrill above the rest. Amiya and Arundati were the first to have their heads shaved. Arundati grew calm as she accepted the gesture. Amiya watched her grey hair fall with growing alarm. Deepaka and Reena stood back.

'You do not have it cut either?'

'I am too old.'

'It is a gesture of devotion.'

'I think not. The temple is rich. The gods do not need my white hair in addition to my prayers.'

'There we agree. It will bring sorrow to Amiya.'

'She said it was a plea to the gods to right things which she has tried to change.'

'Does she believe that?'

'No, it makes the saying easier.'

'And the others?'

'Arundati mourns. The others do it because they think it is custom. Some ask for more grandsons.'

'The men?'

'Who knows?'

'Narend has asked Rhunu not to be shaved.'

'Of course.'

'Uma?'

'A first grandchild is in her thoughts.'

'We are strange. You pray before all and I tell stories, and all these who let their hair fall for no reason. I am often puzzled.'

'So am I.'

'But still you pray?'

'There are few ways to comfort those who suffer. Perhaps the gods will show the way.'

'I have not heard you doubt before.'

'I do not know if comfort is only our duty and not a concern of the gods, or if they do comfort us. The Muslims pray before our goddesses too, for sons, or when the diseases come. But when they are in sorrow, with whom do they weep? With their god? With their neighbours? And are we different? The priest said all priests should comfort, but the sadhus do not attend to others. What makes a man close to the gods? Is it closeness to his neighbours, as we told the priest? Is it closeness to the temple, as Bankim thinks? Or is it as Surendra feels, to know joy when it comes?'

'You have many questions.'

'Reena, all my life I have not asked them. Not even when the children died.'

'Children die without the gods noticing.'

'True, though we still pray for the children.'

'It makes no sense. The tales do not tell us if Parvati wept over dead children and prayed to Lord Siva her husband.'

'The children of the gods must not die.'

'All children are in danger.'

'Then why do we pray?'

'Because if our neighbours do not hear us when we need to speak to them, we must have someone to listen.'

'Or perhaps we are trained to say things to stones and not to our neighbours who might hear.'

'Deepaka, Deepaka! Where are you? Amiya runs!'

Rhunu's voice reached the two women just as Amiya burst upon them out of the crowd.

'Ah fat frog, I have found you. They have cut it off and I have prayed to the gods, but my doubt remains. It is too late. There is no hope that what is done may now be changed. Ah, Deepaka, what have I done?'

'I do not know. But you have made good service here, now let us go down. I find no joy in watching these priests.'

'Go down?'

'Away from the hill, to the bus. Take my hand and I will lead.'

'You are right. We must go away from the gods, there is no help.'

'There may be some, there may be none, but it is good to pray as you have done.'

'No, it is too late. Nothing will change.'

'What is fate? Was it fate that brought us on this journey?'

'Truly, truly.'

'No, it was the wish of Uma-didi. Think of the times you nursed her. You did not think you would see the places she had seen.'

'I should not have nursed her. Uma-didi has died, perhaps she would have lived.'

'You speak forgetfully, you know well that Uma-didi had a sickness that none could help. Watch your step, there are many who come up.'

'Fat frog, you are now my staff when once you were my tail.'

'There is far to go.'

'No, there is no farther to go. It is too late to go any more.'

They spoke constantly through the long descent, riddles to any who listened, but listening carefully each to the other. They were the first into the bus and slept while they waited. When they returned to Madras the shaven women were shy before one another and the men followed behind aware that they were unwelcome. A cup of tea broke their long fast. Arundati cried again on seeing the letter, but the crying was quiet and the others left her to her memories. At last they slept and only the flash of the watchman's lantern disturbed them, for they were used to the wailing and bumping of trains.

At dawn there was a banging on the door of the carriage. There were guards and an eager crowd.

'What is it? What is it?' Surendra shouted and he rose from his bunk. The answer was in Tamil. After a moment he had the carriage door open and the guard pulled and pleaded with him. Surendra understood he was wanted. Narend and Elder De followed closely. They were pushed and pulled up the track by the guards to where another crowd stood quietly across the main line. Surendra blinked and let himself be pushed through the crowd. Then he was standing against the cold feet of Amiya. She had been crushed by a train. The station master explained that the driver had made every effort to stop and to warn her, but she had crouched in the track unmoving and the train had hit her even as it braked. Narend bent and pulled the sari over the crumpled body. Elder De was sick. Then, ignoring the comments about police, apologies, no protests, and so on, which the station master repeated urgently, Surendra bent and tried to lift Amiya. He stumbled and would have dropped the body had not Narend caught them both. Then the two old men carried Amiya to the grass of the siding, straightened her figure and covered it. There they waited for the others.

10
Homeward

'She was burned yesterday, Mr De, they all went together . . . No, today some have stayed by the train, but others went out to see the city. They say there need be no investigation.'

In the pause as he listened the station master looked at the several figures crouched in his office. His distress was obvious to his uniformed clerks, but the villagers were unperturbed.

'Their leader? I think they have no leader. There is an old man with glasses who weeps much, he is an elder in the village. Do you mean that one? . . . A farmer? The big one is very quiet, but he sent them out on the tour; or there is a writer who records all that I say and what has happened. Or do you mean the white haired widow who was a friend of the dead one? She stopped the anger, and said all is as it was meant to be . . . No, another? There is the one who came first when we found the woman. A thin old man who is a friend of the porters of my station? Yes, he is here. Then there is nothing for me to do? . . . I see, I see. That will be done. Here you, come and speak with Mr De. Why he should want to speak to you I do not know.' The station master turned away from the telephone as Surendra took it. Harischandra moved closer, and Deepaka watched with wonder as Surendra talked into the instrument.

'Good evening, Mr De. We speak only when there is sad news.'

'I am sorry, Surendra. Do you know why Amiya wished to die?'

'Yes, she was broken. There was no sense to her living because she felt she had meddled with the fates and failed. She has long looked towards death, I fear her life was not a happy one.'

'How are the others?'

'Some are shocked, some are sad, but most of them are relieved to be free of the fear of her madness. They all want to get back to the village. I think we must stop the tour once we reach Calcutta. Another group can see the eastern Himalaya, though I would like to go north with them when they do.'

'Do you think they can finish that much of the tour without trouble?'

'Yes, Deepaka has told them that death is written. We are all old, whether we die here or in the village matters little. What matters is that

283

we do as Uma-didi wished and learn from this journey. Amiya was not willing to learn. It is women's talk maybe.'

'Does Elder De want an investigation?'

'No, he knows it was her wish, and no fault of the train. He is weeping again for Ashin. The loud ones who spoke of an investigation have been hushed. There is nothing but trouble to be gained from such things. No questions can help Amiya now.'

'Have you the money from the bank?'

'Yes, I have your letter and I fetched the money before we paid for the wood yesterday.'

'Are they healthy?'

'They sleep as babes on the train and Uma has kept us eating well.'

'Then there is nothing to say but to wish you strength on the homeward journey.'

'It is good, sahib. I like this southern rice. We go to see the eastern sea. It is not all the same as I said in Delhi!'

'Then you find the journey good despite the two dead?'

'I miss my bullocks. But now my feet go wandering after new sights each day. Perhaps it will be hard not to carry my rucksack in the village.'

'You carry a rucksack?'

'Yes, Narend and I bought two from foreign children in Bombay. We carry the maps and some of the food. It is easy and I can smoke as I walk.'

'The doctor sends you greetings.'

'Give the doctor sahib my salute. He will be sad to hear of Amiya.'

'Yes, he thought her very fine.'

'I must stop Mr De, the station master wishes his talking machine.'

'Will you wire me, with the telegraph when you reach the village, and ask Harischandra to write me a letter?'

'I will do so with my own hand.'

'Then farewell, friend.'

'Good-bye Mr De.'

The station master sent the villagers back to the train. They talked of the decision to stop the journey in Calcutta. Deepaka sighed and packed away the bundles containing Amiya's things.

'Better that they be out of sight for a time,' she muttered, but Elder De replied:

'Yes, though the hardest time will be explaining to the others in the village.'

'No, for just as Sundara-devi knew of Ashin's death, so they will know. They will know from her letter that she will not return.'

'How do you know?'

'The letter brought news that her granddaughter has won a scholarship to go to Calcutta, and Amiya replied that it was too late.'

'How will the girl go to college now that the grandmother is gone?'

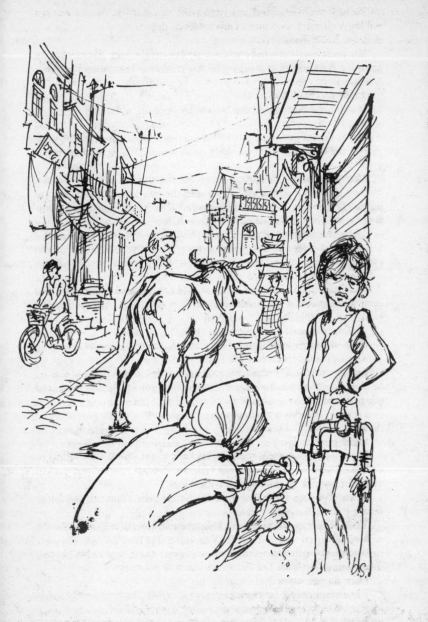

'Probably the father will marry her off.'

'Then we must stop him. Amiya wanted this much, we must see it is done as she wished.'

'Who can say if she truly wished it? At one moment she felt it right for the girl to go and at another she felt schooling brought only trouble and sorrow.'

'The last is foolishness. The journey has shown us all that only those knowing more than we do can help us to get more to eat and the babies to live.'

'Has it shown us that, Elder De? Sometimes we see more of the ways that we are kept poor and those with power gain all. That is what Amiya saw.'

'No, there is hope, but we must go, Surendra calls.'

Over the next days the villagers toured the museums of the city, went out to the temples of Mahabalipuram and Kanchipuram, listened to the singers, watched the students of a dance school and examined the shops of the southern capital. Babla, secretly, bought seed grains as Narend and Surendra had done. Mitu returned again and again to look at the bronze statues in the museum and took Rhunu with him once to share his excitement. Reena matched skills with a southern storyteller and the villagers were shocked to find that she could hold the audience mesmerized even when they did not understand her language. Harischandra found a bookshop and library and from then on did not go on excursions with the others. Narend wandered alone, speaking to no one, unwilling to share his thoughts with Rhunu. The last evening as he was returning to the carriage after the others he heard loud cries of beggars crying for alms. The voices had a bravado and insistence he had not often heard and he turned aside to see the source. Coming down the platform, the last of the passengers leaving a train, was a tall figure Narend thought familiar. It was surrounded by a circling pack of beggars. The whole group moved dreadfully slowly. Then Narend grinned and in a few strides had come up beside the foreign girl, taken her case, and scattered the beggars.

'Welcome, daughter, we meet again.'

'Thank you, uncle. Seeing your face, I am at rest.'

'You must not let the beggars bother you.'

'I rarely give to these, but I do to the children. They all expect so much. I feel ashamed that there is nothing to give.'

'They are wrong to expect it. They treat all travellers like that.'

'No, you speak to comfort me. You know that they do not. They are right to think that we who come from across the seas have riches beyond their dreams.'

'Your money is for study, not for beggars.'

'I fear it cannot be otherwise.'

'Ah, child, you have learned too much. There will still be food if we hurry.'

In the carriage the greetings were loud and happy. The girl was embraced by the women, patted by the men, and drawn down at last to sit between Deepaka and Elder De as Uma loaded a tali and berated the foreigner for not having eaten since last they had seen her. As she ate they questioned her as to where she had been, what she had seen, commenting and scolding the while with all the warmth of affection and loneliness. They told her of Amiya and she wept.

'Why does she weep? Amiya is not her dead.'

'Look, a foreigner weeping for us!'

'Ah, child. Do not cry. She was old. You are young. It is for the old to weep for the young, and the young to laugh. Do not weep.'

Back and forth they spoke, and throughout the night they talked, telling the girl of all the times in the village when Amiya had led them, of the strange bitterness each young bride felt when first she presented her mother-in-law with a son. He was her liberation from the bondage, yet he was the final cement to the bonds as well. They spoke of the journey and the homeward way. Over and over again they asked the girl where she would go and whether she could go with them. At dawn, they were still talking. Rhunu and Mitu had both sketched the scene. Surendra had smoked all the biris in the carriage. The morning shunting in the yards began. The girl stretched out on Amiya's bunk and slept, watched by Reena, while the others rested. In the warmth of the morning the station master came to tell the villagers to prepare to leave. The women rushed to buy food. Surendra made a last check of maps and tickets. They watched as the shunting engine pulled them to the rest of the train. They laughed at the worried confusion of the other passengers pushing and rushing to find seats. The girl swung down to the platform and the villagers wept as the train pulled away, leaving her standing alone, both hands raised high and pressed together as the final salute.

The train moved north along the sea coast. The villagers slept and talked little. Harischandra tried to interest some in the history of Orissa. Reena told him to hush, now was a time of silence. A day and a night later they pulled into Cuttack and watched a family of naked tribesmen cook their meal while lingering for another train. Back they went to Bubaneswar and descending, found that the land was not rocking. In the wide square before the station even the pigeons walked carefully in the shadows. There was a red dust everywhere. It tasted of metal and oil and spice, and clung to the teeth like strong tea. When the town roused from the midday sleep, Uma found a market. She and the women shared a good gossip with the Bengali merchants. The men talked of the crops, and whether the rains would be good. They returned to the carriage at ease.

It took two days to see the temples of Bubaneswar and the caves at Udagiri. Each time the bus passed glistening ricksha men pulling other tourists in the heat, many of the villagers spoke of their shame at being so luxuriously treated. Everywhere the farms were poor, the land dry, the people more sullen than in the south. The talk was of drought and there was fear in the land. When the villagers' way turned towards the coast, they were relieved to smell the salt on the wind and watch reeds growing in the sand beside the road. They wound past the dunes for many miles. Sometimes there was a village, sometimes a stunted, sea-blown forest. At last they moved with traffic, and realized they had reached Puri, the home of Jagannath, Lord of the Universe. The bus took them along the edge of the city to a modern building above the pounding sea. This was the tourist bungalow, and for three nights the villagers felt themselves to be living amid opulence. The building was new, the rooms small and discreetly furnished. For the first time in her life Deepaka slept in a room alone, and was afraid. Each morning the villagers rose to rich cooking smells and feasted on the fish and hot food of sea-going people. Ever in their thoughts, thudding against every effort to walk, was the rhythmic roaring of the sea. The Bay of Bengal was blue but belligerent, and in these days never still beneath the full moon. Arundati played in the foam like a child. Reena and Surendra sat and watched the ebb and flow silently, for hours. Narend and Rhunu walked miles beside it under the sun, and close together in the bright darkness. When the guides came to show the villagers this and that in the town, they gathered away from the water reluctantly, and returned to it with all the cries and fluttering of sea birds.

The guide took them up and down small side streets to weaving shops and tanneries where wizened men with bright eyes offered them snake skins for luck. They walked along one small avenue where painters made small images of the great gods of Puri. Mitu thought them poor and the others agreed with him. Along a wide avenue they joined the stream of pilgrims buying little dolls of Jagannath, beads, lamps and prayer shawls. Sometimes they stopped long to watch a carver, or a craftsman at his work, but usually they were hurried by the guide and the crowds. The first day they did not go into the temple, but saw its environs. By sunset they were exhausted. Next morning they went to worship the Lord of the Universe and each bowed before the enormity of the towers and the staring eyes of the god. They watched the other worshippers and were lectured by the priest on their duties before this god. When at last they returned to the house by the sea they were spent of adoration and sat licking their fingers of the rice set before them for supper, and joked with the fishermen spreading their long black nets out before the night.

'Do you walk again, husband?' asked Rhunu quietly.

'Do you come?'

Rhunu nodded and the two walked out among the dunes. When the moon came up Rhunu stopped, tired, and sat on the sand.

'It is time you spoke, Narend. We shall soon be back in the village where even the walls gossip.'

'I have been thinking of that.'

'And of what else?'

'Of the granddaughter of Amiya. Amiya made me promise to see that she goes to college, I must find a way to do it.'

'But Amiya wrote that she would put her jewels of dowry to pay the expenses of the girl.'

'There will be none to speak for the girl now. Her father has never known me to meddle in his compound. I think they will try to arrange a marriage quickly.'

'Just as with Amiya.'

'Yes, and the jewels can be worth little, after all.'

'Perhaps it would be best, if she must stand the long studies alone.'

'That would not be Amiya's wish. The fates are not written twice the same.'

'What would you do?'

'I do not know. I fear to speak, yet I feel the girl must have her chance.'

'They will know that you heard the wishes of Amiya before the madness took her, and Deepaka will support what you say.'

'There is a way, wife, but it is difficult . . . I fear to speak of it to you.'

'Speak.'

'We have raised two fine sons and married them well. The dowry money from both girls sits untouched in a bank, for there I placed it and we have never spent that much.'

'You have not told me.'

'No, it seemed better not to, for then there would be the wish to use the money for trials which we could stand without it.'

'That is true.'

'If the son of Amiya makes difficulty for his daughter, I propose that we adopt her.'

'What, husband?'

'It is often done with sons, why not for us with a daughter?'

'But she is young and we are old and her parents are of the same village.'

'That is true, but we could make it possible for her to study, and later be responsible for her dowry and marriage.'

'But we should be bound to another's child. What if our own should need help?'

'Our sons did not wish to study, though both write when there is need. They came to the land and have done well. You know that only the sons of Deepaka are as good farmers as our boys, and they all work together to better their plots. When we die there will be little more for them. They need never suffer more than the others of the village in times of want, but we have kept nothing back from them now in their youth. I propose to ask them if they will help the girl.'

'Ask the wives to give up their dowries so that another remains unmarried? Husband, have you caught Amiya's madness?'

'Our daughters-in-law have much courage, and their lives are full. They know the girl and how she yearns to leave the compound. It is not all.'

'You would do this thing without my counsel?'

'What is your counsel?'

'Do not speak to the children of the dowry money in the bank. They will think, as I have thought, that it has long ago been spent on bullocks and ploughs. Wait. If there is difficulty speak to the girl alone. Find out if she truly wishes to study. Perhaps her yearning is merely to leave her father's house. Perhaps she wants to be married to someone far off. If she wishes to study and there is trouble, speak of Amiya and her wish. Then speak of the fates and the dowry jewels of Amiya. They will send the girl to the city for a trial, and once she is away from the village you can offer help. Then there will be no gossip. She will be untied to us as well.'

'You speak, as always, of secrecy.'

'There is nothing to be gained from calling like a peacock for all to hear.'

'We shall do as you wish, but only if you will support the girl.'

'She is not my child. Have I not done my duty as a wife?'

'None better and all know it. But you are more than a wife.'

'I do not understand.'

'The gift of your hands is something of honour. You are a better artist than Mitu and he has said it.'

'I have been foolish, though Reena knows it has troubled me.'

'Of what does Reena not know, but her own death? But I speak of you. There is little now to keep you in the village.'

'Are not you there, and my children and their children?'

'And how often have you hated us for binding you?'

'Forgive me, lord husband.'

'Hush now, and listen. I have been thinking of this for a long time. Will you not go to the city, too? Will you not take Amiya's granddaughter in your care, but go to study art, as once you wished to do when the missionaries spoke of such things?'

'You would send me alone to the city?'

'Not alone, I have just said, you would be with the girl.'

'Are you tired of your wife?'

'I shall be a lonely man, and you know it well.'

'Will you stay in the village?'

'May I not visit you from time to time?'

'I thought you and Surendra wanted to walk to the high hills.'

'You have been listening in the dark. We are but old fools.'

'True, but you have grown sons to plough your fields.'

'I shall plough my own fields. We do not go until after harvest.'

'Is it settled then, without my hearing?'

'If you wish to study, it is settled.'

'Like Parvati must I weep, while my Lord goes wandering.'

'I am no yogi, I shall not forget to come back.'

'No, but you would leave.'

'You will not go to study if I stay.'

'True, though what you offer is but a dream and not fate.'

'You must draw what you love, and all those things which Amiya said we must not forget. Attend, attend she said. There is little time for us, we must attend to all with care, and use the time now for dreams.'

'You are much grieved.'

'Amiya was often silent. I feel I knew her well, though we talked only on this journey. Like Deepaka she is part of me. Now that part is gone.'

'You should come and study and Bengal will have such a poet as Tagore once again.'

'Then you will go?'

'Yes, lord husband, I will go.'

'Hush then, let us speak no more.'

Hours later, when they crept to their beds in the hostel they saw that a bus was parked outside. In the early dawn they and all the other villagers were herded into it for the journey to Konarak. On the sun temple horses pulled the chariot of the sun across the sky. On each wheel nymphs danced to some silent tune, on the flank of the chariot couples loved in the graceful charms of lila: the play of the gods, of life, of love, of death, of remembering and forgetting. In the van the horses' nostrils flared and the stone seemed to sweat with their effort. It took hours to see the carvings. The figures beckoned and the warm stone was alive under examining hands. First a watcher stood near and looked at the jewels on the dancers, the fine anklets perfectly still. Then he moved back among the grasses and looked at the whole, awed that the stone was not truly moving across the sky. Back again to climb up to a ledge to gaze into a goddess's eyes, or trace a vine as it climbed from one figure to another. Mitu and Rhunu were beside themselves. Reena crouched and sang to herself the stories of Surya, the sun. Narend and Surendra set off before the horses, wondering, talking little of this greatest of all wonders. Sunset. Time to go. On the bus Uma said, 'For this alone the journey has brought us near to the gods.'

The bus stopped in a small village while the driver visited some friends. The villagers watched an old man making his worship before a tree. His hair was matted and hung in heavy ropes where he had filled it with dung. Around his body was a strange half-brown, half-red cloth which had been sewn with the feet and tails of various small animals. At each ankle he wore a heavy circlet of bone. Over one shoulder he carried a cloth pouch. In one hand was a heavy staff. He was slightly bent though young, and his looks towards the bus were of anger, resentment and great pride. He circled the tree slowly, muttering the while. Gradually his pace quickened and he drew out of the pouch a small brass pot. When his back was directly to the villagers he stopped, poured something on the tree and then began his circling again, now cupping the pot in one hand. Seven times he went round the great trunk, pouring his libation. Then he stopped, crouched and sat still. So the villagers left him, each wondering and questioning what he had been worshipping there at the tree. Back in Puri the wail of the megaphones blaring film music reminded them that they must journey in the morning away from the sea. They spent the night listening and dreaming, with the rushed and sucking tide close-by.

North again briefly to Cuttack where they were shown a barren city hiding a rich and colourful handicraft industry, then on to the hills near Balasore. Here they stopped and were taken out to see hill temples and mining near by. No longer did they attend to the sights, for they had Surendra's map and knew that tomorrow they would be in Bengal and with the dawn at Howrah. No matter what the guides said, they chattered about the village. They were thin, even Arundati had muscles and could keep up with the rest without complaint. They teased back and forth that this one would find his house more orderly than ever it had been run previously, that that one would find his fields unprepared and his sons asleep by the hearth. They wondered what they would do in Calcutta. Memories of Howrah hushed them. At last they wept and then the talk became open and they argued long over all they had seen and done. Just as they were ready to sleep the train stopped at Midnapore station. There was a clamour and a shout and two figures pushed their way into the carriage.

'Hai, you sleepers, awake and welcome your fellows!'

'Come, show us that we are your honoured guests!'

'What?'

'Strangers!'

'Listen to the fool. He has seen the demons of the south and does not recognize his own people.'

'Nirmal, Bankim! How do you come to be here?'

'What is this? What is this?'

'Waken. Is there tea for Nirmal and Bankim?'

'Where do you come from?'

'How do you meet us?'

'Have you not been to the village?'

At last they were awake and the greetings and questions hushed so that Nirmal, looking jaunty and mischievous, explained. Bankim grinned beside him and kept nodding at the familiar faces.

'We decided to finish the journey with you, so I stole the money for our tickets to Calcutta from my daughter's pot—she scolds less than the daughter-in-law, you know—and came to the station of Howrah. With much trouble I got the station master to find out where you were and he said at last that you would be here this night. We came yesterday and have been waiting.'

'He said he was the messenger from Baroda House,' said Bankim.

'But how was it in the village?'

'When did you leave?'

'How are they?'

'There is trouble coming in the east, there have been three families wanting to stop in the village. But we are all eager for the news. Do we go north now to Himalaya?'

'No, we stop in Calcutta.'

'What? Have we come this way for half a night's journey?'

'Why, why do you not go on?'

'The ticket has been paid to the north.'

'Yes, the ticket has been paid.'

'Then why stop?'

There was silence. At last Deepaka spoke:

'Do you see none missing, teacher?'

'Ai, let me look. Surely all are here. But wait, where is Amiya?'

'Where is Amiya? I have not yet been scolded.'

'She sat and waited for a train to crush her in Madras.' The others gasped at Deepaka's brutal clarity.

'Oh Ma. It is not so.'

'What a fate has followed this journey!'

'Say it not. Amiya's fate was written on her forehead alone, it was for none other.'

'In the village she was always strong.'

'Stern, but not strong. She helped us, she scolded us, she gave us her skills, but there was always a bitterness about her, is it not so?'

'Truly, truly. But Oh Ma, what a death.'

'It could have been one of the slow illnesses and then we would all have shared her pain for longer.'

'You think it was no fault of the journey?'

'Death is no fault. It was her time to meet the boatmen.'

'So it must be, so it must be. How her son will be angry!'

'Why? Will he not now have title to her lands?'

'Title? There have been no titles since the famine of 1943 when she was a bride. We all lost any titles then.'

'Her pride was not from land, but from her hopes. When she lost them it killed her pride. It is not good to link our pride with hope.'

'We watched the pride go after Ashin's death.'

'Then she died?'

'Then she died.'

'Ah, so it is. All is written. All is cast by the great ones. I see now you do not go on from grief for the village.'

'Few will go on, some of us will take the journey with the next group.'

'They will say in the village there is to be no next group. Ashin's death was a portent of ill fate. With this second ill news, none will go.'

'All will go in the end.'

'No, you are wrong. They have said they will petition Ashin's widow to get the money from Baroda House and build a village school in his name. Then none will need to go around all India.'

'And who would send the children? You never had pupils three days out of four, Nirmal.'

'True and I am of your thought, for if the school is in the village it is soon dismissed as of no importance.'

'Sundara-devi, what does she think?'

'She says nothing, she still mourns. But she talks to her children of the day when they will go with her on a journey made possible by Uma-didi, and see the things viewed by their father.'

'Then she will have nothing of the plan.'

'That depends on Elder De.'

'It will not be possible to see that the others understand that the journey is needed.'

'No one will board a train when they hear of Amiya.'

'Then we must show them that we who return have gained.'

'So, Deepaka, have we gained from your worship in the temples of filth?' asked Bankim.

'From my worship only I can gain. From the journey is this talk possible. Never before have we sat as now and spoken of schools and travel and the foolishness of our children. There is much gained.'

'You, Mitu, the quiet one, and of the poorest of the village. Has there been gain?'

Mitu stayed silent. Narend spoke:

'Mitu has become an artist whose work is now sought by wise men in far places. He is no more the village potter.'

'What, Mitu, do you sell clay pieces for money?'

'No, they are not worth money.'

'You do not speak the truth, brother. One piece you have sold to me, and another to the priest, who gives as well the promise of help when you return to him in the far south.'

'That is so.'

'Oh Ma, is it true? Does Narend give money for clay?'

'It is my money, if little.'

'Are the others, are we all now artists and famous?'

'There is no need for all to be artists, Bankim, but all are more than they once were.'

'You speak in riddles.'

'Then, fool, listen, listen.' Reena glared.

'What would you tell us, mother?' Nirmal intervened between the old enemies. He was no more the adamant pedant, no more the moral guide. He had learned to laugh.

'Did the great Garuda awaken your heart, teacher?'

'Oh Ma, I thought it would break my ears. It was all my own foolishness in shouting at you who saved my life. It is a good lesson to know that yours is not the only pain. When Surendra loosened the hurt of my head I saw that none other had screamed at the worthy devotion of a faithful servant.'

'Speak only what is true, not of fancy,' Deepaka's face took on a sudden hardness.

'I came to the village in the car of the doctor of Delhi. He sent a telegram to his family and they took us to the village and told the villagers of all that must be done, and all that had passed. We travelled as rajahs of old must have done. Is there more tea?'

'Imagine, the doctor asking his family to help!'

'Ai, Amiya would be happy.'

'With a car, to the village!'

'We stayed the first night in a clinic, and a doctor took pictures of the inside of Nirmal's head.'

'What magic?'

'Is there a sorcerer?'

'Were you more hurt?'

'No, no, it is just a medical machine to catch the special sight of the great gods. He gave me the picture, I can show you in the village. My head is very big.'

'And that brings wisdom, no doubt.'

'Ai, you should have seen the faces when we came in the car. Your grandchild Narend was the first to see and he went running ahead for all to come.'

'Then my grandson is well?'

'And growing more each day. You will not be the tallest for long.'

'And the new granddaughter?'

'She can walk.'

'And my grandsons?'

'And mine?'

'How is it with my daughter?'

'Is my boy's foot better?'

'Why have you not spoken of my grandson's death? Is my grand-daughter not well?'

'My sorrow to you, Babla, and you, Arundati-ma. I did not know if you had heard and none wishes to be the first to tell of a boy's death. It was over quickly for him, all say it is better so. His trials would be terrible once you his parents had gone. The girl is well though she eats too little from worrying that you will judge her. She would be a good teacher, she helps me and Sundara-devi with the children.'

'My sorrow as well, Babla. It was an ill fate written at his birth, perhaps he will now find a better one.'

'How to learn if my boy has now been born into a happier home?'

'Oh Ma, that is a task only for the best astrologers.'

'They say there is a woman of Calcutta who has contact with the newly dead and can tell where each is reborn.'

'She will cost money.'

'Some, but she is just a simple woman.'

'Then we must try to find her, I do not wish to return to an empty house until I know that the boy has another mother.'

'What said the palm?'

'I do not know of that. It is nonsense.' Nirmal stretched as if to sleep.

'Ai, they read it, but could see nothing. There was no mark for death and none to show the fits would take him.' Bankim spoke as if ashamed.

'That is true, there was no mark to show he would have the fits or that his mind would not be good.'

'What sense is there in the palm tales?'

'Why, is there another way to read the fates?'

'Amiya's palm showed nothing, only strength.'

'And the marks of work with the grinder and in the fields.'

'All our hands show that.'

'Is that not the fate of all?'

'Hush this talk. There have been no other deaths?'

'No, we old are away and it is not yet the time of sickness. The young wife of the boatman's younger son will have no child again. Two of the bullocks of Jaydev were lame for a time but Narend's son has made them well. He takes them out with his own, so you need have no worry, Jaydev.'

'Has my son brought news of his wedding?'

'He came at Holi. The bride is from Murshidabad, so you will have a long journey before this moon has died.'

'This moon?'

'Do you not know? The star readers have said that there must be no marriages after the end of this moon, for there is great trouble coming from the east.'

'Ai, a wedding so soon.'

'I do not like to journey to Murshidabad.'

'Are you not become a wanderer too, Jaydev?'

'No, I want my own soil in my feet, and to lay new pipe to a pump.'

'What are the lights ahead?'

'Do you not know your own land? Those are the lights of Calcutta.'

'So it is at an end.'

'Not yet, not yet. We still have the city to see.'

'Where do we stay, Surendra?'

'I do not know.'

'The station master said in a hostel of some mission.'

'Of more foreigners?'

'No, one of the Ramakrishna places, I think.'

'Ai, who can pay for that?'

'Wait and see.'

Dawn was awakening the city when they slowly pulled into the darkness of Howrah station. This time the carriage was not shunted to a special place and no one came to greet them. Eventually sweepers chased them from the carriage. They crouched among the bundles on the platform while Surendra went in search of an official. Nirmal was clucking and strutting, but the villagers were no longer talkative. They mourned with the birds above them on the rafters. Deepaka alone counted parcels, retied cloth bindings and distributed the loads. Reena sat looking back along the track and would not speak with Harischandra. Uma started a quarrel with Rhunu over who should carry Amiya's bundle. Soon the whole platform was a cacophonous array of animosity. The men fought over whether their lands would be in order or whether this one or that one had done too little to share the burdens of the journey. The women fought over their souvenirs, accused one another of squandering the money, decried the cooking and even turned against the waiting children in the village. When Surendra returned, accompanied, the noise ceased abruptly and the villagers sulked, ashamed of their disgrace. The officer told them that because they had come early, beds could be found only for fifteen; the rest would have to sleep in a courtyard of the mission. He drew a circle on their map showing where they must go and bade them a curt good-bye.

'Is that all? Is there no word from Baroda House?'

'Do we not warrant a feast at the end?'

'Will there be no speeches?'

'I have sent a telegram to Mr De. There is a letter which says we must fetch our tickets at Sealdah in three days' time.'

'Are we to have no guide?'

'The station master is relieved to see us go. Word has come from Madras of what happened. We are no longer welcome.'

For a long time the villagers watched the familiar chaos of the station. Finally they gathered themselves together and moved out, across the square, and up to the bridge in a silent grey file. There was no panting, no chivvying of the laggards, they kept the pace well. Even in the crowds each knew where some of the others walked. Babla and Arundati were side by side on this return, their faces thinner, still shadowed by sadness, but there was an ease between them, and a greater dignity. Harischandra walked with Mitu while Mitu sketched the faces on the bridge. He stumbled often because his bedding and box were slung awkwardly across his back. Narend by custom brought up the rear, Rhunu beside him. Deepaka walked alone, but her shuffle was gone, and so too was most of her plumpness. Her white head caught the sunlight. Only once did she stop to look down at the boats on the water. Most of the others walked as on most days—seeing what was strange, laughing with one another, struggling with an excess of tiffin carriers and bedding. Reena was again intrigued by the bridge, and she stopped often to look at the beggars coming and going, the men pulling carts, the buses, the police. At the far side she caught Surendra and told him:

'I wish to watch this bridge through one day. Tell me the name of the hostel and I will find you before it is time to go to Sealdah.'

'Do you not fear, mother?'

'No, nothing. Walk well.' The bent figure was gone, back into the crowds and traffic before Surendra could oppose her.

'Has Reena gone?' Jaydev asked simply as he came up.

'Yes, she will meet us in two nights.'

'Then Uma and I will go, too. We wish to find our sons and find out what plans have been made for the wedding. Uma must go back with you to the village, but I must stay or travel to Murshidabad.'

'Will you bring Uma to Sealdah?'

'Yes, in three days. Show me on the map.'

In a moment two more were gone. The group around Surendra comprised the full company. Mitu, Narend and Rhunu spoke together. Then they told Elder De, 'We shall go. We have work to see the museums in these days, and the others have little interest. We shall join you at Sealdah.'

'May I come?' Harischandra asked shyly.

'Of course, brother.'

The four moved away down the slope into the streets of the financial centre of the city.

All of a sudden Deepaka said, 'Are there any who wish to accompany me to the temples?' No one spoke.

'Then I go alone.'

'You have no map, how will you find the way?'

'I can ask, and I know that I must come to Sealdah, which all will know.' The white head bowed over the folded hands and then Deepaka too slipped away with the crowd.

'This is great foolishness. We must stay together.' Elder De and Nirmal spoke at once.

'I leave you to keep the herd, for I too wish to go alone. Nirmal knows the way, and Bankim. You will do well at the mission to be fewer. I will come in the dawn of the second night.' Surendra grinned, saluted the astonished faces and was gone, leaving behind the distressed shouts and pleas of those remaining.

It took a few moments for Nirmal to reassure them while Elder De made a forlorn study of the map. By noon they were well on their way across the city, recognizing points they had seen before. By evening they were safely in the hostel, explaining why they were fewer and enjoying the hospitality of the widows who staffed the mission. Nirmal and Elder De sat up late, speaking of the village and the old teacher listened with surprise to the timid elder express hopes for a deeper well, a new irrigation system, and proper storage sheds for the rice. Again and again one of them would say, 'It cannot be done, it will not happen,' but they went to bed full of hope and plans of change.

Reena moved back through the crowd away from Surendra, smiling to herself. It had been all very well these weeks of travel, but she hated sleeping and eating and thinking in the sight of others. Back in the village she could often slip away up the river in the night, perhaps finding Narend bent on the same solitude. Now as she walked and pushed with the crowd on Howrah bridge, she began again to talk to herself. The others were too intent on their own coming and going to pay her heed. Midway across the bridge she found an empty spot against the girders, put her bundles down and settled to watch. She knew the villagers would not look for her here. Beside her a blind man stretched in sleep against a girl. Two children plucked flies and dirt from the sores on their legs while their parent searched for something in her rags. Reena watched them little, bending forwards on her crossed legs to watch back down the slope of the bridge to the crowds ascending. Once a policeman came waving his staff and telling them all to move along. At that moment Reena sat amidst a crowd of goats. Since they did not obey, neither did she. When she left the bridge she moved with the lighter traffic past large bank buildings and uniformed watchmen at the doors. At a busy corner she again sat to watch and was greeted on this occasion by a young man:

'Are you lost, mother?'

'No.'

'Where do you wish to go?'

'Where I will.'

'Where might that be for a son to help?'

'To the library of Belvedere.'

'And why would my mother wish to see a place of books?'

'That is no concern of yours.'

'Truly, but here you sit on a corner where often the great cars of the rich must wait in lines. None of them is bound for a library. Why would my mother sit here and then seek that place?'

'What is your concern?'

'I know the city well.'

'I see there are no others like you.'

'None who can give such service.'

'What service can you give?'

'I can take the old one to the library. Then she will not be tired by walking the wrong path.'

'Why do you wish to take any anywhere?'

'Perhaps a few paisa . . .'

'You, a man of healthy legs and sound eyes, have a head of straw. Why do you not work, like those who pull the rickshas, or that one who carries parcels?'

'Do you not know that a man who pulls a ricksha will never live to see his grandchild? He dies perhaps two or three harvests after he picks up the traces.'

'Some are greyed. They have been pulling for more than three harvests.'

'They are the few blessed by the goddess. Most die. Those who carry parcels may be asked to carry a packet of post or a crate of books, or a bale of jute. Then are their bones crooked, and they must ever walk as beasts, with their hands to the ground. They die of the pain of their bones.'

'All die. They eat rice they have earned, not stolen or begged.'

'Is it theft to help the old? Is it begging to serve another?'

'Those whose tongues were blessed often have evil hearts.'

'Then you will not let me guide you?'

'Go, find some other carrion to pick.'

'You have described yourself well, old one. How many have you starved?'

Shouting insults, the man went off. Reena assembled her baggage, watched, and crossed with the lights in the crowd. Soon she was on the Maidan and there she supped with a family newly come to the city to seek cash, or fortune. The man had no work, the woman would not beg, so the children had become adept thieves of the market stalls. They ate well, but always on the Maidan, far from others, ready to flee in a moment. At the sight of Reena the children had not bothered to move away from the single pot. The man stood until he saw that the bent figure harboured no threat. The woman spoke:

'Come, mother, eat. You are covered with the dust of the city and must find shelter before the night. Come, there is food.'

'Thank you, child. I need little.'

'Do not fear. There is enough this night and pulses, too.'

The family told their story under the prodding of Reena's eyes. She ate much less than even she would normally have done, but said she was replete and wanted nothing more.

'Since there is no work, why not go back to the village?' she asked the man.

'I cannot.'

'Is not your family there?'

'Alas, yes.'

'Ah, I see there has been a quarrel.'

'It was not of my asking.'

'Are there brothers?'

'Two elder.'

'Their duty is to care for you.'

'That is not the way of blood.'

'Is there no plot to plough, are not all hands needed?'

'They say we are too many.'

'Where there are brothers, there is distance.'

'So says the proverb, but sisters are no better.'

'Why so, daughter?'

'Duty to the husband, love for the children, curses to the sister. Each would have ghee every day, if one has a son, the other must scream. When I saved seed in my brass pot, it was the sisters first who screamed.'

'There is no refuge. Where do you sleep?'

'Up at the end of the Maidan there is a wood. It shelters many.'

'You must not fear tigers, aunt.'

'Why not, most clever of children? Do they stalk in this city?'

'No, but they sing in the night. The wood is by the zoo. The beasts are in boxes and do not know what the wood is like.'

'Pity the beasts. Is there room for one more this night?'

'None says nay to another here.'

'Come, these engines give pain to my head. Let us find sweeter air.'

The young man led the way and the children harried Reena across the acres of grass, poking at her bundles and asking where she had been and where she was going. She told them nothing but teased them enough that by the time they had reached a little hill, they were anxious to have her tell them tales all night. The dust of the rush hour was beginning to settle as they walked up the road. The lights around the Victoria Memorial were a beacon off to the right. They crossed a bridge and Reena realized there were many, dressed in varying decrepitude, keeping to the ditch and shadows, but walking in the same way. On the left a high wall and trees beyond intrigued Reena. She asked what it was.

'That is the place called Belvedere. There are watchmen there. Take care.'

They moved across the road, though Reena looked back at her planned destination, and followed the others into a thicket. From the smell, before she heard the beasts, Reena knew it must be the zoo. The night was warm, and those who slept hidden in the thicket were untroubled by the damp ground of springtime. Reena found the smells intruded even to her sleep, so she sat and watched. Most were like her young family, whole and still healthy. Shy and hopeful they had come from the villages, and were not yet flailed to their kernels by the cruelty of the city. One or two of the women were nursing infants. Reena wondered how long they would keep these helpless ones, or if the bodies would shrivel in death before their mothers left them on a doorstep. In the mists of dawn the sleepers awoke and showed Reena a tap where they bathed. Someone made a fire. Reena shared a cup of tea with the children, still groggy and not yet as cunning as the day would demand.

'Where do you go?'

'Some say there is work in Budge-Budge with the jute. We take the road south.'

'Is it far?'

'With the children, yes.'

'And where do you go, mother?'

'There, into Belvedere.'

'You must not.'

'There are guards.'

'It is a place for the rich, and the foreigners.'

'There is great danger.'

'Some say it is a place of books and sorcerers.'

'Beware.'

'Stay, mother. We will look after you in this city.'

'No. I must go. Alas I do not return your food and shelter.'

'You have been our guest. There is no need of thanks.'

'Then the blessings of the traveller will be with you. Lakshmi-ma will bless you at Budge-Budge.'

'Do not tempt the jealousy of the goddess by foolish words. It is best to go in silence. Stay away from the places of the rich, mother.'

They parted. The little family paced the slow morning traffic. Reena followed the wall around to a gate. There was no guard so she entered and found herself near an enormous banyan tree. Beyond it was a mansion. There were rooks and pigeons searching for food among the pebbles. Reena was hailed.

'Mother, where do you go?' She looked for the source of the voice. Some men in khaki uniform were sitting on the grass. They had tea and were smoking.

'Is this not Belvedere?'

'Even so. What do you seek?' The question was friendly, and Reena easily joined the watchmen.

'I come to see the books.'

'What has an old one to do with books?'

'Are books only for the young and idle?'

'Most who come are old priests.'

'No, the foreigners are all young.'

'They are always young.'

'Even those with greyed hair walk as one whose first son has but lately been born.'

'And what have you, who were lately babes, to do with a place of books?'

'We guard against thieves.'

'And old women?'

'If they mean harm. You must show a pass at the door to see the books.'

'Where may I get a pass?'

'From the office of the director, though he is very busy. You may not see him for many days.'

'I have but one day.'

'Why do you wish to see books?'

'That is my affair. How does one see the director?'

'With a letter from a place of learning.'

'Cannot one see first the lesser clerks?'

'Perhaps, some are friendly. That one who works at the mission for widows. He might help.'

'True, he is a good man. He has two daughters.'

'How will he marry them?'

'To another lesser clerk.'

'But they are not schooled, and he has no dowries.'

'True, but he can help a man get work, and that is much.'

'Where do I find this saint?'

'He comes when the sun is high. We will show you.'

'Then I am in your debt for more than tea.'

'It is not each day that a village crone comes to see our books. What do you say to a gamble on her getting in, brother?'

'Now there is some fun. Let us go and tell the others. We may have paisa for meat tonight.'

'Where do you come from?' Reena asked as they walked through the garden.

'From Orissa and Bihar and north in the mountains. We come to get cash, and then go home to work in the planting and harvest. See, there we sleep, and over there the students eat.'

'It is very large.'

'It is the national library for India. There is none bigger.'

'Truly?'

'So it is said.'

'Siv, the clerk comes early today. See, there, on the bicycle.'

'Hurry, mother.'

Reena walked quickly after the young guard, who approached the clerk with none of the bravado he had shown hitherto. The clerk was plump and somehow sad. Reena saw that his face was shy as the guard spoke obsequiously, and she moved to speak for herself:

'Greetings, clerk of the place of books.'

'Blessings, mother.'

'This one can tell my tale less well than I.'

'I have little time, mother, but tell it.'

'I am a storyteller. I come from the village of Uma Sen to the north. In the early months of winter Uma Sen died and her will was read at the tree of the village. We were told that her money had been given to Baroda House for Indian Railways so that all of our village could go around India and learn what wisdom there is in the places of pilgrimage. We, the elders, were to go first. Yesterday morning we returned to Howrah. We saw all the places where Siva cast Sati, where the government is, and where the southern seas bathe the end of our land. In each new place I have bought books of tales, so that when I tell tales in the evening I can tell of these places. The children must learn. My books tell me that the best books of tales are here at Belvedere. I would see them, read them, remember those I do not know. May it be done?'

'It is a tale more of the gods than of men, and thus I will tell it to the director. You have been much blessed, mother.'

Reena bowed to the watchmen and laughed to see them making more bets as she followed the clerk up the warm steps and along a passage of cabinets. The sad man went ahead. He was speaking pleadingly to a woman, and there was a sharp reply. Another voice, again the sad man. Suddenly he emerged and beckoned Reena to come forward. She entered an office of fighting secretaries, and then a dim room where a man waited alone at a desk.

'You come from the village of Uma Sen?'

'Yes, sahib.'

'My friend Ashin Mukherjee went with you and now is dead. Is it so?'

'Alas, the truth, sahib.'

'Then tell me the tale that I may know the last days of my friend.'

Reena told of the journey and Ashin's death but did not stop there. When she had at last spun the words back to Howrah and the return to the village on the morrow, the gentleman was watching her with sorrow, amazement and obvious respect. The clerk had long ago disappeared. The man wrote something and handed it to Reena:

'I can do no more, in memory of Ashin, than give you this. It tells the staff to help you. Tell Sundara-devi of my help and wish her well.'

Reena moved again into the corridor and was directed to an enormous reading room. It was dingy, it was crowded, but here there were books. Looking up at the towers of them, Reena did not hear the rude question of the attendant. When at last she took notice of the helper, she merely thrust the director's letter at him and waited. At once the face of the official changed from disdain, to surprise and disapproval. He returned the letter and took her to a large desk. Again the letter had the same effect, but the man at the desk asked her what she would like to see. Reena produced from her pouch a paper-bound book, flipped quickly to the back and read out several titles. The officer noted them and sent off a runner. Reena's notebook would have foiled an attempt at prying, for it was a confused conglomeration of symbols. One phrase might be in Bengali, another in strangely phonetic English in Bengali script, and there were cryptograms, a well, a tree, a crown. For Reena it was enough.

Her day was a busy one, full of disappointments, for often she could not read the books, and as often the ink had long ago faded beyond the help of any eyes. When she emerged in the evening Reena found she was very tired. She collected her bundles and descended the steps. At the bottom one of the watchmen waited for her.

'Have you been reading, mother?'

'Yes.'

'We have been told how you made the director weep with your tales.'

'I saw no tears.'

'His secretary said so. You must be a good teller of tales to do that, and in his working hours too.'

'He was a friend of one who travelled with us.'

'No matter. I come to ask if you will take food with us and tell us a tale.'

'Yes, I will come, though food cooked by lonely men does not make a feast.'

'There is one among us, from Orissa, who can cook better than my mother, bless her memory. You will not be disappointed.'

Nor was Reena, for the stew of vegetables, the rice, the pulses, were better fare than she had eaten for days, and there was plenty of it. The young cook was pleased by her praises. The evening grew cool as they spoke of food and the ways to enjoy it. Late in the cold a man reminded her of her promise of a tale. She told them an old one of a wandering son, beset by troubles, who returned victorious to save his brothers from disaster. They all were complimented by Reena's analogy, but before they grew restless she began another of snakes and their magic over men. The watchmen became as children, drawing away from Reena's voice as she writhed and glittered with the tale. She concluded with her own tale and bade them praise Uma Sen as she rose to go.

'You cannot go out in the night. There are thieves.'

'What have I worth stealing?'

'They will hit your head first and search after.'

'I want to see the city as it sleeps.'

'Why? There is nothing.'

'You are tired, rest in safety with us. Go in the dawn.'

'By dawn I must be with my companions before they rise to give thanks at Kalighat. There are no dangers for one as old as I.'

All night Reena walked, looking at the sleepers in a doorway here, at the merry-making near a brothel there, at the scuttling around a market beyond. Dawn found her asleep against her own bedding roll within the courtyard of the mission. Elder De found her with relief and together they planned the last day. No one but Harischandra, in his last sickness, ever asked Reena what she had done in those days alone.

Jaydev and Uma spent much of the first day going from one building of

Calcutta University to another, finding each shut and barred because of riots. The first residence they found was also empty, though a corridor of open lockers, discarded sandals and loose pages of books did not convey the desertion at first glance. The walls were smeared with quickly painted slogans. Everywhere there was an atmosphere of haste and thoughtlessness. They moved close together, silently, to the next building. Here students were packing and Jaydev had difficulty attracting their attention. No, they knew of none by that name. Most of the literature students were across the compound. How long had there been riots? Oh, for years now, riots were more a part of the university than classes. But what of examinations and degrees, and jobs beyond? Who knows? Those who can will buy a piece of paper from someone, those who cannot must wait.

The pair were now well worried and crossed the compound quickly. For some hard minutes the remaining students denied any knowledge of the two sons, but then a boy with a bandage around his head came over to them:

'Who are you who seek Jhoti?' Uma started at the name of her younger son on a stranger's lips.

'His father and mother, come back from a tour of India.'

'Did you truly go by train all around?'

'Yes, we came this morning into Howrah. We seek our sons. The elder is to be married before the end of this moon.'

'That is so, Jhoti said his dada would go to the house of his girl when the trouble started.'

'Where is that?'

'I do not know. He is in the class ahead.'

'Are you a man of Jhoti's class?'

'Yes.'

'Where is Jhoti?'

'Are you a father who beats his sons?'

'What is this?'

'Jhoti is hiding.'

'Why?'

'Where?'

'You see my bandage. How do you think I got it?'

'From the students.'

'No, from the police.'

'The police?'

'They came to stop the riot, all who were watching were beaten if they did not run fast enough. Many were taken to jail.'

'You were fighting?'

'I have been here now three years and have had only enough teaching to take the examinations for one year. There is no more money. I will

have no degree, get no job. Yes, I was fighting. There is nothing else to
do.'

'And Jhoti?'

'He is a clever boy, but he does not run very fast'

'Oh Ma, is he hurt?'

'A little.'

'Where is my son?'

'Will you fetch the police?'

'Against my son?'

'Come, but carefully.'

Jaydev followed the boy up into the attics of the building, being pushed
all the time by Uma. Well-concealed behind a pile of old beds and
mattresses running with mould they found their younger son. He started
up with pleasure to see the other boy, but fell back in shock and shame
at the sight of the worried faces pressing behind. Then his hands touched
his parents' feet, his eyes filled with tears, and he was cradled as in years
before. After a long whispered talk Jaydev and Uma spread out their
bedding and Uma went in search of food. Father scolded son for trouble,
son blamed father for not understanding, but then there came the soothing
medicine of Uma's delight in seeing the boy. He told them of his brother
and the bride, who would be a teacher too:

'He has got a post at the new school in the big town. They will go
up after the wedding.'

'And when is this wedding, I would like to be told?'

'In ten days' time, mother. Did you not get the letter to Madras?'

'Not one which told us of a date for the marriage.'

'The astrologer has set the hour. It is to be here in Calcutta in the
house of the aunt, for there has been a death in Murshidabad and it is not
lucky to go there. The parents are here now.'

'Is she a pretty girl, fair?'

'Not so fair as I would like. She wears glasses, but my brother does not
mind. She is tall, and very quiet. A good student and a good teacher, but
probably a very bad daughter-in-law for you, mother.'

'You tease me.'

'Yes—for I think there will be no mother-in-law like you in all Bengal.
You will spoil your daughters as you have spoiled your sons.'

'Hark, he says daughters. Do you marry, too?'

'No, I am too young. But listen. I am but little bruised, only my back
hurts from the beating. May I not come home with you? When do you
go?'

'We go the day after tomorrow. We meet the others at Sealdah. But
what of your studies?'

'Father, there is no more hope for any degree. I have failed you. This
place is good for others, but not good for me. I cannot return to it, and

it will now be closed for a long time. May I not come home and work beside you until I am well?'

'That is the first son of mine wishing to work in the fields!'

'I can learn.'

'Truly, come and be well under your mother's care again. I should be angry with you for wasting these years, but I am not. There is much to be done in the village and a man who can write well will be of much help. But my heart is full. Let us sleep.'

Mother and son whispered longer. In the morning Jaydev found an old cart discarded near the building and the trio set off to the house of the bride. Uma sat long with the women talking and came to the conclusion that no daughter-in-law could possibly be better than this one chosen by her son. She learned from the girl of her wish to teach beside her husband, that they one day build a school where all the children would come out of love, not duty. She heard the tales of how they had met and studied together at least five times from three different mouths. She saw the wedding sari, the ghot and all that would be used while she sat alone in the village waiting. When she slept, Uma hardly remembered the train and her journey of the days past.

Harischandra felt shy as he walked behind the other three. They had decided to go together to the museums. Perhaps he was an intruder. The old shame crept over his frame and he began to lag behind. Narend turned to him and asked which way they should go. Suddenly Harischandra was again the friend and traveller, not the failure of the village. He moved forward and matched his stride to Narend's long one. Behind, Rhunu told Mitu of the plan for Amiya's granddaughter, and Narend's request that she too, should go, and study art.

'Oh Ma. You who tell no one anything tell me this. It is what I have dreamed to do since first I saw the museum. But I am but the potter of the village, not even for a season could I go as you do. Will you sometimes share with me your lessons, devi?'

'Do not speak so, Mitu. You are the true artist. If you wish to study, there will be a way for it, even the foreign priest of the south wished that you make your figures for all, not just the village. Do not believe that I shall go and you not.'

'You try to deceive me with kindness. There is no way for a potter to be other than a potter.'

'Hush now. I told Narend that none should hear his plan. There will be gossip.'

'What use is there in speaking of dreams?'

'Is it better to draw dreams?'

'None can tell if what is drawn is a dream or what has been seen.'

'Perhaps it is better.'

'What will you do with your books of pictures? What must I do with mine?'

'I had thought to put mine in the temple where all could come and see what we have seen.'

'It is well.'

'We will put them before the goddess.'

'Come, wife, Mitu. We are almost before the museum. Harischandra has guided us well.'

For the hours of the afternoon they wandered around the national museum while Narend said he would look about outside. Harischandra read and told the others about the displays they admired. Each wonder seemed the greater to Mitu, and he stood in awe before the beautiful heads of the early artisans. Rhunu saw oil paintings for the first time and all but picked them apart trying to see how they were made, so different from her own chalks. Towards evening they were accosted by a clerk who said they were wanted in an office. There sat Narend with their luggage, and across a large desk was a gentleman of authority. On the desk were Mitu's two clay figures, one of Deepaka and Ashin, the other of Narend and Rhunu. Beside the figures were the sketchbooks, open, exposed. Rhunu blushed and crouched against the wall behind Narend. He drew her forward and placed her in a chair beside him. Mitu he almost pushed into the third chair, and the official smiled at the drama. Harischandra squatted and drew out his notebook.

'Madam, your husband tells me that you made these drawings?'

'Yes, sahib,' mumbled Rhunu.

'And you, sir, are the artist who made these pieces?'

'Yes, sahib,' echoed Mitu.

'I wish to buy these pieces for our museum, for they are the finest I have seen by a sculptor from the villages. Will you sell them?'

Mitu stared and did not answer. The question was repeated. Narend interrupted:

'It is all right, Mitu, have no fear. I have told him our story.'

'Please, do you wish to sell your figures?'

'I had thought that the one would go in the temple, and the other Narend says he wishes to buy.' Mitu did not raise his head.

'They are of fired clay. Can you not make others at your leisure?'

'I have no fire as the strong priest had.'

'I have heard of this priest,' the gentleman looked towards Narend and back at Mitu. 'Does the priest have many images in his house?'

For a long time Mitu described the marvels he had seen. No attempt was made to hush him. Only Harischandra's pen scratched.

'He is one I have heard of. He is a great collector. He has asked you to come and make images for him?' the director asked Mitu.

'He said it would give him pleasure.'

'He is one whose judgment I trust. What do you do with these books of pictures of the village and your travels?'

'They will go in the temple, before the goddess as our thanks.'

'Is that true for yours of the colours?'

'Yes, sahib.'

'What of the books of pictures only of the village?'

'I suppose we will keep them.'

'Where?'

'In the house.'

'And there they will be eaten by ants, dampened by rain, and used for toys by children.'

'Perhaps, sir.'

'Then I wish to buy those books from both of you.'

'Buy them?'

'Yes. They are too precious to stay in your village if there is no place to keep them, and I would have them seen by others.'

'These are not fine like the things of your museum.'

'There are things in this museum which tell us about the great and the rich, but there are few which tell us of life in the villages of Bengal.'

'I am just a potter, not an artist like these must have been.'

'Who becomes an artist is in the hands of gods, not in the hands of fathers who make us carry on their work. You are an artist of what you know and love. It is enough to be so blessed. Do not judge yourself by what you must do for your daily rice. Your hands have been blessed.'

A clerk came in and called that the museum was closing. He was sent off.

'Are you the director of this museum?' Rhunu asked suddenly.

'No, no, just one of his servants. I am charged with the care of modern works. That is why when your husband asked to see someone who would look at your figures he was brought to me. Now we come again to this question of your study of art. There is no good school in Calcutta as there is in Bombay, but what I suggest is this. You come to me. I will arrange that each week you see other artists: there is the Kalighat school, with many artists, there are painters in oils, and there are good workers with batik. Then, besides, there are those called draughtsmen, theirs is a skill worth mastering. If you come to these, you can do in one season what many would take years to do.'

'But we cannot ask you to become a guru.'

'Ai, and I am not a guru. Do not worry. I will ask you to make alpana for me. Then I will have photographs made. I will work her very hard and she will be glad to go back to the pounding of grain.' This last was to Narend, who did not respond with the expected smile.

'Can it be?'

'Truly it will be. And you, my friend, have you thought what price I must pay for your books and these figures?'

'I know no prices but for pots.'

'Then I make you a proposition. Come back now when the rains start and there is little work for a potter. Come back and make your pots for me until harvest time and then go south to the priest with the other villagers who travel. There spend as long as you will with him, but bring me, one day, some of the figures you make. I will pay for each of these books fifty rupees, and for each of the figures 100 rupees. I will give you the use of a kiln in Calcutta so that you can make the two figures again before you go south. Is it agreed?'

There was silence. Narend's face was a study in shock and pride fighting for dominance. Harischandra dropped his book. Rhunu began to weep. Mitu stared, and at last he spoke:

'It is more money than any man can have.'

'No, it is but a modest price. They would fetch much more in the markets of the West.'

'You would pay so much?'

'Yes, but not to take in cash to the village to be stolen. To be put into a good bank here to await your return to me and pay for your journey south.'

'Where would I live in this city?'

'You will live with Rhunu and Amiya's granddaughter and keep them from harm. It could not be better.' Narend was beginning to smile.

'Lord husband, I would know how you have plotted this?'

'Ah, wife, I asked the foreign girl how to preserve your skills and Mitu's from our carelessness, and she told me to come here. It is she you must bless.'

'No, it is the one who cared enough to ask.'

'Where will the granddaughter study?' When the college was named, the official smiled. 'It is not far from my home. I will ask my wife to find you a place near to us.'

'You will truly buy my books?' Rhunu asked.

'Yes, each of them, for fifty rupees. Do you have more in the village?'

'No, I have burned all.'

'Do not burn any again. Do you want more chalks?'

'These are still good.'

'Let me see.' Rhunu found the box and opened it. The pastels were broken and worn.

'You must have new. When you come tomorrow we will get some.'

'Are we to come tomorrow?'

'Of course, I must pay you, and take you to see the artists and the potters where you two will study. Is that approved by the husband?'

'We can come tomorrow, but must leave with the others on the morning following.'

'Then all is in order. You, who have been so long writing, have you kept a record of all that is said?'

'Yes sahib,' Harischandra moved to conceal his book.

'It stands as record of my contract. But wait, have you kept a record of the entire journey?'

'Truly, and he has been chasing our storyteller, making a record of her village tales.'

'What?'

'It is so, sahib. I have written all that she can remember or will tell me, and I have kept a record of the talks on the train.'

'May I see?'

Harischandra opened his bundle, smallest of all, and brought out a sheaf of the simplest notebooks, pages already loose. On each was crammed his tiny script. The officer had no difficulty seeing that here was another treasure. The four sat in silence while he read. Suddenly he said:

'Will you sell me these books?'

'I . . . I have no other souvenirs of the journey.'

'Will you come, with the others, and make copies and sell me those?'

'That could be done.'

'And will you make a record of all that now happens in the village just as you have done for the journey?'

'Of what purpose is that?'

'Tomorrow you come with the others and I will take you to one who works in the anthropological survey of India. He will tell you what use this is. He will tell me what price I must pay you for them, but it will not be less than what I pay for the other books.'

'Fifty rupees?'

'I should say much more. There are many, many tales here.'

'I will come.'

'Do you wish to study also?'

'No, sahib, I wish to follow Reena until she goes to the river.'

'Who is Reena?'

'Our village story-teller. Maybe also a witch, sahib, I do not know.'

'Would she come and tell tales into a machine which keeps a record of her voice for others to hear?'

'She would find it a fine adventure, I think.'

'Then come with the potter, when the rains begin, and bring her. I will pay you all.'

'It shall be done, sir.'

'Oh Ma, I have not had a day such as this for many years. You have made me feel there is hope for India, all of you.'

'I do not understand,' Narend bent forward.

'Listen, friend, for I will talk too long. It is close to my heart. What gives a people hope? Is it good harvests? Is it the weddings? Is it a feast? No, these are pleasures which pass. We hope because we have children and we see again all things new in their eyes. You say that cannot be so for all, since all do not have children, and all who have them are not happy? Yes? Is it so? Listen, again. For a nation, for a land of many people, children are the times to come, the lives we have not yet led, the houses not yet built, the pictures not yet made. All that gives us hope, gives us reason to struggle through the illnesses and the loneliness and the years of drought. Why? I shall tell you. Because we are taught by all we know of the past that what each can do becomes greater if his chances become greater. We think we do not know what comes in the future, but we think it will not be the same as the past. There will be other chances and other problems. The fate is not written twice in the same way, you of the villages say. Out of each that is different, out of each of us living through something alone, comes something new which gives another hope. You have just lived through something which one year ago could not have happened. Out of it you have made a treasure for those who come after. Maybe those will never know a village, or an alpana, or a singer at evening. What more you will make of it I do not know, but it gives me hope that all that is good can never be crushed away and hidden. There must be a remembering. As long as there is remembering there is hope. The power of India lies in the cities, and mostly I think it is wicked. But what endures all powers? The village. The life you lead which is here in your pictures. That is the memory which India must hold to hope and withstand whatever the powers do. You have given this to more than you will ever know, for long after you and your children have gone others will come to see what we have kept of our past. India has no money to give to keep the books, and soon all will be as dust from the ants and the heat. Much that was written in the time of our grandfathers has now vanished, though you say Reena remembers. Now you keep this for others to remember. Yes, you have given me much hope. I bless you all.'

'Sahib, I wish that what you say is true. But many can be hurt by the cruel powers and we have seen some who had a little schooling but thought themselves wise. If those have power then soon the few like you will stand no more.'

'It is not the ones like me who matter, though we help. It is those like Mitu and Rhunu and this writer here who pass on the record to the young. Once the young know that there is something beyond the cruelties of power they will yearn for it and dream of it and someday make it real.'

'But a village is not all good. There is cruelty and foolishness and suffering in good measure.'

'Mother, what you say is true, and of all the lives of men. The village changes whenever there is a new family begun or an old one dies. It is what is kept and how the change is made which you record and which I call the remembering.'

'Do we come tomorrow?'

'Yes, but the museum is closed. I will await you. Now I must go down and let you out.'

The officer wrapped and put away Mitu's figures in a cupboard, then the sketchbooks after them and the villagers watched their possessions vanish with sorrow. Then they were walking through the corridors of the museum and out to the street.

'Ai, I did not know it was so late. It is dark and all have gone.'

'Yes, we have talked long.'

'Lord husband, where will we sleep?'

'Have you no place?'

'No.'

'Come with me to my home. It is small but there is a hall where you can spread the bedding. It will give me much pleasure to have you.'

'We do nothing but accept your favour. I think you must be Lakshmi-ma herself disguised.'

'Hush such talk. Come, it is not far.'

That night and the next the four slept in the apartment of the officer and were treated as celebrities by his wife. On the day between they chased the officer the length and breadth of the city while he introduced them and encouraged them. By evening a room had been rented for Rhunu and Mitu and Amiya's granddaughter. Only Narend did not sleep easily that last night and the tall man sat by the door listening and watching and wondering where Surendra had gone wandering. When the sun banished the mists, the wife of the officer loaded them with treats from the city sweet shops and they set off for Sealdah. Narend was the last to pass through the gates of the station and receive the welcome of the others.

A moment after she had left the villagers, Deepaka realized she did not mean to go alone and really did not want to see the temples of Calcutta. It was too late to turn back, there were crowds between and she knew there was little chance that she could find them. Ahead were two days and two nights in a strange place with none by her side to lead the way. Deepaka remembered the night in the room alone in Puri and shuddered, but she kept walking. She was clumsy with her own bundles and the bag of Amiya's things. Often she was cursed and told to stand aside by the ones rushing. Sometimes she would follow a figure she had felt was friendly, or she would follow another family struggling with bundles. In this way she made her way to the busiest market section of the city by noon. Near a shop selling baskets she found an open, shaded spot and sat down upon her bedding. In the weeks of the journey her hair had gone from grey to white, her face had lost its plump sheen, and her eyes had lost their sleepiness. She sat, a crumpled life, and slept in the afternoon heat. Dogs sometimes nosed at her bundles, and once an urchin tried to pull away a parcel, but failed and ran.

Deepaka awakened with a start at being splashed by water. She was being shouted at and told to go:

'Move, hag. Can you not find a tree?'

Again she was splashed, but this time she moved. By the time the bundles were hoisted they were wet and heavy and Deepaka was cold from her dousing. It was evening. Gaily dressed girls walked in clusters here and there. Jasmine sellers plied their wares along the sidewalks. A blind boy played a flute and begged. Coarse-looking lads with wide grins were stirring hot pulses whose nutty smell made Deepaka even more tired. Prosperous families enjoyed the promenade. The children ran before in their Western clothes of frills and lace, the parents walked slowly nodding to acquaintances now and again. Everywhere ice-cream sellers were out, their calls like prolonged belches echoing against the buildings of the city. Sometimes a yellow taxi would come racing down the avenue sending the promenaders jumping until the sikh who drove it would bring his steed to an abrupt halt and bleat the horn. The first time Deepaka was abused by such a horn she looked about for the beast which was making such a noise, but seeing none did not then associate the sound with the vehicle close in front. The driver leaned out and treated her to his skills as a public curser, and the audience of the streets called out in praise. Deepaka moved to the side of the road, counted her bundles and stared back at the vehicle. The Sikh was standing beside it laughing and talking while the traffic behind displayed his own customary impatience. Then he was off and Deepaka was sprayed with dirt.

The crowd thinned. No longer did any abuse her. Gradually the lights went out, the traffic drew away from the centre of the city. Beggars chose their doorways. There were dogs. Deepaka walked on not daring to ask any where she might be. These strangers might be thieves getting ready for the night of work. That woman of paint was surely a low one going somewhere in haste. Deepaka drew away from the rushing harlot. The sky had first blushed and then sulked in violet. Now a deep cowl of purple concealed its mood and Deepaka wondered why she could not see as well in the city as in the village. The street lights bore clouds of newborn insects and their help was diminished. A policeman asked Deepaka where she was bound and she cowered and crept from him in fear. He laughed and joked to himself about widows just in from the country. Twice she stumbled at broken curbs and had to recount her bundles. In the darker streets where there were only houses, Deepaka began to fear less. She sought a place to rest and found a corner step where no other had staked a claim. The shawl which she had not used for many nights was pulled out. Deepaka slept.

She dreamed of the rocking train and the chatter of wheels. Then of a child of long ago, placed in her arms still damp. Then she was a new

widow weeping while her mother-in-law screamed at her for having
sapped the life of her husband and the dead sons. She moved on the step
but found there was a small, warm body pressed against her. She wakened
at once without moving, from long practice, and looked down. There
was a small girl, a corner of Deepaka's shawl pulled around her. Even
in the night Deepaka could see that the hair was brown and dull with
dirt. The dress was thin and indecently short, even for one so young. At
every joint of the body Deepaka could see the curve of the bones and the
hollows as they met, the skin stretched almost transparent around them.
Deepaka's arm went down along the curve of the small back and drew
the child closer. The girl started not at all but sighed gently. Then
Deepaka slept with care, part of her alert to every breath of the new
being who sought her warmth.

They wakened to the call of the milkman bringing his buffalo along
the street, and the clatter of the shutters above and around them as the
cooks opened the houses to call out to him. The little girl went and
crouched by the farmer's knee, touching his feet. As he milked he would
sometimes send a spray of the warm nourishment into her waiting, open
mouth. When he was done he kicked her away and shouted to the buffalo
to move along down the alley. Deepaka sat looking at the girl. The girl
stood, wiping her chin of milk, staring at Deepaka. The old woman rose
stiffly, loaded the bundles, and the girl came to help. Together they
walked behind the buffalo, enjoying the steam from the beasts and the
greetings shouted to the morning from one window to another all along
the street.

In a square not far away they found a tap. Deepaka stopped and, to the
girl's shock, began to scrub her from head to foot, singing and laughing
the while. Then she bathed herself and rubbed them both dry with her
shawl. There was only one other sari in her bundle and Deepaka knew
it was not clean, so she did not change, but she made the girl clutch the
shawl around her while the little dress dried in the dawn. Deepaka
searched again in her bundles and found a small tin. There was some old
rice in it, dry, and part of a rotten banana. On this the two feasted well.
Once again they set off and now they began to talk.

'Where do you go?' asked the child.

'I do not know. To Kalighat, perhaps.'

'Why have you come, then?'

'I came on the train.'

'Where did you come from?'

'From the south.'

'You are not of the south.'

'Ai, you are wise. No, I am of a village to the north. Tomorrow I
must go back from the station they call Sealdah.'

'I know the place. It is over there. Far.'

'I said you were wise. Where is your own place?'

'Here.' The girl waved her arms to include all the city and dropped the parcel she had been carrying for Deepaka.

'All of it?'

'Yes.'

'And do you sleep where you will?'

'Of course, there are none to stop me.'

'The police?'

'Ai, the police. They do not bother children unless we go begging down by the big hotels.'

'Do you beg?'

'In the winter, if I cannot get food.'

'Where do you find food?'

'Do you not know?'

'No.'

'From the market, and the temples. There is much waste.'

'There is waste of food?'

'Much is left to lie if it falls. Have you travelled without food? You do not know how to find it.'

'Food was given.'

'By the gods I suppose.'

'Why such bitter words from such a small mouth?'

'All say pray to the gods and they will give you better than you have. They give nothing.'

'What have you prayed for?'

'Mostly for food.'

'And not mostly?'

'For a blanket in winter, or a mother again.' This last was an aside not meant to be heard by Deepaka, but she heard it.

'What happened to your mother?'

'She died.'

'Long ago?'

'I do not know. This dress was long for me then. It was my brother's shirt.'

'Then it must have been more than two harvests ago.'

'I do not know.'

'What happened to your brother?'

'He ran away weeping when she died and I have not seen him since.'

'How do you live?'

'As now. I learned from the others.'

'Had you no father, no aunts, no uncles?'

'What has a whore to do with a father?'

'Your mother?' Deepaka's shocked voice asked.

'Yes, but she was no longer good at it. She was eaten by a sickness and ugly to see.'

'You saw that?'

'Of course, she was my mother. We got her food, my brother and I, when she could not stand properly. She said her head was always turning, though to us it stayed still.'

'Who took her to the river?'

'What?'

'Your mother. Who took her body to the river?'

'No one. Why should she go to the river?'

'Oh Ma. We in the village take our dead to the river, where they are given the blessings of the gods of the holy waters. What do you do with dead in the city?'

'Let them lie. They are taken away before the dogs get to them.'

'What do you say?'

'Are you sick?'

'Not yet.'

'Shall we rest?'

'Perhaps. Where are we?'

'We come near to Kalighat.'

'Ai, that is good. I would talk to a priest there.'

'There are too many priests.'

'But it is a place of much power. Have you not been?'

'I fear it. The priests are cruel.'

'How so?'

'They chase us away and do not let us eat the prasad, though there is too much for them to eat. There are always police, for there are always rich pilgrims.'

'Who are the others? You always speak of us.'

'Those like myself.'

'Your friends?'

'No, ones who wander.'

'It is not good to be alone.'

'It is safer. Why do you wish to speak to a priest?'

'A friend has died. I wish to ask for prayers.'

'He will ask much money.'

'I have none.'

'Why go?'

'She was a good friend.'

'We come to the alley of the temple.'

'Truly, I have been before.'

'You have been many places for one who knows so little.'

'That is so.'

'Do you not like your home place that you travel away from it?'

'I like it well.'

'Then why travel?'

'It was written that it should be so.'

'Nothing is written.'

'All is written.'

'Then why should such a fate be written upon me?'

Deepaka looked down and saw that the earnest face was serious in the question:

'I do not know. Perhaps you are right in this as in all, perhaps nothing is written. These are words of old women.'

'Why pray to the gods?'

'That is my affair. Now please sit and watch my bundles. I will not be long.'

The child was astonished by the ignorance which had placed the trust upon her, and sat down to wait. In the warmth of the sun she slept again, with the constant tiredness of the malnourished. Deepaka had vanished within the portals of Kali's temple. The widow sought and to her relief found the young priest who had given her the lotus. He was sitting with others near the place of sacrifice. The temple was quiet. Deepaka had seen it only amid the excitement of one of the days open to public worship. The priests glanced at the poor figure and went back to their own talk. Deepaka bowed. The young priest looked at her in puzzlement:

'Why do you wait, mother? There is no puja this day.'

'Hail, giver of the lotus. I am returned to question you.'

'Truly, it is the one of the sad eyes who came with adoration before Kali-ma while the others looked to see if their marks of blessing were large. You were with the tourists of the village. There was much talk from the seller of saras about you. So Mother, have you seen the places of the gods?'

'Some.'

'And have you been blessed often with the lotus?'

'No.'

'That was error, for your eyes are now even more sad.'

'I come to ask for prayers for one dead.'

'One who travelled with you?'

'Even so.'

'Did I see that one?'

'She was tall, proud, and knew many ways to help others with her hands. Her heart was pained as a bride and had not healed.'

'She came before you to Kali-ma?'

'Yes.'

'I remember. She walked like this?'

'Yes.'

'How has she died?'

'She sat and waited for a train to crush her.'

'Oh Ma, what was written upon her forehead? What a death!'

'We bought wood and I bring the ashes back to the river of the village.'

'All is well done. What would you that I do?'

'I have heard that there are some who can pray for the dead, that they may be reborn happier than they were in this life. I ask you to make prayers for her. Her name was Amiya.'

'That is a custom of prayer I do not know. Perhaps Saraswati, who grants wisdom, will bless her. I can pray for that if you wish.'

'The child says you will want money. I have none.'

'Money matters little when I hear such a tale. Who is the child?'

'I do not know. She came and slept against me in the street. She says her mother was a low one who died of an eating disease. Is there no place in this city to shelter such a little one? Everywhere in India I have found children alone like this, but there have been homes for them in large cities. Often, or most, were homes of foreign ladies. Is there none such in Calcutta?'

'There are, but would the child stay? One of the streets is often a trouble to those who wish to care for her.'

'She is lonely, and has not had enough food for years. For a time she will be eager for the food, but only if the hand were light would she stay.'

'You must find a house of the Loreto nuns. They are also foreigners, though we think they have been touched by Kali-ma herself. Even the great and rich do their bidding when their ears are opened.'

'How do I find such a house?'

'There is one close. I will show you.'

'Why do you help me?'

'Kali-ma tells me I must.'

'It must be a comfort to speak directly with such a one.'

'Why so? You do not sound devoted?'

'Each says one way is right, or one way is wrong. Surely the goddess must tell you the truth.'

'I believed it to be so.'

'Then that is a comfort.'

By this time Deepaka and the priest were together looking down at the frail child asleep on Deepaka's bundles. Something told her of their presence for she stood with a start and asked Deepaka angrily, 'Why have you brought a priest?'

'She did not bring me. I offered to come. We who know the city must show her where to go.'

'That is true, she knows nothing though she has white hair.'

'Then come and help me guide her a little way.' Deepaka and the girl walked a little behind the priest. His dhoti swung. His only other decoration was the sacred thread looped across his chest. Deepaka was often scolded by the street crowds, but the girl helped and cursed in return. At last they came to a wall and a gate. The priest did something which brought a face to the grate and then they were inside a compound crowded with activity. Everywhere there were nuns and girls running or walking hastily. From somewhere came the sound of children singing.

Elsewhere someone was cooking. Deepaka was reminded of a train station: no one here intended to stay long. The priest followed the nun and left the child and Deepaka together. They crouched to watch, sometimes one asking the other what was meant. The child was frightened by the clothes of the nuns and drew close to Deepaka. When the priest returned with another nun he found them huddled against each other, again asleep. Gently he shook Deepaka:

'Mother, mother. They say you should rest inside. Go with the lady. I shall make prayers for the one born as Amiya. Alas, I have no lotus.'

Deepaka touched his feet but was distracted by the tugging of the urchin:

'Come, we must go. They must be lady police.'

'What?'

'Look. They all wear keys. Why are there so many of them?'

'There are not many of us, too few for the work we do. Come with me. The old one must rest or she will be ill, and you must eat. You have brought her safely across the city, bring her now safely to bed.'

'Is there a place of rest here?'

The old and the young followed the nun and were soon seated before a large amount of food. Deepaka could not eat. The child finished everything and was promptly sick. While she was being washed again, under protest, Deepaka told the nuns all she knew and guessed of the child, and made her plea:

'Please, will you give her shelter, and teach her some skill so that she will not die on the streets or follow the way of her mother? She will not take up much room in your house. But I have seen in times of famine, when those shadows around the bones show, death is not far off. We see many children die. You have food here. Can you give it to her? Can you teach her something? In Benares in the home of the foreign ladies they teach the girls beautiful sewing. Do you teach that?'

'Here we teach nursing. There is food to share, and I agree that the hand of death is upon the child. See, she sleeps again. Maybe she will not stay. Maybe she will run away. Then we can do nothing.'

'What do you ask in such times?'

'If the child has no one to run to, there is little way we can find it. If someone has brought the child, usually the little one runs to that one. Then sometimes there is a chance to help.'

'Do you ask for money?'

'If there is money to give.'

'And if not?'

'Then how can we ask?'

'I will make you a promise. I will come to see the girl and take her to my village in the times when you do not teach her. If she will promise to stay until I come, then I think she will keep her word.'

'Will your family not be angry?'

'An old one is allowed much foolishness.'

'We will ask the child.'

The nun wakened the little body. Slowly the two women explained all that they had spoken of. Deepaka asked if she would stay and learn to nurse sick ones with the nuns if she Deepaka would come and fetch her home to the village during times when there was no teaching. The child thought and replied:

'What will you do now?'

'I must be at the Sealdah station in the morning. I must find my way.'

'But you know nothing of the city. If I had not been with you, thieves would have killed you in the night.'

'Yes, you protected me well. But once I come to the station I will be with my own people.'

'It is not safe to let her go. She is an old fool.' The child was distinctly worried and the nun recognized the sense in what she said.

'Then let us show her where you will stay, and you two will sleep together again tonight. In the morning when our truck goes, we shall take her to Sealdah. Is it well?'

'It is well.'

Together the two spent the rest of the day listening to the sisters, exploring the hospital, the school, the dormitories and the convent. The child thought herself in prison until the evening, when they went out with the nuns on the rounds of collecting the sick and the very young from the places where beggars sought sanctuary. At this the girl was gifted, for the street people trusted her and she knew it. When they slept at last, she told Deepaka:

'I will stay here until you come. I think I can help them, and the food is good.'

'It will be well for you, but someday you must thank the priest.'

'I will thank him when next he brings a stranger to the door.'

In the morning the nun presented Deepaka with a long paper which she could not read, but which outlined the arrangements they had made.

'But I do not know your name?' the nun asked of the child.

'My mother called me Guriya.'

'It is no name, it means dolly.'

'I know.'

'Then I will give you the name which will tie you to me,' said Deepaka. 'Is it agreed?'

'Yes.'

'I name you Amiya, but you must learn to be a good nurse, for she of that name was a great healer.'

'Then so shall I be. Amiya. Amiya. Yes, write that. I shall be Amiya.' The nun wrote and Deepaka did not smile. She boarded the truck with several others, counted the bundles and waved briefly to the child as the truck pulled away from the gates.

'She will be best off in the village. She is very ignorant. Do you know, she even asked me to guard her bundles?'

'And you did. Let us go and see the doctor, Amiya. She likes to meet girls who wish to become her helpers.'

Deepaka was delivered in style to the station and tumbled down from the truck almost on top of Reena, who was fetching water.

'Ai, an unexpected meeting. The others are here. It is time to get our tickets.'

Surendra loped along to the Maidan, frolicking in his freedom. At the first seller he bought fresh biri, and as soon as he was on the grass removed his shoes. Then he stretched for a moment and wriggled about on the ground. He lay smoking and watching the sky. A goat came near and examined his possibilities, unimpressed by Surendra's address to it as an old friend. The goat boy ventured near and the two discussed the problems of feeding the flock. Then Surendra sniffed the air, spat and moved on. Soon he was across the area of the grand shops. Near a hotel he took out his map. A doorman came over to see what the ragamuffin was reading. He offered his help and answered the unusual cultivator's questions. They shared a smoke and with a salute Surendra was gone. The doorman had no explanation of why this man of letters walked in rags with his shoes tied to a foreigner's rucksack. Life was odd in this city. For a moment the doorman wished himself back to the hills near Darjeeling.

At a barn sheltering a market Surendra found a shop of tools. With great care he chose a knife with many blades, even one for fixing the feet of the bullocks, bargained with the shopman until the price was right and moved away again. With astonishing speed he entered a sari shop, bought a simple cotton sari with a red border for his daughter-in-law and placed it in the rucksack. Then he was moving swiftly south towards the river. He circled the lands of Fort William and at last found what he sought — an easy bank to descend to the water. Twice as he walked downstream he shared tea with idlers on the bank. No one asked his purpose. When the shadows lengthened, some of the small boats pulled towards shore and Surendra knew his chance would come soon. He asked several before one of the fisherfolk agreed to take him south. They slept through the early night and then rode down the tide. Once on the boat Surendra did little. He was asked to help now and then, but his hand was quick and his eye faster to learn, so he found the work light. He watched the sun come over the wide water. The boatmen told him tales of pirates and sang to him of floods. They refused to take him farther than Diamond Harbour, where they put in. Surendra walked south beyond the port town until he came to a village. There he asked after tigers. None had

seen a tiger since the time of the grandfathers. Perhaps farther south? No
one could say. Surendra went to the next village.

'Why do you ask after tigers? You do not look like a hunter.'

'I have been round India. I have seen Himalaya and the southern sea.
I have learned to read. But never have I seen a tiger.'

'Man, man, where is the rice beer? You are talking from drink.'

'If you do not know of tigers, then tell me of the trains from Diamond
Harbour. When do they go back to Calcutta?'

'They go only to Alipore. They go in the dawn and the twilight.'

'Then I must reach the one of twilight.'

'Have you a ticket?'

'I have a ticket to see all the cities of India. I tell you, you look on one
who has been to Kailash and stepped in the waters of Cormorin.'

'This one is mad. We do not want your talk here. Send him from the
village. Quickly, quickly—Go!'

Surendra went, followed by a pack of dogs who viewed him as a friend
and accompanied him for pleasure rather than principle. Again he walked
the afternoon away, threading across fields back to the town. He found
the station and asked after the train. Yes, there was a train but the office
was closed. Did he have a ticket? Yes, he had a ticket. He had not bought
it earlier when the officer was on duty. No, he had not. Then it was
probably not a good ticket. He ought not to try to ride the train. Surendra
would try. The porter offered him tea, for which the cultivator paid a
biri. The train came, he was aboard, it moved north. No ticket collector
ever roused Surendra from his luggage rack so he was denied his last
chance of flourishing the grand ticket. Once they stopped Surendra joined
a line of workers walking from one factory to another. They talked easily
of their work and Surendra found it dull. He thought himself well off.
Towards dawn he knew he was near Sealdah so traced his way to the
hostel and found the others at breakfast. When asked what he had done,
he would only say nothing at all. It was not until he was alone with
Narend on a hill in Sikkim many months later that he admitted he had
spent his last day looking for a tiger. Narend laughed as he had never
done. From then on between them it was a private code of amusement
which lightened many a journey.

When all the villagers had been counted, when Deepaka had told of her
return to Kalighat, when Jhoti had been introduced, and Rhunu had
dismissed the museum as of little interest to the others, Elder De sent
them one by one to the ticket office to fetch their last tickets homeward.
They climbed aboard the train at noon. When they arrived at the station
in the big town the pale lights had been lit, and they still swung in the
wind, which still sang a monotone among the rafters. The station master
bade them sleep on the platform:

'There is trouble in the east. Do not go out in darkness. Do not talk with strangers. Stay until it is light and then walk to the boats. There are bad times coming.' He hurried away. The guard locked them into the station and they settled on their bedding for sleep. After the last train had gone some groups of beggars came scavenging along the tracks. Deepaka called to them and threw down Amiya's bedding and sari. The woman rushed away with the treasure. Deepaka watched. At last her tears for Amiya came.

'Hush, aunt. it is over. Tomorrow you will see your grandchildren. It is over, sleep now.'

'You are yourself awake.'

'There is much ahead.'

'And how much sorrow?'

'Perhaps less now that we have so many memories.'

'Have we returned to wait out the days until death?'

'There is always work for hands.'

'Is that not work also a waiting?'

'You are talking in riddles again.'

'Amiya was not alone in her dreams. On this journey you have learned to smile. Perhaps I have learned to weep. Do we now grind rice until fever takes us and gives our families peace?'

'Your family has never suffered because of you.'

'Nor have they gained much. The oldest one is given most from honour not from sense.'

'What would you do?'

'Now? Weep. Tomorrow? Speak of Amiya's death to her son. And then? Try to sing in my old voice? No, too much is finished.'

'And too much has never been tried.'

'Will I find a new adventure in my cooking pots? Or in the pieces of my youngest grandchild's toys?'

'Sleep, aunt, it is well over.' Rhunu slept herself, but Deepaka sat awake with Reena and watched for the dawn.

They were off as soon as the gates were opened. The long walk back seemed interminable. At last they stood on the shore and the boatmen were asking where were the boxes of jewels and gold. When they were half-way across the river and began the long loop back up, a shrill cry came over the water.

'They come, they come!'

They saw a boy flash up the bank and through the trees. The boat in which he was riding nearly capsized while Narend stood shouting, 'That is my grandson, and see how he has grown.'

The babble of excitement heralded the villagers' approach to the shore—waving, shouting, reaching out to pull the first boat to land and tumble all its occupants into an embrace and the mud. At last the boats were emptied, the boatmen paid and slowly poling down the bank.

Narend and the boy stood hand in hand watching them go. When they were out of sight, Narend swung the boy up to his shoulders: 'Come, there are tales for you to hear.' They were the last to plod up the bank and disappear into the fastness of the village.

Epilogue

In the second week of the rains Mr De made his way disconsolately to his office. Baroda House was dismal in the rains. All the corridors were carpeted with beetles. He brushed them away and found on his desk a letter from Bengal. He read:

Dear Mr De,
The cultivator Surendra writes his first letter. I beg your forgiveness for the time of waiting. There was much to be done in the village for the young are very foolish and the old very impatient. I have put the money which was left over into the bank in the big town. Two of the elders and myself must sign for it. Harischandra has written out the accounts for you which I enclose. He tells me that is how to say it. Sundara-devi sends you her blessings and asks you to arrange that she and those with children of school age may travel in the next winter holiday. All the others say they will not go, and travel has brought nothing but death and troubles. Mitu is gone to Calcutta to make figures to sell as his sons now have only coloured plastic and the hard steel in their shop. Amiya's son has shed his tears of duty but is much relieved. His daughter has become a great trouble to him since her grandmother taught her to want more than her father could give. She goes with Rhunu to the city after harvest, though why Rhunu goes no one says. The rice from the south grows quickly, it is hoped the rains will be enough. The ground is dry and my bullocks thin from loneliness. Jaydev began to lay water pipes as soon as the wedding was over. Jhoti, the younger son, is worse than a troop of apes among the fields. Elder De would have me write a speech of thanks but I have said he must pay Harischandra for that. Narend and I will go north after the harvest to see the eastern hills. The pen is a great pain to my fingers. I am sorry that you must spend your days with one in your hand, for the hours spent making these marks are very long. Reena calls down all the gods to bless you. My salute to the doctor sahib.

Surendra

Months later, when the lights of Deepavali had come and gone and there was word of a poor harvest in Bengal, Mr De received another letter. The postmark read Darjeeling. This time Mr De recognized the hand which tried so hard to make the letters steady and clear. He read:

Dear Mr De,
The cultivator Surendra writes from the hills. I have sent many letters in the rains and now all is ready for those to go who wish, if it pleases you that they should. Sundara-devi will guide them and Mitu goes with them to the place of the priest in the hills of the south. He brings with him for you a fine statue which you must put away in a safe place for your grandchildren, for Mitu sells his clay for more than ever a harvest brought me. The money left over will pay for the tickets to Sealdah, good medicine, and maps. It would be best if the long tickets were waiting at Howrah for Sundara-devi before the end of the next moon. Elder De speaks of going too, but will probably not as he is ill. Harischandra has a wasting disease and dies slowly, but is in Reena's care, so happy. He sends to you a copy, with Sundara-devi, of the book he made of all that we did and said on the first journey. Your servant Surendra has watched two bullocks die so has no heart to stay in the village and Narend finds his house empty with Rhunu gone to draw in the city. We have come to the hills quickly by riding the trains as we were taught by the beggar boys of the south. I hope this does not offend you for since the harvest was poor we had no money for tickets. We go along the valleys of snow and will return before the time of planting. I beg you give aid to Sundara-devi. Her eldest son is a good boy and I have told him what to do and where they must guard. Deepaka is now restless but brought a beggar girl from a convent to the village after harvest and her family is now angry that she has disgraced them. I think if she would go to Calcutta with Rhunu it would be best, but Narend says no. Others fight, but many go to look in the books of pictures of the journey now at the temple. There are families come out of the east who do not believe we went and bow to the books. This is a very foolish land. The mountains here are cold, but the tea is good.

> Your servant,
> Surendra

It was another year, during which he had had many letters from Sundara-devi and the others, before Mr De had another from Surendra. This time he read:

Epilogue

Dear Mr De,

You will not perhaps remember the cultivator Surendra from Uma Sen's village. He remembers you well and the doctor sahib too. The village is much changed by the fighting and bad times, for there are more new than old families. Rhunu died in the bad winter. They tell me there is a room in Calcutta filled with pictures with her name on them. Harischandra died before her, and Elder De before Sundaradevi had returned. Reena with Babla's daughter has taken over the school from Nirmal, who is very deaf. Jaydev and Uma have gone to live in the big town with their elder son. The young one ran off to fight in the war. Deepaka has become a saint and many come from far to ask her counsel and bow to her feet. She is often angry these days and says it is no wish of hers that they come. She sees into their troubles with the eyes of the gods. Narend's grandson is gone off to school with his cousins, so we are travelling again. This time we go to the spring festival of Katmandu. I have a new rucksack and my map has many lines upon it. In the next winter we walk south to Chittagong and I shall try to see a tiger. It will be a long route for we must go first to Shillong and then down. That is your home place so I write you to say we shall be there. There was a ring around the moon this month. Narend sends his salute.

Surendra

After that there were no more letters. Mr De was transferred to another post away from the tourist information service. One night in the village a fire started in the thatch and spread from house to house. When the old temple burned, the books of sketches within were reduced to ash.

Glossary

Adi-Ganga Old bed of the Ganges running through Calcutta
alpana coloured powder drawings done on the earth or floor in Bengal
arre expression of surprise as, for instance, I say
ayurvedic Indian homeopathic medicine
biri cigarette
bhut a ghost or spirit of malevolent inclinations
burkah the concealing robe worn by Muslim women
chappatis unleavened, soft, bread
didi, dada honorific terms for elder sister and elder brother, used
   generally
darshan to take the sight of and thus the blessing of a special presence
ghazals laments or love songs sung by Muslims
ghot clay pot over which the hands of the married couple are bound
   together
Gita the Song of God, referred to often by illiterates from memory
gondas gangs—thieves, robbers, or unruly people
Gotra clan, blood associations within a caste
gram household, also hot pulses or fried grains
Han-ji Yes Sir, ji is the honorific suffix
Hannumanji the monkey king and god, servant and helper of Ram
Imambara A great hall or building, often with a mosque, maintained
   by Shi' a Muslims
iddlis rice cakes or pancakes
jatra travelling theatre or drama performed by a travelling group of
   actors
Kasi Benares
Krishna one of the incarnations of Vishnu, a playful and friendly figure
   to Bengalis
kurta long tunic or dress worn over trousers
Lakshmi goddess of luck, fortune and wealth
Lingam symbol of Siva, said to be phallic
maidan parade-ground, large open green
mela fair, celebration

Nandi   the bull of Siva

paisa, paisa-wallah   smallest coin, divisions of the rupee, thus a gatherer of money

pan   concoction of betel, tobacco, spices, lime chewed by many Indians

Parvati, Purush/Prakriti,   the original man and woman, Parvati refers to Siva's wife

prasad   the blessed offerings of food given to an image

puja   worship, ritual before an image or deity

pujaris   priests, performers of ritual

pukka   substantial; permanent

Ram   warrior king incarnation of Vishnu

sadhus   wandering or recognized holy men, usually solitaries

sangam   conjunction, joining

sandesh   Bengali sweets made from milk

sannyasis   wandering holy men or ascetics, often feared by ordinary folk

sara   a plate or tray, sometimes a winnowing fan

Saraswati-puja   worship of the goddess of wisdom and music

supari   spiced nut chewed by women in Bengal

stupa   a mound associated with the worship of Buddha

tali   a plate or platter on which food is served

toddy   a rice beer

tonga   a horse-pulled carriage

Tourist Rest House   hostels run by the government for travellers

FOR THE BEST IN PAPERBACKS, LOOK FOR THE

In every corner of the world, on every subject under the sun, Penguin represents quality and variety – the very best in publishing today.

For complete information about books available from Penguin – including Pelicans, Puffins, Peregrines and Penguin Classics – and how to order them, write to us at the appropriate address below. Please note that for copyright reasons the selection of books varies from country to country.

In the United Kingdom: For a complete list of books available from Penguin in the U.K., please write to *Dept E.P., Penguin Books Ltd, Harmondsworth, Middlesex, UB7 0DA*

In the United States: For a complete list of books available from Penguin in the U.S., please write to *Dept BA, Penguin, 299 Murray Hill Parkway, East Rutherford, New Jersey 07073*

In Canada: For a complete list of books available from Penguin in Canada, please write to *Penguin Books Canada Ltd, 2801 John Street, Markham, Ontario L3R 1B4*

In Australia: For a complete list of books available from Penguin in Australia, please write to the *Marketing Department, Penguin Books Australia Ltd, P.O. Box 257, Ringwood, Victoria 3134*

In New Zealand: For a complete list of books available from Penguin in New Zealand, please write to the *Marketing Department, Penguin Books (NZ) Ltd, Private Bag, Takapuna, Auckland 9*

In India: For a complete list of books available from Penguin, please write to *Penguin Overseas Ltd, 706 Eros Apartments, 56 Nehru Place, New Delhi, 110019*

In Holland: For a complete list of books available from Penguin in Holland, please write to *Penguin Books Nederland B.V., Postbus 195, NL–1380AD Weesp, Netherlands*

In Germany: For a complete list of books available from Penguin, please write to *Penguin Books Ltd, Friedrichstrasse 10 – 12, D–6000 Frankfurt Main 1, Federal Republic of Germany*

In Spain: For a complete list of books available from Penguin in Spain, please write to *Longman Penguin España, Calle San Nicolas 15, E–28013 Madrid, Spain*

RUTH PRAWER JHABVALA
IN PENGUINS

A selection

'One questions whether any western writer has had a keener, cooler understanding of the temperament of urban India' – *Guardian*

'A writer of genius . . . a writer of world class – a master storyteller' – *Sunday Times*

'Someone once said that the definition of the highest art is that one should feel that life is this and not otherwise. I do not know of a writer living who gives that feeling with more unqualified certainty than Mrs Jhabvala' – C. P. Snow

Get Ready for Battle

In a series of wittily observed scenes Ruth Jhabvala draws a sharp and perceptive, yet always compassionate, portrait of middle-class family life in contemporary Delhi, through a group of people who are all ready for battle – with each other and themselves. But beneath the ironies, the personal problems and conflicts, we catch a glimpse of India's terrifying social problems, and also of the deep moral consciousness which may prove her salvation.

A Backward Place

The trouble with Bal was not his lack of ideas but the fact that they tended to be rather grand long-term visions whereas his life was organized on a decidedly short-term basis. And for Judy his English wife, Etta the ageing sophisticate, Clarissa the upper middle-class drop-out from the English establishment, the worthy Hochstadts on a two-year exchange visit, and all the other characters who figure in this enchanting novel, India always poses a host of contradictions.

R. K. NARAYAN IN PENGUINS

A selection

The Man-Eater of Malgudi

Nataraj, owner of a small, friendly printing press in the enchanted city of Malgudi, has never been very successful at making enemies. Until, that is, he meets Vasu. Almost accidentally Vasu, a pugnacious taxidermist, moves into Nataraj's attic, bringing an alarming stuffed jungle of hyenas, pythons and tigers and an assortment of dancing girls that clump up and down the printer's private stairs.

Vasu is definitely not a man to tangle with. But when, in search of bigger game, he threatens the beloved temple elephant, Nataraj rises to the occasion – and Narayan invests it with all his warm, wicked and delightful sense of comedy.

'Connoisseurs have known for years that the city of Malgudi ... is the place to go for some of the best, wisest and slyest scenes from the human comedy' – *Observer*

The Painter of Signs

Raman was considering giving up sign-painting (the business was sinking to new levels of meanness in the town) when he met Daisy of the Family Planning Centre. Slender, high-minded, thrillingly independent, Daisy has made up her mind to be modern and is now dedicated to bringing birth control to the people. In such circumstances, Raman's mounting, insistent passion, coupled with Daisy's determination to disregard the messy, wayward concerns of the heart, can only lead to conflict.

R. K. Narayan's magical creation, the city of Malgudi, provides the setting for this wryly funny, bittersweet story of love getting in the way of progress.

'Since the death of Evelyn Waugh, Narayan is the novelist I most admire in the English language' – Graham Greene

CLASSIC NOVELS ABOUT INDIA
IN PENGUINS

All About H. Hatterr

G. V. DESANI

H. Hatterr is an engagingly shrewd-naïve Anglo-Indian seeking wisdom from the seven sages of India. It proves a punishing process: he is robbed and hit by pukka muggers, falls foul of dubious swamis, falls for frustrating Rosie of the riding breeches ('carnal to the core') and experiences much else that wouldn't normally 'bear talking about in one's autobiographical'.

All About H. Hatterr first appeared in 1948 and was greeted with rare enthusiasm by T. S. Eliot and many other distinguished critics. It then, inexplicably, went underground to emerge twenty years later as a modern classic that defies classification.

A Passage to India

E. M. FORSTER

'That Marabar Case' was an event which threw the city of Chandrapore into a fever of racial feeling. Miss Quested, on a visit from England to the man she expected to marry, showed an interest in Indian ways of life which was frowned upon by the sun-baked British community. And the prejudice which most of them felt and expressed against any social contacts between the British and the Indians appeared, at first, to be justified when she returned, alone and distressed, from an excursion to the caves in the company of a young Indian doctor. He was arrested on a charge of attempted assault, but when the case came to trial Miss Quested withdrew her accusation and the doctor was set free. Was she the victim of an hallucination, a complex, an unidentified intruder, or what? In this dramatic story E. M. Forster depicts, with sympathy and discernment, the complicated Oriental reaction to British rule in India, and reveals the conflict of temperament and tradition involved in that relationship.

A CHOICE OF PENGUINS

Castaway Lucy Irvine

'Writer seeks "wife" for a year on a tropical island.' This is the extraordinary, candid, sometimes shocking account of what happened when Lucy Irvine answered the advertisement, and found herself embroiled in what was not exactly a desert island dream. 'Fascinating' – *Daily Mail*

Out of Africa Karen Blixen (Isak Dinesen)

After the failure of her coffee-farm in Kenya, where she lived from 1913 to 1931, Karen Blixen went home to Denmark and wrote this unforgettable account of her experiences. 'No reader can put the book down without some share in the author's poignant farewell to her farm' – *Observer*

The Lisle Letters Edited by Muriel St Clare Byrne

An intimate, immediate and wholly fascinating picture of a family in the reign of Henry VIII. 'Remarkable . . . we can really hear the people of early Tudor England talking' – Keith Thomas in the *Sunday Times*. 'One of the most extraordinary works to be published this century' – J. H. Plumb

In My Wildest Dreams Leslie Thomas

The autobiography of Leslie Thomas, author of *The Magic Army* and *The Dearest and the Best*. From Barnardo boy to original virgin soldier, from apprentice journalist to famous novelist, it is an amazing story. 'Hugely enjoyable' – *Daily Express*

India: The Siege Within M. J. Akbar

'A thoughtful and well-researched history of the conflict, 2,500 years old, between centralizing and separatist forces in the sub-continent. And remarkably, for a work of this kind, it's concise, elegantly written and entertaining' – Zareer Masani in the *New Statesman*

The Winning Streak Walter Goldsmith and David Clutterbuck

Marks and Spencer, Saatchi and Saatchi, United Biscuits, G.E.C. . . . . The U.K.'s top companies reveal their formulas for success, in an important and stimulating book that no British manager can afford to ignore.

A CHOICE OF PENGUINS

Adieux: A Farewell to Sartre   Simone de Beauvoir

A devastatingly frank account of the last years of Sartre's life, and his death, by the woman who for more than half a century shared that life. 'A true labour of love, there is about it a touching sadness, a mingling of the personal with the impersonal and timeless which Sartre himself would surely have liked and understood' – *Listener*

Business Wargames   James Barrie

How did BMW overtake Mercedes? Why did Laker crash? How did McDonalds grab the hamburger market? Drawing on the tragic mistakes and brilliant victories of military history, this remarkable book draws countless fascinating parallels with case histories from industry world-wide.

Metamagical Themas   Douglas R. Hofstadter

This astonishing sequel to the best-selling, Pulitzer Prize-winning *Gödel, Escher, Bach* swarms with 'extraordinary ideas, brilliant fables, deep philosophical questions and Carrollian word play' – Martin Gardner

Into the Heart of Borneo   Redmond O'Hanlon

'Perceptive, hilarious and at the same time a serious natural-history journey into one of the last remaining unspoilt paradises' – *New Statesman*. 'Consistently exciting, often funny and erudite without ever being overwhelming' – *Punch*

A Better Class of Person   John Osborne

The playwright's autobiography, 1929–56. 'Splendidly enjoyable' – John Mortimer. 'One of the best, richest and most bitterly truthful autobiographies that I have ever read' – Melvyn Bragg

The Secrets of a Woman's Heart   Hilary Spurling

The later life of Ivy Compton-Burnett, 1920–69. 'A biographical triumph . . . elegant, stylish, witty, tender, immensely acute – dazzles and exhilarates . . . a great achievement' – Kay Dick in the *Literary Review*. 'One of the most important literary biographies of the century' – *New Statesman*